...edded in a classic sci-fi
...that'll make you shiver..."
...s. Buckell, *New York Times* bestselling author
of *Halo: The Cole Protocol*

"Christopher puts sci-fi in a metaphysical choke-hold
—*The Burning Dark* makes reality tap out."
Scott Sigler, *New York Times* bestselling author of *Contagious*

"A riveting sci-fi mystery reminiscent of Shirley Jackson's
The Haunting of Hill House."
Martha Wells, author of *Star Wars: Empire* and
Rebellion—Razor's Edge

"Smart, intricate, and viscerally gripping...
Adam Christopher carves a place for himself
among the stars of his genre."
V.E. Schwab, author of *Vicious*

"Christopher mines the terror of a setting that feels both
tremendously vast and nerve-wrackingly claustrophobic.
The Burning Dark will have readers hesitating before
glancing at the night sky or turning on their radios."
Robert Jackson Bennett, author of *Mr. Shivers* and *American Elsewhere*

469 059 67 9

THE BURNING DARK

ADAM
CHRISTOPHER
THE BURNING DARK

TITANBOOKS

The Burning Dark
Print edition ISBN: 9781783292011
E-book edition ISBN: 9781783292028

Published by Titan Books
A division of Titan Publishing Group Ltd
144 Southwark Street, London SE1 0UP

First edition: March 2014
1 3 5 7 9 10 8 6 4 2

A CIP catalogue record for this title is available from the British Library.

Printed and bound in Great Britain by CPI Group Ltd.

Did you enjoy this book? We love to hear from our readers. Please email us at: readerfeedback@titanemail.com, or write to us at the above address.

To receive advance information, news, competitions, and exclusive offers online, please sign up for the Titan newsletter on our website.
www.titanbooks.com

For Sandra, always

YOMI

In the shadowland of the dead, she sat and cried for her husband, but the prison was sealed and she could not leave and nobody could hear her.

The shadows surrounded her, swarming like living, breathing creatures. The shadows caressed her skin, holding the rotting flesh onto her bones. Things crawled over her and ate the flesh, but the shadows kept her firm, kept her whole as the things ate, and ate, and ate.

It was too late.

She had eaten the food of the underworld, and she could not return. So she sat in the shadows, and cried for her husband, and things ate her flesh.

Abandoned, imprisoned in the dark, her fury burned like a black sun. Trapped in the basement of the world, she waited, and grew resentful. Her mind didn't break, not exactly, but it grew as black as the walls of the prison in which she sat. The walls that rippled and cracked and filled her head with the roar of the ocean when she touched them, but that did not yield or break. They were solid, inviolable.

He had left her here, left her trapped while he returned to the land of the living. He had tricked her and betrayed her. The one she loved had betrayed her.

They were *one*; they were *kindred*. Yet here she sat, in the dark, imprisoned beyond time, beyond space. In the dark, her despair turned to hate.

She knew now that she could not return, that she was changed and that the world had changed. She also knew that he would pay, one day. She would have vengeance. She would have revenge.

Her tears dried as the last scraps of flesh were eaten from her face. The endless night of her prison grew even blacker as her dead eyes were sucked from their sockets like rotting eggs by something crawling and screaming in the shadows. In their place a blue light shone, the cold blue light of the end of the world. Her eyes lit the prison. The things that crawled squirmed to escape her.

In the dark she burned.

She stood in her prison for the first time in eternity and screamed for revenge. She would return to the world outside, not to life, never again to life, but to find him, and punish him, from here to the end of time. This she vowed.

Then she sat in the black nothingness and waited. Her husband had sent her here; there was no way out. Someone would need to free her. But she knew someone would, in time. The living were curious, and the dead were patient.

And then it came: a knock and a voice, from somewhere else, somehow. An offering, a proposal. A way out. And it was so simple, all it needed was power, just enough to crack the walls of the prison. And if there was a crack, she could reach out and touch the world. She could reach out and drink her fill of life, a thousand souls a day, until she was whole again. And then, when she was whole, she would be able to break free. She would be able to escape, and her husband would not be able to flee her wrath.

In the dark she burned, and she pressed her skull to the wall, and she listened.

THE RELIEF OF TAU RETORE

This is how the shit went down. Lemme tell you about it, right now.

We came out of quickspace at oh-fifteen, which, even pushing warp as we were, was still too damn late. And when we popped back into the universe above Tau Retore, there was already a gap in the arrowhead. One ship hadn't made it—engine burnout in quickspace, or some such. That can happen, and the loss—hell, any loss—was a shock. But we had a job to do first and my crew was fast, filling the gap without even needing an order, sliding the pack of cruisers together just *so*. It was pretty sweet, lemme tell you.

So, formation tight, one ship down. We spin down into planetary orbit, braking hard so the cone of warp exit didn't knock the goddamn planet off its axis. That's why you don't pop quickspace until you're far off out into the unknown. It's bad enough pushing just a spaceship through the gap between *now* and *now*, but, trust me, you don't want a planet dragging in your wake. The whole universe shakes when a single mote of dust leaves it to fly quickspace. Shove a spaceship through the hole, the universe shakes, gets mightily pissed off, and then gives you a smack at the other end. Universal punishment. God doesn't like you messing with his shit, that's for sure. That's what the quantum dampeners are for. A whole planet? *Forget about it.* They don't make dampeners big enough for *that*.

Anyway.

We came in hot and close, but we were too late. They were there already, on the other side of Tau Retore, and we couldn't see the main body, but we could see its claws stuck deep into the mantle of the planet, the liquid interior spilling out around the talons like hot blood. And the claws. *Jesus.* Shit, man, I've seen them do it before, the way they crack a planet open, then spin it—*spin it!*—like a spider. Don't know how they do it, how they find the sheer mass to build machines as big as moons. At the heart of a Mother Spider lies the guttering embers of a star, we know that much, and as the claws reach the core of their victim, the planet's magnetosphere gets all fucked up to shit, and they siphon the energy off that too. That's some crazy tech, way beyond what we got. And it's an amazing sight, the death of a planet—a planet physically pulled into pieces by the biggest fucking machine in the universe. You don't forget a sight like that, not in any kind of hurry.

You could hear it on the bridge. The viewscreens were green with the shitstorm of quickspace, then they flashed, then we're almost in fucking orbit around Tau Retore and that *thing* sucking the power and the life out of it. And everyone, everyone on the bridge of each of the twenty-three ships left in the arrowhead cries out in horror, and the captains give their pilots the command to decelerate and change course to deflect the nose of the warp cone past the planet, but they're already doing it and cursing blind as they do. Because in front of us there's a Mother Spider eating a planet, and the planet is bleeding. And on our ships, the comms channel is choked with one hundred people shouting in surprise and praying to whatever gods or goddesses they hold dear and precious.

I mean... *Jesus...*

Anyway.

We were too late to save it, really. We knew it, but that didn't mean we weren't going to try. So the arrowhead is in formation and we push the warp cone up just as it fizzes out over Tau Retore's north pole and we slam it toward the Mother Spider. If we can take that out, then the planet will at least stay in orbit, and if it stays in one piece, then when this whole crazy shit is over they can send out some terraformers to reconstitute the landscape and restabilize the core while whoever is left alive goes on vacation to Elesti or Alta or somewhere nice with beaches and sunsets.

Now things start to get interesting, because the Mother Spider has seen us. It's weird, it really is. I don't think the Spiders have actual spiders wherever they're from, but they sure as hell built their whole space tech around them. You know those little spider egg sacs, those balls of web on a leaf that you flick and then they break and about a million of the shits swarm out over everything? Just like that. The Mother Spider's still chowing down and we're flying toward it—and the U-Star *Boston Brand* is right in front, leading the charge, because I'm goddamn Fleet Admiral for the day and I want to get there first— when the main body *splits*, kinda like one of those paper folding games that girls make in school. You know, it's a kinda pyramid, you stick your fingers in, and it opens up, like a flower, and there's writing and jokes and suggestions about who loves who.

You know?

Anyway.

The Mother Spider opens and more Spiders come out—little small ones, half the size of our U-Stars, coming out of these shells that they shuck off like cocoons, and then they unfold their legs and head toward us. There's some more swearing but I order comms silence. Then—*Bang!* The ship that filled the gap in the arrowhead? Gone. These Spider babies are like their momma. They don't have weapons; they have *claws*. So they close in and latch on to your hull, and start chewing it up, and with so many of them swarming—hundreds, *thousands* maybe—they take just a second or two to reduce a U-Star to particulate matter. I don't know whether they ever developed projected energy, or even projectile weapons. Maybe they just think eating enemy ships is funny. So: *Bang!* U-Star *Gothamite* is history, nothing but metal and vapor. But we're in comms silence now, and that seems to keep everyone cool, I guess because they're now looking at me for instructions and trying not to think about how a U-Star can be taken out just like that. It takes the responsibility off them, lets them disengage, the conscious mind giving way to training and experience. Which is good for battle. You need your cool, and you don't need your emotions. Plenty of time for that later.

Of course, I'm standing there watching the other Spider babies getting too close and I'm as angry and scared as the rest of them, but nobody knows that. I signal my pilot and then hit the comms, ordering the arrowhead to break up. So long as everyone stays the hell out of one another's way and shoots at the right thing, hunting season is officially open. The Spiders are going straight to whatever hell their creepy insect intelligence believes in.

I can see the arrowhead split on the screens to the left and right. About a dozen ships on each flank peel upward and apart like an aerobatic display, and a few seconds later the same screens are filled with flashes and sparks and flames as the Spider babies are put into the grinder. I let myself smile, just a little, because I know that everyone on the bridge isn't watching the fireworks outside, they're watching my face, waiting for their orders. And if I smile—just a little—they'll smile too and they'll do their jobs just another one percent better than before. That's leadership, *yessir*. You gotta show and *project* it to everyone. They're depending on you, and this time it's not just the arrowhead; it's Tau Retore. That's a whole planet with a giant machine Spider trying to crack it open to make a galactic omelet. We're here to save the day again.

I'm smiling because, although we're still blasting toward the center of the big Mother Spider, right about where the main body splits to spit out the babies, I see the U-Star *Stripes* and its twin ship the *Stars* swing in ahead, rocketing in from underneath the *Boston Brand*. I smile because when the *Stars* and the *Stripes* are flying side by side, they're cool as shit. Those are the cruisers that everyone wants to be assigned to. They've got the kudos, the cachet, the shiniest damned paint jobs in the whole of Fleetspace. But, I mean, what a mouthful. The U-Star *Stars*? Huh.

Anyway.

So the *Stars* and the *Stripes* pull up ahead, and the screen goes pink automatically as the pair empty all their torpedo tubes at once at big momma's belly and the *Boston Brand*'s AI doesn't want its crew to go blind. Ammo spent, the two cruisers curve off out of the way. It's going to take a few seconds for the missiles to hit, and that's when I decide to give them a little push on their way.

Now, you gotta understand, I've got no rep in particular. I don't take risks. I do things by the book, and I know how to lead, and I get results. And that's what counts—boy, does the Fleet need results. And true, there have been those who have taken risks and acted with rash strokes of genius, but those guys are mostly assholes and mostly dead.

But look. When you see a Spider up close, it's one thing. When you see a Mother Spider with twelve legs, each ten thousand klicks long, *eating* a planet like it's a goddamn apple, it affects you. Something stirs in the back of your brain, like you're watching a movie or having a dream. So sometimes you get ideas, and then you know what it's like to be one of those assholes, and you start hoping to hell you're not about to find out what it's like to be one of those *dead* assholes.

I think somebody on my bridge says something but my head is buzzing and my ears are full of cotton wool, and not just because I've got a pink-tinted Fourth of July show outside. Do they still do that back on Earth? They must. I haven't been back in… Well, I'm not *that* old, but sometimes a five-year tour on the edge of the galaxy can feel a lot longer. Could be worse. There was this friend of mine, commander on one of the *really* big ships. "Wraiths" is what their crews call them, these ships that stay out for so long, hiding like an old-fashioned submarine just in case the Spiders pop up. After his last tour, he found me at Fleet Command and he said to me, Ida, he said…

Um. Anyway.

I'm sure somebody says something but I'm on the first pilot's back, pulling his position around and grabbing the sticks. Maybe it's the other pilot saying something, but then he sees what I'm doing, and looks at the screen ahead, following the green trail of the torpedoes through the pink wash—and that looks fucking freaky, I tell you—

and he grabs his sticks and nods. That's it. He sits there, and nods, and looks ahead.

See? That's leadership, right there. He trusts me and is ready to follow me into hell if need be. Which actually isn't far from the truth, because I count to three and open quickspace right there, with the torpedoes in front of us and the Mother Spider in front of *them*. The warp cone pops ahead of our nose, and the screen goes from pink to blue.

Well, it's crazy and suicidal, and now people really are standing up and shouting at me, and the comms kicks into life with so many people all screaming at me that it sounds just like the wild roar of the universe.

But it works. The warp cone shunts the torpedoes forward at a speed way, way, *way* beyond their design tolerance, and when they hit the big fat Spider, they don't just explode, they go fucking *nova*, the energy spilling from our warp cone the same as throwing gasoline on a barbecue. You ever done that? Well, next time you're planet-side and can afford to take a trip out somewhere natural and you don't mind a little smoke. But this, it's like a new star has just sparked up, right over Tau Retore, right in our flight path. If there's anything left of the Mother Spider

(The star falling and burning as though it were a lamp and then they died one and all and)

we never found it. The only shit left was a few trillion tons of scrap metal and a high percentage of helium floating in high orbit around the planet.

But we're still heading right into this fucking mega-explosion and the warp cone is decaying quickly, so I give the order and we pop quickspace for just a second and fly *through* the explosion, and then the second pilot—promoted, needless to say—kills the engine and we slide back into space just a million klicks north. Of course we cooked the engines and the nav computer went offline to run a diagnostic, or maybe it was just really pissed off that we popped quickspace without telling it first and it went into a sulk. It was a rough ride too, and something burns out in the control console in front of the pilot and then there's a bang and something pings against my leg, but I don't notice, not yet. We've got enough juice in the tank to turn her around and coast back in. All the baby Spiders have been mopped up too, with only a few U-Stars damaged. One of which was the *Stripes*, and already someone has cracked a joke about scratching the paint job. Goddamn boys and their toys.

And you know what? We *were* in time. Tau Retore took a fucking pounding, but they'd been clever and got nearly everyone evacuated just as soon as the Spider appeared in the system. Just about the whole planet was saved, almost three hundred million of them…

Now, that's a result. We actually won something, and won it big. I mean, I don't know if you heard, but things… well, things are not all rosy in this great and wonderful war. The Fleet is mighty and the Fleet is all, but, the Spiders? They might not think like us or act like us, but, goddammit, there are so many of them. I mean, it seems like we're taking one step forward and two steps back all the damn time and…

Anyway.

So guess what? I'm a hero. A genuine, bona fide heroic sonovabitch. So then I call up the commander of the U-Star *Castle Rock*, which I see up ahead, and I ask her about how many medals she'd like to have, and then someone says my leg is bleeding and…

"Abraham?"

"Hmm?" Ida paused, hand reaching for the cup. His head was a little light but his throat was dry… if someone would just be so kind as to pour another shot of the strawberry liqueur, that would do nicely, very nicely indeed. He rolled the thought around in his mind and glanced at Zia Hollywood, seeing nothing but his own reflection in her mining goggles.

"Shut the fuck up."

Zia's lips hadn't moved. The woman's voice was coming from the other side of the table. Ida frowned and turned his head too quickly. The room spun in surprising and interesting ways.

"Excuse me… Serra?"

She'd called him Abraham. He hated that.

Serra shook her head, looking at him with a mixture of disgust and pity. It wasn't a pretty expression, no matter how perfect her olive-skinned face was. She stood up and pushed her chair back, looking away.

"Come on, let's go." Serra's voice was almost a whisper. Disgust was now outright embarrassment. Carter, her inseparable lover, six and a quarter feet of military might wrapped in tight olive fatigues, nodded and muttered under his breath, but Serra was already stalking away from the table. Carter stood and threw Ida a look you might call dirty.

"Jackass."

And then they were gone, and Ida was left with the two VIPs. Fathead's permanent grin was as wide as ever, and oddly hypnotic to Ida's pickled brain. Zia's face was set, expressionless, and he noticed she hadn't had much of her drink.

Ida's head settled a little, and he glanced around the canteen. It was late now, but a couple other crewmen of the U-Star *Coast City* were still here, backs turned to Ida's table, apparently happy to keep out of the way of the space station's guests.

Zia Hollywood said nothing as she stood and tapped Fathead's shoulder. She walked off in silence, leaving her big-haired crewman to pull Ida's empty cup away from him before picking up the red bottle and the bag it came in from the floor and following his boss out.

Ida was alone at the table. His hands played at nothing in front of him. He wished the cup would rematerialize.

Well, fuck you very much.

Ida stood quickly, chin high, chest out, and he took a breath. He was better than this. He took a step toward the canteen's serving bar. Then his knee protested, and he relaxed his stiff-backed posture into his more regular, round-shouldered limp. The servos in his artificial joint didn't seem to like alcohol much.

Alcohol was forbidden on all U-Stars, and while the expensive liqueur had been brought in by the famous crew of the *Bloom County*, Ida wondered if there was some of the marines' homebrewed engine juice around. Didn't hurt to ask.

"Hey, can I get a drink, my friend? Something… *special*. Anything you recommend?"

The canteen server had his back to him. Ida coughed, but the man didn't turn around.

"You've had enough. Any more trouble and I'll be talking to the marshal."

Ida blinked. "Huh," he said, tapping the counter. No progress then. Four weeks on board and he was still Captain No-Friends. The U-Star *Coast City* was turning out to be a real nice place.

Ida turned, regarded the silent backs of the other crewmen still seated at the other table, and limped out the door.

It was late in the cycle and the station's corridors were cast in an artificial purple night. Three turns and one elevator later, Ida was back in his cabin. He flicked the main light on, the autodimmer keeping it to a warm, low, white yellow. He tended to dim it during "daylight" as well, as the low light helped hide the nasty, functional nature of his quarters. What you couldn't see, your mind filled in for you. He liked to imagine the dark shadowed corners were crafted out of fine mahogany and teak paneling. Just like he had at home.

"Ida?"

Captain Abraham Idaho Cleveland was called Ida by his friends. Nearly everyone on the station called him Abraham, or worse. Mostly they called him nothing at all.

But not her.

He smiled, limped to his bed, and lay back. The damn knee… Ida raised his leg and flexed it, trying to get the psi-fi connection between the prosthetic and his brain to repair manually, but his leg was heavier than he remembered and lifting it made him feel dizzy. He dropped his leg and sighed, and closed his eyes.

"Hello, Ludmila," he said.

The woman's voice crackled with static as she laughed. It was high, beautiful. It made Ida smile.

"How was your night?" the voice asked.

Ida waved a hand—then, remembering he was alone in his cabin, switched the gesture for another dramatic sigh. "It was… bah. Who cares how my night was. How's yours going?"

The voice tutted. "You've been drinking, haven't you, Ida?" Ida's smile returned. "Oh, maybe one or two."

The laugh again, each giggle cut with noise. She was so very, very far away. "Time for bed?"

Ida nodded and turned over. "Yeah, time for bed. Good night, Ludmila."

"Good night, Ida."

The room fell quiet, and the lights autodimmed again to match the purple dark of the rest of the station. Ida's breathing slowed and became heavy. Underneath the sound of his slumber the room pulsed with static, faint and distant.

Ida dreamed; he dreamed of the house on the farm. The red paint on the barn behind it shed like crimson dandruff in the sun and the same sun shone in the blond hair of the girl as she beckoned him to come with her, come into the house. But when he held out his hand to touch her, he was holding her father's Bible, the one that sour old man had pressed into his hands the very day he'd first met him, insisting Ida read the damn thing each and every night.

Ida felt afraid. He would not go into the house. He looked into the sky, at the sun, but saw that the sun was a violet disk, its edge streaming black lines. He frowned. An eclipse? There hadn't been an eclipse that day. He turned back to the girl, but she was gone and the door of the house was open, a rectangular black portal. Had her father sent her away already? Ida wasn't sure… it hadn't been then, had it? He and Astrid had another summer left, surely.

He took a step forward, and as he breathed the country air, the farmyard pulsed with static, faint and distant.

* * *

The static from the radio cracked sharply, and Ida jerked awake, dream forgotten.

"Mmm?"

"Ida?"

"Mmm?"

"Can you tell me the story again?"

Ida shifted. His bed was soft and the dark was pleasant on his eyes. He lay on his back and looked up into nothing. His knee seemed to have sorted itself out and didn't hurt anymore. He had a vague recollection of a red barn and a heavy book, but he shrugged the thought away.

"You mean Tau Retore?"

"Yes. Tell me again."

Ida chuckled and turned over. The still, blue light of the space radio was now the only light in the room. Ida stared into it, imagining Ludmila, wherever she was, watching her own light in the dark.

"Well," said Ida. "This is how the shit went down. Lemme tell you about it…"

SOME KIND OF HERO

>>...please wait...
>> FLEET_WIKIA_REVISION_889
>> ~cleveland_AI_835401
>>...please wait...
>> last login: Sun Jan 12 06:18:53
>> WELCOME BACK, CAPTAIN
>> /rpos_intro_CC-SECURE.rtz
>> password: ********************
Union-Class, Fleet Starship; Research Platform and
Observation Station (RPOS) configuration. Catalog reference:
Psi Upsilon Psi. Nameplate: COAST CITY.

SUMMARY:
The U-Star COAST CITY was one of only two RPOS-configured
stationary orbital platforms put into service by the Fleet.
Although twenty-four such space stations were ordered,
production problems with kitset modules for both the COAST
CITY and its sister COLLINSPORT resulted in curtailing of
the RPOS program by then-Fleet Admiral LAUREN AVALON. After

a leadin time of seven years, the Fleet station program was retooled, resulting in the now ubiquitous Multipurpose Orbital Platforms (MOPs), the STAR CITY, the METROPOLIS, and the [REDACTED] being the first science platform and command center stations put into operation.

After the COAST CITY and COLLINSPORT were commissioned, a series of [REDACTED] structural failures and robotic system malfunctions during assembly at each site resulted in [REDACTED]. While both stations were completed and activated to schedule, their history made them unpopular tours for Fleet personnel and both facilities were plagued with morale problems and petty crime. Following an [REDACTED]

The COLLINSPORT was decommissioned after twelve years of service, its demise hastened by a failure of the main power pack and [REDACTED]. Originally designed as a monitoring station and launch point in the Oort cloud for Fleet craft entering and exiting the Home System, the unpowered U-Star was towed to Jovian orbit, where it was disassembled. Components of the station were recycled and reused as part of the helium-3 robotic mining systems in orbit around that planet. For more information, please see /JMC_27s_intro_CC-SECURE.rtz, "History of the Jovian Corporation."

The COAST CITY was assembled in a stationary orbit at a distance of 1.2 AU around SHADOW, an asymptotic giant branch technetium star in the constellation of Upsilon. The COAST CITY served a dual role as science base for the study of the star and the properties of its radiated energy and also as a forward warning post against SPIDER aggression in the SHADOW system, as it was believed at one point that the sentient machine race would attempt to harness the unusual properties of the star as part of an attack on Fleet space. This concern proved to be unwarranted and no SPIDER activity

was ever recorded in the system. For more information, please
see /antag_SPIDER_techspec_high_CC-SECURE.rtz, "Spider high-
energy experimentation and special weapons development."

The COAST CITY was placed under the command of Commandant
PRICE ELBRIDGE, seconded from the PSI-MARINE CORPS on the
personal orders of [REDACTED]

SPECIFICATIONS:
Station hub
Diameter: 1,627 meters
Circumference: 5,112 meters; housing 23 levels of habitable
space plus robotic service levels
Spire
Length: 2,063 meters (including communication antenna and
sensor probe packs)
Diameter: 200 meters (widest point, housing bridge and command
centers [habitable space] plus robotic service levels and
computer bays) tapering to 13 meters
Power pack
Three Rolls-Royce Dreadnought cold fusion reactors, output
3.9 GW per unit
Crew complement
2,200; consisting of crew, executive and scientific personnel,
one Marine battalion, and one Psi-Marine company

"Long way out, sir."

Ida looked up from the screen. Sitting in front of him in the
shuttle, the pilot didn't turn around but nodded at the viewscreen
that occupied the entire forward wall of the cockpit, wrapping
around each side a little to simulate an actual window. Ida let the
computer pad rest on his leg and adjusted himself in the narrow seat,
the leather beneath him creaking.

"It sure is," said Ida. Background reading on his destination forgotten for the moment, he took in the spectacular view.

The U-Star *Coast City* was a giant doughnut floating on its side against a starry background bruised purple with the expanded gas cloud that enveloped the Shadow system. The pilot rotated the shuttle, and the *Coast City* flipped to the horizontal. At this angle, a more natural one that followed the station's design, Ida could make out the windows of the bridge and other structures familiar from a hundred other platforms. Everything in the Fleet was constructed from the same prefabricated sections, after all; everything from tiny one-man hotseats, used on extended EVAs, to cruisers to the largest star bases. The entire Fleet was modular, allowing for an infinite number of combinations and functions, limited only by the imagination of the Marine-Engineer Corps—which meant that, actually, the vehicles of the Fleet only came in about five different forms. Efficiency was a higher priority than imagination, so really there was no need to mess with tried and tested configurations. And every war machine produced by the Fleet was given the Union-Class Fleet Starship designation, which no doubt made the accountancy and logistics departments of the Earth government happy, but it meant you couldn't tell what a ship was from just the name. Including the U-Star *Coast City*, which, in this case, was a space station.

As familiar as Ida was with Fleet "vehicles," the *Coast City* was an older boat, and, as he'd just learned, one of only two of this type assembled, so while the shape was more or less what he expected, the torus was a little fatter, perhaps, and the spire that punched through the center of the hub had antenna extensions that were far longer than standard.

Ida hadn't quite seen one like this before, and he'd never seen one being taken apart either. As the curved outer ring of the station moved around in the viewscreen, the shiny solidity of the hub changed to a ragged, torn framework. The superstructure was all still there, leaving the torus and spire shape perfectly intact. But as the shuttle orbited the station, its skeletal innards were revealed. Lights flickered here and there, betraying the progress of construction drones carefully separating plates, girders, bolts, and rivets, making sure not a single stray particle was left floating in space as they repackaged the kitset form of the station back into a series of long, cuboid boxes that stuck like limpets at irregular intervals on the strongest parts of the exposed frame.

A minute later and the shuttle had returned to the intact half of *Coast City*, all solid metal and lights and Fleet insignia. Ida saw another shuttle, similar to the one he was currently in, heading away from the docking bay. Even during demolition, Fleet routine held sway; the Shadow system was clearly still being patrolled for Spider activity, the secondary function of any platform.

The *Coast City* had primarily been pushed into orbit around Shadow to research the peculiar properties of the star. Ida leaned in toward the shuttle's curved viewscreen; glancing to the left, he could just see the very edge of the star's violet corona. He let out a low, long whistle. The light from the star was described as "toxic" in his briefing and the Fleet wikia reported it as "unusual," but that was all he knew. Now, seeing it even via the viewscreen, which processed the light as much as possible, he thought he might agree. When he looked back toward the station, his vision flashed purple and he felt a little dizzy and sick, like he'd been standing on the top of something very tall and someone had come by and given him a shove in the small of his back. He blinked for a few seconds and the feeling dissipated.

"You here on leave, sir?" The pilot's hands moved over the controls, lining the shuttle up for docking.

The question surprised Ida. He was in uniform, so he supposed there was no reason why anyone wouldn't think he was still on active duty if they didn't know. But this pilot was positively chatty. Ida considered reprimanding him, telling him to focus on his job, which was 90 percent automated. One last little flex of power, perhaps. Then Ida laughed.

"Sir?" Now the pilot turned his huge fly-eye goggles to his passenger. Ida saw a dozen tiny reflections of himself, then turned back to the screen.

The *Coast City* now filled nearly the whole view. On a small display inset into the console that showed the rear, the U-Star *Athansor* was just a hulking silhouette with a few rows of lights that might have been nothing but far-distant stars. Only the ship's nameplate, lit in neon red, was any indication that the black mass was an artificial construct.

Ida clapped a hand on the back of the pilot's seat, and then quickly removed it, realizing that while the docking procedure was nearly automatic, the pilot probably needed to keep concentrating as they made the final approach. Ida slid the computer pad on top of the console beside him and adjusted his straps.

"I'm retired," Ida said. "But I've one last duty for the Fleet, signing the final decommission order for this old crate. That and getting some TLC for this thing." He knocked on his right knee, and the sound came back hard and dead. The pilot nodded, although he wasn't looking.

The window was now showing an expanse of metal, tinged purple by the evil light from Shadow. In the center of the metallic wall, an octagonal patch of light allowed them to see into the station's shuttle hangar.

"Early retirement," said the pilot. "Sounds nice." Then he activated the main comms and began swapping technical chatter with the hangar controller on board the station.

Ida sat back with his hands linked behind his head. He smiled and closed his eyes. The purple spots had gone, at least.

Yes, sounds nice.

"Groups four and five, embark."

Finally, things were moving again. Serra swallowed, her throat dry, as she glanced to her left. Half her row turned smartly, fell out, then grabbed their bags and kit and jogged over to the ramp leading up into the gaping loading bay of the transport.

"Taking them long enough. Jesus Christ."

Serra nodded. Beside her, Carter was chewing his lip as he watched the marines get herded into the back of the ship.

He was right. It was taking fucking forever. This was the last-but-one transport ship off the *Coast City*, and it was supposed to take nearly everyone that was left aboard, leaving just essential support crew. Having nearly a whole battalion of marines stuck at the ass-end of the galaxy was not much use to the Fleet, not when the Spiders were making moves all over the damn show. The sooner the station was disassembled and the sooner the combat troops and other Fleet personnel were off it and doing something useful somewhere else, the better.

They'd been standing around in the *Coast City's* hangar for a couple of hours now. The operation was supposed to be efficient, the whole production running practically on automatic. But there was something up with the computer on board the U-Star *Sunken Treasure*. Something about the manifest system getting stuck, refusing to update the catalog of personnel sitting patiently on the transport. Apparently it had been rebooted several times already, but until it was working, they couldn't load any more. But, finally, things seemed to be happening.

The *Coast City* had four berths available in its hangar: two small bays for shuttles, two for larger ships, including troop carriers like the *Sunken Treasure*. The carrier itself belonged to a larger U-Star, *Athansor*, which sat out in space a few hundred klicks away. As well as picking up the bulk of the remaining station crew, it was here to drop someone off. Why anyone new would come to the station at the end of its life, with half its structure nothing more than a delicate framework of girders and open space, Serra didn't know. She didn't care either. All she cared about was getting off the damn thing. She didn't like it here. She never had, not really, but over the last few weeks there was something else bothering her.

On the other side of the hangar, away from the huge featureless box that was the *Sunken Treasure*, the first small bay was empty, the station's own shuttle out on routine patrol. In the other bay sat another shuttle, the one from the *Athansor*. It looked newer than their own craft.

As the marines began to be loaded into the transport again, Carter and Serra stood, kit at their feet, waiting for their group to be called. As they idled, they both watched the new shuttle as a single passenger disembarked. He was middle-aged and uniformed—an officer, although it was impossible to see his rank from this distance.

Carter tilted his head as though that would give him a better look. "Any idea who that is?"

Serra shrugged, but from the row of marines behind her came a deep voice as DeJohn leaned forward, his breath hot on the back of her neck.

"Heard he was some kind of hero. Supposed to have saved a whole planet, or some shit. But fucked if I've heard of him."

Serra felt Carter stiffen as he stood next to her. He craned his neck around to DeJohn.

"What, there's no record of it? That means Black Ops."

Ah, shit. Serra glanced at Carter and saw his face blush red. DeJohn gave a *Hey, don't look at me* expression and stepped back.

"Charlie…" Serra whispered. Carter looked at her, his eyes narrow.

Black Ops. DeJohn didn't know—nobody aboard the *Coast City* did outside of the officers, and of them only a small, select group—about a small but important slice of Carter's service history. Serra knew, of course; Carter had told her, even though it would mean court-martial and an unpleasant, violent end for the both of them if it ever got out.

Black Ops. It was not a topic to bring up, not around Carter. Serra mouthed "Charlie" to him, and he seemed to relax a little, his shoulders falling and the heat leaving his cheeks.

Serra turned and watched as the new arrival was met by the station's temporary commander, the provost marshal. The marshal was supposed to be in charge of security, but with the commandant suddenly absent, he'd stepped in as the last officer of sufficient rank on board, all the other senior officers having left on the previous transport. Serra frowned.

"And you know this how, exactly, Corporal?" Carter asked.

DeJohn sniffed. "Didn't you read the briefing?"

Carter grinned and turned around. "Wait, you can read?"

Serra laughed along with the other two. That was better. Good.

"Shame the commandant isn't here to meet him, then," she said.

Behind her, DeJohn sighed. "Not this again."

"Look," said Serra, turning. "It's fucked up. How come the

commandant isn't here? Isn't he supposed to stay on the station until the very end?"

DeJohn laughed. He was standing with his hands behind his back, his own row of marines forming a scraggly, disorganized group as they waited for their orders.

"You expecting this boat to sink, marine?"

Serra spun around and snapped to attention. The warrant officer in front of her held a computer pad in one hand, his attention apparently fixed on it as he tapped at the screen with his finger. Carter stood to attention too, but snuck a sideways glance at Serra, his lip curled in a smirk.

"Well, Psi-Sergeant Serra?" The warrant officer's eyes didn't leave his pad.

"No, sir," said Serra. Damn, did she want to get off this boat.

Nobody said anything for a moment. The warrant officer continued to tap on his pad. Serra and Carter stood rigid. Serra could hear DeJohn breathing behind her.

Finally the warrant officer dropped the pad to his side. He took a step back and raised his voice to address the several ranks of marines still waiting in the hangar.

"Okay, there is still a problem with the transport manifest, so we can't take everyone. Groups six to nine will embark on my order. Groups ten and up, you're staying put."

The sound of several dozen marines, all packed up and ready to go, sick to death of their current posting and sick to death of standing around in the hangar, murmuring their displeasure as they shuffled to collect their kits, filled the hangar. DeJohn sighed more dramatically than the rest.

"The fuck?" he said, and then added, "Sir."

The warrant officer glanced over Serra's shoulder at the marine. "Them is, as they say, marine, the breaks. Any problem, you're free to take it up with Commandant Elbridge."

"The commandant isn't even on board this U-Star," said DeJohn, "*Sir.*"

"And life is hard and unfair, marine."

Serra tried very hard not to smile. From the corner of her eye, she could see Carter having even more difficulty.

Over on the other side of the hangar, the new arrival and the provost marshal were heading out.

The warrant officer stepped closer to Serra and raised his computer pad again.

"Fleet regulation specifies that at least one psi-marine is to remain on any U-Star at all times. Lafferty drew the card and is on the way out, which leaves you on duty, Psi-Sergeant."

At this, Carter and Serra exchanged a look. As much as she wanted to get off this godforsaken space station and out of this system with its fucking evil star and all the crap its fucked-up light was causing, she didn't want to be away from Carter. She could see it in his eyes too. One day they'd leave the Fleet altogether, the both of them, get married, move out to a quiet colony, have kids. Carter was getting an itch, and Serra would follow him wherever he needed to go.

The warrant officer sniffed. "Problem, marine?"

Serra stood to attention, eyes-front. "No, sir."

The warrant officer glanced at Carter, catching the tail end of his grin. He raised an eyebrow, then shook his head and began tapping on his pad again. Then he walked off without another word.

Serra relaxed. When she looked at Carter, she was grinning too.

A heavy hand clapped her on the shoulder, making her jump. DeJohn leaned between the two of them, his shaved scalp glistening in the hangar lights.

"Looks like time to have a party, girls and boys."

"If by 'party' you mean make sure the demolition drones don't take us apart when they go haywire," said Carter, "then sure, let's party." He grabbed his kit and motioned to Serra. She nodded and picked hers up.

"Hey," said DeJohn, stepping forward as his row of marines fell out. Carter turned but Serra made a point of keeping herself pointed toward the exit. If she was staying on board for the remainder of the station's life, she would unpack her kit in Carter's cabin. Being the sole occupant of the psi-marine berth was going to be a real drag, and there was no one left aboard who was likely to make a fuss about her and Carter breaking Fleet regulations by sharing quarters. DeJohn was right, in his own, stupid way. It was party time at the edge of Fleetspace.

"Hey," said DeJohn again. Serra turned with a much-exaggerated display of boredom, but DeJohn didn't notice. He waved them back over and dropped his voice.

"Look," he said, "it's just us. We got this whole damn boat to ourselves—"

"And two hundred other marines," said Carter, folding his arms. DeJohn screwed his face up like he'd just bitten something very sour.

"Naw, I mean us. We're a fireteam now, am I right? One marine, one marine-engineer, one psi-marine."

Serra folded her arms too. "Your point?"

"Think we need to say hello to our so-called hero. Show him a thing or two, you know?"

DeJohn rubbed his fist into the palm of the other hand with relish. Carter stood still, not doing anything except sucking in his cheeks. Then he turned quickly and patted Serra's shoulder for her to follow.

Out of DeJohn's earshot, Serra asked her lover if he was okay, but he didn't answer.

Ida shifted on the couch. Looking up, he was blinded by the light that hung in the steel globe directly overhead. He turned his head to look at the medic, a young Japanese woman who had introduced herself as Izanami.

Ida wasn't sure this was entirely necessary—the only part of him that needed medical attention was his robot knee, and only as part of a routine check. He was on his way *out* of the Fleet, not a raw recruit whose psychopathic tendencies were to be identified and, if possible, developed. But psychotherapy was all part of standard Fleet procedure, and his training died hard.

Izanami sat perfectly still, hands clasped in her lap. She smiled, the white of her teeth matching the white of her medic's tunic and skirt, contrasting a little—but not that much—with her pale skin. She was practically monochromatic.

Ida had been on board not quite two cycles, and so far Izanami was the only person other than the provost marshal who had spoken more than a few words to him. She'd turned up at his cabin, knocking politely on the door before appearing around the frame with a big, friendly smile. She introduced herself as a neurotherapist, but like most of the station's crew, she was no longer on active duty, merely stuck on the *Coast City* until the final transport ship arrived. With a skeleton crew of just over two hundred—and a full complement of medical drones capable of dealing, at the extreme end of the spectrum, with ten thousand war-wounded—she was surplus to requirements.

Ida shifted on the fake leather couch. To hell with it. The couch was comfortable.

"So, tell me about yourself," said Izanami.

Ida laughed. "Please don't tell me they teach you that opening line at the academy?"

"Sorry," said Izanami. She gestured to the room. "Old habits! I haven't had much to do here. I'm clearly dying to psychoanalyze someone, and you seem to be a willing victim, Captain."

Ida waved a hand, dismissing her apology. "I'm joking. But, let's see… I was born in Avebury, England, 2920, Anno Domini. But only by accident. My father worked for the Fleet, so we traveled around a lot and were only in the Britannic States for a couple of months when I decided to make an early appearance. He was from Idaho—well, what used to be Idaho, before the Fleet Confederacy reorganized the United States in… *whenever*. He still called it that, anyway."

Izanami smiled, but there was something off about the expression, and Ida didn't like it. It was years since he'd been on a Fleet shrink's couch, and he thought perhaps he was straying from the point. He frowned and tried to find a better place from which to continue his personal history. He turned back to face the ceiling, closing his eyes against the dazzling light globe directly above. He cleared his throat.

"Well…"

For a second Ida thought he felt Izanami's hand on his bare forearm. Her fingers were cold, almost painfully so, and he flinched, jerking his head up from the couch to look.

Izanami hadn't moved, her fingers woven together on her lap. Her smile was somehow warmer now. Ida felt himself relax. He was jumpy; that was for sure. Maybe the whispers he'd heard around the place were worrying him more than he thought.

"So," Izanami said, "who are you going home to, now you're retired?"

Ida looked at Izanami, annoyed at the question. But, of course, she didn't know. She sat still in her chair, clearly expecting an answer.

"Oh," he began, then paused. "Not much time for family life in a job like mine. But... there was someone, though. Once."

Ida stopped, and frowned. He hoped Izanami would move on.

"Tell me about her."

No such luck. Ida coughed. "Ah, well, her name was Astrid. She had blond hair, and she... she died." He raised himself up on one elbow. "Do we need to talk about this now?"

The room seemed colder. Izanami met Ida's gaze, her face now expressionless. Her eyes seemed to catch a reflection from the steel lamp and flashed blue for a second.

"I have a husband," she said.

Ida raised an eyebrow.

"He left me," she continued. "Sometimes I think that is harder than death."

Ida's jaw worked as his brain tried to catch up with the conversation.

"I'm... ah..." Ida lay back on the couch. He squinted into the lamp; when he looked away he saw purple spots and streaking shadows until he blinked them gone.

"It's okay," said Izanami.

Ida glanced sideways at her and she was smiling again, and for a moment he was lost in her eyes. Then he saw that they actually *were* blue, a rare color indeed for a Japanese woman.

* * *

"You're not serious?"

DeJohn's face split into a wide grin. Serra looked across the canteen table at Carter, daring to hope he at least saw some sense, but he was smiling too. Except… there was something else, something behind the smile, behind his eyes. He was bored—hell, they were all bored—and he seemed content to let DeJohn take the lead on practically everything now. Carter was better than that; she knew it. If only he'd snap the hell out of it. If only DeJohn would just let it go.

"Hey, hey," said DeJohn. He looked first over one shoulder, then the other, like he was worried someone else in the canteen would overhear them. That was bullshit too; DeJohn didn't give a flying fuck what anyone else heard. But he still leaned in to the table and lowered his voice. All part of his stupid game.

"He's an officer with a Fleet Medal, jackass," Serra hissed at DeJohn. Her eyes remained on Carter's face, though. His smile thinned a little.

"He ain't no such goddamn thing, marine," said DeJohn. "Some kind of hero, right? Bullshit. I checked. Bull*shit*. There's no record of him or anything. Saved a planet? There's no way we wouldn't know about that. No *way*! Hell, save a planet? That doesn't happen. That's called winning. Which is something we sure as hell ain't doing."

"But if he was Black Ops, he wouldn't have a record, would he," said Carter quietly.

"Bah!" said DeJohn, sitting back in his chair. "You telling me Black Ops are saving planets now? A little difficult to keep something like that quiet. And you're telling me they hand out Fleet Medals in Black Ops? Black Ops is called Black Ops for a reason. They do the nasty shit so we don't have to. They don't give out medals for that."

Serra tried to catch Carter's eye, but he was staring, unblinking, at DeJohn. She glanced down—she couldn't help it—at the silver bar sewn into his tunic.

FOR SERVICES RENDERED

"You're right," said Carter. Serra blinked. There was a light in Carter's eyes, a fire. His smile crept up at the corners. "He's a goddamn liar."

Serra slumped in her chair as DeJohn laughed. *Damn. It.* She'd try to talk him down, but later, not here.

"So," said Carter, leaning in across the table, "what do you think we should do about it?"

Serra folded her arms and gazed into the air somewhere above the table as DeJohn told Carter exactly what he had in mind.

Idiots, she thought.

This had to be it, surely. Ida checked the computer pad in his hand, rotating the screen to view the station map from a different angle.

Left, Corridor Eleven, Omega Deck. Then left again, and then straight on. Service elevator to the next level, keep on going. Ida traced the route on the pad, his finger leaving a red trail on the station schematic. He tapped the "home" button and stroked the station locator icon on the pad's main screen. The device bleated, then came back with an error. Ida looked around, but the plating had been taken off this section of corridor already, taking with it the level and corridor ident signs.

Somebody had screwed up. His duties weren't exactly onerous— he was officially retired and merely an observer on the station. But as such he'd been given a few minor chores, including demolition sign-offs for each section, as well as a list of station modules already packed away that he had to cross-check against the master manifest. It was stupid, really. They were the kind of checks that the demolition crews would be doing anyway, so all Ida was doing was duplicating the paperwork and, no doubt, pissing off the skeleton crew who were doing their best to get on with their difficult and dangerous work without him slowing them down. King too—the provost marshal hadn't been exactly thrilled to welcome him on board and had been a little frosty ever since. Perhaps he thought that by sending Ida here, Fleet Command were butting in, questioning whether the marshal was capable of running a tight operation.

So far, the one adjective Ida thought of when describing the marshal was exactly that: tight.

But this? Either his pad was bugged or they'd sent him on a wild goose chase to get him out of their hair. One of the greatest heroes of the Fleet, stuck down a maintenance access tunnel on the toilet deck of the station with a glitching computer pad.

Ida frowned at the notebook-sized screen and thumbed the station layout again. The two-dimensional map sprang into life, showing an area of the *Coast City* Ida was pretty sure was nowhere near where he was. He was right out on the far edge of the station torus, as far from the inhabited section as it was possible to get. This whole segment of the base was not only unused but in the process of being dismantled as well. The walls and flooring were bare metal grilling, revealing a mess of cables and pipes behind the façade. It was also cold, the life support automatically cycled down to minimum just to keep atmospheric integrity with the rest of the station.

Ida turned, but as with the life support, the lighting was also on auto-minimum. As he'd passed each section of corridor, the next section lit in front of him, and the one he'd just been through turned off. Which, when you're lost with a bugged map and no corridor markers, in a station you've been in only a few cycles, was a real pain in the ass. There weren't even any comms boxes—or at least Ida couldn't see any, being stuck in a bubble of light between two near-black envelopes ahead and behind. And they hadn't given him an internal comms badge and ident tag yet either.

Ida took a deep breath and coughed, his throat catching on the cold air. He took a few paces forward, and the next corridor section faded into view as the lighting powered up. Satisfied, he set off to try to retrace his steps.

Now that he thought about it, this was a rather interesting section of the *Coast City* hub to be in, away from where the rest of the crew were installed. He wondered if there were any empty berths nearby, or whether the cabins had all been stripped by the demolition drones. If not, it wouldn't be a bad place to haul his gear and set up camp.

Ida walked on for a few minutes, following the grilled but otherwise featureless corridor, then slowed as he noticed his breath steaming even more in front of his face. Perhaps he was taking it too fast for the atmospherics to power up and keep the corridor heated. Ida stopped and, holding the pad firmly in one hand, patted his arms around his body to try to warm up.

No, it was too far around the hub, and the section was in too fragile a state to be comfortable. He'd settle for the regular crew quarters, but he could at least shift right to the end of the berths, put a little distance between him and the rest of the crew, even if it was just a handful of empty cabins. Better than nothing. Out here, the cold made his knee hurt.

Then the lights went out, and Ida was in darkness punctuated only by the glowing screen of the station control pad in his right hand.

"Well, that's nice," said Ida. He flicked the pad back to the home screen and selected the notepad feature. The screen lit with a blank cream page so bright in the total dark of the corridor that Ida squinted before he turned the screen away from him to act as a flashlight. It was remarkably effective, throwing a whitish light several feet ahead. Enough to get back to the service elevator, for sure. Ida kept walking, surprised at the loud, metallic sound his footfalls were making on the bare grille decking. The dark was playing tricks.

Ida stopped when he realized his boots *weren't* making that sound at all, but the sound stopped at the same time he did. He turned, holding the control pad in front of him like a shield. The corridor was empty, but while the light from the pad was bright, it was diffuse, producing a glow that left the edges of the corridor in shadow. Ida watched his breath puff out in front of his face.

There. Again, the sound. He swore it sounded like footsteps, but whoever was walking around was a long, long way off, the sound echoing from some distant corridor. Ida took a step forward. Then he shook his head. He'd had enough of this game.

"Hello?" His voice didn't carry as far as he'd thought it would. The rough grilled surface of the walls, floor, ceiling dampened the sound.

When the footsteps sounded again, Ida felt his heartbeat quicken. The footsteps *were* echoing, no matter what the corridors were lined with. They continued for a few seconds, getting fainter as the mystery walker moved away.

"Huh," said Ida, feeling stupid but also wondering if this was all part of the joke. He turned and, pad lighting the way, headed for the elevator in the opposite direction of where he thought the footsteps had come from.

As he turned the corner, Ida pulled up quickly to prevent himself from walking straight into two huge men in regulation olive green T-shirts.

Ida shone the light up, into the faces of the two marines, but their heads were wrapped awkwardly in more olive cloth. The disguise was childish, but quite effective in hiding everything but their eyes.

Those eyes had a spark in them. Ida had seen that light before, in the heat of battle. It was the light in the eyes of a killer that the Fleet selectors looked for when choosing frontline troops. And now Ida appeared to be locked in a space station with them, all clearly with a touch of cabin fever.

"Abe, Abe, Abe," said one of the marines, stepping forward. "Fancy meeting you here."

Ida shook his head. Enough of this nonsense. "Stand aside, marines." He took a step forward, only to be stopped by a large hand pressing into his chest. The marine turned to his companion.

"You hear what he's been telling everyone?"

"You mean that bullshit about saving a planet?"

Ida knocked the hand away. "What the hell are you talking about?"

"Some jack-shit story, right?" said the first marine. "Nice little tale for the grunts out in deep space, eh? Because those fucking space apes will believe any shit, right?"

The second marine shook his head and turned back to Ida. "He's a goddamn liar."

Ida felt his heart rate spike. "Now, wait one minute—"

"Serving the Fleet is an honor, you sonovabitch," said the first marine. "Now, you tell me what kind of cowardly shit would make up a story like that, huh?"

Ida made to turn, but it was too late.

* * *

"Look, Captain…"

Ida closed his eyes, took a deep breath, and began to count. It was supposed to be relaxing, helping him clear his head and focus.

Now the deep breathing just hurt, as somewhere inside, a cracked rib creaked. He winced, skipped from three to ten in his head, and opened the one eye that could still open. The ready room flipped in his vision in a way that made Ida nauseated, just a little, and when it righted itself it was fuzzy at the edges and slightly out of focus. Not good.

"Sir, do you expect me to explain how I fell down some stairs last night? Take a look. A good, long look. It was two of your marines, Carter and DeJohn. I know it was."

King leaned back, pressing his body into his leather chair, and looked at Ida down the length of his not insubstantial nose. There was no chair on the other side of the desk. The commandant—who should have been occupying the ready room—probably didn't want to wear out his fancy rug. Importing it from Earth, along with the fancy wooden desk and the fancy leather chair, had cost the Fleet a fortune; of that Ida had no doubt, no doubt at all. So he just stood and ignored the shooting pains that tap-danced down his side from armpit to ankle, and tried to ignore the fact that Provost Marshal King was the most obtuse officer in the galaxy and that he really, *really* wished the commandant himself was still on board.

"Captain Cleveland," King said. He kept looking down that mother of a nose.

Ida supposed this was his idea of appearing all-important and commanding to his subordinates; considering the jackasses left on the empty hulk that was the U-Star *Coast City*, perhaps it worked. On Ida? Not so much. Not least of all because the space station's security chief was a couple years younger than he was. Didn't King know who he was talking to? Who he was trying—and failing—to make sweat on the fancy little rug? Ida had been busy saving a whole goddamn planet from the Spiders while the provost marshal here got the *Coast City*'s canteen roster nice and straight. And now, with the commandant gone, King was the ranking officer.

Maybe it was just lack of experience, the self-important paper-pusher suddenly finding himself elevated to commander of a powerful, if only partially active, piece of Fleet military hardware. He seemed a born bureaucrat, content to manage the affairs of the Fleet from a safe distance while field servicemen like Ida were actually out there, taking the fight to the Spiders. Except now he was supposed to be in charge of the station and in control of its personnel, and Ida had just told him that he was anything but. The marines knew something was wrong—Ida had sensed that already, the commandant's absence clearly a sore point among the station's crew. And, Ida thought, the marines also knew that the marshal wasn't capable of replacing their respected commandant, even temporarily. Ida started to feel sorry for King.

King coughed. "Something funny, Cleveland?"

The feeling quickly passed. Ida tried opening his black eye, but all he could see through that one before it filled with tears was the provost marshal framed in a dark, grainy slit. Ida let it close again, and noted that King had not only dropped Ida's title but gone from his first name to his last. King was slipping, beginning to think Ida was part of the shitty little crew of the *Coast City*. And Ida wasn't going to let that pass.

"It's Captain, sir, and there is a whole lot that I find amusing on board this U-Star. Not the least of which is the deliberate obfuscation of a criminal act, namely the attack on myself by two crewmen under your direct command."

King pretended to look busy behind the desk, turning his attention to a stack of papers in front of him that were in desperate need of alphabetizing. He seemed uncomfortable, nervous even. "Captain Cleveland, let me assure you I take such accusations with a certain level of seriousness."

Paper shuffling while you told someone who was clearly an annoyance to get the hell out of your office was standard procedure. Ida had used that old trick countless times himself. Back in the day, before saving a planet and getting a robot knee had brought him here, to the back end of a particularly nasty little nowhere.

"But..."

Here it came.

"... right now we're in the middle of a complex mission, and we're against the clock. I need all of this station's personnel working to capacity. Taking apart a platform like this is a difficult and dangerous operation—I don't think I need to tell you that. While I'm in command I need this ship running as smoothly as possible. I'm happy to discuss your report, when we're back at Fleet Command, but until then we have a job to do. All of us." King looked up at Ida, papers suddenly still.

Ida felt his molars grind together. So, he was right. King was out of his depth. Pushing the matter would do little. At the moment, anyway.

"Sir." Ida shifted his weight from right foot to left but this only amplified the pain in his side so he shifted back. He kept his breathing controlled and tight, but he sure as hell needed to lie down right about now. At least the knee wasn't acting up again.

King put the papers down and tapped his fingernails on the top of the desk. "The Fleet, in its infinite wisdom, sent you here to oversee the final phase of the demolition. I'm not entirely sure your presence is strictly necessary, but if that's the way they want to do things, then I'm not going to complain. Orders are orders. But let's make it easier on ourselves. Carry out your assigned duties, such as they are, but if you can stay out of my way, then I'll stay out of yours, and then maybe we can get this job done quickly and get out of here."

"And your marines? Carter and DeJohn?"

The marshal gave a curt nod. "The marines, Carter and DeJohn, everyone."

Ida relaxed his jaw. To hell with it. "Sounds like a plan, Marshal."

"Look. It's just a few more months. I know time may hang heavy on your shoulders—you're supposed to be a guest here, and your assignments are hardly taxing."

"That's true, sir."

"So fill your time. Read something. Take up a hobby. The station's facilities—what's left of them—are at your disposal."

Ida considered the marshal's proposal. Maybe that wasn't such a bad idea. Distraction, something to pass the time, something he could do on his own that would keep him out of the way of space apes like Carter and DeJohn.

Ida had an idea.

"Well, when I first joined the Fleet, I built, ah… I built things."

King's eyebrow went up. "You built things?"

"Well, electronics. I dabbled, here and there. Just little projects. My father taught me back when—"

The provost marshal held up his hand. "Fine. Electrical stores are yours, help yourself."

"Thank you, sir."

"Is it on?"

The device was six inches square and two inches tall, just a low silver box sitting on Ida's table. There were four large screws at each corner, flush with the top, and across the front was a row of small embossed buttons that ended in a larger dark circle.

"It's on," said Ida.

Izanami reached forward and scratched at the LED with an immaculate fingernail. "Are you sure? I don't hear anything. Is this light supposed to be on?"

Ida's hand dwarfed Izanami's, and he gently brushed the medic's delicate, almost skeletally thin fingers away so he could fiddle with the controls.

"Huh," he said. He hit the box with his fist. The light flickered white briefly, then began to glow, dark purple at first, brightening to a near-white blue.

Izanami clapped excitedly. With Ida bent over the space radio, she laid a hand on his shoulder. She was cold; he could feel it through his shirt.

"Well done, Ida!"

Ida smiled and tightened the radio's housing with an old-fashioned screwdriver, then stood back to admire his handiwork. Izanami's hand fell away, and she stepped back politely. When he glanced over his shoulder, he saw her smile was as wide as his.

Ida scratched his chin with the blade of the screwdriver. He regarded the plain silver box with the glowing blue light; then he slid his finger over the surface, like he was wiping dust off the spotless device.

A space radio. It had taken just two cycles to assemble it, using components from the electrical stores and the plans Ida had committed to memory nearly thirty years before. The device was actually quite simple, certainly easy enough for the ten-year-old Abraham Cleveland to build with a little help from his father.

Izanami tilted her head, clearly intrigued by Ida's handiwork. "So, what can you listen to?"

Ida looked into the blue light of the device. This was going to be fun.

"Well, that's a good question," he said. "Let's see, shall we?"

PART ONE

THE SIGNAL

1

"You ever seen a chick from Polaris? I mean, holy schnikes. You need level-ten protective eyewear just to look at them. Naw, seriously, they radiate UV when they get turned on. Some kinda survival mechanism. So yeah, it's risky and you need to prebook yourself ten weeks in a class-three ICU afterwards to get your DNA rebuilt, but man, what a rush. What a *goddamn* rush. There was this one time—"

Ida flicked the volume of the radio set down by half. It was Clive's Friday night. Let him have it.

Clive was a pilot orbiting a lump of ice near Polaris. In a few hours he was due to break cover from behind his asteroid and spearhead a lightning strike on the hidden Omoto base on Polarii Inferior. Chances were this time tomorrow Clive would be a patch of brown radioactive dust drifting in the Polarii solar wind, the residue of his beloved Polarii women with him. Because no matter what the outcome of the attack—be it Fleet victory or a successful defense by the Omoto—there wasn't going to be any sentient life left on the planet afterwards.

So, let him command the air awhile. Ida felt bad and hoped Clive made it, but he wondered if perhaps he should stay off the radio in the next cycle or so, busy himself with those damn checklists he'd let slide. As boring as Clive was, he wasn't sure it would be the same without him, and he wasn't sure he wanted to hear about the outcome of the Omoto sortie, good or bad.

It was a waste, one that Ida objected to. Strategically important but ultimately futile. The universe was a big place and maybe the Omoto could keep their base. The Omoto weren't even the Spiders, and wasn't the Fleet supposed to be fighting those mechanical creeps instead of starting little wars over lumps of ice? Given how the war was going, Ida wondered if maybe the Fleet wasn't focusing on the right thing sometimes.

A little interference on the line was obscuring select moments of Clive's monologue.

Ida flicked through a set of diagnostic routines on the space radio's three-dimensional interface. What was a hobby for, if not to present a series of tiny challenges that needed to be overcome, one by one? Talking to others out in space was only half of it.

The white noise of interference spiked. Ida leaned his chair back to the upright and cast an eye over one of the screens that hung on an arm over the desk. It wasn't part of the radio set, it was just a display from his cabin's computer, but he'd patched it into the solar observatory located at the very top of the station's spire. He found the data useful. It had been ten cycles since Ida first turned the radio on, and he'd quickly discovered that the physics of Shadow frequently threw a spanner in the works. And tonight it was no different.

But he had to admit it was really quite a fascinating academic study on the interaction between the star's strange light and the station's own artificial magnetosphere. As the amber glow of data flowed across the screen, he noted a few spikes of stellar activity that corresponded to the static on the set. He could try to retune, or perhaps, given an hour, come up with an algorithm to work the mess out of his signal. Ida poked at the screen, the amber of its data tables and the blue light of the radio the only illumination in the cabin.

Clive kept talking. Castle, a civilian mining engineer whose job supervising the construction of a drill head on one of the moons of Arbitri clearly left too much free time on his hands, butted in occasionally to express his satisfaction with the juicier aspects of Clive's adventures in Polarii love and to ask respectfully for more technical data on the difficulties of human–Polarii anatomical interaction. A newcomer too, calling himself Captain Midnight—Ida wasn't sure whether this was his rank and name or some kind of superhero identity—seemed to be enjoying the chat. Ida didn't quite believe he was calling from inside a black hole, but, hey, the radio hams of the galaxy were a bunch of sad, lonely losers with nothing better to do. If Captain Midnight wanted to be inside a black hole, then let him be inside a black hole. On the radio you could be anyone and anywhere you liked.

Ida wondered whether he should tell them about his adventures over the skies of Tau Retore, and whether he'd get a better reception here than among the jarheads that inhabited the *Coast City*.

DeJohn had been quite right about Fleet service being an honor. In the middle of a difficult, decades-long war against an alien machine intelligence, a citizen could do no greater service for humanity than enlist in the Fleet. And Ida knew full well how he would feel if he came across someone claiming a heroic action that they had no right to.

But was he really so far out on the edge of Fleetspace that the news about Tau Retore hadn't made it? He'd saved a planet and seen off a whole Spider cluster—including a *Mother* Spider. Why else did they think he'd been awarded with the Fleet Medal?

And, he thought, an artificial knee, an enforced honorable retirement, and a final posting to one of the most remote backwaters in Fleetspace. To oversee the decommissioning of an unremarkable space station well past its use-by date.

Ida absently flexed his robot knee, which had grown stiff as he sat at the desk.

He sat and thought.

Something was well and truly FUBAR, and not just on the *Coast City*, but at Fleet Command itself.

Something that, maybe, he should look into.

2

Space is black. Everyone said so—in verse, prose, even song. Except in the Shadow system, space wasn't black; it was *purple*.

Serra took a breath. She stared at the violet-tinged metal wall in front of her, her eyes flicking over the green HUD projected onto the inside of her helmet visor. Among other things—suit status and integrity, temperature, oxygen, constant (and pointless) system notifications from the *Coast City*'s main computer—the HUD's main features were two glowing brackets on either side and an upside-down T right in the center, showing which way was up and which was down. Although such things lost meaning in space, the Fleet liked to impose its own order on the universe. The slice of it occupied by humans wasn't called Fleetspace for nothing.

She wanted to turn around, but, clamped on to the outer hull of the space station, she could only manage to get her helmet around enough to look awkwardly over one shoulder. She wanted to turn, *needed* to look, but she was afraid.

"Carminita… "

The voice again.

"*Date la vuelta, m'ija.*"

Turn around, my child.

It echoed inside her helmet, washed with static, and she swore whenever it spoke the comms indicator on the HUD flickered. But she knew the voice wasn't coming from the station. And it certainly wasn't coming from Carter, working just a few meters away on the hull.

"Carminita, está bien, nena..."

It's okay, baby.

Serra closed her eyes and took another breath, pulling on the atmosphere a little harder than the suit expected. She heard a whirr as it compensated.

"That's it. Cycle the power again."

Serra opened her eyes and turned her head slowly. The front of her visor was an inch from the station's hull, and she watched the metal slide out of her vision until it was replaced by the black—by the *purple*—of space. Until there, just at the edge, she saw something brighter, a violet-tinted white.

Immediately her suit's HUD changed from regular green to a bright, angry red. A countdown appeared, superimposed over the inverted T in the center: *4'38"*, and a third column that spun too fast to read.

"Ahí estás, Carminita!"

There you are!

She closed her eyes.

"Serra?"

Serra blinked and gasped, but the suit ignored it and didn't broadcast her sharp intake of breath to Carter. She turned back to the hull, and the HUD turned green and the counter froze on four minutes thirty-one seconds and remained in view for a few more heartbeats, just to make sure the reader got the message.

Serra got it: The light of Shadow will fuck you up. It wasn't hard to understand. First it would eat through the shielding on your visor; then it would burn your mind out through your optic nerve. Shadow was an evil mother.

"Earth to Carmina Serra. Come in, please."

Carter's voice was loud, exasperated—not quiet, not female, like the… *other*. The comm caught the rasp as he scraped his chin against the padding inside his helmet.

Serra turned and her partner propelled himself toward her. As he approached, he reached past her helmet and yanked at the manual power override switch she was floating right in front of. Serra watched the fabric of his suit's sleeve press against her visor, but it made no sound.

Carter sighed and pushed off again, back to where he had a service panel open. "You awake in there?"

"*Carajo*. Sorry, sorry." Serra shook her head. Should she tell him?

No. A psi-marine hearing voices—*a* voice—wasn't usually taken well by the regular crew. The psi-marines were essential to the Fleet, now more than ever as the fight against the Spiders seemed to be getting harder and harder. While this earned her class respect, she knew some found specialists like her more than a little creepy. She didn't want to give them the excuse. Not that Carter would tell anyone, but sometimes he joined in with the ribbing with the rest of them.

"Don't blame you if you need a little shut-eye," Carter said as he worked, arms deep inside the skin of the space station. "Didn't get much sleep last night."

Serra shook her head and smiled as Carter's laugh snorted across the comm. She wondered whether anyone in the station's bridge was listening in. She wondered whether she cared. The ship's manifest would have shown the two of them spending most nights in each other's cabins anyway.

"You hear what our honored guest has going on?"

Serra turned back to Carter. "Cleveland?"

Carter snorted again. He pulled something out of the service panel, checked a connection, and pushed it back in. "Got himself hooked up with a space radio."

"Oh." Serra wasn't interested. She wished she had more to do out here. She didn't like being in Shadow's light, but EVAs always had to be done in pairs and Carter had assigned her a simple task. "I didn't know they still used those."

"They don't. Nobody does. Seems he's a bit of a geek, among other things."

"We need to talk about that, Charlie."

"Not now." Carter grunted and floated a few feet back. He had another part in his hands, a long black pipe with silver connectors at either end. He held one end up to his visor, then the other. "Damned if I can find anything wrong with this thing. It's not the coolant conduits. I think in engineering terms, this whole thing is fucked."

Serra laughed. Carter's helmet turned slightly in her direction, and she could see her own golden-mirrored visor reflected in his.

And... something else. A black shape, like there was someone else out there, stuck on the side of the hull like a clam, just behind her.

Serra gasped. The comms ignored it again.

"Bridge, come in, please." Carter spun the black pipe and let go. It continued to revolve in the vacuum between him and the *Coast City*.

Serra turned her head quickly, the joint between her helmet and the neck of her suit clacking loudly. There was no one else outside. Of course there wasn't.

"M'ija, no tengas miedo..."

My child, do not be afraid.

Serra closed her eyes and turned back around to the hull. It was the light of Shadow—that fucking magical radiation from the technetium star—that was the root cause of all their problems. The voices in her head. The instability of the station's internal environment system. Shadows where there shouldn't be.

Her comms clicked again. It pulsed a little with static as Shadow's light played with the data stream.

"Sergeant Major, I have Marshal King here."

"Sir, no faults out here," reported Carter. He pushed off a little from the hull and looked up. Above them, a demolition drone was crouched on the hull, parked temporarily but with a green winking light on its back indicating it was just waiting to continue its job. "The drone didn't report anything, because there's nothing to report. Fault must be elsewhere."

There was a pause before the provost marshal responded. He must have been holding the comms link open with his thumb, because Serra could hear a rushing sound in the background for a second before he spoke.

"Okay, back in. We'll just have to keep monitoring."

"Roger that, sir."

The comms beeped and went dead. Carter grabbed his spinning part and grabbed on to the door of the service panel to pull himself back toward the hull.

"Cycle the power back off, lemme get this piece of shit back together."

Serra nodded, and then realized Carter couldn't see it behind her mirrored visor. She acknowledged over the comm and flipped the lever back to the off position. She gave a thumbs-up, and Carter got back to work.

Serra closed her eyes and said, "Do you think there's anything out there?"

Carter grunted as he worked, but after a few seconds she heard his considered reply. "There's always something out there."

When Serra opened her eyes, the metal wall in front of her still had the alien violet hue. She could *feel* the star behind her, and… something else. A presence, something real, something alive right at her shoulder. It was impossible, they were alone, but—

"But the Shadow system is uninhabited, if that's what you're talking about," said Carter, the sudden appearance of his voice in her ear making Serra jump. "No planets. Nothing but slowrocks and dust. Not exactly the kind of light you can grow plant protein under, right?"

Serra laughed.

Carter reappeared from behind the service panel. "Tell you what, though, those slowrocks are probably worth a bit. I heard the marshal a couple of cycles back. High yield of lucanol. Said something about someone coming out to take a look soon."

"Uh-huh," said Serra with total disinterest. If someone wanted to come out this far to look at some asteroids, then they were welcome to them. But there was something else in the Shadow system, she *knew*. Something watching, waiting for… something.

Carmina Serra blinked behind her visor, then turned her head back around to the left. The hull slid away, the purple of space reappeared, the glow of Shadow at the edge, her HUD red.

4:31

4:30

4:29

3

Ida lay on his bed. The lights were off and the room was dark but too cold and not particularly conducive to sleep. Even here, just on the edge of the occupied deck of living quarters, the station's systems were struggling. But at least he was left alone—there was nothing much beyond his cabin that hadn't already been sliced by drones and packed away, and the only person who bothered coming along to his end of the deck was Izanami, which suited him just fine.

But the environment was dodgy all over the station, with wild temperature fluctuations and deviations in the standard air pressure. A side effect of the deconstruction process. Ida had heard a crew went on an EVA to try to rig a fix, but so far they didn't seem to be having much success.

Not that he really *could* sleep. Ida was furious, but he'd pushed the feeling away and gotten on with his work, even though the remaining crew were not shy about their annoyance at his interruptions. Now, in the small hours, on his own, that ball of anger had changed into something colder, bitter.

He sat up and quickly swept off the covers, then slipped the top blanket off the bed and wrapped it tightly around his shoulders as he stood. Damn, it was cold, the temperature dropping even since he'd left the warmth of his bed. His breath didn't quite steam as it left his mouth, but the metal floor was ice on his bare feet.

He turned and hopped to the environment controls near the door, set the heating on full power, and then kicked his boots from where they lay against the wall into the upright position and slid into them. He hobbled to his work desk, boot tongues flapping against his shins. Sitting and securing the blanket around himself, he pulled one of the computer screens toward him on its articulated arm. He checked the clock in the top center of the home screen. It was three in the morning.

The *Coast City*, like every other U-Star in the Fleet, no matter if they were ships or stations or something in between, and no matter how far from home they were, was synched to a daily cycle that matched the rotation of the Earth, specifically to a cycle that matched the day and time at Fleet Command in the former state of Utah. Three in the morning there was three in the morning in space, no matter where you were hiding or the light of which star was shining on you. It didn't matter. War was a round-the-clock operation anyway.

He started poking at the display. Proving his involvement in the action at Tau Retore would be easy enough. All he had to do was access Fleet records and call it all up. Even jarheads like DeJohn and Carter wouldn't be able to deny one of the greatest—not to say *rarest*—heroic actions in Fleet history.

"E.T., phone home," he said, tapping the communications browser. The screen filled with the spinning insignia of the Fleet—rendered as a particularly nasty and old-fashioned three-dimensional model in scratchy blue—before resolving into a black empty square. Ida saw himself in a smaller window in the top left, and laughed. What the hell did he look like?

"Name, rank, and serial number," asked a voice from behind the black window. Ida gave his details, and an icon at the bottom of the screen flicked to green as the video link switched suddenly on. Facing him was an operator at Fleet Command, his chin the only visible feature of the man's face underneath a large, almost comical communications headset. Every minute movement of the operator's head made the insectlike eyes of his headset wiggle and catch the light on its myriad surfaces. Crew who worked as operators—the definition included nearly everything that was vaguely technical or skilled, whether it be communications, logistics, or even pilots—had two nicknames. The official one was Ops. The unofficial one, but the one much more widely used, was Flyeye.

"Ah, hi there," said Ida, pulling the blanket tighter but sitting up a little straighter in his chair. He didn't want anyone to think that a Fleet Captain—even a former one—was a slouch. "Put me through to Archives, please."

"Connecting you now," said the Flyeye; the video flickered with white lines before going black again. Huh. The interference from Shadow was getting worse, crossing over into the supposedly impervious lightspeed link channel. Sunspot activity or some such, no doubt. Ida made a note to check on the readings from the solar observatory again.

Ida waited, and waited. He peered at the tiny view of himself in the top corner. He frowned, and rubbed his face, and tried to flatten his bed hair. With the room heating up, he was beginning to feel drowsy. He shuffled, trying to get comfortable, and then was distracted by one corner of the blanket that had gotten caught under his chair. The room was dark, lit only by the glare of the computer screen and the few small lights on equipment scattered around the room.

Ida sighed and tugged at the corner of the blanket. He leaned down and freed the thick fabric from under the wheel, then sat back up and looked into the screen as he readjusted the blanket around his shoulders. He blinked and peered into the dark, reflective window where he expected a Flyeye from Archives to appear any second. He blinked again and his breath caught in his throat.

There was someone standing behind him.

Another blink, and it was gone, although there was a blur of movement on the screen that might just have been his eyelashes sweeping up and down. Ida felt his heart kick for a beat or two, and spun the chair around on its swivel.

Nothing. He wasn't sure who had been assigned to the room originally—it was large, clearly designed for an officer, maybe one with a higher rank than Ida's own. The cabin's door was on his left. On his right was the bed, which reached to just over halfway into the circular chamber. There was a low bedside cupboard on the side of the bed closest, stacking high with personal belongings not yet tidied away. On the other side of the cabin were a couple of tall lockers, still empty, waiting to be co-opted into use. There was nothing else in the room, no place for anyone to hide unless they were on the floor on the opposite side of the bed or had squeezed themselves into one of the lockers.

Ridiculous. But Ida got up and checked anyway. There was nobody beside the bed. The cupboards were empty, and, besides, the doors were stiff and impossible to open without a harsh metal-on-metal scraping amplified by the quiet of the night-cycle. The main door was closed, and on the bulkhead control panel beside it the indicator glowed a pale red, *locked*, next to the environment control sliders. Nobody had come in or out.

Ida stood and flapped toward the panel, then stopped after a few steps, unhappy about the sound his unlaced boots were making. He had the sudden urge to be very, very quiet, and with the room warmed up, he shucked them off. Barefoot, he crossed the rest of the floor to the room controls, double-checked the lock—as though the red LED could give a false reading of security—and tapped the environment down a couple degrees.

When he turned back to the table and chair and faced the rest of the room, he found himself doing it with some trepidation. He was a career military man, and he didn't like being spooked—mainly because he never was. But he was tired and worried, and he knew sleep deprivation, no matter how mild, could amplify anxiety about the smallest things. He felt a surge of anger. The fucking space apes who inhabited this godforsaken space station were getting to him.

The video link flared into life again. Ida scooted to the chair and sat down again, blanket now abandoned.

"Archives," said the Flyeye, this time female. "What is your request, please?"

The video link rolled, for just the blink of an eye, and when it restabilized, it took a second or two for the white lines of interference to vanish. Ida ignored it.

"Reference Fleet action 2961, May to September. Sortie of the First Fleet Arrowhead to Tau Retore. List of commendations and awards, please."

"Thank you," said his new Flyeye. "One moment, please."

Ida tapped the mute and pushed the screen back on its arm to give him some room as he leaned forward on the desk. Head in hands, he massaged his cheeks, trying to wake himself up. He wondered if he should go down to the canteen to get some coffee. He quickly decided against it.

The Flyeye's head tilted. "Tau Retore System, 2961, sir?"

"Yes, Operator," said Ida before realizing he was still muted. He tapped the screen and repeated for the Flyeye.

"No commendation list available. The last Fleet action for the Tau Retore system is… December 2960."

Ida felt an adrenalized pang in his chest, enough to snap him to full wakefulness.

"Can you confirm, Operator? Tau Retore, 2961."

The operator paused only a moment, her multifaceted goggles bobbing as she inclined her head again to read the data off a display out of sight of the camera. When she spoke again, she was shaking her head.

"Sorry, sir. Do you have the correct reference? 2960 is the last action. I have the authenticated order command on file."

"Okay," said Ida. He rubbed his chin again, and then pulled his hand away. It was shaking. He slapped it down on the desk and hoped the operator didn't notice.

"Can you pull sortie sheets for Fleet ships?"

"Yes, sir. Nameplate and date?"

"U-Star *Boston Brand*. May 2961. No, wait… make that September 2961. Should be a log of repairs out in one of the dockyards. She took quite a battering. Warpcore was burnt clean out."

Ida tapped his fingers on the desk while the operator a thousand light-years away searched the servers of Fleet Command. He smiled to himself. Yep, the warpcore burned clean out because he had a bright idea that ripped the solar heart right out of a Mother Spider.

(Burning as if it were a lamp and then they died one and all and)

Ida coughed.

The search took longer than it should have, long enough for Ida to find his socks and pull them on. He felt a dull ache creep up his chest with every passing moment.

Something was up.

"U-Star Kappa Alpha Omega Omega. *Boston Brand*. Listed as out of service, January through November 2961."

Ida felt dizzy. "The hell?"

"That's what it says here, sir."

"Reason?" Ida snapped, causing the operator on the video link to jerk back at her console. Another pause. Ida could just see the top of the op's hands as she typed.

"Q-Gen coil failure. Replacement of the whole coil assembly. Any further information requires engineering classification, sir."

Ida swore, just remembering to hit the mute as he did so. The Q-Gen coil was the part of a U-Star's engine—a tiny component compared with the rest of the thing, but a vital one—that tore a hole in the universe and let the ship push into quickspace. He knew exactly how it worked—all U-Star commanders had to know the mechanics of quickspace and the technology that allowed them to abuse it. He knew that the Q-Gen coil had nothing whatsoever to do with the warpcore, the central component of the main engines that did the actual business of moving the ship past lightspeed. He also knew that such repair work was exceptionally rare and, as indicated by the operator, took nearly a year to complete.

The mute came off again.

"Q-Gen coil failure? The Q-Gen coil was fine. The warpcore needed replacing because I was the one who burnt it out. We pushed quickspace without engine warming!"

The operator said nothing. Then she licked her lips. To Ida she looked less like a fly and more like a praying mantis considering its next meal.

"I don't have any more information, sir."

Ida felt like reprimanding the operator, but he knew she was just reading what the terminal showed her.

"What about the U-Star *Stars* and the U-Star *Stripes*? And the *Carcosa*." He clicked his fingers. "Yes, the *Carcosa*. Gotta be a big report on that one. Same system and flight time."

The Flyeye glanced down, and Ida heard some tapping as she pulled the data sheets up.

"The *Stars* and the *Stripes* are both out of service. No further engineering notes. No entry on the... *Carcosa*?" The Flyeye repeated the name, then spelled it out. Ida confirmed it was correct.

Ida felt that deep, sinking feeling in his stomach, a mix of nausea and adrenaline that left him hollow and dizzy.

Maybe he was dreaming. Maybe he could just slide back into bed, and Astrid would be waiting for him. He remembered the farmhouse and the red barn. He'd been seeing those a lot, lately.

The Flyeye moved her head to look at someone off-screen; exaggerated by the operator's headset, the motion was enough to snap Ida out of his reverie.

The Flyeye turned back to her camera. "Do you have another request, sir?"

Ida considered. He had a hundred requests, a thousand individual entries he wanted the operator to look up. The flight histories of every ship in the First Arrowhead for the last two years. Service records and notes on every crewman on board the *Boston Brand*. The same again for everyone in the whole Arrowhead, including the list of the dead from the U-Star *Carcosa*. Reports on Tau Retore for the same period. News items. Observations on Spider movement and activity in the Tau Retore system and the next dozen closest.

He wanted a detailed listing of his own service history, including retirement remarks, commendations, and awards, along with medical records.

"Sir?"

Ida sighed and reached forward, hand hovering over the "terminate call" button.

"No further requests," he said, tapping the screen. It went dark. "Thank you," he said, all too late.

4

The "food" was spicier than usual, but Serra didn't mind. Next to her at the table, Carter spooned in mouthful after mouthful of the stuff. He normally hated anything remotely approaching hot, but even just a few hours outside the station on another EVA to try to fix the environment controls seemed to have spurred his hunger.

Serra didn't mind at all. In fact, she rather enjoyed it, the pleasant glow in her mouth replacing that thing called "flavor" that she thought she could remember if she tried hard enough.

"Heard the Omoto got fucking hammered," said DeJohn. "Heard it over the link. That rock was fucking toasted."

"Damn!" Carter held his hand up, and DeJohn gave him a high-five.

Serra grinned. Nothing better than news of a victory, no matter how far away, no matter how small. Victories were few and far between, moments to be savored, celebrated.

DeJohn sucked a sporkful of protein slime over his teeth. The sound was revolting, but manners weren't high on the priority list for combat troops. Combat troops taking apart a stupid space station. She shook her head and took her next mouthful.

"What?"

Serra glanced up. DeJohn was looking right at her, but it was Carter who had spoken. He had half turned toward her and seemed to be staring at her plate.

"What?" she said.

"You shook your head."

"I guess that's the end of the Polarii," said Serra. She tapped her spork on her tray and winked sideways at Carter before looking at DeJohn. "Shame."

Carter collapsed in mirth. Serra and he both knew about DeJohn's predilection for Polarii women. DeJohn looked slightly worried as he processed the information, before Carter reached forward and slapped his shoulder across the table.

"Relax!" he said. "Man, you are *so* easy."

DeJohn laughed, but it was unconvincing. Carter rattled his tray on the table and stood.

"Gonna get some more," he said, glancing at Serra. "Coming?"

Serra's tray was half full. "Nah, I'm good."

Carter gestured to DeJohn, but DeJohn waved him off. Carter stood and joined the back of the queue of marines slowly shuffling past the serving counter.

Serra ate some more, but there was no conversation. When she looked up after a few mouthfuls, she saw DeJohn was looking at her. Fuck. She shouldn't have mentioned the Polarii. Now DeJohn was wired, and when he was wired he was a fucking pain in the ass.

Serra shifted in her chair. She was smaller than he was, but still muscular; any difference in strength between the two marines would have been compensated by Serra's increased agility. She shook her head again and returned to her food. DeJohn was fine, but he was also a creep sometimes, especially when he started thinking with his dick. It didn't particularly bother Serra—life in the Fleet, am I right?—but it was fucking boring. Then again, maybe she didn't blame him. Months and months out on this wreck and hardly a female left among the crew. She was pretty sure there was something about shore leave that Fleet Command had conveniently ignored.

They ate in silence for a while, Serra doing her best to ignore DeJohn's gaze. By the time Carter returned, she'd nearly finished her tray. Carter dropped into his seat, spork hanging from his mouth and fresh mountain of something grayish green on the table in front of him. He pulled the spork out with a wet sucking.

DeJohn tore his eyes off Serra. "Been around the hub lately?"

"Nope," said Carter, hunched over his new tray. "Why?"

"Heard that fuck Cleveland shifted his shit around to the end of the officer's row on Omega Deck. Fucking prick scared as shit." DeJohn laughed.

Serra and Carter exchanged a look. "King said to keep away, remember?" Carter said before popping another mouthful.

"Fuck King," said DeJohn. "And we can just take a look. I wanna know what that prick is doing here, anyway."

Serra frowned and turned back to her plate.

"Carminita?"

Serra looked up. "What?"

Carter and DeJohn slowed their chewing. Carter raised an eyebrow. "Huh?"

Serra bit the inside of her cheek. She felt cold, and… somehow she didn't feel alone. She was in a canteen full of crew, sharing a table like she always did with Carter and DeJohn, but she had this feeling that there was someone else, somebody sitting in the empty chair to her right.

And she looked, just to be sure. The chair was empty, of course.

"I think we should stay away from Omega Deck," said Serra, her voice almost a whisper. She blinked and turned back to her food.

Where did that come from? She didn't know. Then again, she didn't know where the voice was coming from either.

DeJohn sniffed loudly. "There's a good little marine. The marshal asks you to suck his dick, would you do that too?"

"It's not King," said Serra. "We should stay away because… just because," she said, feeling stupid. She stopped eating and pushed her tray away. She saw DeJohn scratch his ear, his eyes flicking between her and Carter.

"Not this shit again," said DeJohn. Carter frowned at him and leaned over the table toward her.

"What's up?"

Serra held his look a moment, then shook her head and returned her attention to her tray.

"Anyway," DeJohn said, "there're better things to do off shift, right?" He nudged Carter, but his friend ignored him.

DeJohn chuckled, low, deep, his eyes crawling over Serra again. She sighed, then stood and began to walk away, empty tray dangling from one hand.

"Hold on, I'm coming," said Carter. She could hear him quickening his pace as he fought to clear his second tray.

Serra nodded but didn't turn around. By the time she'd dumped her tray on the collection trolley by the canteen's doorway she was unsteady on her feet. But only when she reached a little farther down the corridor, where there were no people around, did she allow herself to lean on the wall. She bent over, hands on knees, fighting the dizziness.

Someone called out her name again, the name only her long-dead grandmother used, but she ignored it, took a deep breath, and then stood up straight and kept walking.

5

Ida found Izanami six hours later, as the *Coast City*'s artificial day cycled toward midmorning.

After he'd cut the connection to Fleet Command, Ida sat in his room in the dark for what felt like a thousand years. There was a hell of a lot to take in.

Stuck in a space station full of jarheads was, in a way, like being back in the academy. All it took was someone taking a dislike to someone for rumors and stories to spread. Ida had seen it happen before. But picking out Ida as a liar who hadn't earned his medals was a surprisingly specific storyline for DeJohn to take up. Ida wondered who had started it. Carter, no doubt. He was the leader of the engineering team DeJohn was in, and the most senior noncommissioned officer left aboard. Maybe that was part of it—Ida had seen the silver bar of the Fleet Medal on Carter's tunic too. The Fleet Medal offered certain privileges that Carter no doubt enjoyed, only now there was someone else aboard—someone with a higher rank, even though no longer on active duty—with those same rights. Carter probably felt threatened, in some way, no longer the special one. And so a whisper about Ida's award being fraudulent had started, with DeJohn just happening to be the loudest.

But it seemed it was more than a whisper campaign. The more Ida thought about his late-night call to Fleet HQ, the more surreal it felt, like it really had been a dream. Maybe he'd given the Flyeye the wrong date, and the Op had looked up the wrong records. Or the Flyeye was working on too much caffeine and had made the mistake herself. Perhaps a computer glitch had caused the wrong data to be displayed; someone had screwed up the entry accidentally or— worse—deliberately.

He needed to do more digging, get it sorted out.

Not that he needed to prove himself to Carter and DeJohn. But... but it *bugged* him. Being sent out to the Shadow system was the most obscure retirement duty he'd ever heard of. If he didn't know better, he would have said that someone at Fleet Command had it in for him.

Izanami was in the surgical unit. She jumped when Ida called her name.

"This a new hobby, sneaking around the station?" She glanced down. Ida followed her gaze, realizing he was still in his socks. He sighed. Bootless, in grubby shorts and T-shirt, he must look crazy. But the feeling of self-consciousness passed as he began to describe the conversation with the Flyeye at Fleet Command. As he explained, Izanami's expression changed from a puzzled smile to a frown, her forehead creasing deeply.

"How is that possible? A mistake with Fleet records?"

Ida scratched his unshaven cheek. "It's possible, but even if it was a mistake, it seems to match with what DeJohn and the others think. None of them have ever heard of Tau Retore. It was six months ago, but this wreck isn't *that* far around the edge of Fleetspace. There's no way the news could have passed by."

Izanami dropped into her chair silently, tapping a pen against her teeth.

"Well," she began with some hesitation, "the lightspeed link hasn't been that reliable."

Ida curled his lip. "Interference from the star? Yeah, I had that myself. But bad enough to cut the station off so they missed the reports? Were you guys cut off?"

Izanami just shrugged. Ida thought maybe she hadn't been on the station then.

"But… you believe me, right?" he asked.

Izanami's pen stopped and she looked at him, her eyes narrowing. "Of course."

"I think you're the only one who does."

Izanami sank deeper into her chair. "What are you going to do? Try Fleet records again? If you asked the marshal—"

Ida shook his head. "It runs higher than him—it has to. If the commandant was still here I could ask him—maybe that's why he left before I arrived. No, I need to talk to Stockley, Stevens. The other commanders of the First Arrowhead. See if they've landed in the same mess." Ida frowned and looked at the floor. "How, though? The lightspeed link to Fleet Command is just going to lead me around the same circle."

Izanami smiled and stood. She reached out and laid a hand on Ida's shoulder. Her touch was cold and so light, he could hardly feel it through his thin T-shirt. "Well, you have your own link now. There's nothing to stop you."

Ida looked at Izanami. "The radio set?" He felt the smile grow on his face. "That might work. If I can find out their current postings, I could try getting in touch directly, bypassing Fleet Command."

"You'll need to use Fleet Command to get their posting first, though?"

"Yeah," Ida said. He frowned again. "Maybe. I'm not sure I have clearance anymore. Maybe I can pull a favor or two…"

Izanami withdrew her hand. "You'll get to the bottom of this. I know you will."

Ida smiled and nodded his thanks and headed back to his cabin. The station was cold again, and he picked up his pace, rubbing his upper arms and looking forward to putting a second pair of socks on his frozen feet.

* * *

Ida slumped on his bed and ordered the cabin lights to darken. He lay still and closed his eyes, collecting his thoughts. He was exhausted, physically and mentally.

His efforts had been fruitless. Talking to Fleet Command via lightspeed link had been a frustrating and time-consuming process, given the clearance required for the information and the endless delays that caused. He'd spent hours on hold, or being transferred between operators and departments, or repeating his original request over and over again to new operators and supervisors who had no clue who he was or what he wanted. His original plan to call in favors owed evaporated when it became clear nobody could locate the people he wanted to speak to.

But it was the interference from Shadow that was the most frustrating. It had grown progressively worse the longer Ida kept the lightspeed link open. Several times it had gotten so bad, the link automatically disconnected. Ida had never seen anything like it, but then he'd never been in orbit around a star like Shadow. When he patched into the *Coast City*'s solar observatory again, the graphs flew wildly over the screen as numbers that meant little to Ida hurtled past. Shadow was active; that was for sure. Flares and sunspots and a lot of stuff Ida had no clue about; the activity even seemed to be affecting his knee, the psi-fi field periodically glitching in time with the rhythms of the star as he sat motionless at the desk.

If Shadow continued to act up like this, the station would be cut off from the rest of Fleetspace. Which, thought Ida, might not be such a bad thing—the last transport wasn't due to swing by and pick up the station's last remaining crew, Ida included, for a couple of months. If the Fleet lost contact with the *Coast City*, they'd more than likely send the ship early. Which suited Ida just fine.

Except right now, when he needed to get answers from Fleet Command, the increased activity of Shadow was just what he *didn't* want.

Between the endless waiting and signal dropouts, what information Ida had managed to gather was next to useless. Even when he had persuaded someone to impart the data he wanted, or even just look the damn thing up in the first place, there were either no records or a single-line description. Commanders Stockley and Stevens, no record. Lieutenants Yung, Martin, and Hazlett—two listed as deployed, with no further information, and the third an empty record. It was the same with all the command crew of the First Arrowhead. Like the U-Stars they had captained just a few short months ago, the men and women who had been under Ida's command were mysteriously unavailable, their records vague, their status indeterminate. Swept under the carpet. Just as Ida had been.

No doubt with proper authorization he could probe further into the records and mission status of the crews, but that would mean convincing Provost Marshal King, as *Coast City* commanding officer in the absence of Commandant Elbridge, to put the request in. Ida once again reflected on the early and unexpected departure of the commandant. There was another situation Ida didn't feel entirely comfortable with.

Ida closed his eyes. His lack of progress was worrying. Something was going on at Fleet Command, something revolving around him, his former compatriots, and the action over Tau Retore. The interference from Shadow was the icing on the cake. He almost felt the star was doing it deliberately.

Ida opened his eyes.

The brightest light in the dark cabin was the blue dot on the front of the radio set. It was the first thing he saw every morning, the pale, sky-colored LED drawing his gaze toward it. It represented so much—not just the effort of building the thing in the first place, but the link it formed with the rest of the galaxy. With the radio, he could escape from the *Coast City* and the weird nightmare he now found himself in. With the radio, perhaps he could find the answers out there in the black. Maybe Izanami had been right.

Ida sat up on the bed, his eyes used to the dim of the cabin, lit in pale blue by the radio, the red and yellow LEDs scattered on the other equipment and the walls of the cabin itself nothing more than an abstract star field of pinprick lights. He pushed himself off the bed with his knuckles and slid into the swivel chair, rolling it back over to the desk.

He coughed and looked around the empty room. He had no idea where to start—if the Fleet didn't know where his former colleagues were, then what chance did he have of finding them?

He waved a finger over the uniformly silver top of the radio set. The blue LED flicked to a brighter setting, and the cabin filled with the background white noise of the universe as it breathed. The sound swam until Ida found his headset. As soon as he snapped it to the sides of his head, the main speaker cut.

Ida was alone with the universe.

He closed his eyes, listening to the rush of static until his brain began to impose order on the sound, introducing patterns and rhythms Ida knew were nothing but figments of his imagination.

As a child, back on the family farm, he used to lie in the dry grass of summer, staring at the brilliant sky until his vision went white. Then he'd roll over, dust tickling his lips and the smell of dry dirt and leaves in his nostrils, and watch the patterns play out in purple black behind his tightly closed eyelids. Sometimes, if you stared long and hard enough, the patterns didn't just form geometric shapes and figures that danced left and right. Sometimes whole narratives played out. How long he used to spend lost in this nonexistent world, he had no idea. Years later he taught Astrid the same trick, and together they would lie in the grass and describe what they were seeing to each other, Astrid weaving intricate fairy tales and scary ghost stories.

Ida blinked and pushed the memory away.

The noise rose and fell, waxed and waned. The echo of the Big Bang, reverberating on for all eternity.

"*Sonovabitch*, where you been?"

The voice that erupted in his ears practically threw Ida out of his chair. Heart thundering, the next thing he heard was howling laughter. Ida coughed as he drew breath.

"Clive! You're alive!"

The laughter cranked up again. "You're a poet, and you know it."

"How was the, ah, sortie?" Ida winced. He wasn't asking about Clive's holiday in the sun, after all.

There was a sloshing sound, followed by a hollow pop. Clive was on the sauce. Probably quite deserved.

"Oh man, we hammered the Omoto. It was a beautiful thing. Also, I rescued some damsels and got me some prime Polarii pussy for the ride home. Listen to this—"

Ida bounced forward on his chair. "Tell you what, maybe later. Good to hear you're in the land of the living."

Clive didn't notice the snub. He supped from his bottle again and gave a friendly holler over the air. "Take it easy, bro!"

"I'll try my best," said Ida, pointing a finger and rotating it in the air. The channel shifted, and the warm static filled his ears. Good old Clive. Nice to hear someone made it.

Ida leaned back and rubbed his face, allowing the virtual dial to keep spinning up as he considered where to start looking.

After a moment, the white noise changed, lowering in pitch, taking on a harsher edge. Ida's eyes flicked open in surprise. He glanced at the display hovering in the air in front of him and sat upright very quickly.

The radio's tuner had cycled down through the regular frequencies but had kept going. All Fleet communications equipment had built-in fail-safes, preventing certain frequencies from being accessed. Ida's rig, constructed entirely from memory, was clearly flawed, as the set should have hit the bottom of the dial and then stopped.

The sound in his ears was different. He was in unknown territory. Dangerous territory.

The set was tuned to subspace.

Ida frowned, hesitant to continue but also hesitant to turn the radio off. The frequencies of subspace were illegal, but despite his misgivings at the alien sounds that now filled his ears, he had to admit he felt a little thrill. Not just because he was breaking Fleet regulations, but also because he was doing so on board the *Coast City*. King would probably burst a blood vessel if he found out what Ida was doing... but what the marshal didn't know wouldn't hurt him, right?

Ida closed his eyes, leaned back, and listened. The sound of subspace wasn't just white noise and it had nothing to do with the Big Bang. The sound of subspace was the angry roar of the nothing that resonated *between* space. It was weird, *alien*. Ida couldn't remember quite what the penalty for accessing subspace frequencies was. He didn't imagine the regulations had been enforced in years. In fact, he wasn't even sure why they'd been drawn up in the first place.

Ida knew what every U-Star crewman knew about the physics of space travel—and maybe a little more than most. That interest was probably the only reason he'd even known *how* to think of pushing a whole U-Star through a Mother Spider via quickspace, the "hidden" dimension of the universe, the one that allowed objects, such as U-Stars, to travel faster than light, and which the Fleet's entire communications net—the misnamed lightspeed link—depended upon.

But subspace… subspace was different. Scary, even.

Back in the day, when quickspace and other dimensions were first probed, everybody thought subspace was *it*. Mankind had hit the jackpot and discovered the legendary hyperspace, the key to interstellar travel and faster-than-light speed, the subject of hundreds of years of science fiction. But, as it turned out, you couldn't push anything through subspace except energy, which made it useless for travel but perfect for communication. Then quickspace technology was developed, and by the time U-Stars were powering toward distant stars, subspace had been long abandoned, the lightspeed link having become Fleet standard.

No, subspace hadn't just been abandoned—it had been *banned* by the Fleet. Ida scratched his cheek, trying to remember the reason, trying to remember if he ever knew it. It had been a long time ago, he knew that much, nothing more than a footnote in Fleet academy textbooks. Nobody thought anything of it.

The noise flared, and Ida opened his eyes again. He blinked in the dark, eyes drawn again to the blue light on the radio set, and he frowned.

Maybe he did remember, just a little.

There was a story—probably just nonsense, a bit of spice to explain why subspace was prohibited—that the sound of subspace, that exotic static, was *bad* for you. Listening to it would drive you mad or rot your brain or make you curse your mother and start drinking at an early age. Some said the sound of subspace was an echo from another dimension, something *deeper*, a place where monsters lurked. A name had even been coined for the imaginary lower level: hellspace.

Hellspace was just a story and the name itself was a joke, but sitting in his cabin in the dark, Ida felt unsettled. The roar in his ears was a little weird, but it sounded more or less like regular white noise… but he had to admit there was something else there, a rolling sound that was beginning to make him feel dizzy. Maybe there was a reason, a real one, stories and legends aside, why the Fleet didn't want anyone tuning in to the roar of subspace.

Ida reached forward and gestured above the radio set, turning it off. The empty noise clicked off sharply.

Ida sat in the silence of his cabin, suddenly feeling alone. The sound of subspace had almost been like a physical presence.

Despite himself, it took Ida a few minutes to get the courage to move to the cabin controls and turn the lights on full.

6

The desk in the commandant's ready room and the green-shaded lamp that sat upon it were not standard Fleet equipment, but by tradition the most senior officers were allowed to bring their most treasured personal effects with them on long tours. Across the U-Star fleet, many wonders were held—rare and valuable books, sculptures, antiques and heirlooms. The officers of the Fleet liked to think they were a cultured lot. And having such objets d'art on display didn't hurt when welcoming representatives of other cultures and planets aboard a Fleet ship. The Fleet had to impress sometimes, and not just with firepower.

Roberto King didn't like the desk, but then it wasn't his desk, and it wasn't his office. The contents of the ready room belonged to Commandant Elbridge; indeed, since taking command of the *Coast City*, the only change the provost marshal had brought to the ready room was an adjustment in the height of the chair, itself as old as the desk it was placed behind. King was less interested in aesthetics and design and more interested in functionality. Give him a psi-couch and an earpiece, and he'd happily sit in the ready room and control without distraction the final few spins of the *Coast City* as it orbited

ADAM CHRISTOPHER

toward full demolition. The chair was less comfortable, the desk less functional, but despite this, King spent most of his time in the ready room anyway.

He reached forward, the ancient springs in the chair protesting as he did so, and flicked to the next page in the book on the desk in front of him. He regarded the image on the thousand-year-old paper with distaste, but when he sat back into his chair he didn't take his eyes off it.

The provost marshal didn't like the desk or the chair (or, for that matter, the rug or the lamp), but he did appreciate the art on the wall behind him. He also appreciated the fact that the art was hung on that wall in particular, because it meant that while sitting in the chair, he didn't have to look at it.

He liked the artwork, wondered at the artistry of it, found the palette interesting and the brushwork exquisite. Of the subject, he was less sure. It was a ship in a stormy sea, the prow of the vessel about to crest a titanic wave that was sure to overwhelm and drown the crew. It was Japanese, and rendered in classic blues and grays and greens that, despite the subject, made the scene bright, if highly stylized. Perhaps Elbridge had a fondness for the art of the Far East. Perhaps he liked it because it showed that, no matter what measures were taken, nature could not be tamed by mere mortals. Perhaps he felt that the picture represented the *Coast City*, its mission to study the technetium star around which it orbited akin to trying to sail in a stormy sea. Shadow was dangerous. King knew that now, and Elbridge certainly had.

Or perhaps there was another reason for having the picture on the wall. Because the picture went with the book, and the book went with the desk.

Elbridge had volunteered to command the *Coast City* from the very inception of the mission. He'd had the desk installed as soon as his office was ready. The desk was made from the timbers of a sailing ship, one with a famous name, although it was a name Elbridge had kept to himself. He'd written about it on the inside front cover of the book—a leather-bound first edition of something called *Spate's*

80

Catalog, published in New York in 1903—which had been hidden in a secret drawer. When King took over the office, that drawer had been left open, and it hadn't taken much to figure out how the mechanism worked.

After only a little reading, King knew full well why the book was hidden. He knew why the desk was here. He knew what the picture on the wall behind the desk showed.

He also knew why Captain Abraham Idaho Cleveland, retired, had been sent to oversee the last orbits of the U-Star *Coast City*. He knew why the station was due to host Zia Hollywood and the famous *Bloom County* in just a short while.

King reached forward and flipped another page, feeling his stomach flip in synch. And then he leaned back again, and this time he closed his eyes.

7

The *Coast City* rotated into Earth-dawn. Ida yawned, stretched. He'd managed a few hours' sleep, at least.

The cabin lights were still on.

He rubbed his eyes, wishing that when the purple shapes appeared he could tell a story about them to Astrid. That wasn't going to happen. Ida's fingers stopped moving, and he sat with them pressed against his eyeballs.

He had to keep it together. He had to get to the bottom of it all.

He sighed, loped out of the cabin and down the hall to the vast communal toilet and shower room. As far as Ida knew, he had the place for his own private use, right on the edge of the habitable deck as he was. The nearest occupied berth was a good three hundred meters back toward the elevator lobby. Not far enough for Ida's liking, but any farther away and the station got a lot less comfortable.

Ida left the door of the stall open as he relieved himself, and thought about whether he could be bothered trekking to the canteen for a proper coffee instead of the caffeine simulant he kept in his cabin.

He zipped up, and stood stock-still for just a moment. He glanced over his shoulder, into the empty men's bathroom, wondering whether it was time for another of Carter and DeJohn's hilarious pranks. The space apes hadn't bothered him for a while.

Ida moved, the rustling of his T-shirt suddenly loud. Then he stopped. He wasn't imagining it. From down the corridor came the unmistakable rise and fall, rise and fall of subspace static. Faint as it was, Ida felt the hairs on the back of his neck prickle. He'd turned the radio off last night, and he hadn't touched it since as far as he could—

Ida drew in a sharp breath. There was something else in the noise—not a rhythmic pattern, but… a voice.

Someone was talking on the subspace channel. It was faint, unintelligible, but Ida could tell it was female. He jogged back to his room.

As he sat down at the desk the static swelled, obscuring the transmission. Ida adjusted the tuning and the roar popped a few times; tapping the panel displaying data from the solar observatory, Ida watched as the popping coincided with spikes of activity from Shadow. More interference, this time strong enough to penetrate even subspace. The purple star at the heart of the system certainly was a strange beast.

There! Faint and distorted, behind the wall of noise. As she spoke, her words punched the static, and it flared and danced around her voice, like Shadow was reacting to the signal, fighting the transmission. Ida brought up the tuning dial and carefully adjusted the channel.

"Hello? This is Captain Abraham Idaho Cleveland of the U-Star *Coast City*. Come in, please."

The static buzzed and popped, and he repeated his call twice, fine-tuning the channel as he did so. Nothing. He'd lost it.

"*Pyat, cheteeree, tree, dva, raz…*" The woman's voice crackled suddenly, filling the room. Whatever she was speaking, it wasn't English. Ida frowned. English was the Fleet's official language, used for all communication. It was hard to tell with all the noise, but it almost sounded Italian.

"Can you repeat? You are very faint." Ida turned up the volume, and then grabbed the headset in a hurry and jammed it on. The rush of static was like a slap to the face, and he quickly turned the volume down again.

"Raz, dva, tree, cheteeree, pyat..."

The woman's voice rose and fell in the unfamiliar accent, making it impossible to tell whether she had realized Ida was on the line and was talking to him or she was in the middle of a conversation with someone else. Ida kept talking, stopping quickly as the woman spoke again, but soon he realized she couldn't hear him. He was eavesdropping.

Words and phrases were being repeated; he could tell that much. There were pauses; then she would repeat a phrase, sometimes quite loudly, as though she was trying to make herself heard. Ida realized that he could hear only one side of the conversation, as the pauses and phrases sometimes sounded like answers to questions, the speaker's temper rising as though whoever she was talking to didn't understand or couldn't hear.

Ida didn't like it. There was something about her tone as she went on, her speech quickening and her voice becoming higher and higher. She sounded scared and angry.

But... he couldn't turn it off, not yet. Who was she? Where was she? Was she in trouble, in danger? He tried to tune out her voice and listen for anything in the background that might provide a clue, but the channel was uniformly awful. The static was punchy, sharp. Ida watched the graph of solar activity crawl over the nearby display. If anything, that scared Ida more than the mysterious and frightened voice broadcasting, impossibly, from the depths of subspace.

But there was nothing he could do. She couldn't hear him, and he couldn't hear who she was talking to. He removed the headset and there was a brief second of silence before the subspace radio's speaker clicked in, filling his cabin with the static and the voice. It echoed oddly around the hard walls of the cabin.

Ida knew he should turn it off, but a part of him wanted to keep listening. It made him feel uncomfortable, and sad, and very, very small. The universe was a big and terrible place, and she was very far away, and there was nothing he could do, even if he knew what the trouble was. He suddenly felt that his own situation—most likely the result of a clerical error—was ludicrously insignificant.

Before he lay on the bed, he checked that the message and data stream was being recorded. If he was lucky, he might be able to analyze it later and get a position on the signal. Not that that would be of any use.

Then he closed his eyes and lay with his hands behind his head. Listening, watching the purple patterns behind his eyes, wondering who she was.

8

M'ija, no tengas miedo.

Serra woke with a start. She might even have called out, she wasn't sure, but what she was sure of was the cold dampness of the sheet and the way her heart was trying to break out of her rib cage. She sat up quickly and breathed shallow and fast in the dark. The voice again. The dreams.

She should have left the station, insisted that Lafferty—whom she outranked—stay instead. But as her pulse slowed she also knew that a psi-marine who regretted past decisions was one with a much abbreviated lifespan.

The cabin was dark, and when she glanced to her left she saw the other side of the bed was empty, the blanket drawn back and the mattress still sunken from the weight of her companion.

There was a click from the other side of the room. Serra jumped again and this time she did call out, something colorful and Spanish that made Carter chuckle as he sat at the table, his naked back to her.

"You scared the crap out of me, Charlie." Serra sat up against the wall and readjusted the blanket around her. Damn, it was cold. The station's faulty atmos controls were becoming a drag, fast. "What are you doing, sitting in the dark?"

The clicking sound came again. Carter sat with his forearms on the desk and he wasn't moving, but Serra saw something bright flash in his hands. A small metal something, narrow and silver. Charlie Carter's Fleet Medal. FOR SERVICES RENDERED.

"You okay, baby?" she said. The Fleet Medal was the highest honor available to them both, but Carter didn't like to wear his, preferring to leave it in its fancy box back in his quarters. He'd said several times that he didn't need to wear it all the time, only for special occasions, and there weren't many of those on the *Coast City*. Besides which, there was a smaller bar, a placeholder for the medal itself, sewn onto the breast pocket of his tunic. It was less conspicuous, which Serra knew suited him just fine.

Serra had learned to stop asking, anyway. Whenever she brought it up, he changed, withdrawing into himself. She knew that if she had a Fleet Medal, she'd wear it all the time and damn well write poetry about it, but Carter's was a different kind of medal. He'd been part of the Fleet Marine Corps Black Ops division—that much Serra knew, but little else. He shouldn't even have told her that. The commendation on the medal was standard, deliberately and officially vague; covering their asses, Carter said whenever she asked him about it. Which was rarely.

Except he'd clearly been thinking about it again, with the arrival of Captain Cleveland. She didn't blame him, especially not with that idiot DeJohn stirring things up.

Serra had thought Carter's medal was locked away in the cupboard where it usually was, but he had it now, at the table, rolling it between his thick fingers. He must have started carrying it around with him.

Carter didn't speak or move, except for the slow motion of his fingers, turning the metal bar over and over and over, the light it caught like a star glittering in the dark.

She tried again. "Can't sleep?"

No answer. Serra drew her legs up to her chest. Her breath was now clouding in the air in front of her face.

"Wanna talk about it?"

The Fleet Medal clattered to the tabletop and Carter got up. He was wearing pants but Serra could see his torso glisten with sweat as he moved across the room toward the door. He must have been freezing.

Almost in tune with her thoughts, he flicked the environment control on the wall next to the door up a couple of notches. Above her head, Serra heard the air unit whirr into life as it began gently blowing in warm air.

She smiled, and then, unsure if he could see, patted the bed next to her.

"Come back to bed."

Carter stopped by the door. "You know what they give out the Fleet Medal for?"

Serra pulled her legs up tighter to her chest. "For services rendered," she said.

" 'For services rendered.' " Carter smiled. "You know what that means when you're in Black Ops?"

"I—"

"Means you weren't afraid to follow orders, no matter what they were. Means you weren't afraid to get your hands dirty. Means you did things for the Fleet that nobody else could know about. Means you did things that sometimes keep you awake at night."

Serra nodded. "You think he was Black Ops too?"

Carter sighed and walked back to the bed. The tension in the room seemed to ease a little as he sat down heavily, rocking Serra on the mattress. She reached out to him. His skin was cold but she ignored it. She was warming up and he would too, soon enough. He rubbed his chin slowly, but said nothing.

"Think he's cooked up that story to, what, cover his involvement with something else?" she asked. "Turning his Black Ops medal into something heroic?"

"Something heroic," said Carter. He laughed and shook his head. "I didn't mean it like that."

Carter nodded and slipped back into the bed, facing her. He didn't look her in the eye, so she took his face in her hands and softly pulled his chin up. His eyes shone in the dark and she kissed him, but his lips only twitched in response.

"You're not okay," she said.

He smiled, but it was a sad expression. He brushed the hair from her forehead and sighed.

"Forget it," he said. "It's just another bad dream."

He settled onto his pillow and pulled the blankets up to his neck and closed his eyes. Serra watched him for a while. He didn't fall asleep, but he seemed calm, more relaxed.

She understood, or maybe understood just a little more, anyway. Carter lived with the shadow of the Black Ops cast over him; whatever it was he had done, whatever it was he had been *ordered* to do, it had affected him—broken him, a little—and they'd given him a goddamn medal for it. He hated the medal; really, deep down, she knew he hated the Fleet too and was looking for a way out.

And now they had Cleveland, a man with no past, with a Fleet Medal of his own, won in an epic and heroic battle that nobody had ever heard of. Here was a moment, a chance for Carter to act on his anger, his self-loathing. Cleveland was everything Carter hated about his own past.

Serra sighed, and she slid down under the covers. Maybe Carter realized that too. Maybe he'd reached a turning point. She glanced at him and saw he was now asleep, his breathing soft.

The room was warming up and she felt a little more comfortable, but as she closed her eyes she thought perhaps the shadows in the room were moving, and as she drifted off into sleep, her face twisted into a grimace of fear and her eyes moved under their lids rapidly.

Ahí estás, Carminita!

And the cabin was still and quiet and dark, and the shadows moved.

9

"My *God*."

Ida raised an eyebrow at Izanami, but the medic was staring at the floor. The subspace recording from the radio looped and echoed around Ida's cabin as the pair sat and listened.

"What?"

Izanami looked up at him, her face drawn. If she'd had any complexion to start with, he would have said she looked quite pale. But it was hard to tell. Her opalescent skin rarely changed hue. "Can't you hear it?"

Fear. He'd heard it before, the first time, but the more he listened, again and again, the worse it sounded. "She is—*was*—in trouble," said Ida. "Some kind of accident?"

Izanami listened for a moment more, and then shrugged. "Have you pinpointed the origin?"

Ida rolled on his chair to the desk. He reached out and stopped the playback; then he pulled a computer screen toward him. His fingers spread over the display as a scrolling table of data transformed into a simple vector map he'd constructed. A solar system. *The* solar system. Proper noun. Home.

"Near Earth, as far as I can make out. There's a lot of data loss in the signal. Most of the information has been stripped out by the interference."

"Interference from Shadow, I presume?"

Ida nodded. He felt Izanami peering over his shoulder at the screen.

"And near Earth? That doesn't make sense."

Ida tapped his index finger against the plastic frame of the computer screen.

"Not much about this does," he said. "Subspace isn't used for communication—it's a banned channel, has been for, oh, years and years—"

"Banned?" Izanami's eyes went wide. "Is this going to get you in trouble?"

Ida waved away her concern. "No one will find out. U-Stars aren't fitted out to monitor subspace, so it's not like anyone can listen in. Anyway, my point is: what's the signal doing there in the first place?" He scratched his chin and regarded the silent silver box on the table. "A signal broadcast from somewhere near the Earth, using a disused, prohibited system, spoken in something other than the Fleet's official language."

He poked the computer display, rotating the map of the solar system, new vectors drawing themselves from several points near the schematic representation of the orbit of Earth, each line suggesting possible source coordinates.

"I wish I knew what she was saying," said Ida. "I don't think anyone on the station speaks Italian, and the signal sounds too poor to feed into the station computer for a translation. If King would let me near it, of course."

"Italian?"

Ida turned and looked at Izanami. She looked confused.

"Don't you hear the accent?" he asked.

"Oh," she said with a shake of the head. "That's not Italian. Russian."

Ida's eyes widened. "And you know that because?"

She shrugged and turned away from Ida. She walked to his bed and sat delicately on the edge. "I worked in Russia once. That's the beginning of the recording—she's counting down, then up, like she's testing something." She held a hand up before Ida could ask the obvious. "That's as much as I can manage, sorry."

Ida crinkled his nose. Then he spun his chair around to the computer, switching the map back to the data tables. He flicked a hand near the radio, and the playback began. On the computer screen, the table began scrolling as the audio ran, a smaller window beneath plotting another graph of the audio analysis.

"She's talking to someone else, that much is clear. I only patched on one side of the transmission."

"Why do you care?"

Ida stopped, hands frozen above the computer's touch screen. He turned slowly. Around them the Russian voice crackled on. "What do you mean?"

Izanami had lain down on Ida's bed. *Well, make yourself at home*, he thought.

"You don't know who the recording is of," she said, looking at the ceiling. "You don't even know where it is from. If she was in an accident, she's probably dead. And even if she is or she isn't, if it was near Earth, the Fleet would have picked her up, because if it was some kind of distress call, or if she was reporting on something, she wouldn't have been using subspace. She'd be on the lightspeed link. What you patched into was an echo. That would explain the quality of the signal."

Ida didn't know what to say. He played his tongue along his teeth, and he felt cold again. Another environmental glitch. But she was right. The signal couldn't have been broadcast in subspace at all. What he'd picked up, completely by chance, was some weird echo bouncing around the hidden dimensions of the universe.

"More to the point," she said, "weren't you supposed to be working on something else? Your old crewmates?"

Ida blew out his cheeks. Why *did* he care? Izanami's question was fair enough: the signal was a distraction, something to keep him from going slowly mad as he tried—fruitlessly, it seemed—to get answers to his own little mystery.

But the lightspeed link was a waste of time now, the interference from Shadow growing so strong as to make it almost unusable. Even if he could break through the static, all he could do was call Fleet Command again and get some Flyeye to read him the same abbreviated reports he'd already heard a dozen times now.

"Ida?"

Ida coughed and looked at Izanami. The recording had looped again. "I'm working on it."

"Okay."

"Yes, okay." Ida felt a tightening in his chest. He sucked cool air over his teeth and changed the subject. "An echo, you think?"

Izanami shrugged. "Could be?"

Ida frowned. He'd never heard of signal leakage from one dimension to another, but it sounded feasible, especially when there was a strange star just next door pulling all kind of tricks on the communications networks.

But Izanami's question scratched at something in his mind. He repeated it over and over to himself, looped like the recording.

Why do you care, Captain Cleveland?

"Hmm," he said at length. He turned his chair around a few degrees and looked at the radio set and computer screen on his desk. She was right, it was a pointless exercise. But…

"Distractions can be useful sometimes," he said, turning back to the medic.

She nodded, and her smile reappeared. "I'm sorry, I didn't mean to make you feel guilty."

Ida laughed, but maybe that's what the feeling was. He tried a smile, and found it worked a little. "And, you know, there's something about her voice… it makes me feel… sad. But in a good way, somehow. I don't know. That doesn't make much sense."

Izanami tilted her head, her frown a thoughtful expression. "Melancholy can be good for the soul."

Ida blinked. "So says the neurotherapist."

They looked at each other, then both laughed. Izanami closed her eyes and pointed at the ceiling as she lay on the bed.

"Play it again."

Ida pushed his screen away, waved at the radio, and sat back with his eyes closed as the Russian woman's voice faded into the cabin.

"Pyat, cheteeree, tree, dva, raz..."

10

After another replay or two, Izanami left Ida to it. It was very late, and Ida wanted to use the main comms deck on the bridge to start a translation running before he tracked down Carter and got the marine to sign off on the next demolition briefing. And boy, was he looking forward to that meeting; he'd delayed it as long as he could, but the paperwork had to be done eventually. Over the last few cycles, Ida had realized his official duties took up maybe an hour per cycle, which made it easy to let them slide altogether. The marines resented having him poking around, giving them small, annoying extra tasks in order to get the demolition signed off. And the provost marshal, despite his apparent love of procedure, hadn't asked to see any completed documentation yet anyway.

Ida shifted on the bed and lay awake for a few minutes, then absently turned the recording loop back on and listened to it as he lay in the dark.

He dozed and dreamed of the farm, Astrid leading him into the red barn. When they got to the door, red paint streaming off it in a breeze that was colder than it should have been in summer, he discovered it led to a corridor of the *Coast City*.

Standing by the door was her father, his eyes narrow as he and Astrid argued. Argued about Ida, probably. But every time the old man opened his mouth, nothing but white noise came out. Astrid screamed and ran off down the corridor.

Ida woke with a start, thinking there was someone standing over the bed, watching him. The cabin was silent, the playback having stopped apparently by itself. Ida sat up and watched the blue light of the radio set for a while, thinking he'd probably turned it off sometime during the night and didn't remember.

He got up, showered, and headed to the bridge, subspace recording in hand and the silver Fleet Medal insignia shining on his breast pocket. As he walked, it crossed his mind that his self-imposed isolation was bad for his health. The last thing he needed now was to have some kind of breakdown.

It was the recording; he knew it. The mystery woman was becoming an obsession. Something mysterious but trivial to ease the wait until the interference on the lightspeed link cleared and he could try again to get some real answers about his missing past.

Ida picked up his pace. He was nervous, and more than once he checked over his shoulder, and more than once he thought he saw someone disappear just out of sight. Someone with blond hair, wearing a blue survival suit, like the one he'd last seen Astrid in.

Ida took a deep breath and shook his head, trying to snap himself out of it.

He felt better as he entered the busier part of the station. Here the lining of the corridors was intact, and the station's remaining crew went about their duties, none paying him much attention as they rushed around. As he got closer to the bridge, he kept an eye out for his special friends, DeJohn and Carter, but he didn't see them among the green- and blue-uniformed personnel.

Normally the bridge of a U-Star was out of bounds except for those with explicit permission to be there or those of a high enough rank to make such a formality meaningless. Ida wasn't sure he had either, not anymore, but the elevator didn't protest as he requested his destination, and as he stepped out of it he fingered the Fleet Medal on his tunic, making sure it was still in place. Its constant presence made him feel a little better, anyway.

Despite the customized design of the space station, the bridge of the *Coast City* was fairly standard: the regular semicircle layout common to all Union-Class Fleet Starships was here extended around to form a completely circular room, with the elevator rising in a column in the center. The column continued up through the ceiling, leading ultimately to the top of the station's main spire.

Ida stood quietly by the elevator, jiggling the recording disk in his hand, scanning the half of the bridge he could see. It looked like only the minimum regulation crew were manning their stations: two pilots, who on a station had damn-all to do; two other officers Ida didn't recognize, both of whom were several rungs down the ladder from him; and a marine-engineer, recognizable in his olive green T-shirt and combat pants, checking something at the science station.

Ida frowned. The marine was DeJohn. But his expansive back was turned, and if Ida went left around the central elevator column, he could reach the unmanned comms deck, placing the column between him and his rival. He wanted to talk to DeJohn at some point, but it could wait.

"Can I help you, Captain?"

Ida jumped. He turned, finding his nose not two inches from Provost Marshal King's face. Ida smiled, trying to ignore the man's garlic breath.

"Comms deck free?"

King's eyes flicked sideways toward the side of the bridge that housed the communications station and then back to Ida. "The comms deck?"

Keeping his smile fixed, Ida casually strolled over to the comms deck and rested his hands on the back of the vacant chair. "May I use the communications deck?"

King stood stock-still near the elevator column, following Ida with only his eyes. He looked nervous. Ida could see it in his face, no matter how hard the bullethead tried to assert his authority. It was like the whole thing was a façade, one the man was desperate not to let slip.

"It won't make any difference," said King finally.

"What won't?"

King clasped his hands behind his back and slowly walked over, a ghost of a smile playing lightly over his lips. "The lightspeed link is down, ship-wide. Interference from our friendly neighborhood star."

Ida frowned. "Happen often?"

The provost marshal shrugged. "Sometimes. The star has unusual properties. It's what this station was built to study, after all." King's smile tightened. "That comms deck will be needed when the channels have cleared."

Ida nodded. "Oh, no doubt. But while the lightspeed link is out of action, maybe I could borrow it for a little while?" He jammed one hand in the back pocket of his fatigues and offered the small black rectangle of plastic that held the subspace recording toward King. "Won't take that long. I just need to run some data from my little radio shack through the mainframe. You know, crosscheck some of my programming. I'm not as good as I used to be."

"Oh yes," said King. "I heard you built a radio set."

Ida grinned and waggled the disk in front of the marshal's face. "You did say I needed a hobby."

King's lips twitched, the tic pulling at one side of his nose. Ida widened his eyes expectantly.

"Very well." King had barely snapped out the words before he turned and marched swiftly back to the elevator. He pressed the call button, but as the elevator indicator light above the door began counting the floors toward the bridge, he turned back to Ida.

"One more thing, Captain." King folded his arms and took a few steps closer.

"Marshal?"

"I know you have relocated from your assigned quarters without authorization." King unfolded a hand from his arms and held it up, stopping Ida's protest before it had started. "And while I would normally issue a reprimand and insist you go through the regular channels, I'm prepared to overlook it for the moment. So long as our mission runs its correct and proper course, I don't care where you sleep at night."

Ida huffed a laugh. King's expression tightened.

"However, the station will be receiving VIPs in the next few cycles. If you could add your new cabin to the list of occupied spaces, I will add that stretch of the hub to the security detail."

Ida nodded. Anything for a quiet life. "Fair enough. I'll do it now."

"Thank you, Captain," said King. "Also, for the duration of the visit, all personnel will be required to wear their station tags and have them turned on at all times."

Ah. There it was. Always a catch. "So you can track my movements?"

King nodded. "So I can track everyone's movements, Captain. This station may not be in active Fleet service, but it is now a construction site. A *dangerous* construction site. For the safety of both our crew and the visiting party, we will need to keep security tight and to restrict access to some parts of the station."

"Don't want any important people stepping through the floor and floating away?"

King ignored the comment, turning away to head back to the elevator. The door slid open with a pleasant tone.

Ida called out after him. "Who's coming anyway? Anyone I know?"

King turned back, arms still folded, and the tight smile returned to his face. Ida didn't like it. Whoever was coming must have been a big deal, the way the provost marshal walked slowly back toward him. It was just short of a swagger. "You've heard of Zia Hollywood?"

Ida frowned and then shrugged. "Can't say that I have. She must be a hell of a VIP, name like that."

King drew an index finger along the bottom edge of his mouth. "She's a starminer."

"Ah," said Ida. That explained the name, then.

"You've been out in the black too long, Captain," the marshal said. "She's the most famous woman in Fleetspace. Hollywood and her crew will be stopping here to refuel on the way to that field of slowrock debris on the other side of Shadow."

Ida nodded, but he didn't care. He had no interest in the so-called celebrities of the Stellar Gold Rush. To have reached the top, she would be young, pretty, and 90 percent silicone, and she would spend her whole stay aboard the *Coast City* peeling frustrated space apes off her. Good luck to her. He'd register his cabin, wear his ID tag—turned on—and stay in his cabin for the duration of this special visit.

Apparently satisfied, the marshal stabbed the elevator button again to open the door and disappeared inside. Ida watched the indicator above the door begin to move again, King heading up the station's main spire.

"Zia Hollywood," said Ida quietly, shaking his head. He dropped himself into the comms chair, slammed the recording disk into one of the free slots in the console, and set to work.

11

The control room of the *Coast City*'s solar observatory was circular, very similar to the main bridge far below but condensed, with only enough room for a half dozen personnel at most. The provost marshal was the only one in the room, but he knew he was not alone.

The screen in front of him showed a view of Shadow, the image filtered with software so only certain wavelengths were displayed at the operator's request. King cycled the view through each in turn, and much as he expected, the image did not much change. The star was violet, light at the center and dark purple at the circumference, and stubbornly remained so no matter which wavelength he selected. The only change was in the corona, a shifting, diffuse halo that streaked off into space from the star's surface. As the images changed, so the corona changed with it, shifting in shape and size.

It was a failing of the solar observatory systems. It had to be. Although the systems were fitted and customized as best as possible for this particular mission, observing Shadow was a difficult task. The light from the star degraded the sensors and cameras with surprising speed, resulting in a constant need for replacement and recalibration.

The light that will fuck you up. King allowed himself a smile. It was a common refrain around the station. Nobody liked being out here, not within touching distance of a star so foreign, so *alien*, that it felt like it was alive, like it was watching. Maybe the *Coast City* wasn't watching the star; maybe the star was watching the *Coast City.*

King reached the end of the available filters, and he paused. He knew the truth, thanks to the book hidden in the desk, but he had to check for himself. Commandant Elbridge's notes may have been written in some personal code, but the comms deck had translated it without any difficulty.

The final filter would show it. King held his breath. He wondered if Elbridge had known what he was doing. Then he turned the selector switch.

The view of Shadow changed, the colors reversing, the bruised black of space a brilliant violet white and the star itself now black. And at the center of the star, the blackness swirled, spiraling inward, black moving on black moving on black, like darkness being pulled in on itself, tumbling into a whirlpool. Darkness falling into an abyss.

King stiffened. The lights in the solar observatory were on low, twilight normal. The observatory was mostly run on automatic, the systems gathering data and piping it back to Fleet Command via the lightspeed link, while researchers who had until recently been stationed on the *Coast City* did their work in more comfortable surroundings down in the hub.

In the reflection on the screen in front of him, in the depths of the black star, King saw her standing behind him. Her eyes were blue, and the hand on his shoulder was as cold as the hull on the dark side of the space station.

"I know what you want," said King. He didn't move, but his jaw clenched as the pain of the cold crept into his bones and made him ache from head to toe. He closed his eyes. "You cannot have him. *Will not* have him."

When he opened his eyes, he was alone, and the observatory control room wasn't as dark as he'd thought it was. On the screen before him was displayed the regular view of Shadow in the visible spectrum, the violet white star a featureless globe, a purple halo licking out around it.

King turned off the display. He walked backwards until he was up against the opposite wall. Then he sank to the floor and wept.

12

"Fuck, Sen, you're a stone cold killer. Remind me never to—"

DeJohn's words were lost as the marine gunner next to him opened fire again with her heavy automatic rifle. Aboard a U-Star, all arms were switched from plasma pellets to soft ceramic shells so the hull wouldn't get punctured should a firefight break out. The shells were safe to use but made a hell of a noise, which made the practice range a popular place during a tour. Marines liked to make a lot of noise, and today the range on the *Coast City* was nearly full, the marines left aboard the station taking advantage of their light duties to get some practice time in.

Serra watched Sen's back as the gunner emptied her weapon at the target a hundred meters down her lane, reducing the somewhat dramatically drawn two-dimensional representation of a Spider groundcrawler to so much shredded fiberboard. Beside her, DeJohn had his hands clapped over his ears, the protectors hanging uselessly around his neck. He was laughing as he watched Sen practice. Heavy weaponry was her specialty, and leering at female troops was his.

A buzzer sounded and green lights lit above each firing point as the range commander called a halt. As the *Coast City*'s complement of marines was lower than normal, a roster had been drawn up; today the range commander was Corporal Ahuriri, and aside from punching the buzzer, Corporal Ahuriri didn't really give a shit. Regulations were loose now there were so few marines left on board, which meant practice at the range was perhaps a little more fun than it should have been. DeJohn even had a plastic drink bottle filled with something that smelled far stronger than their standard electrolyte solution sitting on the shelf in his firing point. Serra wondered if she cared enough to report it, and wondered if sucking on engine juice while holding a live weapon made DeJohn more dangerous or less.

The light on the barrel of Sen's rifle flicked to blue as she raised it, smoking, to the ceiling, balancing the stock on her hip and glancing sideways at DeJohn's grinning face. Serra couldn't resist grinning herself as Sen turned and, weapon safe, gave her a nod. DeJohn, meanwhile, started getting his own weapon ready on the shelf in front of him. He whooped as he checked his magazines.

"Some things a man never gets sick of," he said. "Am I right or am I right?"

Serra took her position at Sen's vacated station. The range of weaponry available to her as a psi-marine wasn't as wide or as heavy as the gunner's, just the standard light rifle and pistol. It was the latter that she was working on today; it had been a while since she'd used it. She positioned her feet carefully and then looked up, but DeJohn hadn't been talking to her. On the other side of him, Carter stood at his own firing point, pistol in hand but barrel end resting on his shelf. He was staring at his target. He didn't seem to be listening.

Serra frowned. Carter was acting like nothing had happened during the night, but he seemed distracted. She knew not to bother him, not after she'd seen the Fleet Medal in his hands. She wondered again about what had happened in his Black Ops tour. Being out on this derelict station probably wasn't helping either, not with DeJohn hanging around, not with Cleveland aboard.

DeJohn didn't seem to notice his friend's snub. He whistled to himself and returned his attention to his weapon. He'd chosen the light rifle. When it was ready, he flicked the safety off and the barrel light went from blue to red. He glanced over his shoulder at Sen, who leaned back against the wall and did nothing except look him up and down with a smirk on her face before pointedly slipping her ear protectors on. DeJohn grinned.

"They say it's not what you've got, it's what you do with it, am I right?"

Serra rolled her eyes. "Oh please," she said, and readjusted her footing before punching the button on her left. A new target slid into her lane fifty meters ahead.

The buzzer buzzed. The indicator lights turned red.

She fired six shots. Then DeJohn opened up with his rifle in the neighboring lane. Further down, a handful of other marines began firing as well, the combined sound of exploding ceramic ammunition pressing on Serra's eardrums despite the protectors. She lowered her weapon, regarded her shots with some disdain, and stepped back.

Carter hadn't moved. He was breathing quietly, his chest rising and falling beneath the tight olive T-shirt. Serra removed the clip from her pistol and walked over to him. She waited for the buzzer to sound again before speaking.

"You okay?"

Carter jumped at her voice, then closed his eyes and sighed. But when he opened them again they came with a grin. She smiled in return, and she felt a little better.

"Yeah, no problem," he said. "Didn't get enough sleep last night."

Serra laughed. "No kidding."

From behind her came a low chuckle from DeJohn. Serra turned and lifted an eyebrow. "You have a one-track mind, marine."

"You'd better believe it," he said, slamming another magazine into his rifle. He winked at Sen, who just shook her head. She was smiling too.

"Never see Captain Asswipe down here," said DeJohn, punching his target button and raising his rifle sight to his eye. "Girl has probably never handled a gun in his life."

Sen smirked and pushed herself off the wall. "Girl, huh?"

DeJohn snickered. Sen trailed a fingertip over his back. "And you'd show him a thing or two, wouldn't you?"

DeJohn lowered his gun. "That I would, marine. That I would."

Sen placed the back of one hand on her forehead and buckled at the knees. "Oh, Captain! My Captain!"

Then she burst out laughing, DeJohn and Serra too.

"Marines, ten-hut!"

There was a clatter of weaponry as the range came to attention, Serra, Carter, and Sen all standing tall. DeJohn stood relaxed, rifle hanging loosely by his side. With his other hand he grabbed his drink bottle and sucked noisily on the straw.

Captain Ida Cleveland stepped toward the insubordinate marine, computer pad under one arm. As he walked forward, his eyes flicked here and there, taking in the others in the firing range. He was frowning, the typical disappointed officer, but Serra could sense a lack of control. He wasn't in charge here, and he knew it. DeJohn knew it too.

"Thirsty, marine?" asked Ida. DeJohn looked him in the eye and kept sucking on the straw for a good few seconds before setting the bottle back on his shelf.

"Thirsty work, being in the Fleet," he said. Then he sniffed and raised his rifle. Pointing the barrel at the ceiling, he thumbed the safety off and manually reloaded the chamber.

Ida didn't move, didn't take his eyes from DeJohn's. "That's thirsty work, being in the Fleet, *sir*."

"I don't see no officer in here." DeJohn nodded at Carter. "You see anyone, Charlie?"

Serra could almost feel Carter vibrating next to her. She glanced sideways and saw his lips flicker, his eyes staring straight ahead.

Nobody moved; nobody spoke. Ida took a step backwards, his footfall loud in the quiet firing range. Then he turned on his heel and offered the computer pad to Carter.

"You're the demo leader on lambda section, marine. I need you to check and authorize the last drone run."

DeJohn hissed and turned back around at his firing station. He began fiddling noisily with his weapon.

Serra turned her head, breaking her stance. Carter looked pale. He licked his lips.

Ida lifted the datapad higher, until it was practically under Carter's nose. "Problem, marine?"

Carter exhaled, blowing the air out with puffed cheeks. He said "No, sir!" and grabbed the computer pad, thumbed the page down three times, then tapped his thick index finger across the screen. He held the pad out to Ida.

"Authorized, sir!"

Ida took the pad slowly, a slight smile on his face. He glanced down at the pad, nodded, then put it back under his arm. He looked around the firing range.

"Carry on," he said, and marched out.

DeJohn turned around as the marines fell out.

"Fuck," he said, then grabbed for his drink bottle. "Comes all the way down here, disturbing the peace, just for that? Like we haven't got enough to do without him making all this extra work for us."

Serra busied herself checking her pistol. "It's hardly that much work."

"Yeah. Well. *Prick*." DeJohn rolled his shoulders and raised his rifle, aiming down his lane. "You don't have to salute him, Charlie. He's not a real captain."

Carter's station was quiet. DeJohn lowered his weapon and glanced at his friend. He shook his head.

"Fuck, clear your head, marine," he said. "Ain't no time for napping when there's Spiders to shoot." He raised his rifle and took aim, adjusting his grip and lowering his cheek to rest on the side of the gun. "Fucker needs to be taught a thing or two about how we work around here. Things would be different if the commandant was around."

Sen sniffed and returned to lean against the wall with her arms folded. "Yeah, but he isn't."

"And ain't that sad fact. Hey, Ahuriri, punch the fucking lights already."

Before the range commander had even pressed the buzzer again, DeJohn opened fire. Serra and Sen stepped back, Serra clutching her ear protectors as she watched him obliterate the target.

Serra frowned. It was easy enough with a rifle, she thought. Pistols were harder. She'd managed only five hits on her own target, all of them marginal. She turned to Carter—but so far he hadn't fired a single shot.

"Hey, come on," she said, putting a little more strength into her voice than she actually felt. But it was what he needed; she was sure of that.

Carter rolled his shoulders and, without another word, raised the gun and fired ten shots in quick succession. With practiced ease he slid the half-full magazine out of the gun's grip, made the weapon safe, then punched the target button. The fiberboard Spider glided toward them.

There was only one hole in the target, ragged and large, in the dead center of the Spider's head section. Carter's aim had been perfect.

DeJohn whistled and shook his head in appreciation, then began reloading his rifle. "That's my man!"

Serra and Carter exchanged a look, and Carter laughed. His shoulders slumped, and under Serra's hands his muscles felt far more relaxed than they had been all day.

He nodded and smiled; she smiled back and walked over to her station and got another target up and ignored the voice in her head that kept calling her name.

13

The cabin was dark when Izanami came by. She stepped half-in, half-out, and looked like she was about to back out when Ida spoke from his position on the bed. Izanami stopped and squinted, and as Ida sat up, the cabin lights warmed to the preset twilight dim. Izanami stepped into the room properly, the door closing behind her and cutting out what little light had crept in.

"Finally!" said Ida.

"Good evening, Captain."

"Where have you been hiding? I've been looking for you."

Izanami smiled and waved her hands vaguely in front of her. "Oh, around. So? Did you manage to run a translation?"

"I did," said Ida, swinging off the bed and walking over to his desk. He stopped before sitting down and turned to face the medic.

Izanami frowned. "Find something?"

He nodded. "Plenty."

He sat, pulled the computer screen toward him, and tapped out a sequence. The rush of static filled the cabin like a warm bath. When the Russian woman spoke again, Ida saw Izanami stiffen. The voice was now speaking in English. It was still distorted, and still heavily accented, the computer simulation a perfect match. And now they could hear what was being said very clearly.

"Five... four... three... two... one... one..."

"You were right about the countdown," said Ida over the next section of dialogue. The static crackled over the top.

"Listen... listen! Come in! Talk to me! I am hot, hot... What? Forty-five? Fifty? Yes, yes... yes? Breathing, breathing oxygen. Yes. I am hot!"

Izanami sank to the edge of the bed, hands clasped tightly in her lap. She was looking at the floor, but when she glanced at Ida, her eyes caught the blue glow of the space radio light again and he suddenly felt odd and had to look away. It was uncomfortable, listening in on someone else's conversation. It felt wrong, but he wanted Izanami to hear the rest.

"So she is in some kind of ship? Smaller than a U-Star?"

Ida nodded but held up a finger. "It gets worse."

The recording popped sharply.

"I am hot... This... Isn't this dangerous?"

Ida heard Izanami gasp. He closed his eyes.

"Yes... What? Talk to me! How should I... Yes? Transmission begins now... Forty-one... Transmission begins... I feel hot!"

"Ida, please."

His eyes snapped open. Izanami was looking at him, her oval eyes shining brightly. As he watched, the shadows in the corner of the cabin behind her seemed to swim a little, but it was just his imagination. "Just listen," Ida said.

He'd told himself, over and over, that he was just listening to a computer-generated interpretation. He knew that, but he couldn't help the tightness in his chest. He knew that no matter what, he'd never be able to listen to the original Russian recording again, ever.

"I can see a flame!"

"Ida!"

"What? I feel hot... I can see a flame! I feel hot... Thirty-one, thirty-two..."

Izanami shifted on the bed. She was looking at the floor again. "An accident," she said, her voice so low, Ida only just heard it over the static.

He nodded, but she wasn't looking.

"I can see a flame! I can see a flame!"

The voice, computerized or not, was heartrending. The woman was clearly trapped and desperate to escape. These were her last moments of life. Of that Ida had no doubt. He also had no doubt that he was going to give up the space radio and never touch it again. He had only a couple of months to go on the *Coast City*. He'd sort out the business with Tau Retore back at Fleet Command. It wasn't like he'd ever see Carter and the others ever again anyway.

"Am I going to crash? Yes, yes! I feel hot... I will reenter, I will reenter. I am listening."

The static snapped off and the silence that filled the cabin was as cold as the air had become. Ida stood and walked to the environment controls, pumping the heat up a few notches to compensate for the faulty atmos. When he turned back, Izanami hadn't moved. She stared at the radio set.

"You said you'd found something else?" she asked, her voice flat, her eyes unmoving from the device.

Ida rubbed his chin and slowly approached the desk. He didn't take his eyes off the radio either. He walked toward it like it was a thing alive and dangerous. Maybe it was.

"You were right about the signal being an echo, but—" Ida slapped his hands against his legs and sighed.

He glanced at Izanami, her eyes reflecting the blue glow of the radio light and, unless he was mistaken, a very slight smile dusting her lips. She was leaning forward a fraction, poised, anticipating.

"It's weird. I can't explain it and the comms deck didn't like it either—damn thing threw up so many errors, I had to check it manually."

Izanami's mouth twitched; her eyes widened. She looked like she was contemplating a meal, but Ida put it down to the odd shadows cast across her face.

"The signal is old. Very old. *Impossibly* old. It was certainly a freak event that I picked it up." When Ida blinked, the shadows moved, so he turned back to the desk and the radio set. "It's not an echo from the lightspeed link. The signal is electromagnetic. It's a *radio* signal—radio, honest-to-God electromagnetic radio waves—and it's been racing toward us, from Earth to Shadow, for the last thousand years."

Ida whistled. He knew that as you traveled out from the Earth, if you could overtake the transmissions as they were beamed into the black, you'd be able to—theoretically—pick up old signals. The farther out, the older the data. Although as far out as Shadow, the signal would be weaker than the background roar of the universe. The signal, somehow, had bounced sideways into subspace and been boosted until it reached the radio set.

He shook his head, trying to fathom the how and the why and, now that he had the translation, the fate that had befallen this woman a thousand years ago. The age of the signal put the transmission sometime around the middle of the twentieth century—it was a relic from the early days of space travel. Now that he knew there was no action he could take to save the sender, who was a millennium dead, Ida thought the hollow ache in his chest should have improved. But somehow it didn't, and the more he thought about the signal, the more anxious he felt.

When he turned around to ask Izanami about that, she'd gone, leaving nothing but the sigh of the door closing behind her.

14

Marine-Engineer Niels DeJohn stood in the corridor on Phi Deck, Level 20, the heels of his boots on the standard metallorubber tiles common to every Fleet U-Star and his toes on the hard grille of the demolition zone. Lights shone through the gapped floor, illuminating the mist that swam lazily, liquidlike at ankle height.

DeJohn stared straight ahead, into the side of the *Coast City* that was more skeleton than whole. It was safe, where he was; the zones open to space were accessible only to the demolition drones. But here, on the edge, the environment controls had a hard time. But nobody was supposed to be here, not really, so what did it matter?

The environment controls were fighting something else as well, not just the stress of the space station being pulled to bits, its mass redistributed, its structure altered, every slice and dice requiring careful recalibration of virtually all systems by the station's central computer, no matter how carefully the demolition drones were programmed, no matter how routine these things were. Taking apart a U-Star, while keeping it functional as long as possible, complete with skeleton crew—now there was a difficult and dangerous task.

DeJohn stared ahead but he couldn't see the corridor, not

anymore. The mist swam around his feet, and his breath plumed out in a great white cloud. Unusual, but not impossible. Out in space in half a station, odd things could happen.

The shadows. Now, they were a problem. The corridor on Phi Deck was dark, twilight-normal, to conserve power, maintain efficiency. The low light created a lot of shadow, but not the sort that moved, the sort that swarmed around the marine, swimming through the mist, caressing his body as he stood, muscles tense—so rigid, he was shaking, like he was being held in place. His eyes twitched, as did his lips, and DeJohn stared ahead, but he couldn't see, not anymore.

And then she was behind him. He knew she was there, knew who she was, but he couldn't move and he couldn't see. He was a Fleet marine, the best of the best, a warrior who had engaged in hand-to-hand combat with the Spiders themselves and lived to tell the tale.

But there were some things he couldn't fight. Somewhere inside he screamed, somewhere deep where the last vestige of his conscious mind scrambled for a foothold. A second later that hold was lost, and the scream faded and echoed until there was nothing left. Nothing but silence and shadows and her standing behind him.

Her eyes glowed blue in the station's night.

"Contact has been established," she whispered. At her words the shadows roiled, peeling out of the corners of the corridor and sweeping around her in a slow orbit. Within moments she was the center of a storm of night. The shadows, alive, kissed her skin.

She reached out and pointed at DeJohn's back. The marine's eyes rolled up until only the whites were showing, and then he jolted like he'd been shocked, and then he turned around. The shadows coalesced around him too, and together the pair stood in the dark on Phi Deck, the world dimming around them until the only light was the light of her eyes, blue and terrible and aflame.

"Serve me and I will soon be here," she said. "Serve me and soon I will end it all."

DeJohn jerked again and blinked. He looked into her blue eyes and laughed, long and hard.

And as he laughed, she smiled, and in the dark, she burned.

THE SITUATION ON WARWORLD 16 HAS BEEN RESOLVED

"For services rendered."

The metal strip was pinned to his tunic. Corporal Charlie Carter saluted the colonel, who stood back, saluted in return, then led the applause, deafening in the confines of the base's operations room. Carter stuck his chest out just that little bit more.

Someone shouted out that Charlie Carter was the best goddamn marine on the planet. Carter laughed, and so did the colonel.

"Please," said the man, and when he said it, his bottom lip quivered like he was begging for forgiveness from his significant other. Which he was. The Fleet was everyone's SO, whether you were enlisted or a citizen. *Especially* if you were a citizen out on a colony. The Fleet looked after you, after everything.

Didn't it?

"Please," said the man again, like he really, honestly, truly damn well meant it even more this time. The sweat on his face glowed in the low light. It was hot underground, in the bunker.

A bead of sweat reached Corporal Carter's top lip as he stood in the dark behind the interrogator. He licked it off and regarded the begging man manacled on the other side of the desk. His own face was hidden in the shadows. To the prisoner, he was just one of two anonymous jarheads standing guard.

His father wouldn't recognize him.

Carter turned his attention to the back of the interrogator's head. Her hair was brilliantly blond and long, much longer than specified in Fleet regulations. But the interrogator was special, her skills unique. Not even the Fleet could tell the Angel of Death what to do or how to wear her hair.

"We trade protein. Only protein." The man's eyes were wide as he spoke to the Angel. In the silence that followed, she tilted her head.

"Oh, but that's not all, is it?" It wasn't a question; it was a statement. Her voice, cool enough and quiet enough to scare even Carter.

Another drop of sweat. Another nervous lick.

The Angel of Death would get the truth out of Carter's father, even if it killed him.

And it would.

Carter found Angel Jones in the bunker's main passage, a wide, low-ceiling tunnel that led to the outside. Carter hadn't been looking, but the moment was opportune.

"Ma'am," he said. Angel Jones didn't seem to have a rank, at least not one that the rest of them knew about. Her uniform was the same as everyone's, save for the absence of any insignia at all.

The Angel of Death smiled. Carter wondered whether she knew what people called her on the base. Of course she did. Nothing escaped her on Warworld 16. That was why she was here.

Carter kept his gaze level, looking politely over her right shoulder. But he saw the Angel smile, and he felt the skin on the back of his neck crawl.

"You've done good work, Corporal," she said.

Carter stood to attention automatically. He tried not to think about his good works, not here, not on Warworld 16. "Ma'am," he said.

The Angel nodded. "Thanks to the information extracted from the insurgents, we've located the supply route from the Omoto to the Spiders. First the Fleet Medal for bravery. Now I intend to recommend promotion."

"Ma'am."

And then she was gone, stalking away, back into the gloom and heat of the bunker. Carter blinked into the glare of the entrance farther ahead.

That was it. He'd had his chance, and he'd blown it. Had his chance to protest, to complain, to offer alternative theories, to make his case that his own intel was wrong, that his parents were just trading protein for vegetables with the local Omoto tribe like his father kept saying. That there was no way they were involved with the Omoto's dirty little secret. That there was no way his parents were guilty of aiding and abetting the enemy, no way that they were just as responsible for the deaths of every marine on Warworld 16 killed by roadside ambushes and suicide bombs as the Omoto tribesman who carried out the attacks.

Carter walked toward the light, the decision already made.

"You and your wife are laboratory technicians."

"Please, we only grow animal protein for trade. Nothing more. Resources are scarce here. The Omoto need protein, and we need the supplements."

"Are you saying the Fleet does not provide for the colony?"

"No, of course not, but—"

"Because that is a lie. The Fleet provides for all its colonies. You make other things in your laboratory, don't you?"

"Please, no, we—"

"Don't you?"

The man begged, the Angel of Death smiled as she gestured to her assistant in the white mask beside her, and Carter closed his eyes and felt the sweat pour from his brow in the dark underground heat of Warworld 16.

* * *

The Omoto called it Tangakia. The first human explorers, Nova Australis. When the war came and the Fleet arrived, it was entered into the catalog of combat theaters as Warworld 16.

There were no Spiders on Warworld 16. There was just a handful of Omoto tribes doing fuck all in the endless savannahs. The Omoto were nomadic, with enough tech to leapfrog from planet to planet but without much ambition to do anything else.

Carter hated the Omoto. All the marines did. The Omoto jumped to a new planet and then built temporary tent cities and sat around smoking the foul-smelling weed that was all they seemed to grow. It was pathetic. The Omoto were nomadic, but when the humans arrived, they stopped moving. Soon enough they were wearing logo-emblazoned T-shirts and hats traded from the colonists.

Pathetic.

As a human colony, Nova Australis wasn't much better. Carter knew that, but while the others on the base regarded the colonists with the same distaste as the Omoto, Carter kept his thoughts to himself. Nova Australis was okay. As far as Carter could tell, it was all farmers and traders and the kind of people who liked to sit around and smoke as much as their Omoto neighbors did. There were worse places to relocate to. Nova Australis was out of the way. If you wanted to start over, here was as good a place as any. His parents had chosen a good spot. That their son was here now was coincidence, pure and simple.

Then the Fleet arrived. Because the Omoto weren't just growing plants and trading them for lab-grown animal protein from the colonists. The Fleet was on Warworld 16 because of the Omoto, but Carter knew that aside from the combat theater designation there would be no official record. The base on Warworld 16 was secret. The Omoto had no part in the Spider conflict, not officially.

Carter liked being part of a Black Ops. You got more money and the rules of engagement were looser. Carter thought it would give him a chance to stretch, to show the Fleet just what he was made of.

After six months he became the youngest marine to receive the Fleet Medal, and now he was being recommended for promotion by the Angel of Death herself. He'd done good work on Warworld 16. He'd confirmed what the Fleet spies already suspected.

The Omoto were helping the Spiders, and the colonists were helping the Omoto.

But... not Carter's parents. The intel was off; it had to be. They'd come to Nova Australis because they wanted a chance to make their own way, to show the Fleet what people could do when left to their own devices. Nova Australis was nice. The Omoto had gotten there first, but they liked the colonists and the colonists liked them.

Carter spit into the dust and turned back to the dark tunnel entrance.

It was now or never.

Carter stood to attention in the operations room as the colonel outlined the endgame for Warworld 16. It was simple enough. They'd found the supply route between the colonists and the Omoto insurgents. The removal of the new targets would be surgical. When the mission was over, life would go on as normal for the colonists of Nova Australis. For the Omoto, things would be different. After 0000 hours CUT, Tangakia would no longer exist.

Carter found that the Fleet Medal meant he could do a lot of things and go a lot of places without anyone paying him much attention, other than snapping a salute to the silver bar on his chest.

The Angel of Death had only just started on his father. For the moment he could still see and he could still walk, just. They'd left his mother alone. She could help her husband.

Carter relieved the marines on duty outside the cage holding the prisoners; then he opened it without signing the manifest authorization. The manifest would simply flag the action and await someone's okay at a later date. Carter just had to log in from the command deck later and punch the acceptance himself.

He led his parents through the service levels of the base and out onto the surface. He gave them a GPS. He pointed them in the right direction. The Omoto would be wiped out in four hours. There was enough time to get away, to get off the planet. When their escape was discovered, Carter would be the one to track them back to the Omoto town. With the town excised from the planet, it would be assumed the two traitors had been disintegrated alongside their Omoto collaborators.

Problem solved, for everyone.

"Very good work, Corporal."

Carter saluted. The colonel nodded appreciatively and glanced sideways at his adjunct.

"I've received a recommendation I intend to honor. A fitting way to commemorate our departure."

Carter dropped his hand. It was 2340 hours. In ten minutes he was due to lead one of the raiding parties to burn the Omoto town.

"Sir?"

The colonel smiled. "At ease, marine. Start prepping. We evac in four hours."

"Sir. The… sortie?"

The colonel patted Carter on the shoulder. Carter flinched, just a little. The colonel noticed, and he smiled. "Change of plan, marine."

They knew.

Carter watched the change of plan from orbit, with everyone else. The featureless black orb of Tangakia/Nova Australis/Warworld 16 filled the screen. Then the black turned to red as an entire hemisphere melted. No more insurgents, no more collaborators. No more Omoto and no more colonists.

Black Ops were black for a reason. The Spiders would be blamed for the loss of Warworld 16—nothing unusual there, the Fleet on the back foot as it was, as it always had been. It would be marked as a setback and used as a rationale to push the conflict to a new level. Statistically, the loss of the colony was insignificant. Strategically, the benefit gained would be great.

The situation on Warworld 16 had been resolved. The Fleet Admiral would make a speech, and there would be a memorial.

Carter left the command deck without permission, but when you had the Fleet Medal on your chest you could do a lot of things without permission.

The engine juice on the U-Star *Bloodflowers* was stronger than Carter liked, but he was developing a taste for it. He took another sip and glanced at the monitor and the surveillance video playing.

There it was. The crappy cart pushed by his father. The Omoto tribesman taking protein packs from it. And something else. They were trying to hide it but they were amateurs and the surveillance from the drone was clear. They were in on it.

They were guilty.

The U-Star *Bloodflowers* had evacuated everyone from the base on Warworld 16. Eight hundred marines and ninety prisoners. At least that's what the manifest said. Carter had logged in and accepted the release query before anyone else had seen it. Angel Jones had already left in her own ship, and nobody else would care even if the discrepancy was noticed. Warworld 16 was now incapable of supporting life, and the U-Star had two less mouths to feed.

Carter flicked the Fleet Medal strip from his breast pocket and tossed it into the trash next to the desk. The Fleet Medal earned with the blood of the innocent and the guilty alike. FOR SERVICES RENDERED. No record of what the services were. No mention of his good works on Warworld 16. The Fleet was never there.

Sergeant Charlie Carter fell back into his bunk. He took another swig of engine juice, looped the surveillance video back to the beginning, and stared into the screen.

DREAMS AND NIGHTMARES

She opened her eyes and realized she'd been dreaming, but it was hot, and she couldn't breathe, so she closed her eyes again and returned to the dream.

Once upon a time there was a girl who lived on a farm. Her parents were very proud and gave her life to the State so she could bring fame and honor. Honor was important. Honor was what kept the subsidies rolling in, was what kept you from being visited in the night and taken away to somewhere very dark and very cold. The girl's father had connections that the State did not approve of, but honor made the people who mattered turn a blind eye. Honor kept them safe.

Because they were proud and because they had decided to give her to the State almost from the beginning, they gave her a beautiful name, a name that sounded like the half-remembered dream of a fairy princess in her tall tower. Her name meant "dear people." Even from the beginning, her destiny was written. She was a tool to be used.

She didn't mind. She embraced the life carved for her by her father (with his connections) and her mother (with a cold fear in her heart). They pushed her and she excelled, but she excelled because she wanted to. She was smart—that was a big help, a blessing from above—and she worked hard, and she did well because it made her parents proud, and it made her village proud, and it made the men in uniforms and hats smile at her when they visited. Once there was a man in a big blue greatcoat, bigger and heavier than anybody else's. He had a kind face, lined and marked with pox scars, and a big gray mustache. Her mother was nervous that day. When she served tea her hand shook and the cup rattled in the saucer. But the man with the mustache thanked her and said what a wonderful home she kept and how well Father was doing on the farm. Everyone smiled.

When she turned seventeen, she was sad to leave the farm but excited to join her new friends at the city. She'd never been to the city before. She remembered her mother and father waving from the road, remembered the soldiers hanging around and waving as well, one hand in the air, the other on their rifles. She stood on the back of the truck's bed as it drove away, fairly bursting with pride, waving so hard, her arm ached for a day afterwards.

The city was a strange place, full of more soldiers and empty streets. Everyone was pleased to meet her, everyone had heard so much about her, and she was introduced at a big meeting in a cold hall, not by the man with the mustache but by a new leader, a fat man who wore a silly white hat. She knew who he was now—who they all were—of course, and as she stood to attention by his side, her back was so rigid and tall that she felt like she could take off through the roof and wouldn't even need the rocket and capsule. Her face hurt from smiling, and when the man had finished speaking everyone in the hall lined up to walk past and shake her hand and salute the fat man. She wished her mother and father could have been there, but they were busy on the farm and now had one hand less to help with all the work.

Mornings were spent on mathematics, physics, and engineering. Afternoons were spent on physical and combat training. She met some people who smiled when they looked at her but frowned when they looked away. She could see them, and sometimes they didn't even try to hide it. She never asked, but somebody said that she was supposed to have come from the military and that there were others more worthy of the honor. But she told them about how well she was doing and how hard she was working. At night it worried her that there were some people who pretended to like her but really didn't, and she didn't know why. But hours of being strapped to gyroscopes and centrifuges left her sick and tired every night, and she never worried for very long before falling into a deep sleep.

Sometimes in the morning she awoke and was worried again, although not about the people who didn't smile. Sometimes she had dreams, and sometimes they were about her mother and father on the farm. Sometimes her dreams were filled with dark shadows and cold mist and a sun that burned with a purple light she could almost taste. In her dreams there were people calling her name and people reaching out to her. When she had those dreams, she woke with a cry and her bedsheets were wet with a cold, cold sweat. Nobody else in the dormitory noticed; they were all busy trying to get their last ten minutes of sleep before being woken by the siren at four o'clock.

The months passed and she got used to the people who talked behind her back and who were rude to her face. She didn't know why some of them treated her like that, because she was doing her military training at the same time as her flight training (and surely doing it at the same time was harder), and when the fat man came to visit the city he always had a private audience with her first, before the others. Surely that meant she was doing well?

But it was her friend—the only true friend she thought she really had, the Japanese medic who was working with her on her training program—who made her understand. She asked her finally, and the medic laughed. She said she was pretty, and being pretty made men angry and women jealous. But the Japanese girl was pretty as well and she'd never seen any of them look at *her*, but her friend laughed again and smiled and told her she would find out why one day.

She was also smart, gifted even, and this *also* made men angry and women jealous. But she couldn't understand that either—it was all being done for the State, not for herself. Her friend laughed and said that she was a true hero and would get a medal after her flight, and this would make people even angrier. There were some, she was told, who had worked for years or even decades on the program, only to be leapfrogged by the newcomer, the simple girl from the country. Did she know that there had been a pilot chosen before she arrived? No? And that before she arrived, the first pilot had been welcomed by the fat man and had been visited by him just as much as her? No?

She watched her friend laugh, late at night, and when she laughed her eyes flashed blue and were filled with stars and suddenly the girl was afraid and she remembered the cold mist and dark shadows of her dreams, before her friend smiled and asked if she wanted another drink.

On the morning of the launch, she awoke refreshed from a deep sleep, but as she ate her special meal in a laboratory while scientists watched scrolling reels of paper and whispered to one another, she remembered a dream she'd had, one with her mother and her father and her friend in it. She ate her protein and carbohydrates and fats and tried to remember more, but she was cold and her eyes were playing tricks on her because everywhere she looked, black shadow-shapes jumped out of corners and streaked away in every direction. The men watching the paper didn't say anything, so she knew it was just the stress and excitement of the launch.

Some of the men who hated her—she understood that now, having thought long and hard about what her Japanese friend had told her—were the first to wish her good luck, the first to smile and shake her hand. As they walked away she saw them smile to one another as well, and she thought that perhaps they really were happy for her now. But there was no time to think about it because the fat man was due to arrive for a final meeting. She was in her suit now and stood proudly with the round helmet under one arm and the insignia of the State in bold red across her chest. There were photos, and the man gave a speech, and everyone smiled and clapped.

She opened her eyes. She'd been cold, so very cold, and every time she looked out the window of the capsule she saw the dark shadows again. They'd been following her, a freak atmospheric effect as the capsule pulled around the Earth for yet another orbit. She realized she'd blacked out again, but the controls made no sense. Seventeen orbits? The plan had been for three. And when the controls stopped responding, the radio went dead. Another fault, perhaps, but it had gone off with a sharp click and now when she turned it on all she got was a pulse, a heartbeat of static. It was dead, like the rest of the capsule. She was alone in the sky, encased in two tons of metal that were melting from the outside in. She could feel the warmth on the panel beside her, heating one side of her body while on the other side the panels cracked with a dense frost. Around her the black shadows swarmed, and if she turned her head, she could swear the shapes were in the capsule with her, sometimes blotting the view of the small square window from the inside.

She opened her eyes. Now it was hot, too hot, and she realized she'd blacked out again. The radio popped and cracked and she reached for the controls, her silver hand cast in orange and yellow by the flames from the window. Someone was calling on the radio, someone from very, very far away. The words were distorted and buried under a roaring she soon realized was the capsule on fire.

She remembered her mother, and she remembered her father, and she remembered standing proudly with the First Secretary in the warm sunshine as the photographer lined the pair of them up against the rocket sitting on the launchpad half a mile behind them.

She remembered her duty and she remembered her country and the sacrifices that must be made. She flicked the radio and made her report. She wasn't sure if she could be heard, but she trusted the Soviet technology that surrounded her, even as it burned, even as the capsule hurtled toward oblivion as it skipped the atmosphere of the Earth too fast, too low.

"Five, four, three, two, one…"

Nothing.

"One, two, three, four, five…"

A pop, a voice, far away. They were listening. Someone was listening.

"Come in, come in, come in. Listen! Come in! Talk to me. I am hot! I am hot. Come in. Please.

"I am hot."

129

PART TWO

DARK SHADOWS

15

Ida spent the next cycle looking for Izanami, but he couldn't find her anywhere. He couldn't even find any signs she was on board at all—the desk in the medical unit looked like it had been packed up, ready for the trip home. After stalking the hub for what felt like hours, Ida was about to give in and get the bridge to put in a station-wide call for her, when there she was, waiting in the corridor by his cabin. As soon as he saw her, he called out. She recoiled from his door in surprise; then her face broke into a broad smile.

"Where have you been?" They both said the words at the same time, and then laughed.

Izanami moved out of Ida's way so he could operate the door panel.

"I've been looking for you." Ida tapped the lock code. The red LED winked to green, but Ida stopped before pressing the open button. "I can't get the damn recording out of my head."

Izanami nodded. "It is unique. You have captured a freak event."

Ida rolled his shoulders. "Well—"

He stopped short just inside the door. Izanami ducked around him to see into the cabin.

"Oh my God!"

Ida strode inside, picking up a handful of clothes as he did so. He tossed them onto the bed, where the blankets and covers were bunched in the middle of the mattress.

Every inch of the cabin was covered with papers, clothes, bits of equipment, and broken items—a smashed ceramic mug here, Ida's deodorant there with its screw-cap a few feet away. The chair was overturned and the main desk had been moved and stuck out of the wall at an angle. Ignoring the rest of the room, Ida headed straight for it.

The computer terminal had been moved and the screens were pushed back on their sprung arms against the wall, but both were undamaged. The space radio hadn't been touched, but the blue LED was on.

"I am seriously losing patience with this place." Ida pushed the computer screens out of the way and shoved at the edge of the desk. It was a heavy table, and it took some considerable effort for him to move it back just an inch before he had to stop to catch his breath. The table was still angled nearly a foot off the wall. Ida blinked and regarded the gap between the table and the wall. Whoever had turned his cabin over had been strong.

"What happened?" Izanami tiptoed through the debris.

Ida swore and the table thudded against the wall as he gave it one almighty shove. "The space apes happened." Ida turned and scooped another armful of clothes from the floor to the bed. "DeJohn, Carter, whoever, I don't care. I came down to this end of the station to keep out of their way. Assholes."

"But what did they want?"

"Damned if I know." Ida sighed. He turned back to the desk and waved a hand over the top of the radio set. The blue LED went dark and a very quiet background rushing sound Ida hadn't noticed suddenly stopped.

"Huh."

Izanami joined him at the desk. "What?"

"Well," said Ida, "they didn't come here to smash the radio. But I didn't turn it on."

"Maybe they didn't know how to work it?"

"If they wanted to use it…" Ida shook his head, took one more look around the cabin, and then headed to the door. He looked back at Izanami. "If we have a VIP on the way, then I doubt King will be able to sweep this one away. You coming?"

Izanami shook her head. "Do you mind if I listen to the recording again?"

Ida opened his mouth, closed it, and then opened it again. "Ah, yeah, sure. Knock yourself out." He turned and began to walk away.

"Wait, Ida!" She ran to the door.

"Yeah?"

"The cabin was locked, wasn't it?"

Ida stepped back toward her and looked at the door panel. The control was simple, a small qwerty keypad with a display above it about two inches square and a series of small LEDs; below that, the touch-sensitive chrome pad. Currently the screen was dark and a green LED was lit, indicating the door was open. Izanami was right—when he'd arrived the LED was red, and he had locked the cabin when he left it a while before. Only Ida knew the PIN to open it—that was something nobody could know or even look up on the station's log. The Fleet was big on security. If anyone on the *Coast City* had managed to breach Ida's privacy in such a manner, it would become a very serious matter. Court-martial and imprisonment, at least.

"*Sonovabitch*," said Ida. He turned on his heel to jog down the corridor. "King has to listen to me now."

Ida disappeared around the corner. Izanami watched the empty corridor for a moment and then turned back into Ida's cabin. The environmental lighting had dimmed automatically when Ida left, but the door remained open. In near darkness, Izanami sat at the desk and turned the radio on.

The woman's voice—the original recording—crackled into life, filling the cabin and echoing down the empty corridor outside it.

At the far end of the corridor, long after Ida had passed by on his way to the elevators, something crossed the faint light cast by the dim yellow service lights. A few moments later, the shadow moved again. In Ida's cabin, Izanami sat still and silent, listening to the recording over and over and over again.

In the dark, she smiled.

"Captain Cleveland," King said, "nobody has been near your cabin. For crying out loud, you're at the other end of the crew berths. There's nothing around there but demolition drones. In fact, your cabin will be spare parts in just a few weeks, so you might want to consider moving back—"

Ida ran a hand through his hair. He'd run onto the bridge and confronted King—even the crew, so expertly practiced at ignoring distraction, had stopped what they were doing to look. King, to his credit, had simply laid his hand on Ida's shoulder without another word and pushed him over to the security console himself.

"You sure this captures everything?" Ida nodded at the computer display. King looked Ida up and down, his face pulled off-center by a scowl. Ida returned the look.

"Yes, Captain," said King. "This captures everything. All doors, locks, bulkheads, panels. Anything that needs to be turned on or off, locked or unlocked, coded or passed on board the station." He pointed to the schematic rendered in green and amber on the large rectangular screen. "Not only do we have the record of the lock and door controls of your cabin, but we've got camera coverage right down the corridor. Look."

King's fingers moved with speed over the touch-sensitive keypad. Ida watched the screen.

The schematic flipped horizontally, replaced by the security camera feed for the corridor outside Ida's cabin. The image was high definition and crystal clear but, given most of the station hub was perpetually in low-energy mode, was lit only in the warm twilight now so familiar to Ida. The corridor was still, silent, and it took Ida a moment to realize that King was fast-forwarding through the camera feed. Then something olive green flashed over the screen, and Ida reached forward to almost, but not quite, tap the screen.

"What was that?"

King glanced up. Then he watched the screen as he tracked back. "That was you, Captain." A few seconds later, Ida watched himself walk backwards toward his cabin door and turn awkwardly on his heel. Ida hated seeing himself on camera, let alone video run in reverse; he was not the ruggedly handsome young man he imagined himself to be. But he recognized the scene as King scrolled backwards along the timeline—his arrival back at his cabin to find Izanami waiting, then his hasty departure to report the break-in. He frowned. Something was wrong with what he was seeing, but he couldn't quite place what it was.

"Nothing, then?" he asked, peering closer at the screen. King had paused the feed just as Ida was pulling a very odd face. He was pretty sure the marshal had done it deliberately.

"Nothing." King tracked again, going back and forth across a large chunk of the last cycle. Ida coming and going, stopping, coming and going again. Ida watched himself but he also checked the background—the camera provided a fish-eyed three-quarters top-down of the whole corridor, positioned as it was on the bulkhead frame at the end of the passageway. He could see the edge of his cabin door and the control panel set into the mesh wall outside it, sticking out after the standard tiling had been removed as part of the demolition of that part of the station.

Nothing. Just him, moving around, coming and going. The odd feeling returned as he watched. His eyes roved the background, seeking out any corner or nook that the intruder could have hidden in to escape the view of the camera. But there was nothing, nobody except Ida.

"And look," said King, this time rapping a knuckle on a smaller display inset in the flat surface of the security console. "No life signs in that area, none except yours for nearly the last seven cycles." He straightened up, adjusting the bottom of his tunic. The look he had in his eye as he met Ida's gaze was a clear invitation to leave his bridge.

Ida raised his hands in surrender. At least King had helped scan the feed with him. King's obsessive attitude toward his own job was, this time, to Ida's advantage.

King made a stiff nod before turning back to the console to shut everything down.

Ida balanced on his heel, and then turned to head back to the elevator. There was something he didn't like, something he didn't quite *get*, about the security feeds King had just shown him. Something buzzed around the back of his mind as he stepped into the waiting elevator.

It was impossible, right? Nobody could have faked the security feed or the monitor readings. And yet someone had turned over his cabin. Even if it was possible to alter or erase data from the *Coast City*'s log—and Ida was pretty sure it wasn't—the amount of time and effort required would classify the act as a conspiracy well beyond the petty bullying he'd been the subject of since arriving on the *Coast City*. That took Carter's space apes out of the picture. And, besides, if they'd broken into his cabin to deliver a message, there wouldn't have been anything left to pick up, let alone the computer terminal and the space radio set left not only perfectly intact but turned on as well.

But no one had been near the cabin except Ida and Izanami, and none of the security systems could be overridden and none of the data could be faked. And Ida didn't believe in ghosts, not least ghosts in space. He stood in the elevator, running scenarios backwards and forward and sideways in his head, replaying King's video feed, still unable to put a finger on what he felt was wrong. He couldn't place it as he left the elevator on his level; he couldn't place it as he walked down the corridor outside his cabin and turned to look back at the security camera up on the bulkhead. He couldn't place it as he walked into his cabin and nodded at Izanami, lying on the bed and listening to the recorded message on repeat. It didn't occur to him as Izanami met his eye with a smile and returned his nod.

Ida sat at the desk and massaged his temples. He had a headache coming on.

16

"And then what did you do?"

Carter didn't answer Serra's question immediately. Instead, he stroked his chin as they walked down a corridor somewhere in the *Coast City*'s middle.

"So what did I do?" he repeated, glancing at Serra and turning on a wicked grin.

My God, that smile, thought Serra. That was the Charlie Carter she knew and loved. He seemed better now, more like his old self. And how long before they were off shift and—

Serra stopped walking.

Carter didn't seem to notice, and kept strolling slowly forward. "I said, 'Yes, sir. Right away, sir. Three bags full, sir.'" He stopped and turned around. "What did you think I said?"

He paused. His eyes played over Serra. "What is it?"

Serra stood motionless, eyes wide, looking to the floor. She held both arms straight down, fingers splayed out like she was preparing to walk a tightrope. She felt alert, suddenly energized, the corridor she and Carter were in and the conversation they were having now a million light-years away.

They were not alone.

Carter pulled in close. She could feel him tense up, could almost see a ripple of gooseflesh crawl up his bare arms.

She knew the feeling. It was the same sensation you felt, out in the field, when a patrol was going too well, the second before the ambush struck or the bomb went off. Serra could almost taste it. She had no doubt Carter could feel it too—all marines had it, the good ones, the ones who came back alive. But for her, it was like being thrown into an ice bath.

Carter's muscles moved under his regulation T-shirt. He was preparing himself, Serra knew, to take on whatever was coming. Serra kept very still; it felt like she couldn't move even if she'd wanted to. She knew she had the best goddamned battle sense in the Fleet, and when it was sharp like this, trouble was coming, thick and fast.

Carter looked to Serra, his brow furrowed. She knew that he was a pro, that he wouldn't do a thing until she gave the word. She flicked her eyes to his and he nodded, almost imperceptibly. She slowed her breathing and listened, reaching out to the world, *feeling* it.

But feeling what? There was nothing on the station but a rag-tag crew, some drone robots, and one washed-up ex-captain on board for some reason nobody really knew.

Serra's mouth was dry. Maybe she wasn't sensing anything but the fatigue of the machine around them. The station was being pulled into little bits. Every day tons of metal and ceramic and plastic were sliced up and boxed up, leaving the humans to walk around a cat's cradle framework. What if something had gone wrong? What if a drone had malfunctioned, or crashed? Or worse, got stuck in some error loop and kept on slicing and dicing the station until it hit the habitable spaces. One stray demolition laser, and the *Coast City*'s atmos would be voided into space, the crew killed instantly by the peculiar light from Shadow.

No… there *was* something. The dreams and the voices and the odd feeling she'd had for weeks, and now… this. A presence, nearby. Someone watching them. Some*thing* watching them.

Then it was over. The corridor was suddenly warmer, and the unpleasant weight in the center of her chest evaporated. Serra relaxed and allowed herself the luxury of oxygen.

Carter sank a little as he lowered himself from his toes. His chest heaved, and he looked sideways at her. "For crying out loud," he whispered. "I hate it when you do that."

Serra walked forward, comfortable enough now. She stopped, then walked back toward Carter and looked into the marine's tight eyes.

"What?"

"Didn't you hear it?" she asked.

Carter glanced up and down the corridor, then back at Serra.

"Nope. What's up?"

His words were light, but that was something else you learned from battle. There was enough death and despair around you without going all down and serious. There was a time and a place for that. Standing in a corridor in a far-distant, decommissioned space station was not one of them.

Serra shrugged, and they resumed their walk. But it was different now. Serra was tense, her eyes flicking around. She was waiting for her grandmother to call her name again. But after a while no voice came, and she tuned back in to Carter's diatribe.

"I mean, what are we here for?" he was saying. "Security and engineering, right? Making sure this hunk of junk is sent back to the Fleet with all the right parts back in the box, right? So why the goddamn hell is a celebrity starminer coming here? Like anybody has time for that."

Serra snickered. "She's hot, you know."

"Oh," said Carter. His surprised expression might or might not have been faked, and she slapped him on the back anyway, not without a smile on her own face. He yelped playfully.

"What—?"

Carter came to a halt, Serra's hand pulling at the back of his shirt. This time Carter pulled himself in close to her side instantly, fists clenched, and glanced up and down the corridor. He opened his mouth to say something, but Serra pushed her hand into his chest and his jaw snapped shut. The sensation of a presence was as thick as a blanket.

As they stood in silence, Serra heard it again. It was another voice, distant but at the same time right over their shoulders. Then the voice stopped, leaving an unsettling, hollow echo. The passage they were in was lined with standard rubberized floor tiles and interlocking plastic panels on the walls, slotted into the underlying metal skeleton of the station. This section was a main thoroughfare and wouldn't be marked for demolition for weeks yet. There was no good surface for that kind of reverberation.

But as the seconds elongated, the bad feeling only increased. When Serra blinked, her vision flashed purple and she couldn't help but flinch back, the weird sensation that there was someone standing right in front of her impossible to dismiss.

This was different, a creeping dread that wasn't battle sense, not this time. This was something older, simpler, something that didn't require Fleet training and pharmaceutical enhancement, something that pulled on the primal, lizard part of Serra's brain. She pressed her hand hard into Carter's chest and focused on the real, physical connection. His chest shook with short, shallow breaths, and she could hear the saliva moving in his mouth as he wet his lips.

He felt it too; she could tell. It wasn't fear they shared, not really. There was no room for that kind of reaction in the Fleet Marine Corps. They faced injury or death constantly, not just from the enemy but also from the million things that could go wrong in space that would end them in a millisecond. That was life in the Fleet. And Serra and Carter were marines, the best of the best.

This... this was something else, something worse.

They were not alone. Now she was sure of it.

"Now what?" Carter's whisper was surprisingly loud.

Serra shushed him, but a second later she gasped herself.

There was someone at the end of the passageway. The light ahead of them was at minimum, part of standard energy conservation. The passage was dark behind them too, the lights of each section dimming after they passed. A few hundred meters farther back was a main intersection, well lit, spilling a pool of light into each of the four corridors that branched from it. Alone in their passage, Carter and Serra were standing in a glowing bubble that stretched just two meters ahead and behind. Standard procedure on any U-Star during the night-cycle, or when a section of a station had a minimal number of crew in it.

Ahead the familiar darkness was punctuated by steady LEDs in three colors that studded door controls and comms panels at regular intervals. In that darkness the figure stood, swaying on its feet. Serra's eyes were drawn past it, to a red light that pulsed on and off as the figure's waist moved side to side—gently, rhythmically blocking and unblocking the light.

The figure was nothing more than a black silhouette against a blacker background, wide and bulky like the person had something on them or around them. The head was large, circular, like they were wearing some kind of helmet.

Serra called out, "Hello?" which seemed redundant. She turned to Carter and watched as he squinted into the dark ahead of them. So it wasn't just her; he could see it too.

"Why hasn't the light come on?" Carter whispered.

That was precisely the problem. Serra turned back to look down the corridor. For a second she saw nothing but dark, and then the darkness moved and she could discern the figure again. She didn't like it. It was fucking creepy as hell.

"Maintenance?"

Serra knew Carter was wrong as soon as he said it, but the explanation helped break the tension, the hesitation, the lead-limbed feeling she had. She felt tired, heavy; the air of the corridor suddenly thick. The sensation was alien but at the same time familiar; the sensation of helplessness and dread from a thousand childhood nightmares. Serra muttered something colorful in Spanish, but it didn't make her feel any better. Carter's breaths were still small and tight.

Serra and Carter turned to each other, and then it was over. Serra could feel her heart beating like a hammer, trying to burst out of her chest, and the feeling of weight was replaced with a slight light-headedness. Carter raised and lowered his arms, flexing his thick fingers. He looked at Serra; then his eyes flicked back down the passage. Serra turned and followed his gaze. It was still half-dark, but the figure had gone along with the weird, oppressive atmosphere.

Serra opened her mouth to form a question, but nothing came to mind.

Carter sighed loudly. "For fuck's sake." He walked heavily to the comms panel just behind them and thumped the control hard with his clenched fist, shaking the plastic wall panel.

"Bridge."

Carter flicked the comms switch more delicately with his thumb, and turned his back to the wall, his eyes scanning ahead.

"Carter on Level Fifty-five West—" He looked across the passage to the wall opposite, reading off the bar code stamped along the edge of the panel nearest the bulkhead. "—Alpha Ninety. Who's on demo on this deck?"

There was a pause. Serra walked up to Carter. She saw the skin of his arms was covered with gooseflesh and noticed how cold it was in the corridor. She wrapped her arms around herself and rubbed at her own icy skin.

"Negative," came the tinny response from the wall. "Demo not booked until alpha ten-ten is taken down."

Carter exhaled, his breath whistling between his teeth. "So who's down here? We got a problem with the environment lights. Someone checking?"

Another pause. Carter tapped his fingers on the wall panel.

"Negative. Scan shows Carter, C, and Serra, C. She there with you?" The Flyeye sounded like he was a million miles away.

Serra leaned forward, arms still folded, balancing on her toes.

"Affirmative, operator." Her eyes met Carter's. Their gaze lingered for just a moment before Carter broke it to look back down the corridor.

"Give me environment control."

There was a click from the other end of the comms, and Serra's eye was caught by an LED on the wall opposite that flicked from red to green. Carter pushed off the wall and punched the panel. The corridor lights increased evenly in brightness until Serra almost needed to squint. The entire passage was illuminated, behind them to the intersection through which they'd come and ahead to the bend in the corridor where whoever it was must have turned out of sight.

While Carter took a few steps down the corridor, almost as though he didn't trust his own eyes to show him the completely empty passage, Serra flicked the comm. "Operator?"

"Standing by."

"Patch me to DeJohn."

Carter turned, mouthing something. Serra waved him off. "Hold a moment, please," came the voice from the wall grille. "DeJohn is not responding."

Carter stomped back toward Serra, shaking his head. He flicked the comm, and Serra stepped back.

"Bridge, what's Corporal DeJohn's twenty?" Carter glanced back over his shoulder. "We'll meet him in person."

"Locating," said the operator.

Carter turned to Serra. "What's DeJohn got to do with it, anyhow?"

Serra shrugged. "He's been wired the last few cycles. Who knows what he might pull." The idea sounded weak, even to her.

Carter turned back to the wall and frowned, and pressed the call button a couple of times. In between each electronic beep came a faint sound from the speaker grille. It sounded like water, or the roaring of air a long, long way away. Serra didn't like it—here was one more fucked-up effect of the star they orbited in a space station missing more than half its regulation shielding. The interference was creeping into everything, even the internal comms network.

But Serra had heard the sound somewhere else, too. It was the sound in her dream, and the last few cycles she'd begun to hear when she was awake, when the voices spoke to her. She decided she was still going to keep that from Carter and the others.

"Operator," Carter said into the comm, "you make me wait any longer, I'm gonna need some hold music, okay?"

The speaker crackled. Serra could hear the operator saying something, but for a second it didn't sound like the Flyeye they had just called. Carter leaned back, eyes scanning the display on the panel in case it was registering a fault. But everything was clear. He flicked the comms switch again.

The operator was back instantly. "Marine, I have the provost marshal here."

Carter frowned, and Serra shook her head. *Gee, great.*

"Carter? This is the marshal. DeJohn's tag is not appearing on the U-Star's manifest."

Carter shot Serra a glance. She felt her forehead crease as she tried to comprehend what the provost marshal had just said.

But what King said wasn't hard to understand; it was *impossible* to understand. Somehow the conversation with King had got all turned around. Serra gestured and Carter pushed the button again. "Sir, I'm not sure I follow."

"DeJohn is not in the ship's manifest, marine."

Carter looked at Serra. She reached forward and pushed the comms with her thumb.

"Marshal, sir, this is Psi-Sergeant Serra. What do you mean, he's not in the manifest? Do we have a twenty on DeJohn?"

The head of security sighed into the receiver, the sound popping the speaker slightly before the background roar faded in again. Serra felt cold. Very, very cold.

"We're running a systems check now, marine. For the moment assume a fault, but the operator tells me you asked for the demo crew for that deck?"

"Affirmative, sir," said Carter. "There is someone down here. The Op said they weren't showing up either."

"Check it, please. The computer must have bugged and removed DeJohn's tag. When you find him, the three of you return to the bridge and we'll get the security system reset. We need to be on our toes with our guests arriving soon."

"Affirmative, sir. Carter out." He released the button and then stood, rubbing his chin.

Serra started walking down the passage. She stopped and turned when she realized Carter wasn't following. "You coming?"

Carter clicked his fingers. "Got it," he said. "Sonovabitch!"

"What?"

"The other day, remember? DeJohn said he needed to show Captain Cleveland how we do things around here. You're right. DeJohn is planning something, and he's taken himself off the security scanner to do it." Carter shook his head with grin. "Clever boy."

Serra frowned. He'd have to be—tampering with the computer system was impossible as far as she knew.

"Come on, let's find him," said Carter, heading down the passage at a trot.

Serra followed.

17

Izanami lay on Ida's bed. He watched her for a few seconds; then he blinked and swiveled his chair around so he was facing the computer screens and the space radio on the desk. The last rush of static faded as the recording came to an end.

They'd been listening to it for what felt like hours. Ida knew every pop and crackle, but it still made him feel scared and ill. At least his head felt better, anyway, the unusual headache finally gone.

Ida turned around in his chair and glanced at Izanami as the recording looped back to the beginning.

Unlike Ida, Izanami had seemed to take a detached, scientific approach, which he envied. Except... her eyes were closed, but at certain points of the recording—when the woman's voice raised to a fearful pitch that sent Ida's stomach flipping, and later when the background static washed in and peaked, almost as though it were trying to interrupt the speaker—Izanami's face was lit by a smile, each and every time. Perhaps Izanami wasn't really listening to the recording, and with her eyes closed was lost in her own thoughts in the half light.

She shifted on the bed, and Ida turned back to the desk. The playback had only a couple seconds left.

"I've had enough, I think," came Izanami's voice from behind him.

Ida slumped back in his chair, suddenly tired. How long had they been listening, and for what, anyway? The hobby had turned into a habit, and not, he thought, a particularly healthy one.

When he turned around again, Izanami was sitting on the edge of the bed.

Ida jerked his thumb over his shoulder, indicating the silver box with the blue light. "Get anything new this time? I think I've heard it enough myself, actually."

Izanami nodded, much to Ida's surprise. "I think so too. I just wanted to hear it a few more times, in case there was something we'd missed."

"Like what?"

She shrugged. "I don't know. But it's fascinating, isn't it?"

Ida frowned. "Yeah, but I'm thinking maybe it's best to leave it for a while. There's no information to be had, nothing that tallies with anything recorded in that time period. The station's computer put the recording in low Earth orbit, but that's probably wrong. Could be anything, from anywhere. The only thing we know is that the message was sent a millennium ago." He slapped both hands down on his thighs. "Not much to go on, really."

"So you managed to get some more time on the comms deck?"

"I did, yes." The corners of Ida's mouth turned up at the thought. King would throw a fit if he found out, but Ida had been clever, disguising his computer time under a stack of fake processes that would swamp any activity list an operator would bring up to check. King seemed to be using the deck to run some analysis of his own, but with the lightspeed link down, it seemed as good a time as any to use the spare capacity. "One last pass, trying to filter the noise out. I've left it running. Should have something tomorrow, I think."

Ida leaned back and closed his eyes, and was halfway into a yawn when a knock came from the cabin door. His jaw snapped shut with an audible clack. He didn't move, thinking King had hauled himself around the hub to berate him personally for using the computer without authorization. The knock came again, and this time Ida quickly got to his feet.

The cabin door had a small square window set at an average head-height. It was a rubbery, thick plastic, scratched and slightly cloudy. As Ida approached, he could see someone moving outside the door, but the corridor was mostly in darkness and the person was just a shadow. The head was large and round, a helmet of some kind, and the person seemed to be bouncing a little, as though he or she were agitated.

Not King. It was Carter, or Serra, or DeJohn, in a better disguise than a T-shirt mask this time. Time really was lying heavy on their hands.

Ida turned, motioning Izanami to get back against the far wall of the cabin. She nodded, expressionless.

Turning back to the door, Ida exhaled quickly, rolling his shoulders, loosening them up. If someone wanted a piece of him, they'd have a fight on their hands.

The cabin door slid sideways the instant Ida jammed his index finger on the control. He held his breath and hopped backwards a little, balancing on his toes, fists clenched.

There was nobody there. Ida darted out into the corridor, checking to the left and right in a half duck, expecting someone to swing out from shadows on either side of the door.

Nothing, nobody. Ida stood to his full height but kept his fists clenched. Turning to reenter the cabin, he glanced up at the security camera he now knew was in the corner of the next bulkhead. This time he'd seen someone at the door. This time there would be evidence and King wouldn't be able to brush him off so easily.

"Who was it?" Izanami was still pressed up against the far wall, peering out from around the edge of one of the floor-to-ceiling cabinets. With the lights at one-quarter power, the cabinet cast a near perfect shadow across the angle in which Izanami hid. The room was cold again, and Ida caught sight of Izanami's eyes reflecting the dim blue glow of the light on the radio set.

"Didn't see, but I have a fair idea," said Ida, pausing at the threshold. "I need to talk to King. The camera should have got the asshole this time." Ida shuffled on his feet. "You coming?"

Izanami shook her head. She must have gotten quite a fright.

"Okay, but stay here and don't let anyone in who isn't me. If someone has it in for me, they might have it in for you as well. You seem to be my only friend around here. Don't think that has gone unnoticed. Back soon."

The door closed behind Ida, cutting the light from the corridor down to a dirty square thrown onto the cabin floor through the small window. Eventually that light dimmed as Ida moved down the passage and out of the section.

Izanami stepped out of the shadow in total silence, her eyes glittering. She padded to the door and, with a smile, placed the flat of her hand against the cold metal.

A shape appeared at the window, a black shadow at first barely distinguishable from the orangey gloom until its face resolved, pressing up hard against the cloudy plastic. Pale skin, sickly and white; yellow eyes wide; mouth pulled into an unnatural grin as the flesh squeezed against the window, revealing teeth as yellow as the eyes.

DeJohn writhed against the door, his hands now appearing beside his face, pressed hard enough against the glass to bleach the color from them. His mouth was open and he rocked his head from side to side, pulling the skin and flab into hard geometric shapes. His grimacing face, shoved hard against the window, was a horrifying, insane mask in the dark corridor. If he was screaming, no sound penetrated the cabin. His eyes rolled, shot through with broken blood vessels.

Izanami watched, the smile growing across her face.

Finally DeJohn calmed, his convulsions becoming less and less. His huge eyes lolled in their sockets until they fixed on the face on the other side of the door.

Izanami drew her hand away from the door, put a finger to her lips, and shushed the engineer. DeJohn's twisted mouth flickered. Then he pulled himself away from the window, leaving a thick, slimy residue of saliva and sweat on the frosted plastic.

Smiling, Izanami opened the door. In the near blink of an eye, it slid to one side.

The corridor beyond was empty.

Izanami stepped into the passage, cast a look at the lens of the security camera high on the bulkhead, and then turned and walked deeper into the hub, into the dark skeleton of the station.

18

"The provost marshal is busy, Captain, I'm sorry," said the Flyeye.

Ida blew out his cheeks and almost jogged on the spot in annoyance. The door to the commandant's ready room was locked, and the Flyeye had been quick to leap from her chair nearby and stop Ida from punching the doorbell.

"What the hell does he do in there?" asked Ida, waving at the sealed bulkhead. "Polish his precious desk?"

The Flyeye didn't speak, but her hand was held out as though to prevent Ida from charging the door with his shoulder.

Ida sighed. If the marshal didn't want any visitors, fine—he could use the security console himself.

As soon as Ida turned on his heel, the lock on the ready room door chimed. Ida turned back to see the indicator change green and the door slide open. King stood on the threshold. Behind him, the ready room was dark, lit only by the old-fashioned green-shaded lamp on the antique desk. Ida could see an open book—a *real* book, made of bound paper.

"Captain?" King's voice was steady, his eyebrow raised in the marshal's favorite expression.

The Flyeye began to explain, but King waved her away. He drew a breath to speak but Ida held up his hand. King sighed and nodded, and began to rub his forehead.

"I saw him this time," said Ida.

King shook his head. "We're a little busy here, Captain. Do you wish to report another burglary?"

Ida realized he was standing on his toes, and he gently rocked back onto his heels.

"No, I don't," he said, ignoring the weary look on King's face. "But I caught him snooping around. He was wearing a helmet, maybe a spacesuit."

King kept his eyes fixed firmly on Ida's.

Ida breathed slowly, trying to keep his cool. What was King waiting for? "Marshal, if one of your crew is wandering around playing practical jokes in a spacesuit, I don't think our incoming guests are going to think much of Fleet discipline."

King blinked, jaw muscles working as he ground his teeth.

"I'm all for a little fun and games," Ida said. This was not strictly true and both Ida and King knew it, so Ida picked up the pace before the marshal would notice. "But aren't you going to have to file a report on Ms. Hollywood's visit? A crewman taking a suit without authorization to fool around in isn't going to sit well with Fleet Command, is it?"

Ida widened his eyes a little, playing the innocent, and King finally clacked his tongue against the roof of his mouth and, arms folded, turned and strolled over to the security desk. Ida was at his heel, checking his step, trying not to overtake the marshal in his impatience.

King tapped the operator, who stopped his furious typing and turned his huge, multifaceted goggles up at his superior. King nodded his head toward Ida and stepped back. Ida exhaled loudly and leaned over the desk, eyes scanning the array of screens suspended above the console. The Flyeye glanced at King and then back at Ida before signaling his readiness.

"Okay, camera feed outside my cabin—there we go. Wind back

about twenty minutes, and also bring up crew scan records for the same period." Ida stood and rubbed his top lip. "No, further—go back an hour, let's see what we have."

"I wouldn't rely too much on that."

Ida turned to King, standing behind him. "The crew scan?"

King nodded. "There's a bug in the manifest. Crew tracking is a little flaky at the moment. That's what Operator Jagger here was busy with, trying to locate and correct the error without having to reboot the entire ship-wide net."

Ida frowned and scratched at the back of his head. He'd never heard of a manifest bugging. Keeping track of everything on board a U-Star was one of the provost marshal's main responsibilities. Everything from pencils to protein sachets, from neutron missiles to the crew itself was traceable and trackable. Their current whereabouts could be called up instantly on the automated system, and any movement watched in real time from the security desk. Fleet personnel had subcutaneous ident tags that couldn't be removed without a lot of blood and trouble—Ida's had been removed when he retired, hence King's requirement he wear an old-fashioned tag card on his belt.

"Huh," said Ida, turning back to the console. The two largest rectangular computer screens were showing the results of his request, the left-hand panel an amber diagram of the section in which Ida had made his quarters, the right showing the camera feed from the passage outside his door.

Ida watched one, then the other, his eyes flicking between the two screens. He saw his green ID indicator on the schematic. It was mostly motionless—him listening to the recording in his cabin, he realized. But the manifest scanner only showed him in his cabin, not Izanami.

"I see what you mean about the manifest," said Ida, glancing sideways at King.

The marshal raised an eyebrow but merely grunted in response.

The camera feed showed the half-lit passageway from the same three-quarters top-down view as it had before. The picture was almost entirely still, and if not for a few red and blue LED studs embedded in various wall panels that periodically flashed or changed color, Ida could have sworn the picture was on a freeze-frame.

"Wind them on together."

The operator acknowledged, fingers moving over analog jog controls on the desk. The pulsing of the LEDs on the security feed increased, and Ida could see his own green indicator on the map wobbling a little as he shuffled around the cabin. But aside from that, nothing was happening.

"Fascinating, Captain."

Ida turned to King. "Watch and wait," he said. He turned back to the desk and saw his green indicator move quickly across the schematic diagram of his circular cabin.

"There!" Ida tapped the desk and the operator slowed the recordings to normal speed.

Ida's green dot stopped by the door, and then moved forward. On the camera feed, he darted out of the now-open cabin door, fell into a crouch, and looked left and right in quick succession. Finally he straightened up and, fists clenched, walked back through the door and out of view.

Looking at the manifest scanner, Ida saw his green dot move back into the cabin a little before turning and leaving in a curved trajectory. On the camera, Ida reappeared briefly as he strode out of his cabin and headed to the bridge, walking under the camera and out of sight.

King sighed, and Ida felt a heavy hand clap him on the shoulder.

"Okay, Captain," said King. He looked at the floor and then flicked his eyes up to meet Ida's. "Thanks for the show. I'll be sure to look out for the rerun. Now, next time you step onto this bridge, I'm going to have a demo droid dismantle you and pack you away in one of the kit boxes along with the section of the hub that your cabin is in. Do we have an understanding?"

Ida shook King's hand off.

King stiffened, his eyes narrow and nostrils flaring.

Ida pointed at the two security screens, both now paused by the Flyeye. "You think I'm making this up? There was someone at my cabin. What? You think I'm seeing ghosts now?"

King clicked his tongue, then sighed and tapped the back of the operator's chair.

"Run it back, just before Captain Cleveland left his cabin the first time. There. Pause. Now go slow."

It was the same as before. Ida's green indicator unmoving in his cabin, then jerking into life and moving to the wall beside the door before passing through it. On the other screen Ida watched himself jumping into the passage and looking left and right.

King pointed at the screen. "Take it back, just a little. Slow, slow."

The Flyeye rotated the jog control, reversing the playback in ultra slow motion.

Bingo. Ida knew it. He pointed at the screen and looked at King. "Told you."

King looked at Ida, eyebrows knitted together over his nose. He looked back at the screen. "Operator, full manifest for that timestamp, please."

Ida folded his arms and took a step back, admiring the view on the two security screens as the operator and King busied themselves at the console.

The more he looked, though, the less he liked it. Ida began to feel a chill, and an odd, tight sensation in his chest, as the feeling of triumph over King abated.

The camera feed on the corridor was paused, a millisecond before Ida was due to make his exit from the cabin. The corridor was empty, except for a faint black shape. Hardly more than an outline, it was the size and shape of a man in an old-fashioned bulky spacesuit, complete with spherical helmet.

But even though the image was still, the form seemed to melt back into the shadows. In fact, the more Ida looked at it, the less it looked like anything at all, certainly less like DeJohn—the marine was a muscle-bound six feet, and the figure in the corridor was shorter, thinner. Ida squinted at the screen. It was a shadow, nothing more, maybe a simulacrum formed by the poor light of the passageway. He began to feel less and less confident.

But it was something, right? He was right. He'd seen something. Even if it meant he was jumping at shadows, this was proof it wasn't all inside his head.

"No suits missing," said King. He turned back to Ida. "Captain?"

Ida shook his head. He blinked and took a step back toward the console, where King was pointing at a smaller display set into the desktop. "No crew either," said the marshal.

"I thought you said the manifest was bugged?"

King pressed his tongue into the side of his cheek. Then he nodded. "Better check it manually."

He flicked the comms panel on the security desk. Nothing happened, and he flicked it again. Static popped sharply, making King jump.

"Problem?" asked Ida.

King whistled between his teeth. "No," he said sharply. Then he swore. "Where the hell is DeJohn? Carter, report, please."

"DeJohn isn't showing on the manifest, and there might be a suit missing. That's it, isn't it? That guy's been itching for me since day one."

King squinted at Ida, then glanced down at the Ops seated beside him. "Get a security detail here. Now."

"That's more like it," said Ida.

King stepped forward. There was something about his expression that Ida didn't like.

"You're right, Captain. It's time we started doing this by the book." King smiled a smile without any pleasure. "We're entering lockdown for the arrival of our guest, and you are operating an unauthorized communications deck. You are to surrender it immediately."

Ida almost took a step backwards. "Excuse me?"

The marshal placed his hands behind his back, now clearly in his element. "When I told you to take up a hobby, I didn't say anything about breaking Fleet regulations. I am aware you have tuned your radio set to subspace, which is a prohibited frequency."

Shit. He knew. Ida's mind raced. How? Clearly someone had told him—probably the same people who had broken into his cabin earlier. Ida wondered if anyone had been listening in on his radio chatter too. He wondered if anyone else had heard the strange message.

"Look, marshal," Ida began. He was on thin ice here, and he knew it. He just hoped that with the operations on the station winding down, King would continue to be lenient. He opened his mouth to speak again when King held up a hand.

King nodded to someone just over Ida's left shoulder. Ida saw King's hand twitch just before a heavy hand enveloped each shoulder.

"Security, escort Captain Cleveland to his quarters and supervise the deactivation of his space radio set. Bring the confiscated equipment to me when you are done."

The grip on Ida's shoulders tightened.

"Captain Cleveland is to remain in his cabin until our VIP has departed." King looked between the two marine escorts and seemed to choose one at random. "Ahuriri, remain outside the cabin. If the captain tries to leave, manacle him to something heavy."

King's eyes flicked back to Ida's. The marshal was in his element now. Ida knew, after months stuck on a barely functioning station, he must have been itching for a chance to reestablish order and control.

"I'm under arrest now?" Ida's voice was almost a whisper.

King regarded Ida and folded his arms. "You are a security risk, Captain. But believe me, I am doing you a favor. If you were on active duty, this would be much worse. Dismissed."

The marines, each fully kitted out in the security detail's helmet and body armor, pulled harder on Ida's shoulders, and he knew if he didn't comply, they'd lift him up and carry him by the armpits back to his cabin. He shrugged them off, holding both hands up in surrender, and turned and walked to the elevator column ahead of his escort.

The walk back to his cabin took nearly ten minutes from the bridge, but Ida barely noticed. Instead his mind was racing. He'd got off easy, for sure, and he should have known not to dabble in the forbidden subspace frequencies, even if he'd found them accidentally in the first place.

But without the radio, he wouldn't have the message, the recording. Which was exactly what needed to happen—provost marshal aside, Ida had to get the damn thing out of his head.

None of which made Ida feel any happier about losing the ghostly, crackling voice of the woman who had died long ago.

"You going to open this door or what?"

Ida's head snapped around, and he looked at himself in the reflection in the marine's helmet. They were standing outside his cabin.

Ida nodded and, glancing up at the security camera on the bulkhead, tapped the entry code into the door panel.

19

Carter swore and slid off Serra's body. She sighed and kicked at the tangle of damp sheets at her feet. He laughed.

"What?" she asked.

Carter helped push the bedding off onto the floor with his feet. They lay together, heat radiating off their slick bodies.

"You," he said. "Aren't girls supposed to sigh delicately and pull the sheets up to their chin when they're done?"

Serra laughed now and stretched her arms above her head. Carter's eyes were fixed on her breasts as they were pulled taut against her rib cage.

His lip curled and his hands moved over her body. Serra giggled and moved in to kiss him, then jolted under his grip, pushing herself up the narrow bed quickly. Carter snarled and poked his tongue between his teeth, but his grin quickly vanished when Serra said "*coño*" and then "fuck," and knocked his hands away.

"What is it?"

Serra looked past him, her eyes searching the cabin, but it was dark, twilight-normal, empty. Carter craned his neck around.

"There was someone looking in." Serra pointed at the door as

Carter rolled over and swung his legs over the edge of the mattress. She sat up and leaned over, scrabbling for the bedsheets so recently discarded.

Carter sat on the edge of the bed, elbows locked as he pressed backwards on the mattress, ready to spring up. After a few seconds his shoulders relaxed and he turned back to Serra.

"There's no one there. You okay? You're pretty edgy, you know?"

Serra frowned and pulled the sheet tight against her chest. It was getting cold in the cabin. She could hear the environment control kick in, faintly roaring like a distant sea.

Carter was right; that was the thing. Serra wished that she'd gone with the other psi-marines instead of Lafferty and met up with her lover back on Earth, later. Life on the *Coast City* was fucking her up.

Carter sniffed and looked back toward the door, apparently oblivious of the dropping temperature. "You think we got a Peeping Tom?"

Serra nodded. She wanted to say more, to tell him about the voices, to tell him about the purple light in her dreams, to tell him that she felt an almost constant presence now, tailing their every move around the station.

But she just pressed the sheet against her chest with her left forearm crossed protectively over it. Carter stared at her, his own face expressionless. But there was something in his eyes. She knew he trusted her instincts. That was her job, after all. He was a frontline marine, one of the best. That was *his* job.

Carter sighed and he pushed himself off the bed, padding over to the door. Placing his hands on either side of the square window, he pressed his nose against the panel and looked left and right as best he could. Serra shuffled on the bed behind him.

"I must have imagined it," she said.

"Huh," said Carter, still trying to look down the passageway outside the cabin without opening the door. "Y'know, if we've got a peeping perv, I have a feeling there's only one person on this boat that it'll be."

"DeJohn?" Shit. It wasn't a surprise. They'd given up trying to find him after nearly two hours of chasing shadows around the hub, Carter finally calling it and reporting back to the marshal. If DeJohn was playing a game, it was a fucking tiresome one.

"Yep. Prick." Carter turned from the door. "You've seen how he's been lately. He's high on engine juice most of the time. This tour is seriously screwing him up." Carter gave one more glance out the window. "Anyway, looks like we're alone now. Maybe it wasn't him. Maybe it was your imagination. Now," he said, turning and advancing toward the bed, a wicked grin on his face. "Where were we, exactly?"

Serra relaxed, letting the sheet slacken as Carter leaned forward to grab it off her. They both laughed, and Serra braced herself for a tug-of-war. Jerking forward, Serra glanced over Carter's shoulder, toward the door.

They weren't alone. She screamed. She couldn't help it.

Carter cried out and tumbled back as Serra's grip on the sheet suddenly loosened. He regained his balance on his heels and slid off the bed, spinning around to face the door, stopping just short of slamming straight into it.

They had a Peeping Tom, all right, and Carter had been right. The face was pressed tightly against the Plexiglas, rolling from side to side, dragging the fleshy cheeks horribly, exposing yellow teeth and sickly pale gums.

"DeJohn!" yelled Carter. "What the fuck?"

Carter slammed a palm against the locking mechanism. The door whined but didn't open, and for a moment DeJohn's distorted face stopped squashing itself against the glass just long enough to look Serra in the eye.

"Fucking *fuck*," said Carter, slapping the door control repeatedly.

There was something wrong with DeJohn, thought Serra. He'd never had the best teeth in the world, but through the slightly cloudy glass of the cabin door they looked yellower than ever, and ragged, almost chipped at the edges, pointed. But it was the eyes—the whites were almost a dark shade of yellow, shot through with a bright spiderweb of red. DeJohn was grinning, his eyes so wide as to be almost perfectly circular.

"Get fucking rid of him," Serra called from the bed. She'd brought her legs up to her chest now and pressed herself against the wall at the head of the bed. On a fucked-up space station like the *Coast City*, the last thing she needed was DeJohn being a fucking *carajo*.

Carter looked down at the door control. "The hell is wrong with this thing?" He slapped it again, his palm smacking with a wet sound against the silver-chrome surface. The door whined again, and this time, after just a second's pause, opened.

The passageway was empty. Carter muttered under his breath as he strode out into the corridor. As soon as he crossed the threshold into the passage Serra saw him tense, his skin suddenly crawling with gooseflesh, the cold outside the cabin enough for him to reflexively pull his head back as though avoiding a blow. His body shone metallically with sweat in the dim light.

As Carter paced outside the cabin, Serra screwed her eyes tight. She was a marine, a fucking marine, and a little cold air and someone being a dick was nothing, *nothing*. But she'd had a surprise, and she was annoyed at her own reaction. She'd been more on edge before than perhaps she realized, and this made her uneasy, uncomfortable. Right now she'd rather have been at the front line of a battle against the Spiders, using her ability to plug into the Spiders' own psi-net and fuck with their communications.

"What the *fuck* is up with the environment control?" Carter's voice drifted out of the passageway. He reappeared at the door, sweat steaming off him as he stepped back into the cabin.

Serra thought of the purple light of Shadow. "I'm not going back outside to try to fix it again," she said quickly.

Carter paused and gave her an odd look. Then he nodded.

"Freezing out there. This hulk is fucked, I tell you. Environment control is all screwed up again." Carter reached behind him and hit the door panel. As the door slid shut, he knocked the cabin's environment control to high and sighed as warm air gently blew in through the vents near the ceiling. Carter walked over to the bed and began separating his clothes from Serra's.

"This demo job is really beginning to piss me off," he said, pulling on his pants. He swore again as his foot got tangled in the leg.

"So what the hell was DeJohn doing out there? Did you tell him to fuck off?"

Carter huffed. "Where's my shirt?" Finding it, he yanked it over his head and unrolled the T-shirt down his chest and back while shaking his head. "There's nobody out there."

Serra stiffened under the thin sheet. "What do you mean? What did you tell him?"

"I said," Carter growled, hopping on one foot as he pulled his boots on, "there's no one fucking out there."

"But… he was there!" Serra pointed at the door, waving her finger around as though that emphasized her words.

Carter glanced up at her and shook his head again. "He must have run out of the section."

"Where are you going?"

Carter hooked a thumb over his shoulder, toward the door. "Gonna see if I can find him, then see King."

"King?"

"Yep. Something isn't right."

Serra buried her chin in the sheet. The Fleet-issue bedding was terribly thin, and despite the warm air filling the cabin, the sweat on her body refused to dry, making her feel wet and cold. But she didn't want to move. It was ridiculous. She was a marine, a trained soldier, just like Carter. And yet… and yet she had to bite back the urge to ask Carter to check under the bed, just in case. *And then when he leaves*, she thought, *I'll lock the cabin door, turn off the lights, and hide in the corner, and wait for him to come back.* She didn't want to be in view of the window in the door. Or, more important, she didn't want to be able to see out of it herself. Because…

"You see his face?" she asked.

Carter blinked at Serra. He was standing over the bed now, dressed. The muscles on his chest were tight, stretching the fabric as he clenched his fists.

"His eyes…" she said quietly.

Carter nodded.

Serra sat up a little. "Is he sick? He looked sick. Maybe that's why he didn't respond earlier?"

Carter nodded again. "Stay here," he said.

But he needn't have bothered. Serra just watched as her lover opened the cabin door, standing in the frame for a good few seconds as he checked left and right and left again. With a final look over his shoulder and a small frown, he disappeared down the passage. The door snicked shut behind him automatically, and the light dimmed as the passageway darkened as he walked away.

In the corner of the room, on the bed, under the thin green sheet, Serra sat, every muscle in her body tense, not wanting to move, not wanting to close her eyes. If she edged back, just a little, the angle of the door window was enough that nobody could see her easily. Perhaps that was enough, but she didn't dare move across the room, not even to get dressed.

Shivering with cold and shivering with fear, Serra lifted the sheet over her head, plunging herself into a world of cold, green dark.

This fucking spaceship.

Carter walked slowly at first, then picked up the pace once he realized the environment control had at last decided to play ball, switching section lights on around him as he moved, keeping the ambient temperature just so. Still, it played havoc with his sinuses. The inside of his nose was cold and dry and it hurt when he sniffed. His lips had a layer of cracked skin on them.

The second passageway, then the third. Each gently curving corridor was separated by a bulkhead and door, the edges of each premade section that, when assembled together in space by the robot drones, formed the kitset space station.

Carter reached the end of the third passage along from the cabin he now shared with Serra. The bulkhead door slid upward silently as he approached, the ship's sensors timing it so that he didn't have to pause to pass through no matter what his travel speed.

Serra. Now, *there* was a marine. Her gunnery scores were higher than those of anyone else Carter had met in service, specialists like Sen aside, helped by that goddamn freaky sixth sense she had going on. But that wasn't the half of it. For the first time, he'd met someone who really understood him, who knew what it was like not just to be a marine but also to be ex-Black Ops. She knew what this meant, more than anyone he'd met who hadn't actually *been* there. She helped him deal with his past—it was a slow process, but he was getting better, he knew it, and it was all down to her, too, not the army of shrinks the Fleet threw at him. Serra was special, in more ways than one. And if they could only escape from the Fleet one day, then he knew, he *knew* she was the one he wanted to grow old with. Time spent with her helped him forget, more and more, about the Fleet and its business.

Carter stopped on the other side of the door, peering ahead. He was heading toward the demolition zone proper, marked by a red line running at eye level on the walls on either side of him. The metallorubber floor tiles had already been lifted, leaving a shallow grid of black metal. The corridor was very long, and although it was nearly pitch dark ahead, the bright red LEDs on the next bulkhead door did a fine job of illuminating the end of the section in a dreamy, misty light.

Carter sighed, tapped his fingers against the doorframe behind him, and then turned to leave. He needed to see King.

Just as he turned, the red light at the end of the passage flared in his peripheral vision. He stopped and snapped his head back around. Something had moved across the red LEDs. A shape, indistinct and blurred.

"DeJohn?" Carter stepped back into the section, trying to see through the mist now filling the dark passage. Lit by the low LEDs on the walls, it created an eerie violet glow.

"DeJohn? Hey, Niels, you there?" He shook his head, muttering, and kicked his feet at the clouds forming near floor level. The environment control had gone loopy again. Mist? "What the—?"

Carter took two steps forward, each footfall ringing out on the metal floor grid. Then he stopped.

He was there.

Standing at the far bulkhead, the figure in the spacesuit was unfocused and rough at the edges, the mist curling around it, crawling up its legs like it was alive, aware. It was standing in front of the door panel, and the glowing air made it look like you could see through it, see the lights behind.

Carter blinked and took another step forward. The door behind him, sensing his progress, closed.

"DeJohn, you fuck. What do you think you're doing? King is going to eject you into space, man. But not before you've explained yourself to me. Hey! I'm talking to you!"

The figure in the spacesuit didn't move. It was DeJohn, wasn't it? They'd seen him at the cabin window, although he'd put his helmet back on now. Although... the figure was somehow shorter and thinner than DeJohn, even in the bulky suit.

Carter suddenly had a feeling he should have ducked into the armory and signed out a sidearm. His fingers curled at his belt, searching for a holster that wasn't there.

But he kept walking forward. The figure in the suit didn't move, not really, although he shimmered in Carter's vision.

Carter's skin was pricking with a cold sweat, chilling him even further in the fucked-up atmosphere of the semi-deconstructed passageway, each step illuminating the next ceiling light tile to half power, enough to make sure you didn't walk into anything but not enough to see properly. Ahead, the figure rippled again.

Carter frowned. The ceiling lights above the figure in the suit were still dark—another environment glitch—but the section where the guy was standing was lit better now by the lights above Carter as he approached. He could see now that the figure in the suit was standing almost hard up against the bulkhead door. The door was unlocked—Carter could see the indicator light through the spacesuit—but remained closed.

Through the spacesuit? Carter stopped and pinched the bridge of his nose between forefinger and thumb. He felt dizzy suddenly. He sighed and strode forward.

"DeJohn, quit fooling around. You shouldn't have that suit out of storage. King is already in a bad mood and you're going to drive him truly apeshit, man."

Carter stopped. He could feel the cold air move around him, the thin mist cloying on his bare arms.

He blinked and was alone in the passageway. The figure in the suit had gone. The bulkhead door was still closed, and he'd never heard it open.

The corner of his mouth curled into an irritated snarl, Carter looked at the frame of the door panel, as though an explanation might be printed there alongside the standard Fleet insignia. He stepped forward, just to check, and at the appropriate proximity the bulkhead door slid open, left to right. Beyond was another corridor in an identical state of deconstruction. The ceiling light across the bulkhead faded on, and, caught in the yellow-white light, Carter watched fingers of the cold mist drift into the clear air of the next section.

Carter swore, then stood and breathed deeply for a while. The nausea had passed, but his chest hurt. It was an unfamiliar feeling, being in a situation in which he wasn't in control. You could never let that happen in space, nor on the battlefield. Calm, control. Think. He shook his head, like that would clear his mind. He focused on facts rather than on supposition, ignoring the uncomfortable way the image of the man in the spacesuit had been a blurring, shifting black shadow in the passage. He quickly came up with a theory, one that better satisfied him.

DeJohn had snapped at the same time the *Coast City* manifest had bugged. He'd dropped off the scan and was now running free around the station, high on engine juice. He must have fallen into a paranoid delusion, stealing the suit, convinced that the U-Star was going to fall apart around him at any moment. He was sick; he needed help. Carter had seen plenty of cases of space madness. The theatrical nature of the environment failures was just triggering the latent, primitive, superstitious parts of DeJohn's mind. Carter understood—lighting and door failures, temperature drops and problems with humidity and condensation, it was enough to flip anyone out. And maybe with the station not altogether there anymore, they weren't shielded from the light of Shadow. Shadow scared even Carter. The light of that star would fuck you up. That was something else to report to King. The *Coast City* may have been decommissioned and in the process of demolition, but it was probably important for the demolition crew itself to survive the process. Maybe they could move the station farther out from the star. There was no scientific crew left aboard to study the stupid thing anyway.

He turned around. The figure in the suit was a couple of meters away, now standing in the passage through which Carter had just come. Carter felt a lump in his throat and instinctively swore just as he took a huge intake of breath. The result was a strangled gasp that didn't quite fill Carter's lungs. He stood, back straight, and whooped for breath again. In an impossible second the figure was now standing right in front of him, close enough to touch. It reached forward.

Carter's last thought before the blackness descended was that it wasn't DeJohn in a spacesuit. It was a woman, her curves unmistakable even under the silver padding. And it wasn't a Fleet-issue spacesuit. It was old-fashioned, like something from an old movie. Silver quilting and white plastic, and across the front, four large, bold letters in red: CCCP.

Carter stared at the closed helmet visor, trying to work out who the reflected image was. A man with cropped hair and a mouth stretched wide and screaming.

20

"What the hell?"

Ida heard the scream, and so did the two armed marines. The one inside his cabin shifted, helmet turning toward the door. Through the semi-frosted square window, Ida saw the guard stationed outside turn his head, looking down the passage. Ida stood quickly from the bed, where he had been reading a book on his computer pad—with no space radio, no mystery recording, he actually felt a lot better, and had started to think about his edited personal history again and what he would do and whom he would see back at Fleet Command in a couple of months to get it sorted out.

He put the pad down beside him and looked at the marine. The marine said nothing but shifted on his feet, clearly itching to check out the sound.

Ida pointed at the door. "Aren't you going to see what that was?"

The marine looked between his prisoner and the cabin door.

"Come on, don't be a jackass," said Ida. "Someone's in trouble. It's your duty to check, marine."

Outside the cabin, the second marine had been joined by somebody else. It was impossible to see who, but they were shorter and weren't dressed in battle gear like the guards. The marine's helmet, nothing but a dark spherical shape, bobbed as he conversed with the newcomer.

"Oh, for crying out loud." Ida took a step forward, hesitating only a moment as his robotic knee panged with pain. *Too much lying idle*, Ida thought.

The marine snapped back to full attention and made a move to stop Ida, but then seemed to think better of it and nodded instead. Ida slapped the chrome control panel next to the door, which snicked open.

"I can't get through to the bridge." It was Serra. She was dressed in her off-duty fatigues, her green singlet damp with sweat; clearly she'd come straight from her cabin at the sound.

"What's going on?" Ida's gaze flicked between the marines.

Serra looked at him; her eyes were wide and wet, her lips parted and quivering slightly with rapid breaths.

"Marine?" Ida looked at his guard.

The guard raised a gauntlet to the side of his helmet, and Ida watched his index finger twitch as he manually cycled through the comms channels. Normally it was automatic, controlled by a combination of jaw movements inside the helmet and selective thoughts as part of the combat suit's low-level psi-fi field. The manual control was there as a backup only.

The marine shook his head. "Some kind of interference on all channels."

Serra's face dropped into a worried frown. "Me too." She tapped the silver comms tag slotted onto her belt.

"Interference?" Ida stepped back and, standing in the doorway to his cabin, reached around to the door control panel. The room's main comms channel control was embedded next to the lock.

Ida thumbed the call button. "Bridge?"

As soon as he released it, the cabin was filled with a harsh burst of static. First the lightspeed link, now the station's internal comms channel? It was impossible. Ida flicked the button a few times, each resulting in a burst of noise. He bent over and absently rubbed his artificial knee, which seemed to throb in time to the static.

There was something else in the noise. Ida depressed the button and held it, focusing on both the sound and the way his knee ached. There was something else buried underneath the random sound. A rhythm, a roar that waxed and waned with a sharp edge that made the edge of Ida's jaw tingle like he was sucking on a lemon.

He'd heard that sound before. He had been listening to it just recently.

The static of subspace.

He hit the button again and again. "Bridge! King, come in." Nothing, just the empty roar of the universe that lay underneath their own.

He pressed the button one more time, but then he saw Serra wobble on her feet, her hands on her forehead. She was a psi-marine, he knew that... Maybe the alien noise of subspace affected her like it affected the psi-fi link between his knee and his brain.

Serra closed her eyes and rubbed them. She muttered something in Spanish, just a whisper, and looked at the floor.

Ida turned to the marine next to her. "Go to the bridge. Inform the provost marshal that we have a ship-wide communication failure and that there may be crew in danger. Go."

The marine turned his visor from Ida to Serra and back again, before looking over Ida's shoulder at his companion now standing in the doorway. The marine who had been guarding Ida nodded, the movement exaggerated by his helmet.

Ida tapped the first marine on the shoulder.

"Go!" he said, gently pushing on the jarhead's armor. The marine finally seemed to make his decision and turned, jogging down the corridor. The marine in the cabin pushed past Ida and made to follow, but Ida grabbed him by the elbow.

"Come with us. You're the only one with a gun. Serra?"

Serra snapped out of her reverie and raised her eyes to Ida's. "Yes?"

"What happened? Who's in trouble?"

"Carter. It's Carter. He... We saw DeJohn. He was acting up, so Carter went to get him. He didn't come back."

That snagged it. DeJohn, the nastiest, stupidest marine on board had finally flipped and jumped Carter. That had to be it. They were all in this together now.

"Come on," he said, and he led the way down the corridor.

They found him by a bulkhead, clockwise around the hub and only a few hundred meters from his own cabin. He was out cold, and Ida was pleased to see Izanami had got there first. The medic was kneeling on the ground beside Carter, his head in her hands, her long white fingers pressed into his face.

Ida was at her side immediately. "Is he okay?"

Serra dropped to her knees and rolled Carter's head toward her, brushing off Izanami's hands. "How should I know? He needs a medic. DeJohn must have jumped him. *Fuck.*"

Ida eased back a bit, giving Serra a good clearance around Carter's supine form. He was breathing, and as Serra clutched at his head he groaned and his eyelids flickered.

Ida looked him over briefly, not really sure what to look for. He wasn't bleeding and he seemed to be in one piece, although his uniform—off-duty greens like Serra's—was crumpled and saturated with cold sweat. Carter coughed and tried to get himself up onto his elbows, hissing in pain as he did so.

"Easy, marine." Ida laid a hand on Carter's shoulder, and the marine gave him a hard look.

But Serra's hand rested on his other shoulder, and she pushed him back. He looked at her and blinked, and seeing her face, he seemed to relax a little.

"What happened?" Ida asked. "Are you hurt?"

Ida gently took Carter's forehead between the fingers of one hand and rolled the marine's head to expose the back of it. There was a grid pattern in his closely cropped hair that showed where he'd lain, and the scalp underneath looked red, but otherwise he was unharmed. If he'd been attacked by DeJohn, the other marine hadn't managed to land a blow to the head.

Carter gave Ida an unfocused look, like he was concentrating on a particularly difficult engineering problem. He blinked again.

Ida recognized the signs of a concussion.

"Ah… that's a very good question, sir," Carter said quietly.

Ida smirked. He'd called him *sir*. Perhaps a concussion was good for him.

Then Carter's hand grabbed at Ida's chest, pulling the front of his shirt into a bunch as he sat up from the floor. Ida looked down and could see the veins bulging in the marine's biceps. His jaw was tight, the muscles under his ears bunched and white. His eyes were wide.

"I… remember…"

"Charlie, what is it, babe?" Serra asked, trailing her fingers around his face.

He flinched at her touch, but then relaxed, the red flush on his face sinking back into his bones. He breathed quickly in a controlled way, trying to calm himself down.

"I saw someone. It… I don't know who it was. A woman. Never found DeJohn. But… nah…" Carter shook his head, his eyes now fixed on the floor between his legs. The armed marine shifted to give him more room. From farther down the passage came the sound of more booted feet, running to the rescue.

Ida turned back to Carter. "Who was it? What did you see?"

Carter laughed. The laugh was empty, spent of emotion, an expression of fear and resignation at impossible things.

"Whoever it was, I don't think she's part of the crew. I didn't recognize the suit either. It was strange. Not Fleet issue. It had letters on it, maybe some kind of insignia." He moved his hand in the air over his own chest, miming his description. "*C—C—C—P.*" He shook his head.

Ida frowned, unsure whether he should recognize the initials or not. He pushed the thought to one side.

Serra looked at Ida and then up at the armed marine. "A stowaway?"

"Or an infiltrator," said Ida. "That would explain the suit."

Serra nodded. "Spacewalk between the hub and their ship?"

"Could be. The manifest bug can't be a coincidence. If they've tampered with the station systems so we can't detect their ship, they might also be able to knock out life scanners *inside* so we can't see them as they sneak around the station. Maybe that's what's caused the manifest to bug, DeJohn to drop off the system. Right?"

But Carter was shaking his head, his agitation returning. He rubbed his greasy temple.

"No, there was something else, like... like they weren't really there, they weren't part of... ah, I dunno."

Ida stood up and stroked his chin in thought. A trio of marines jogged around the corner, pulling up as they saw the group standing around the man on the floor. Ida's former guard stepped toward the newcomers and filled them in on what was happening.

Ida glanced over at Izanami, who was standing well back in the shadows at the edge of the passageway, giving everybody room. He nodded to her, and then looked back at Carter.

"Okay, we'll let the medic take care of you, and then we've got to take this to King. This facility is supposed to be on lockdown."

Serra looked up at him. "He's not going to like this."

"Well, he can like it or he can lump it, but this time he can't brush it off." Ida rolled his neck a little, conscious now that he was bringing the subject back to himself. He felt everyone's eyes on him and quickly moved back to business. "We have an intruder. That's about as serious as it gets."

Ida turned on his heel. The marine at the front of the new group brought himself to a quiet attention, but Ida wasn't looking at him. He was looking past him.

Ida looked at Izanami. In the half dark of the corridor her eyes flashed with pale blue light.

Ida looked over his shoulder, down at Carter. "Do you think you can walk, marine?"

Carter snorted and bent his knees. "I'm not a cripple."

Ida smiled. Carter's old attitude was coming back, which meant he was feeling better. Damn.

Carter stood, Serra and a marine on each side for support. Ida stuffed his hands in his pockets and stepped back, eyeing Carter up and down, making sure there wasn't an injury he'd missed.

Carter froze.

Serra's eyes searched his face. "What is it?" she mouthed.

But he wasn't looking at her. He was staring straight ahead, into the shadows. His face blanched to a deathly white, and when he opened his mouth, his scream was long and high.

Ida swore and turned, following Carter's eye line. But there was no one there except Izanami, standing apart from the group, keeping out of everyone's way. Smiling in the darkness. Her eyes moved from Carter to Ida. Then she turned and walked away toward the bulkhead door.

Ida frowned. Behind him, Carter collapsed into the arms of Serra and the other marine.

21

"This is exactly what I don't need."

Ida snorted and shifted the weight on his feet. The provost marshal paced back and forth in the ready room, apparently talking to himself. Ida wasn't sure whether King was more concerned about possible infiltrators attacking his marines or about this screwing up his carefully planned schedule.

King stopped pacing and glanced at Ida and Serra. Serra stood to attention, looking pale and ill as she stared at the wall behind King's commandeered desk. Ida followed her gaze to the painting there—a print, Japanese, of some nautical disaster. It must have been as expensive as the desk and the rug. The desk was clear, the book Ida had seen open there now absent.

"Where is Sergeant Major Carter now?" asked the marshal.

Serra's heels clicked together. "He's been admitted to the infirmary, sir, and is under sedation, sir."

King nodded. "Very well. I'm moving this station to alert status. Our guests are due in just two cycles. We are going to sweep this station from top to bottom and get rid of our rats. Captain Cleveland..."

Here it came. Confined to quarters to twiddle his thumbs. He wondered if Izanami would at least keep him company. Ida glanced to his left, where she was standing demurely, smiling but staring ahead, her eyes apparently focused on the same point as Serra's. Maybe she knew what the print was about. Ida wondered who was looking after Carter.

"You and Psi-Sergeant Serra will lead the search. Dismissed."

Ida blinked, then coughed politely into his fist. "I don't believe I heard you correctly, Marshal."

King ground his teeth. "This station is operating on a skeleton crew, if you hadn't noticed. Retired or not, you hold the second-highest rank on board. For the moment I'm going to forget about the radio—"

Ida drew breath to speak but the marshal held up a hand.

"I said *for the moment*. Until we get this situation under control, I'm officially reinstating you to service."

Ida opened his mouth again, but he wasn't sure what to say. King raised an eyebrow.

Reinstated to service? It was a surprise, but it made sense. Orders changed all the time in war, often suddenly; Ida had plenty of experience with that. And King was right. If the station was under threat, they needed everyone to pull together.

Ida felt a smile grow on his face. He saw King look at him, and quickly brought himself to attention. He snapped a salute.

"Captain Abraham Idaho Cleveland reporting for duty, *sir*!"

King nodded and moved back around behind his desk. With the marshal's back turned, Ida glanced sideways at Serra, but she was motionless, her glazed eyes fixed on the wall. On Ida's other side, Izanami had that damn smile on her face again.

"At ease, Captain," King said as he sat behind the desk. "We need to flush out our rats, and quick. This station needs to be secure for our VIPs. I'm giving you a chance here, Captain. You say you're a hero? Show us. You and Psi-Sergeant Serra will assemble your teams. Dismissed."

Serra's heels clicked as she came to life. "Understood, sir." The marine spun elegantly around, snapped her heels again, and left the office at a formal march.

Ida and King regarded each other for a few moments. Then King nodded, and this time the smile on his face seemed genuine. Ida saluted and glanced at Izanami, who at last tore her eyes off the wall and looked at him, her smile still firmly in place. Ida turned back to the marshal, said "sir," then waved at Izanami. "Come on," he said, and he turned to leave.

"I'll monitor from here, Captain," said King.

Ida turned back. "Ah... yes, sir." He frowned, nodded at Izanami, and left.

Each of the twenty-three decks of the vast torus structure that formed the bulk of the *Coast City* had a series of large atriums at the four compass points that housed both passenger and service elevators and other access points. Ida had picked the northern lobby on Deck 20 as the closest one to Carter's incident. Ida told Serra he'd meet her in twenty minutes at the assembly point nearest to her cabin.

Then he returned to his quarters to prepare for the bug hunt. While the *Coast City* had an ample supply of uniforms, fatigues, and combat suits, Ida preferred his own, custom suit, brought with him from his own U-Star. He'd clung to it like a safety blanket, a reminder that he wasn't crazy, that he had served the Fleet and retired with honor. As he stood in his cabin, holding the combat jacket in his hands, he rubbed a thumb over the rank insignia and the small silver bar sewn onto the left breast. *You don't get that*, he thought, *from being a liar.*

Ida was surprised to find himself needing the combat suit again, surprised to find himself suddenly wielding authority after his confinement to quarters. But damn, did it feel good. He'd given his life to the Fleet, only to end up in forced retirement. But now the provost marshal had stepped up, shown his faith, and Ida was a captain again, combat suit and all.

Unfortunately, he'd have to wear it incomplete—the helmet sat on a shelf in the cupboard, the psi-fi link between it and the rest of the suit somehow unable to pair, no matter how many times Ida cycled the system.

"Are you excited?"

He turned, looking up from the jacket. Izanami was standing in the cabin's open door, and he realized that he'd been rude, leaving her to trail behind him while he was lost in his own world.

"How's Carter?"

Izanami stepped in, her eyes glittering in the cabin's subdued lighting. "Oh, he'll be fine. He's well looked after."

"Good, good." Ida tossed the jacket onto the bed and went to drag the rest of his combat gear out of one of the lockers. He thought he heard her soft footfalls on the floor and then a rustle behind him as she sat on his bed. He was about to ask who, exactly, was looking after Carter, but then he found the rest of his combat suit. He yanked it from under a pile of other bits and turned around.

Ida paused, then looked over at his desk. The silver oblong of the space radio was there, plugged in, the blue LED shining bright. Which was odd, since he didn't remember seeing it as he'd come into his cabin, and the blue light really was bright in the half-lit cabin. He walked over to the desk, running a finger along the top of the radio. He couldn't believe it was there.

"What's this—?"

"I brought it back," said Izanami. "Thought you might like to listen to her again."

Ida whistled. "King is going to throw you out of an air lock when he finds out." He turned to the bed. Izanami's words bothered him more than he cared to admit as he picked up the last pieces of his kit—gloves, belt, shoulder utility harness covered in pouches and metal snap-rings for holding additional equipment. "Time to get this bug hunt under way. Will you stay here? If there are rats, they may run. I can get a marine on the door."

Izanami shook her head. "I'll be fine. I'll lock the door."

Ida nodded. "Keep it quiet and keep it dark," he said. He adjusted his gloves and then nodded a farewell.

"She's a mystery, isn't she?"

Ida froze at the cabin door. "Um..."

"She blasted off from Baikonur Cosmodrome in May 1961 and never returned."

When he turned around, Izanami was standing right behind him. She smiled and Ida felt cold, even under his intelligent combat suit.

"A space pioneer," she said, "lost on reentry." Her eyes flashed blue, reflecting the light of the subspace radio. "Dead for a thousand years."

Why Izanami found the whole thing so amusing, Ida wasn't sure. But there wasn't time to discuss it now. She was right, the message *was* a mystery, and clearly she'd spent some more time unpicking the signal, getting a better fix on its origin. But now there was real work to be done, hunting down the infiltrators and securing the station. As King had said, he had a chance now to show who he really was. It was time to move on.

"Fine," he said, surprising himself with the hardness of his voice. He pointed at the subspace radio. "As soon as we've secured the station, that needs to go back to wherever King stowed it."

Izanami took a step backwards, never letting her gaze drop from Ida's. Ida shivered. He supposed the recording had become a little obsession for her too. After all, she had nothing to do around the station. But he knew now that he should never have built the damned thing. Getting rid of it would be the best decision, for Izanami and for him.

"But right now I need you to stay here." Ida turned and headed toward Serra's rendezvous, adjusting the buckle on his equipment harness as he did, trying to remember why Carter's description of the red letters *CCCP* on the infiltrator's space suit was familiar.

22

Serra was waiting for Ida, and suddenly Ida felt he was out of place, his earlier bravado evaporating. His combat suit was a dark blue and he was missing the helmet, while Serra and her team were clad in the *Coast City*'s olive green battlesuits.

Get it together, Captain.

As he approached, Serra turned and flipped the visor of her helmet up and looked him up and down. Ida smiled tightly but Serra didn't say anything, instead tossing him a small rifle identical to the one she and the others were carrying. Ida caught the weapon and checked the small ammunition indicator display on the butt. It was loaded with soft ceramic shells, lethal to flesh and blood but, in the event of a full-on shoot-out, unable to penetrate far into the interior skin of the space station. The last thing you wanted to do in a crisis was breach the hull and pop everyone inside the station like overripe grapes.

"Thanks," said Ida, clipping the weapon to the webbing across the front of his combat suit. He felt better. "What's the plan, marine?"

Serra glanced over the assembled troops—Ida counted the two security officers who had kept him confined to his cabin among the ten marines present. The task force was a small but impressive one. Fully armored up and with helmet visors closed, they looked like a cluster of particularly angry turtles standing on their hind legs.

"The central core of the *Coast City* is locked off with marines patrolling key thoroughfares and junctions," said Serra. "Observation drones are monitoring other access points. That leaves us with the hub itself, eighty percent of which is uninhabitable."

"Observation drones?"

Serra nodded. "We've borrowed some demolition robots and set them to cover the access wells leading to the bridge and spire. Those areas are open to space, but might make an ideal access point for our rats."

Ida smirked. "I'd hate to come up against a demolition drone programmed to be a security guard."

Serra's mouth twitched into a smile. "Exactly."

"With the lockdown active, how many levels do we need to cover?"

"Just eleven. We split into two teams, start at opposite ends, top and bottom, then spiral toward the center clockwise and anticlockwise. Even if the rats manage to keep ahead of us, we'll have them squeezed between the two groups." Serra pulled a narrow rectangular computer pad from the holster on her thigh and held it up to Ida. As he watched, her gauntleted finger traced a map of their route through the station.

It was a nice plan, and a simple one. Ida had wondered whether scouring an entire space station was beyond the capabilities of the skeleton crew, even with him freshly recruited, but with the patrol points and observation drones doing most of their work, all they had to accomplish was a coordinated sweep that would force any infiltrators out into the open. Serra had done a good job, and he said so.

"Thank you, Captain."

Ida smiled. *Captain.* Yep, it was a good feeling. He was back at work.

Serra seemed to notice and grinned; then she turned to the other marines. "Decker, Blackmoore, Ahuriri, Reitman, with me. Lawrence, Perrett, Leena, Newman, follow Captain Cleveland."

She turned back to Ida. "Top or bottom?"

He looked at the ceiling. "Up, please."

Serra nodded. "Let's roll."

For the first time in... oh, a *long* time, Ida felt less like a spare part and more like the old Captain Cleveland. Taking point of his party of five, stalking forward slowly, rifle raised and sighted all the way, he immersed himself in the mission, losing himself in years of training and combat experience. He was in control, and that felt good, but there was more to it. He was *needed* and *trusted*. King's vote of confidence seemed to have brought Serra around too, which was, Ida thought, a small first step on the long journey to winning back the respect he deserved aboard the *Coast City*.

Ida stepped forward slowly, bulkhead to bulkhead, door to door, sweeping his weapon in front of him. It was pretty quiet so far, just the gentle tapping of the marines' boots behind him and the occasional plastic creak of their armor.

The provost marshal wasn't so bad. Uptight, sure. A manager rather than a warrior, but the Fleet needed both. It was just a shame, Ida thought, that the commandant wasn't aboard. He'd liked to have met him.

They kept moving. The passageways were still on minimum power, with the automatics turned off so that their progress wouldn't be heralded by the ceiling tiles lighting up as they moved. Ida regretted his lack of helmet, as it meant he had to rely on the enhanced sight on his rifle to see his way ahead clearly in the low light well.

"Leena," said Ida, still walking forward in formation, rifle sight playing the empty space in front of him as the squad crawled forward.

"Sir," came the marine's reply, her voice echoing electronically from behind her visor.

"When did the commandant leave?"

"He left before the last transport, sir."

Ida clicked his tongue, and they passed a bulkhead and began following the curve of the outer wall.

"Wasn't the one before that months ago? I thought he'd left recently?"

There was a pause before Leena answered. Ida could hear her breathing get heavier behind her helmet microphone. "He left just before you arrived... I think."

Ida pursed his lips. "So he somehow managed to get off the station *between* transports?"

"Sir, I don't understand?"

"Never mind."

They walked on in silence. What had *really* happened to the commandant? Maybe Leena had got mixed up and he had left in a transport. That was the most obvious explanation, but with the current situation aboard the *Coast City*, Ida found his thoughts stirring some nastier suspicions. Had there been a coup, or a mutiny, King overthrowing his commanding officer? No, King didn't want to be in charge; that much was clear. Perhaps the commandant had been kidnapped by the infiltrators. Maybe what was left of his body was in orbit around Shadow, a carbonized ember floating in that star's toxic light a million klicks from the station. Maybe...

"Sir, shall we continue?"

Ida blinked and raised his eye from the gun sight to look back at Leena, following immediately behind. He realized he'd stopped moving. A trickle of sweat, salty and cold, ran onto his upper lip. Dammit, he needed to focus. But his knee had started hurting, and—

"Marine, what ambient temperature does your suit read?"

"Eighteen point five, environment normal."

"*External* ambient."

Leena's helmet tilted just a little as she called up the display inside her visor and scanned the data.

"Fourteen point three. No, point oh... thirteen two... thirteen... twelve five... twelve... eleven... ten five..." The temperature was dropping rapidly. Ida nodded, and Leena stopped reading out her display. The marines behind her looked at one another.

The sweat on Ida's face was now like an icy cloth stuck to his skin. Environment failure had become an increasingly common occurrence on board the *Coast City*, and Ida knew it meant just one thing: Something unusual was about to happen. Something else was giving him a warning too—the psi-fi link in his knee was acting up. Interference.

There was a sharp click in Ida's ear. He let go of his rifle with one hand and touched the comms link on his collar.

"Receiving."

"Captain?" It was Serra, calling from several decks below his feet.

"Reading you, marine. Found any vermin yet?"

"I don't know. We're on Level Fifteen, Gamma Eleven-Two. Do you have any environment problems up there?"

"Affirmative. Temperature just took a dive in the last thirty seconds."

No reply.

"Hello?"

Ida thumbed the comms link twice, and suddenly it sparked back into life with a burst of static, loud enough to make him cry out in surprise. The sound receded quickly, but remained in the background as Serra's voice broke through. He couldn't catch her words, and asked her to repeat.

"Same here," she said. "We've tried the manual controls, but even the lights won't come on. Looks like some kind of general power failure."

Ida looked back at his team of marines. Leena was standing, gun down, listening to the conversation. Perrett and Lawrence remained alert, covering the front, rifles up. Newman had her back to the group, covering the rear with her rifle.

It was deliberate sabotage; it had to be. Which meant they were closing in.

Serra's voice was edged with white noise over the comms. "Captain, we've got company. There's someone up ahead."

Leena lifted her rifle and aimed just a notch over Ida's shoulder. Then she nodded at him. "Sir."

Ida snapped his head around. At the end of the passage, against the next bulkhead, was a dark figure, humanoid but bulky. Someone wearing a spacesuit. Ida clicked the comms.

"Serra, confirmed, so do we."

White noise, static.

"Serra? Come in?"

Nothing. Nothing but the angry roar of subspace.

Ida kept his eye on the figure ahead, noting that the bulkhead door hadn't opened despite the proximity of the intruder. That was it—they were controlling the environment, turning the lights off when it suited them, overriding the doors somehow, disabling the manifest and life scanners so they could move through the wreck of the *Coast City* unnoticed. Reducing the ambient temperature because—

Ida's comm sprang into life with a roar of white noise, just as the passage lights above Ida and his team flickered on to full for a second before falling back to the system minimum. The flare hurt Ida's eyes, and he drew an arm up instinctively to shield his face.

Ahead, the figure in the suit was somehow hard to focus on. Ida squinted. The outline was furry at the edges, streaking out like it was a reflection from somewhere being bent in the air. The shadows seemed to move, clustering around it like iron filings to a magnet.

More noise from the comms. Ida thumbed the control again and again, but each time, the roar seemed to come back louder and louder.

"Serra? Serra, come in."

Click, *static*, click, *static*.

"Sir?" Leena raised her rifle.

Behind her, Newman had turned from covering the rear and brought her gun to bear on the intruder. Lawrence and Perrett did the same. Ida pulled his own gun back to his face and put his eye to the sight, but the intruder ahead melted into the background in the computer-enhanced view. Ida released his safety and took a step forward. His boot crunched something on the floor; glancing down, Ida felt the blood drain from his face. It was his imagination, it had to be. The flakes of paint on the floor were red on one side, pale on the other. They swam around his ankles like autumn leaves on a nonexistent breeze.

He took a sharp intake of breath and realigned the gun sight with his target.

"Halt and identify yourself!"

The intruder began to walk forward, very slowly. With each step, the temperature in the passageway plummeted, and within seconds Ida's breath plumed in a cloud of steam in front of his face. The ceiling lights, already on minimum, dipped as the intruder passed underneath, almost as though their power were being siphoned away.

Ida adjusted his grip on the gun. As he shifted his weight, his boots crunched again. Something inside him screamed out, but he ignored it. "If you do not halt, you will be shot. You are unauthorized personnel. Prepare to be detained. Halt and identify yourself."

The intruder didn't stop. Ida felt his rifle, pressed hard against his bare cheek, become a cold, slippery block of metal as a dusting of frost began to grow on its surface. He shifted his grip again, pushing the sight hard enough into his eye socket to hurt. With the lighting fading, the scope automatically adjusted, enhancing the view even more so Ida had a crystal clear, if green-tinged, view of the passage ahead. He could see ahead to the closed bulkhead, but the corridor was completely empty.

Ida swore and raised his head from the gun. The intruder was still there, shuffling forward slowly like a sleepwalker. He checked the scope again. Nothing. More tricks?

"Marines," he called over his shoulder. "Do not use your scopes. Our equipment may be compromised."

"Sir," came the chorus of quiet replies.

Ida's comms link chimed. "Cleveland…"

Ida's hand shot to his collar. "Marshal?" The channel was clear enough, although the white noise pulsed steadily in the background, like the universe breathing. Or like a giant heartbeat.

"This is Commandant Elbridge. They're… here… don't let them get the… book… the ready room… the ready room… the…"

The commandant sounded like he was shouting in a hurricane, the roar that Ida knew was the sound of subspace drowning him out.

"Commandant? Come in, please. Where are you?"

The comm clicked and the white noise was so loud, Ida flinched, his hand a moment away from pulling the piece out of his ear.

The intruder stepped forward again. As it got closer, the edges of the suit seemed to resolve, as though the figure was coming into focus. A metallic blue spacesuit and narrow, elliptical helmet. A U-Star survival suit.

Ida's hand dropped and frowned. He recalled Carter's description of the intruder, but something didn't match. Behind him, Leena gave the order for the squad to take up a firing position. Ida automatically fell into a firing stance himself. His boots crunched; he glanced down again, willing the thick, heavy flakes of red paint to vanish in the same way they had magically appeared. Perhaps he was dreaming again. Perhaps, if he turned around, the bulkhead door would be made of rough wood, paint peeling off in a summer breeze. He closed his eyes and opened them again, but the paint flakes were still on the floor. He jerked his gun up. "That's enough. Stop right there."

The suited figure stopped just a few yards ahead. It was a woman, Ida could see now, as solid and as real as anyone.

"Identify yourself."

"Ida, it's me."

The barrel of Ida's rifle dropped an inch.

"It's me," she said again. The figure raised her hands to the sides of the helmet, twisting the globe anticlockwise until it clicked, and then lifting it off.

The woman was in her early thirties, strands of blond hair streaked with bright red and pink visible around the edges of the skullcap she wore.

Ida took a step forward, lowering his gun.

Leena took a step forward, gun rock steady and level, ready to shoot. "Sir?"

Ida waved her off. He was staring at the woman in the suit, his mouth hanging open, forehead creased. Was it hot, or was it cold?

"Astrid?"

She smiled, her teeth shining pale blue in the low light and her eyes burning with the same color.

"It's good to see you, Ida."

Ida walked forward, mimicking the glacial pace Astrid had taken when she appeared at the bulkhead. He smiled, but his eyes were still narrowed in confusion.

"Astrid? I…"

She shook her head. "It's okay, Ida, don't worry. I forgive you."

Ida stopped and raised his gun, pointing it directly at Astrid's forehead. He slowly curled his head down to the sight. It showed nothing but empty corridor in front of him. He raised his head again. There she was. The barrel of the gun was less than six inches from her head.

"Come with me," she said. Astrid glanced behind Ida at the tight pack of marines, each with a gun pointed in her direction. "All of you. Come."

"Astrid… I…"

Astrid smiled. "Come with me."

"Astrid, you're dead."

"All of you. Come."

"You died. You all died."

"Oh, Ida." She laughed.

The sound made Ida dizzy, but he pushed his cheek so hard into the side of the rifle that it hurt.

Astrid tilted her head. "You can't stop us," she said. "Come with me."

Ida touched the comms tag on his collar, and when he spoke, it was through clenched teeth.

"Serra? Come in! Serra, you there?"

When he released the call button, the static popped out again, rising and falling, like the winds of a storm pressing against the shuttered windows of Ida's old family farmstead, back on Earth.

"Serra, dammit, come in."

Astrid smiled and reached out a hand.

Ida froze, rooted to the spot. He tried to turn around, to direct his marines, but suddenly he was swimming through syrup, trapped in a slow-motion nightmare. With a huge effort, Ida pushed himself back and opened his mouth to shout an order to his troops.

The order never came. The comms flared into life again with the screams of Serra's team, decks below them. He recognized her voice at first, before it melted into the wails of the marines with her, impossibly loud for the tiny earpiece pumping the sound into Ida's skull.

Ida let go of his gun, letting it drop and then swing from the short line clipped to his chest. He yanked the earpiece out then pressed the heels of his hands into his ears, trying to shut out the terrible cacophony, the sound of pure primal terror that reverberated around and down the passageway.

The marines didn't seem to hear it, couldn't have heard it, because they just stood, ready for action, frozen. Ida's artificial knee sent a pain signal so pure, so intense that the whole side of his body felt like it was on fire. Then it disconnected from his psi-fi field. The knee buckled, and Ida fell. Even that seemed to be in slow motion as the force, a presence so thick, emanating from all around them, threatened to swamp his senses.

Then he saw them, the shapes, tall and thin and black. As the overhead lights flickered and dimmed, each new shadow moved of its own accord, peeling itself off the wall, forming a misshapen, unfinished figure. Long, flaring human silhouettes flickered like guttering candle flame. Within moments they surrounded Ida's team, and he found himself separated from the marines by an ever-decreasing circle of darkness.

It was only when the circle of figures finally closed in that the marines sprang to life. Beneath the screams of Serra's team, piped out of the earpiece dangling over Ida's shoulder, Ida heard his own unit cry out. Two of them fired their guns, lighting the passage in brilliant flashes of white-blue light, each flare showing a passageway entirely empty. Ida looked back over his shoulder and watched as Astrid's image flickered in time with the gunshot flashes. He winced at the sound of the shots, each loud enough to punch through the roaring static and the wailing screams, and within seconds he could feel hot gritty dust coating his bare face as the soft ceramic shells were pulverized against the walls of the passageway. The marines were shooting at nothing. Ida found his voice and called on the troops to cease fire.

More barrel flashes and he felt something tug at the fabric of his combat suit, then an odd, wet sensation. Ida's leg jerked, a blackened smear appearing on the side of his robot knee. Underneath the torn fabric of his suit, the silvery surface of artificial joint shone through a web of dark blood.

The static and the screaming suddenly increased in volume—so loud, Ida let himself slide against the wall as he pulled his hands to the side of his head. Ida cried out in surprise and pain, and looking up, watched as the black shadows drew to within touching distance of the marines. Watched as the marines—trained professionals, conditioned for space battle in the most deadly environments it was possible to exist in—turned to blind fear, throwing their arms in the air and wailing like cornered animals.

"Come with us. All of you. Come."

Astrid's voice was inside his head. Looking back at her, he could see her lips moving as she spoke, but her words echoed somewhere inside his own skull, her voice edged with metal and fire. She took a step forward, her outstretched hand now turned palm-up as she offered her help to Ida.

Ida looked back at the marines. They were writhing shapes, shadows cocooned in a deep black envelope, a frictionless absence of light that was impossible to focus on. Ida closed his eyes.

Astrid was dead. He remembered her scream and her plea for help as it echoed around the bridge of the *Boston Brand*. He remembered the faces of his crew as they listened to the dying cries of those on Tau Retore who hadn't escaped. The one part of his heroic victory tale that he never told: how he'd been responsible for saving an entire planet, but he'd also been the reason many on the planet's surface died, the ones who had stayed behind. Including Astrid, who had been taken away from him and sent to Tau Retore by her father, the Fleet Admiral. Astrid, the love of Ida's life. When he closed his eyes he could see the stellar core of the Mother Spider drop, released from the heart of the machine, and plunge down toward the planet.

the star falling as though it were a lamp burning shining bright annihilation holocaust extinction

He opened his eyes.

"You're dead, Astrid."

Astrid smiled widely. Her eyes were burning blue ovals, deep and impossible like the black shadows that swarmed the corridor around them. "Come with me."

Ida shook his head. He didn't know what she meant. Nothing made any sense. As he lay on the floor of a corridor on the U-Star *Coast City*, his hands dropped from his head, and his fingers curled on the flakes of red paint beneath him.

He said, "No."

Then Ida blinked, and he was alone in the passageway. The paint flakes were gone, and the floor had an icy sheen, cold against his cheek as his head flopped sideways. The ceiling lights stabilized and returned to the system minimum, spotlighting his prone form.

He lay on the floor, alone. The image of Astrid was gone, and the black shadows had evaporated, taking the marines with them.

23

"Help me, somebody!"

Maybe he'd been asleep. He felt stiff, tired, cold, and his right leg was wet. He moved, and a sharp pain shot up from his robot knee, all the way up to his shoulder. He'd been shot, he remembered now. He'd been talking to Astrid and someone said...

Ida jerked his head off the floor. One side of his face was numb, and the saliva in his mouth was cold. He swallowed, and coughed, and looked up and down the passageway. He could hear the environment system purring, bringing the temperature back to ambient normal. The lights were on and tinged with purple. It was night on board the *Coast City*.

"Hello? Can anyone hear me?"

Ida pulled his right leg around to a better angle. He could move his toes, and his knee still seemed to work, luckily undamaged by the ceramic round. For the first time, Ida was thankful the joint was artificial—the shot would have completely destroyed it otherwise. Thank God the passage hadn't been stripped of the rubberized floor tiles yet, either; otherwise, he'd have a head injury as well.

"Come in, please, somebody."

He looked left and right and up and down. He was alone. They'd gotten the marines, taken them. And they'd sent Astrid to get him. A ghost from the past to tempt Ida away to… what? He shook his head. They? Who were "they," anyway?

"Help me, please, somebody."

It took Ida a few seconds to realize a woman was speaking. He closed his eyes and listened. Maybe he had a concussion. Yes, a concussion. Hit his head, not thinking straight. He'd been dreaming too, a woman's voice, far away, calling out. They'd sent Astrid to get him, and Astrid was dead. They'd…

"Can anybody hear me?"

Ida's eyes snapped open, and he swore. He had to get moving. Someone was calling, not over the comms but from somewhere on the same level, from behind the next bulkhead. Maybe Serra had escaped and made it to Ida's deck. Maybe she'd been hurt too.

Pulling himself awkwardly to his feet, using his good leg and the wall to support himself, he tested his knee. Each flex stung like all hell and his leg felt weak, but he could manage a limp. He'd get Izanami to patch him up. Gingerly testing his weight, Ida pushed off the wall and stood in the middle of the empty passage.

"Help me, please."

The voice was from the left, and it didn't sound like Serra. Maybe it was one of the other marines? Leena? Or Newman? No, the voice was different—it was hollow and had a strange accent.

Ida limped down the corridor, through the bulkhead door, and toward the next section. The voice kept calling out, getting louder all the time. Ida replied, shouting that he was coming, but his voice sounded quiet and weak. The woman's voice had a crackle behind it, some sound that was so familiar to Ida, but he couldn't put a finger on it.

Hobbling as fast as he could, hissing at the pain and his own too-slow progress, he cleared the next passage and bulkhead and kept going. The woman's voice was getting stronger, and now Ida realized he was in familiar territory. Level 12, Delta-12. Omega Deck. The very edge of the crew quarters. His own cabin was just ahead.

He stopped. What if the voice was a trick, like Astrid and the dark shadows that had taken the marines? It *had* been her, hadn't it? Or had he dreamed the whole thing?

Ida closed his eyes and felt dizzy. He was confused, trying to untangle a million illogical thoughts.

"Help me, please!"

Ida sucked in a breath. He had to keep moving. Concussion and confusion were clouding his thinking. Someone was injured and needed his help. Someone familiar, if only he could place the voice.

Ida reached his cabin and punched the door control. As he stepped inside, the lights swelled to twilight-normal. On the desk in front of him, the blue light of the space radio pulsed softly.

"Is there anybody there? Come in, please!"

The woman's voice was coming from the radio set, punctuated by static, echoing across one thousand light-years of space. Ida recognized the accent, and recognized the voice. Moving to the desk, he saw that the radio wasn't set to receive; it was set on playback. The recording—the last communiqué of the lost cosmonaut—was running. Ida recognized the static and white noise and the distinctive crackle burnt into the signal as it criss-crossed space and time, bouncing around in subspace, across channels that didn't even exist in the real universe.

The recording of the woman dying in space, one thousand years ago.

The recording was speaking to him.

Ida coughed and gripped the back of his chair. It was a dream; it had to be. Or a nightmare. He was lying on the floor of the corridor, bleeding to death. He'd been shot and the station was under attack from saboteurs and infiltrators and assassins. The hull had been ruptured and he was being barbecued by the fucked-up light from the purple star. This was not the real world; this was a violet-tinged nightmare.

"Who's there?"

Ida flinched, looking at the radio. He cleared his throat.

"Who's there, please? I can hear you. Can you boost your signal?"

Mouth dry and leg on fire, Ida found himself reaching forward, adjusting the radio's controls. It was ridiculous, farcical even, increasing the antenna gain when the radio wasn't even on. It was just playing back the dead recording. The dead recording that was speaking to him.

Ida cleared his throat again. "This is Captain Abraham Idaho Cleveland of the U-Star *Coast City*. Please identify yourself."

He idly wondered who would find him first. Maybe the shadows had taken the entire crew off the station, and he'd condemned himself to a slow, lingering death alone in the corridor in deep space by refusing to go with Astrid. Or maybe Serra and her squad had fought off the attackers on the lower levels and were right now running up the maintenance stairs to his position.

"My name is Ludmila. Help me! Help me, I am lost."

Ida slumped into his chair. He felt his breath leave him in a warm, shallow stream, and then white stars filled his vision and the room turned sideways and then upside down, and everything went black.

THE STARCHILD

The Private-Profiteer *Bloom County* cruised lazily through space, in the light of the star Shadow, toward the skeletal remains of a large, doughnut-shaped space station.

It was Zia's father, Milo Hollywood, who had built the ship. True enough, at the heart of the vessel was an ordinary cargo barge—the original ship, the P-Prof *Herculanium Lady*, which had given Milo years of good use before being used as the framework for the *County*. But after the Spider attack on Earth—the historic battle that killed three billion and destroyed a hemisphere—it was Milo who saw the opportunity. He watched from the asteroid belt as the Spiders were defeated; then he piloted his barge into the shattered remnants of the moon to salvage what mineral wealth there was.

Well, he said, scotch on the rocks in one hand and flight joystick in the other, the moon was gone, no point crying about it, and hell if there wasn't 7.3×1022 tons of lunar rock just floating around in space that wasn't no good to anyone, not to mention it being one heck of a hazard to the spaceways, or it *would* be once the spaceways were cleared of any last baby Spiders. Okay, so maybe a few people protested the blatant capitalism, and maybe a few people registered their disgust at the desecration of the moon, at his turning the disaster into profit, but come on, it was the Spiders that chewed it up and spit it out like they had something to prove.

You can't fathom the alien mind. That's what Milo said when he announced his trip, and that's what he kept saying as the *Herculanium Lady* blasted off toward the Earth, skirting the cordon of damned hippie protest boats whining about the horror of moon mining. That's what he said again and again as the *Lady* weaved through the brand-new asteroid field a quarter of a million klicks out from the Earth, a slow-moving morass of gray tombstone rock and bone-white dust, a vast lunar graveyard. And Milo kept talking, even though, inside, he found it hard himself as the *Lady*'s belly was filled with the valuable mineral ore. Even though two of his crew nigh-on had nervous breakdowns at the very thought of scooping up great chunks of the moon—the *moon*, for God's sake. Even though perhaps he realized it *was* an act of desecration, pissing on the grave of three billion dead.

In fact, Milo kept saying you can't fathom the alien mind even as he cashed in the ore—making more money than existed in theory on the entire planet and plunging the Earth into a huge debt to its myriad colonies—and took off in the *Lady* with his riches, never to return home again.

Well, he couldn't, not really. The richest man in Fleetspace was persona non grata like nobody else. Sometimes, in the moments before sleep took him, Milo agreed with all his heart and all his soul.

But it was worth it. Because Milo Hollywood and his crew had found something else floating among the debris.

There was Fleet wreckage, of course, and whatever was left of the lunar colonies, but Milo didn't really stop to check, because the herculanium that formed the walls of the lunar bases and the engine housings of the U-Star hulks could be recycled just as well as the mineral ore could be processed from the gray lunar rock. The Fleet didn't seem to take any notice, being too busy patching that great hole in the Earth. The moon? Milo could have it.

But the near-intact Spiderbaby, barely a scratch on it—now, *there* was a prize. It had taken up nearly an entire bay of the *Herculanium Lady*'s mineral skip, and it had cost nearly a whole cycle of mining time retrieving it, but the loss in profit was well worth it. Because Milo Hollywood was one to tinker—tinkering with the *Lady* was what had enabled him to turn the standard G-class cargo barge into something bigger and faster, reaching the asteroid fields before his rivals and carving out the Hollywood mining empire. And now he had a Spiderbaby, its gigantic articulated legs neatly folded around its spherical body in the instinctive protective formation as it slept.

Milo couldn't exactly fathom why it was inactive. Perhaps this one was immature and underdeveloped, never having left its mother's belly with its hundred thousand siblings, and had somehow survived as the Mother Spider was blown to bits by the Fleet's finest all around it. *Whatever.* There it was, and it was his. All that alien tech, that living, thinking, adapting machine, eight giant legs and the beginnings of a mouth that would, in time—as the Spiderbaby became a Spider and perhaps even a Mother Spider—be able to render the ruined fragments of whole planets into so much particulate matter to fuel its growth and organo-technological systems.

Milo saw the potential. Sitting in his hopper was the perfect technology to pull open an asteroid like a piece of overripe fruit and process the mineral ore there and then, negating the need for bulk cargo trailers or unmanned barges to fill with raw, unprocessed ore and push back to home base on microkinetic rockets. The current technology was cheap but some of the haulers could take years to find their way back home, and some of them never did, each loss reducing the paycheck by a painful margin. If he could crack the alien tech, if he could turn the Spiderbaby into a mining ship, he'd go from commercial king to economic legend.

And Milo Hollywood was good, and he did crack it. It took twenty years, and most of his crew had by then left his employ, convinced the old man's mind had cracked just like the Earth's crust. But that was fine; he didn't need them. The *Herculanium Lady* drifted through space with no set course, stopping here and there only to refuel and restock protein and carbohydrate packs for the two remaining crew,

Milo and his wife, Honey. Even without a running mine operation, their bank balance was large enough for colonial governors to offer their own beds for the duration of each port call. It didn't matter, none of it mattered, until the Spiderbaby had been cracked.

When he'd finished, the P-Prof *Herculanium Lady* was unrecognizable, its classic—if functional—lines hidden deep at the center of a new structure, eight insectoid legs folded around a cuboidal body, ready to twitch and grab and grasp at anything Milo landed on. The Spiderbaby's primitive mind was left intact, and it still slept, but the legs could operate independently and automatically. The new chimeric ship wasn't sentient, but it was alive, certainly.

Honey demanded the vessel be rechristened. The original ship had been named for her, but there was something alien and horrid about the new version that kept her awake at night. Sometimes her dreams were filled with dark shadows and alien whispers and the roar of the ocean, and sometimes when she awoke in a cold sweat in the middle of the night-cycle she felt she wasn't alone. It was the Spiderbaby; it had to be. She knew it wasn't dead, merely inactive, held in check by Milo's ingenuity and quantum dampeners, but really only temporarily imprisoned.

Milo eventually agreed, although he could never figure out what the darned fuss was about. You cannot fathom a woman's mind; that's what he said as he dug out the registration certificate and scrubbed the ship's name off with a short, thick finger, leaving the slightest trace of black dust on the pad screen as he did so.

It wasn't until later that he found the new name. Once the original registration had been deleted, they were theoretically illegal and weren't able to make port until the new registration had been filed. One cycle out from Arb-Niner and the little lady was giving him the ear about the state of supplies, so he had to do something. They had enough credits in the bank to buy all the real estate on Arb-Niner twice over, and as she paced the living quarters on board the *Herculanium*... the *whatever-the-hell-it-was-called-now*, she said she might well do that and evict the entire planet's population if Milo didn't take some responsibility for a change and maybe invest a few precious credits in something a little better than the compressed protein and carbohydrate ration packs that had been their diet for the past twenty years.

And maybe at five years old, their only child, Zia, could have some real food, and maybe they could even stop over for a while and Zia could meet some other people planetside. Zia was a starchild, born in space, schooled in space. Zia knew nothing but her ma and her pa and the tiny metal world of the *Herculanium*... the *something-something*.

You can't fathom a woman's mind; that's what Milo said as he watched his wife read to Zia in bed, the light of the pad she held shining brightly on their faces in the dark. There wasn't much use for reading when you're out there in the inky black, sorting rocks by the teraton, he thought, but the kid liked it and the little lady liked it, and if they were happy, then Milo was happy. Maybe they should settle down for a while, and maybe Arb-Niner was a decent enough patch. He lay on the bed next to his wife and his child, squinting at the too-bright screen that showed something from one heck of a long time ago, all small and black and white and like something Zia might draw herself. He asked them what they were reading. *Bloom County* came the answer. His wife said Zia didn't understand it; but Zia jumped up on the bed and said she liked the penguin, which tickled old Milo something. Later that night, he was sitting in the cockpit of his mighty new ship, watching lights on the panel flicker as the Spiderbaby's legs convulsed reflexively underneath them, when his wife came by, gave him a kiss, and told him to fix the ship reg or he'd have to swim the rest of the way to Arb-Niner. She laughed and he laughed too, but there was a hardness in her eyes. Goddamn it if the woman wasn't speaking the truth.

Milo Hollywood picked up his pad, called up the ship reg, remembered the penguin and the happiness on Zia's face, and thought of a name.

And so the famous P-Prof *Herculanium Lady* vanished, and the legendary P-Prof *Bloom County* was born.

PART THREE

THE GHOSTS OF SUBSPACE

24

Whispers in the dark.

Zia Hollywood's head jerked against the back of her command chair. She'd dropped off. It had been a long journey. Her three crew members, seated in front of her in the flight deck, each turned their heads around at the sudden leathery creak of her movement. She met their eyes, one by one, then nodded slightly. The crew turned back around.

Beep.

"*Bloom County*, this is *Coast City*. Welcome to the neighborhood, friend. Please transmit your preassigned clearance codes and security authorization. Channels are open."

Across space, a pencil-thin beam punched the radiation-soaked vacuum, carrying vital data from the *Bloom County* to the shadowed hulk of the station. The light from Shadow, the technetium star a hundred million klicks away, sucked at the transmission, stripping energy and data from it, introducing a rhythmic pattern of interference that sounded like a heartbeat, if anyone had listened to the raw feed. The computer on the *Bloom County* noted the energy loss automatically and boosted the signal; Zia glanced at the comms display on the arm of her chair, noticing a data transfer failure of more than 80 percent.

Beep.

"*Bloom County*, you are cleared for approach. Set your docking computer to ready and we'll guide you in. Enjoy the ride."

The message ended, and the air pulsed with static for just a second. Zia heard it, even if no one else did. The static was odd, tinged with something metallic, something... screeching. She knew about the star, of course. Maybe, without her realizing it, it had made her anxious, because she had heard the sound in her purple-tinged dream too.

She leaned back, and the chair creaked again, and a warning tone sounded as the docking computer went online.

Beep.

One of her crew, Dathan, ran a finger along a data readout and flicked the comms channel back on.

"*Coast City*, this is *Bloom County*. Systems report a second-class alert on board our destination. We've been trying to contact you on the lightspeed link for several cycles. Can you confirm the nature of your alert and advise if your port is open? Please acknowledge."

Static swarmed. Zia leaned forward again, and somebody swore under his breath. The hub of the space station was an empty black void on the viewscreen ahead, a nothingness framed by the flickering violet light of the evil star beyond.

Beep.

"P-Prof *Bloom County*, this is the U-Star *Coast City*. Alert status negative. We have a minor technical issue due to the ongoing demolition of this platform, and increased solar activity is affecting the lightspeed link. Proceed as normal, no special instructions required."

"*Bloom County* confirmed. See you on the other side."

25

The ready room felt huge without the desk.

They—whoever "they" were—had attacked the beating heart of the station, somehow making it to the ready room and turning it over, turning Commandant Elbridge's expensive desk into so much expensive matchwood, at the same time as Ida's and Serra's squads had been confronted. "They" had got past guards, crew, Flyeyes at their posts, the works. The first anyone knew something was wrong was when the comms were filled with the roar of the ocean and the sound of destruction came from behind the ready room's closed door. When that door was opened, the room was a mess, the desk shattered, the provost marshal insensible in a corner.

Ida knew something had happened, even before he stepped inside and saw the wreckage. The commandant himself had tried to warn him that something was happening, something to do with the ready room. Ida didn't mention that to anyone. Not yet.

Whatever force, whoever the enemy was, they'd escaped, vanishing from the station with the eight marines led by Serra and Ida—they were the only two who were left behind. Worse than that, the station's manifest now reported less than half the crew there had been before. Those left aboard the *Coast City* were in a state of shock, impotent, with nothing to do but put armed guards everywhere and pretend to their VIPs that nothing was wrong. Pretend that the security was normal and that shadows and the cold were just an artifact of the station's half-demolished condition and that everyone was just tense because the end of the road was in sight, is all. And Ida pretended that the voice of the commandant hadn't come through his comm, that the absent commander hadn't tried to contact him, give a warning, as all hell broke loose.

Ida wasn't even sure that had happened, not anymore. Just a cycle later and he and Serra were standing in the ready room, he with his arms folded and she staring at the picture on the wall, which had survived intact. Ida glanced at her: she looked empty, burnt out. He knew she was a psi-marine, the last left on board, and he wondered what she was feeling and seeing and hearing that nobody else was. Like him, perhaps. He thought about the commandant's voice and about Astrid and paint flakes on the floor. Neither of which made him happy, not at all.

The ruins of the wooden desk had been removed. Now King had only a computer pad and a chair, and it looked as though he was making do with just that. There was hardly any point in refitting the room for the last months before the final sections of the *Coast City* were packed into their crates and rocketed on the long drag homeward.

Provost Marshal King stood square in the center of the room, arms folded, chin held high. Behind him, Ida heard the armor of the guard at the door crackle as he shifted on his feet. Red alert. Battle stations.

"So, what happens next?" asked Ida. Serra finally turned her head from the painting to look at him, but when Ida met her eye, her expression was still blank, like she was somewhere else entirely.

King's nostrils flared, but he remained otherwise motionless. "Next, Captain?"

Ida tightened the loop of his folded arms. "Yes, next. We have personnel missing. We have firsthand proof of intrusion. We have to tackle this now."

King shook his head. Then he held up his hand as Ida made to protest.

"Captain, I agree, but our VIPs have docked. We've put the station on alert and have armed guards covering as much of the hub as possible, but we're spread thin. We need to hold out until our guests have left, and then maybe we can accelerate the demolition. We have barely enough personnel to maintain operations, let alone go chasing after ghosts."

Ida found King's choice of words interesting. He raised an eyebrow. "Ghosts?"

"Intruders, then," said the marshal. "And with the lightspeed link down we can't alert other stations or call for any help, either. We're alone out here. We need to focus on internal security right now. We have a very valuable guest to look after. Her safety, and that of her crew, is paramount."

Ida folded his arms. "Where's Elbridge?"

King flinched, the corners of his mouth twitching downward. "What?"

"The Commandant, Price Elbridge. Do you know where he is?"

King turned away and paced back to his chair. He reached down and ran his hand along the edge of the computer pad as though he were about to pick it up. Then he seemed to change his mind, and he straightened up.

Ida stepped forward. "I was expecting him to be here when I arrived, but apparently he left before the last transport, but somehow after the one before that."

King's shoulders sagged. When the marshal turned back to Ida, his face was gray and the skin around his eyes tight.

"The station has two shuttles," said Ida. "One has been packed away and the other is still in use to patrol the system."

"I—"

"So where is he? Where did he go?"

Ida and King regarded each other in silence in the ready room. King knew something. He was hiding something. Ida knew it. He had to tell him about the voice on the comms, about the absent commandant getting in touch, or at least trying to. And then—

"Marshal, our VIP has arrived."

The Flyeye's appearance at Ida's shoulder broke the spell. Ida turned, suddenly angry, forcing himself to relax and to breathe, breathe, breathe.

Ida turned back to King. "Marshal, please."

But it was too late. King nodded at the Flyeye and strode from the room, leaving Ida and Serra and the marine on the door.

Ida sighed, and tried to think of something to say to Serra when he noticed she was squinting, like she was in pain.

"You okay?"

Serra rubbed her temples, spat out "fine," and turned on her heel. As she left, Izanami stepped out of the shadows on the other side of the room. Ida blinked. He'd had no idea she was there with them. In the dim light her eyes seemed to shine blue. Then she laughed.

"Sorry!" she said. "I didn't mean to intrude." She looked at the marine stationed at the door.

"I'm hungry," she said. She walked toward the door. "Come on, let's eat."

26

The woman on the screen cast a lazy look around the bridge, eyes hidden behind large rectangular dark glasses, while her entourage laughed at something. Beside her, King smiled, but everyone else on the bridge was as stiff as a board, standing to attention during the official tour. Armed marines stood against practically every clear spot of wall, conspicuous in their green armor.

Ida took another bite of the protein stick and peered closer at the screen hanging above the table in his cabin. The official welcome was, despite the current situation, being done by the book, broadcast on the station-wide information channel like any other important bit of Fleet business.

"She's pretty."

Ida looked over his shoulder. Izanami had crept up behind him and was peering around his folded arms.

Zia Hollywood was not pretty. She was flat-out gorgeous. Deep auburn hair streaked with black, cut into a long, angled bob that framed a delicate face with a snub nose. She was wearing black overalls, the top half folded down at the waist and the arms tied around her middle in a big knot, revealing a black sleeveless singlet.

There she was, clad in the practical work gear of a space miner and somehow she outshone the stars. Her left arm was heavily tattooed, geometric patterns and floral motifs slowly moving over her skin. Intelligent, mobile ink was expensive. Her moving tattoo had probably cost as much as the pile of antique kindling that had been the commandant's desk.

Ida watched her on the screen as she glanced here and there, her eyes hidden behind what he could see now were square mining goggles. At the center of her entourage, she was silent and otherwise still. Her crew consisted only of three men. They were grimier than their boss, their overalls patched and marked, the bare biceps of one of them—a tall, thin man with an alarming scarlet Mohawk—matted with scar tissue. Ida had caught him being referred to as Dathan. He looked like he'd been handsome once, but his nose was angled strangely and the rest of his face was flat as a plate. He scowled at the camera and sniffed, the movement pulling his broken nose to one side. The other two were Ivanhoe—a very short, muscular older man, bald with a long graying beard—and an average-looking thirty-something with a huge, spherical Afro haircut who seemed to go by the name Fathead.

Ida shivered. Pulling himself away from the screen, he walked over to the environment controls near the door and poked at them. He didn't expect much to happen. The lights were now stuck on twilight-normal around most of the hub, and—sudden failures aside—the whole station seemed to be getting steadily colder. He thought Izanami must have been terribly cold in her thin, short-sleeved white medical tunic, but the temperature didn't seem to bother her.

The controls responded and warm air began to blow into the cabin. Satisfied for the moment, Ida turned back around.

"Where were you, anyway?" he asked. "Did you see anything when it happened?" *It* being the security breach.

"I locked myself in the med unit. Didn't see anything." She turned back to the screen and then she asked, "Why don't you like her?"

"Who?"

"Zia Hollywood. You don't like her, or her crew."

"Says who?"

Izanami brushed her hair from her eyes. "You don't like anyone, Abraham."

Ida worked his mouth. She... Actually, she was right, and he knew it, but her tone was surprisingly hard. And she had called him Abraham.

Ida turned back to watch the Hollywood gang fidget as King lectured them on the wheres and why-fors of station procedure before they were taken on a tour of the facilities. They were too far away to be heard over King's monotone on the feed, but Ida saw the Mohawked man glance at the Fleet personnel around him and then rock on his heels in a suppressed laugh, although what he could possibly find funny about being surrounded by a squad of marines in full field battle kit was beyond Ida. Behind Dathan, Ivanhoe and Fathead had lost interest in the briefing and were playing some kind of hand-slapping game while their boss stood, arms folded, mouth set, and expression unreadable behind the protective eyewear. Fathead gave his bald companion's hand one last sharp slap and then, laughing, sidled over to Ms. Hollywood. He trailed his hand over her arm as he swung around behind her. Then with one fingernail he traced the moving tattoo on her arm, the ink swirling like liquid under his touch. Hollywood remained still, but Ida thought she turned her head a little to look into the security camera.

"Admit it, you don't like her."

He found himself rubbing his chest through his shirt, trying to ease the tight feeling he now felt around his heart. "I don't even know her."

"Exactly," said Izanami, and she walked toward the door, and then out of it.

Ida bit his thumbnail and watched the empty space where she had stood, then sighed.

"What's wrong?" said the voice, thin and edged with static like the rolling waves of the sea. The space radio popped and crackled and Ida felt his heart kick.

Ludmila. She was real, apparently—an electromagnetic ghost bouncing around subspace, her voice echoing out of nothing but only when the recording was on playback. She was impossible. She was real. When she spoke, Ida felt afraid, knowing that he couldn't, shouldn't be talking to her. But then the fear faded, melting away, leaving Ida dizzy. They'd been in contact for little more than a cycle, but already he felt that he'd known her for years, that they had some weird connection, two spacefarers trapped in situations they had no control over.

Ida closed his eyes. If he thought about it too hard, none of it made sense, but there at the back of his mind he recalled a story he'd read years and years ago, a tall tale if ever there was one, but one that now made him take pause for thought. The story was that Marconi, the guy who had invented radio in the first place, hadn't been trying to build a new form of communication; he'd been trying to find a way to talk to his dead brother. That scared Ida too, and he was perhaps a little grateful that the lightspeed link was down, as he wasn't sure checking the veracity of an urban legend like that would do him any good.

"Nothing," he said, opening his eyes. "I'm glad you stuck around, though." This much was true. She was a welcome distraction.

Ludmila laughed. Ida liked it when she laughed; the sound was high and young, and very happy. The background static pulsed in time with it, and then she sighed, the sound cut like dry leaves in an autumn wind. Ida couldn't remember the last autumn he'd had on Earth. He got as far as thinking it was red and orange before the memory was too fuzzy. He'd spent too long in space, too much time in Fleet service. He preferred to remember the summers on the farm, anyway. Or... he had, until recently.

Ida moved back to the door and glanced through the semi-frosted window, but the corridor to the right was just a faint orange smudge.

Then Ida looked to his left, and saw Izanami standing in the passage. He recoiled from the window in surprise; then he hit the control panel with his palm. The door snicked open.

"Izanami?"

Izanami took his arm, her fingers like ice even through Ida's sleeve. For a moment her eyes seemed to catch the light in an odd way, like they were spun blue with stars. Then the space radio popped and went quiet and Ida blinked, and the light was gone.

"I just walked around the deck," she said, pursing her lips. "I'm sorry, I didn't mean what I said before."

Ida smiled weakly, and gestured for her to enter his cabin.

27

The P-Prof *Bloom County* crouched on the side of the U-Star *Coast City* like the Spiderbaby it really was, customized mining legs folded into a symmetrical array of scalene triangles. From a distance it looked like a complex communications pod, myriad antennae pointing out into the inky black. Closer, it looked like a parasitic insect, a strange locust–spider hybrid, clamped to the side of the station, sucking from the belly of its prey. They hadn't used the station's hangar. They didn't need to—thanks to its unique design, the *Bloom County* could just sucker onto the side of the station, air lock to air lock.

There were many theories about the origin of the Spiders, about how an organo-metallic life-form might have evolved—or been *created*. About why the planet-eating, intelligent but not quite self-aware machine race looked so much like spiders. About why they had any interest in human affairs anyway. But for the crew of the *Bloom County*, the Spiderbaby at the heart of the ship was merely a very, very effective tool that helped them do their jobs. Out on the ragged edge of space, there was no time for theories.

* * *

The short, bald member of the Hollywood gang, who went by the name Ivanhoe, flicked a switch, dimming the lights in the *Bloom County*'s control cabin, and leaned back in the navigator's seat. He'd been born in the stars—just like the rest of the crew, each handpicked by Zia Hollywood with starbirth the most important parameter—and far preferred their light to the artificial illumination on board the ship. And while Shadow, the technetium star, was hidden on the other side of the space station, its high-energy emissions floodlit a shell of dust that enclosed the whole system nearly a tenth of a light-year out, giving the normally infinite black canvas of space an eerie—and with the cabin lights off, quite bright enough to work by—purple glow. This far out on the galactic rim, the star field beyond the glow was not as dense as Ivanhoe knew, or liked, but the scattering of distant suns that were visible were large and bright. So Ivanhoe sat for a spell, eyes flicking from one tiny solar body to the next, watching their outlines curl and flicker behind the dust cloud. He was happy to have gotten out of the VIP tour of the space station and glad to be able to look at the stars, even if he had a lot of work to do. They'd been lying about the security alert; that much was obvious from the number of marines on guard at every doorway. Unlike his crewmates, Ivanhoe didn't like guns much. Especially guns on board a spaceship.

Someone knocked a tool off the bench behind him. Dathan, probably, either finally managing to pull himself away from their boss or finally being told by said boss to go and fix the motherfucking ship. Either option was good for Ivanhoe. Tracing the fault in the navigation pod would be much easier with two people, and besides, if someone had to go out onto the hull and open up the pod itself, he'd rather it wasn't him. It wasn't the light of Shadow that bothered him. The pod, a box shaped like half an egg three feet in length, was within reach of the mining claws. *That* was what bothered him.

One day, Ivanhoe knew, just *knew*, those claws would turn on them. Zia said she knew what she was doing, and Ivanhoe had no doubt about that. But nobody really *understood* Spider tech, not her, not her father. And, well, those claws were *alive*, my brother. They twitched, and sometimes they even grasped, as the Spiderbaby slept. There, they were doing it now. Ivanhoe's eyes moved to the blinking indicator on the control desk in front of him. Two legs out of the four on the portside array were moving. Just a bit, just a flex, like someone who has sat on their hand for too long rolling their fingers to get the circulation back. Damn, it was as creepy as hell. But creepy as hell was paying the bills. Good old Spiderbaby. Sleep tight.

"I'll tell you now," said Ivanhoe to the shadows behind him, "I ain't going out there. Let's see if we can't get the nav pod rejacked from here, my brother."

Silence. Ivanhoe tore his eyes from the flickering indicator and slowly revolved the navigator's chair around. The control cabin was empty, and the door was closed. The fallen tool—just a regular screwdriver—was on the floor in the middle of the cabin.

Ivanhoe sighed, pushed himself to his feet, picked up the screwdriver, and dropped it back on the tray of tools on the bench, not really thinking about how far the screwdriver had fallen from one side of the room to the other, not really thinking about how hot the metal tool had felt in his hand. It didn't matter. Space was strange. Artificial gravity wasn't perfect. Ivanhoe didn't trust it—he'd been born in zero-G, my brother, and like the water babies of Earth, anything else just wasn't natural. Falling through starlight. That's how he liked to describe it. It impressed the ladies, anyway.

He turned back to the control deck and put his hands behind his head, scratching his bare scalp as he did so. The mining leg motion indicator had gone dark, but the data screen showing the nav pod output was still a wash of amber nonsense.

"Well, fuck you very much, you spiky-haired freak show." It was clear what had happened. Even if Zia had told Dathan to go and help him, he'd probably stopped by the nearest dark corner of the station for a quick jerk-off. That prick had the slimy dirty hots for their boss. He made no secret of it, but it seemed to suit Ms. Hollywood. He'd jump to anything she said. To Ivanhoe and Fathead, it was free entertainment.

Ivanhoe stood from the seat and, reaching one leg forward,

dragged a wheeled tool tray out from below the console with the toe of his boot. He looked at the tray for a minute; then he selected two or three items before kicking it across the floor over to the pilot's console on the other side of the flight deck. So, there it was. Once again it was up to him. Hours on his back under the consoles wasn't Ivanhoe's favorite horizontal activity, but the nav pod had to be fixed if they were going to find their prize on the other side of Shadow. And if he could fix the pod from here and not have to crawl out over the outside of the ship and take a look at it in person, all the better.

"*Dominos...*"

Ivanhoe jumped, dropping his tools with a clatter across the pilot's station. An electric socket wrench with a heavy handle bounced on the edge of the console and hit the floor, rolling noisily across it.

"Hello?"

There was no one. He was alone in the cabin, but someone had very clearly called his name. His real name, one that he hadn't heard in fifteen years and that, of the crew, only Zia knew.

He swore and stormed to the cabin door. Dathan again, playing some kind of trick. Maybe Zia had let his real name slip. Ivanhoe never wanted to hear that name ever again, and if she'd told Dathan, even accidentally, he was now officially pissed.

"Day, you fuck."

The wheel on the door spun counterclockwise for a few seconds. Ivanhoe watched it impatiently, knocking his knuckles against the heavy metal frame of it. Dathan was a dead man.

The door beeped as it unlocked. Grabbing the wheel with one hand, Ivanhoe pushed it to his left. Beyond was a short corridor leading to a ladder that went up to the crew quarters and down to the hopper and the working end of the ship.

The corridor was empty, and the hatches in the floor and ceiling were closed.

The *Bloom County*'s navigator drummed his permanently blackened fingernails against the doorframe, the thin metal plating making a harsh, tinny rattle as he tapped. The hatches were closed. The latches on both shone with the orange glow of the engaged indicator. Besides, the hatches beeped in the control cabin when the latch was shunted to green for open.

Well, if someone was playing games, they'd have to play by his rules. Ivanhoe walked the short corridor, hopped up the first two rungs of the ladder, and flicked the ceiling hatch from engaged to locked. Jumping off, he locked the floor hatch. If anyone was coming, they'd have to damn well ring the doorbell.

"Dominos Tararaz... Where is he?"

Ivanhoe spun around just in time to see someone duck around the lip of the open control cabin hatch. The corridor was only twenty feet long and just wide enough for two people to pass. With the hatches locked and in full view in front of him, Ivanhoe was positive nobody had come in. He'd been in the cabin for a couple of hours and he knew the ship was empty, the rest of the crew accompanying Zia on the formal tour of the U-Star.

A stowaway was impossible—the crew made it their habit, each of them, to inspect personally near to every damn rivet in the ship before a flight. There was no room, no room at all. Which meant...

Intruder.

"Mother*fucker*," said Ivanhoe, shaking his head in disbelief. Some bored grunt from the station taking a look around and messing with his head. Shit, did that piss him off. He had a lot of work to do, and nobody but nobody got into the *Bloom County* without his permission—even the famous and rich Zia Hollywood, who *owned* the ship, asked him before allowing any visitors aboard. As navigator, Ivanhoe was responsible for steering the ship true toward riches and glory and, more important, away from and out of trouble. The lives of the crew and the safe and secure transit of their valuable cargo were in his hands. If they went in the wrong direction, if the charts were off and they missed their mark and lost a paycheck, it was his fault.

"Hey, come out here so I can kick your green-covered ass!"

Something clanked from beyond the door. It sounded like one of the tools being picked up. Fucker was arming himself.

"The hell you do," Ivanhoe muttered, and he jogged down the

corridor. "You picked the wrong ship to play hide-and-seek in, my brother."

The control cabin was dark, much darker than it had been. Ivanhoe squinted in the gloom. The main window shutters were wide open and the purple light of the dust cloud shone in, a smattering of large white stars still visible. But there was something else inside the cabin, obscuring the windows with a blackish haze. Ivanhoe absently waved a hand in front of his face, but the mist (was it mist?) didn't move, didn't react like it should. He stood still, unable to decide whether this was smoke and something was on fire. But the blackness had no odor or taste, and it didn't move in the air. It was more like shadow, like swirling patches of air that were somehow less inclined to let light pass through them.

"Hello?" People were constantly asking him whether he liked the dark, or the night, considering he was a starchild. He usually answered that while space might be black, it was really full of light, as bright as can be, in every color—total baloney, but not many people he met were familiar with Olbers' paradox. And it hid the fact that no, Ivanhoe did not like the dark. In fact, he hated the dark.

Now, in the control cabin of the *Bloom County*, the black shadows disturbed him more than he liked.

"Dominos..."

He ducked away from the sound, a harsh whisper with an odd accent right in his ear. He banged the tool bench with his thigh and gasped at the pain, one hand automatically brushing at the side of his head. For a second he imagined the tickling sensation of someone's breath in his ear as the voice spoke to him.

"Where are you?" He squinted again. Something silver flashed in front of him, then another, then a third. Glinting with light, the objects wobbled in the air.

The tools. Two crescent wrenches, brand-new and still nicely chromed, and the heavy electric socket driver. They hovered five feet from the floor, dipping a little around their balance points, like someone was dangling them from above on thin wire.

"The poisoned sky weeps for my husband..."

The navigator jerked his head away again as the whispering voice came from the other side. The intruder would have had to be crouching right on the control desk, up against the right-hand window pane, to breathe into his ear like that. The voice, feminine but not human. Empty and black. Like the dark shadows themselves were speaking.

The floating tools ducked and dived, then stabilized. Ivanhoe couldn't tear his eyes from them. He kept his distance as he walked around the edge of the control cabin, toward the main consoles.

What the hell was going on? It was that star, had to be, something to do with its light. The data sheet fed to them by the Fleet said it was "toxic"—whatever the hell that meant—and earlier one of the jarheads on the station had even said "that light will fuck you up," like it was some kind of a joke, although he hadn't been laughing. But the way their nav pod had scrambled as soon as they'd hit the system's heliosphere made Ivanhoe think again.

"*Dominos Tararaz...*"

The light. It had to be the light. The weird star and its weird starlight. That light will fuck you up.

Behind him the malfunctioning nav pod output screen flickered with new data, and the ship's computer alerted the navigator to that fact with a loud chime. Were those shapes moving around there? Long, thin figures, pulling themselves together out of the mist? Ivanhoe risked a glance over his shoulder. He saw enough on the output screen to know the nav pod had apparently not only fixed itself but aligned itself with the system's star. The information streaming across the screen didn't make much sense, consisting of a list of coordinates that looked okay but, he saw at a glance, were inverted, *negative*, like the computer was looking *through* the star and into someplace else, which was fucking nuts but—

The mining legs. Ivanhoe was drawn to the indicator lights, all eight flashing as all eight legs flexed. The Spiderbaby was dreaming, and dreaming deep. Maybe he was as well.

Ivanhoe looked up at the window, hoping for a reassuring, familiar look at the stars. But the windows were almost completely black now, the view transformed into a dull mirror. He saw nothing but his own face, floating in the shadows, lit from underneath by the scrolling amber text of the nav pod output and the flashing indicators.

Then over his right shoulder, another face. Ghastly white, angular, with a sharp chin and oval eyes that burned with a bright baby blue light. The face was that of a woman, pale and Japanese. Her hair was long and black and straight and blew in a nonexistent wind across her face. She looked Ivanhoe in the eye and smiled a smile from hell.

"Where is he, Dominos? Where is he?"

Ivanhoe's scream was not as manly as he'd hoped. But what the hell. The conscious centers of his brain relinquished the last vestige of control to his brain stem, and as his bladder emptied, everything spun to blackness.

28

Maybe I'm getting old.

Ida ran the thought through his head. He was forty years old, and he was tired and sick of spooning the blue protein gloop from plate to mouth in the canteen. Too much time in space. He was alone on one side of the eating area, watching Carter's space apes and the Hollywood gang merge into one shouting, swearing mass. Carter had recovered from his ordeal and seemed to be back to his old self. Serra sat by his side and laughed at the right moments but said nothing herself, and over the top of his spoon Ida could see her eyes narrow again, like she was fighting against a migraine.

The visiting crew of the *Bloom County* laughed and joked and slapped sides with their hosts, but they also exchanged looks and smirks and eye rolls among themselves that Carter's friends didn't notice. Ida did. It cheered him up no end.

Ida realized he was staring at the group when he saw Zia Hollywood returning the look. Eyes still wrapped in the mining goggles, she sat at the head of the table, cradling a shallow beaker of engine juice, the toxic liquid DeJohn had distilled out of the space station's cooling system before he'd gone missing. Ida had seen her laugh too, smile at the right people, but she wasn't really part of the group. She could never be—the fame and fortune attached to her name kept her distant from everyone around her, even her own crew.

Ida smiled, but not at Ms. Hollywood. In the time she'd spent returning his stare, she'd probably earned more in pure interest than the annual wages of everyone on the *Coast City* combined. She had the kind of wealth that could buy planets.

Ida sucked the spoonful of protein past his teeth and returned his attention to his plate.

"Fancy pulling up a pew and joining the party?"

Ida looked up. It was the first time he'd heard her speak. Her voice was strong and melodic, deeper than he expected and bathed in a golden accent. Her voice had a breathless quality; it crossed Ida's mind that she might be a good singer.

Zia's call had halted all conversation at her table, and Ida felt his face grow hot. Carter frowned at him, but Serra kept her eyes on the table. Ida knew he'd have to talk to her, and soon.

"We brought some food from our ship. Condensed nutrient from Earth, farm fresh."

Carter muttered something, and Serra touched his elbow. A few of the others laughed and turned back to the table.

"Well, I'm honored, but—"

"It tastes like chicken."

Ida dropped his spoon and pushed the metal tray away from him. "Count me in."

He picked a spot two seats down from Zia, on the opposite side of the table to Carter. Ida made sure he smiled and made eye contact with everyone at the table. On his right, between him and Zia, Fathead worked his jaw, the wet sound of his chewing obscenely loud as he looked Ida up and down.

"Now, ain't you gonna introduce us?" asked Zia Hollywood, seemingly to the table at large. Her chest moved as she spoke, the black singlet featureless but tight. Ida found himself swallowing a trickle of hot saliva. Oh, she was good. Being a genuine A-lister meant being able to turn it on and play the game anytime, anywhere.

Carter coughed, and Ida stuck out his hand. Ms. Hollywood looked at it and didn't move. Izanami's earlier comment played at the back of his mind.

"Captain Abraham Idaho Cleveland, ma'am. Pleased to make your acquaintance."

Hollywood pulled her bottom lip—pierced with a small silver loop just to the left of center—into her mouth, and Ida watched as she chewed it with her top teeth. Up close her square goggles had a greenish hue but were completely opaque, showing nothing but a double reflection of Ida grinning back at himself.

"Ain't captains supposed to salute?"

Ida let his hand fall away. "I'm retired, ma'am." He frowned. "Or... I was, and then I wasn't. It's a little complicated."

Fathead chuckled through clenched teeth, eyes half-closed in amusement. "You don't sound too sure. If you were retired, why are you here?" he asked.

"Good question," said Carter.

Zia raised a hand to the opposite shoulder, and from the corner of his eye, Ida thought he saw her moving tattoo dive down from her shoulder to her wrist, a thin twisting veil of black shadow forming a strange, streaking figurelike shape. He jerked his head back in surprise and blinked.

"Can't rightly say," he said, clearing his head. "Although upon the retirement of a senior officer—that's me, by the way—Fleet command is at liberty to issue one final set of orders. Usually it's a friendly gesture, like reporting to the Fleet college library to present your final log file to the custodian of special collections. Happened to a friend of mine. Sounded nice. Or it might be something more formal, like christening a new U-Star."

"And you?" Zia asked.

Ida laughed. "And then there's me. Well, apparently I have to close this hunk of junk down." He looked Carter in the eye. "Can't happen soon enough."

Fathead snickered and jogged Ida's elbow, passing him a plastic container stacked with gelatinous beige cubes. "Dig in, bro. It's on us."

Ida took the container and loaded his plate, then paused before carefully placing it back to the center of the table. He counted around the table again.

"Am I in someone's seat?"

Zia shook her head, mouth in her beaker. "Ivanhoe is back on the *County*, taking care of some last-minute work." Ida could hear the wet pop as Hollywood's lips parted when she spoke.

When she finished speaking, she held her mouth just so, in a moody pout perfect for the camera lens. Perhaps she wasn't just good, thought Ida. Perhaps she was a natural. "Our nav pod is temperamental, always has been. The Spider tech interferes with it something fierce. It went offline completely when we entered this system."

Ida nodded and started to say something about the nature of the star in this particular system, but as he squashed a cube of nutrient between his tongue and the roof of his mouth he was hit by the note-perfect taste of hot roast chicken, fresh from a farm oven. His words tailed off and he sighed, just a little.

Fathead jostled his elbow again. "Good, no?" He looked over the table at Carter. "Eh?"

Carter grinned and raised his spork in a toast. "Sure is, my man. I haven't eaten like this in years."

There was a murmur of agreement from the other marines, most of whom Ida didn't know by name. Ida caught Dathan and Fathead exchanging another look. This was the night's entertainment for them.

"The radiation from Shadow has a strange effect on electronics," said Ida, picking up the thread of his thoughts. "It's taken out our lightspeed link already. I presume you've got the right shielding on the pod?"

"Yeah," said Zia. "We're all good. Just needs recalibrating."

Dathan leaned forward on the table, peering around Ida at his boss. "We're gonna need that pod working if we're going to hit our target, Zia."

"Cool your boots. We're good."

Ida took another mouthful. The gelatin cube crushed to mush in his mouth, and when he breathed in through his nose he could feel the moisture of the steam rising from the nonexistent chicken meal.

Ida turned to Zia. "And what are *you* doing out here? Or is that a secret known only to you and Fleet command?"

"No secret, Cap'n." Zia seemed to relax, putting aside her beaker of drink and tipping a few food cubes onto her plate. On the other side of the table, Carter and his marines began talking among themselves, clearly refusing to be part of a conversation started by Ida. Zia chewed slowly and spoke with her mouth full. He watched his own reflection in her goggles as she ate.

"There's a small field of asteroids on the other side of Shadow. Hardly rocks even, more like a debris field of some kind. Maybe a half dozen big chunks, and a lot of dust and sand. They read mighty strange. Slowrocks. Nearly pure lucanol, ninety-eight percent, according to the readouts from your very own station computer. Lucky we got word before your lightspeed went south. So we hightailed it across Fleetspace to take a look-see. Your station is a pit stop. A bit of free PR for the Fleet in exchange for the tip-off."

Ida whistled and then dabbed his mouth with a canteen paper napkin. "Didn't think that was possible, an entire asteroid made of lucanol. How does it hold together? Must be as soft as your chicken cubes."

The two greenish black windows shielding her eyes were still pointed in Ida's direction, so he assumed she was looking at him. Then she smiled.

It was a beautiful smile, the kind of smile the paparazzi would have paid a fortune to see and to broadcast around the Earth and all her outposts. Ida thought he was probably very privileged to see it firsthand, sitting not one foot from the famous lips. Zia had a blue gray gem embedded in one of her upper teeth—spoils of her profession, no doubt. Ida suspected the tiny sparkling stone was worth more than the rug, the painting, and the matchwood in King's ready room put together. Ida knew at once that hardly anybody had a smile like this. This was the smile of a person rich and famous for a very good reason.

"That's what we're gonna go and find out," she said.

"And the Fleet just fed you the readings from this station, just like that? Would have thought that kind of data would be classified." Ida smiled. "Or encrypted, at least."

"That's what *they* think," said Dathan, tapping his metal spoon against the side of his tray four times, each tap with more force than the last until he let go of the utensil, letting it clatter across the table. Carter and the marines halted their conversation and looked at the spoon and then Zia's crewman.

Zia's expression tightened. "Go and help Ivanhoe with the nav pod."

The spoonless Dathan began rocking the edge of his food tray against the tabletop, making an annoying metallic clacking that increased in volume. Ida suddenly didn't feel like sitting between him and his boss.

"What in the name of Satan's tits are we doing here, Zia? We've come a hell of a long way on some spotty numbers. What if it's the starlight fucking with our instruments?"

"You'll get your cut."

"Oh, really? And what if there's nothing there? What if there's nothing shiny and gold at the end of your spectrograph?"

"Go and help Ivanhoe."

"Are you even listening to me?"

Zia leaned forward quickly, her expression tight, and when she spoke her voice was low and quiet. "If there's nothing there, I'll damn well pay you anyway. How does that sound, peaches?"

Everyone at the table looked at Dathan. He'd stopped rocking the dinner tray but his fingers were pressed against the rim, holding it up at an angle of several degrees. Dathan hesitated, perhaps aware that he'd pushed too far and the personal argument had become public. He sighed and let the tray drop with a crash. In the next few seconds, the only sound was Fathead chewing wetly on his chicken cube.

Then Dathan pushed his chair back and left the canteen without a word. Fathead was the only one who moved, turning to watch his fellow crewman walk out the door. Then he turned back to the table, grinning like this was the best night out ever.

"He always like that?" Carter finally broke the game of statues, reaching for another container of food cubes.

Zia's enigmatic smile reappeared. Ida was sure she'd been staring at him again. If only she'd take off the goggles. Ida felt that he'd not really even met Zia Hollywood yet. He was spending all his time talking to his own reflection.

Zia nodded, then tipped her drained beaker toward Fathead. The crewman reached down to a shoulder bag sitting at his feet. From it he extracted a tall, thin red bottle. It was elegant, expensive, and quite, quite illegal. Alcohol. The real thing.

"Oh yes!" Carter clapped his hands, and there was a murmur of appreciation from the other marines.

Zia took the bottle from Fathead. "Line it up, boys." She glanced and looked toward the door. "Your marshal isn't likely to walk in, is he?"

"Nah," said Carter. "Spends all his time in the ready room, if he's not asleep already."

Zia nodded and offered the bottle to Ida. Ida took it, calculating as he did the proportion of his wages that just a single shot of this would cost him on the black market, and how many years on a labor planet possession of a bottle that size would earn him.

By the time Ida had poured himself a careful measure of the liquid—revealed to be as bright in color as the glass of the bottle—Fathead had downed three shots. His face got redder and his smile wider. He bounced on his chair as he licked the remnants of the drink from his teeth, looking for all the world like a self-aware ventriloquist's dummy, the old kind Ida had once seen as a child. Fathead's eyes moved in the same way, keeping a glassy look on Ida as his head wobbled from side to side.

"So you're a real space hero, my good captain?" asked Fathead, grinning like a loon.

Ida paused, focusing on the intense fireball that exploded on his tongue as soon as it touched the red liqueur. He closed his eyes and willed them not to water. He heard Carter hiss out a laugh between his teeth.

When Ida opened his eyes, everyone at the table was looking at him. Carter with his favorite frown, Fathead with his smile. And for the first time since the incident down on the hub, even Serra seemed to be paying attention.

"Heard you were a hero." Carter and Ida both turned to Hollywood. She was, apparently, looking straight at Ida as she spoke, but with her mining goggles it was hard to tell. "I also heard you were a coward and a liar."

Ida couldn't take his eyes off her face, which was now completely, totally unreadable. Whose side was she on? "That so?"

Carter downed another shot of the liqueur. "Yeah, you going to tell them about that, old man?" he asked, his voice raspy with the kiss of the hard alcohol.

Ida allowed himself a slow smile and drained the remainder of his shot. He exhaled hotly through his nose, and immediately Fathead reached forward and topped his glass up. He made a wet clicking sound behind his fixed grin, which Ida took to be a sign of approval. Ida raised his shot to him as a toast, and then to Zia, and then sank it back. His mouth and throat were stung but numbing nicely. His tongue flopped fatly against the back of his teeth. He looked at Carter.

"Marine, I'm flattered my reputation preceded me across all of Fleetspace, but it's the utmost shame that it was a load of BS that got here first rather than the truth. Because, frankly, I'm not sure you can fit more than one idea and a half in that brainbox of yours."

Carter gave Ida a steely look, his face reddening a little, but Ida just leaned back and laughed. Whatever the liqueur was, it was starting to work. Serra smiled. Ida liked that.

"I'd like to hear the truth."

Ida looked at Zia and was surprised that when his head stopped turning, his eyes kept going. For a second Ms. Hollywood's image doubled, then trebled, clicking sideways in rapid succession like an out-of-synch video feed, throwing multiple silhouettes like a whole bunch of people standing behind her chair. He focused and held his glass out to Fathead. Fathead made the clicking sound and topped him up. Ida raised the glass a second time.

"Much obliged, man with the hair. And to you too, ma'am."

He drained the shot in one gulp. The alcohol burn was hot, hot, hot, but now he could taste the drink. His mouth filled with rich wild strawberry. Now he knew why Fathead was so damn happy all the time. He could get used to this. He idly wondered if the *Bloom County* was in need of a retired—formerly retired—Fleet captain with a robot knee.

Ida waved his arms as though to draw the people sitting at the table closer over his campfire. Nobody moved, but he didn't notice. He had the stage. It was time to tell the truth.

"This is how the shit went down. Lemme tell you about it, right now."

29

Ida jerked up onto his elbows, eyes playing around the dark room, lit only by the faint blue LED of the radio set. A few seconds later and his head pounded, *onetwothree-twotwothree*, then settled into a steady, slower beat. That strawberry liqueur had been mighty fine. Too fine.

As he turned his head side to side, the rush of white noise swam with his movement. He imagined Ludmila listening, watching him sleep from her magical nowhere.

"Did you hear that?" Ida whispered, cocking his head. He'd been woken by a scream, but dreams and nightmares were becoming increasingly common. Maybe Izanami would prescribe something. If he could find her. The station medic seemed to be keeping to herself more and more since Ludmila had made contact.

There came a rustling across the subspace waves, like someone brushing against a microphone. "Mmm... Ida?"

"I'm here. Did you hear anything?" He squinted as his head thumped.

A pause, another rustle. "Maybe... I don't know. I was dreaming, I think. There was a girl, with black hair..."

Ludmila was cut off by a second scream. It was very real, and not so far away. Ida was on his feet and at the cabin door, ignoring his headache. He stood at the threshold in the dim nightlight of the hub corridor. From inside the cabin it was hard to figure out from which direction the cry had come.

Ida stepped into the corridor, and the door slid shut behind him. For now, all was quiet. Ida noticed that the floor-level nightlights had come on for the first time he could remember. Their light was a soft blue, simulating the natural ambience of nightfall on some planet or another, he vaguely recalled. The *Boston Brand* had had them. Usually it was nice. But at times like this, the up and down angles of the light cast odd shadows that made Ida feel uncomfortable. When he looked down toward the far bulkhead door heading away into the demolition zone, blinking made it look like there were people moving in the dark corners of the passageway that weren't directly illuminated. And in his peripheral vision, Ida kept seeing fast sideways movement, startling enough to make his heart race. All tricks of the light, because the passageway was clearly empty, and Ida was alone.

He kept telling himself this for the next minute or so as he stood, unmoving, working up the courage to pick a direction and take a look. He was a Fleet captain, for God's sake. Getting spooked by shadows? *Gimme a break.*

For once the station wasn't an icebox, but the crosshatch flooring was hard on his bare feet. Ida was considering getting dressed when the scream tore the night air into little bits a third time, followed quickly now by the sound of running feet.

"Get in your cabin, let us handle this!" Carter appeared, shod in unlaced boots and stripped down to a stained olive singlet, carrying a plasma rifle. Behind him were two marines, armed and armored, with Zia Hollywood and Fathead bringing up the rear. Fathead was carrying a weapon as long as he was tall with a barrel approximately as wide at the business end as his hair.

"Where's Serra?"

Carter snarled. "Staying put where she was told to stay put. You gonna be difficult with me now?"

Fathead looked between the two men and waggled his finger at the pair. "I sense tension. Do you two need a moment?" He snickered.

Ida ignored him and looked at Carter. "The intruders didn't leave, did they?"

The marine looked him in the eye, his stare diamond hard. Then he nodded almost imperceptibly.

"Intruders?" Fathead turned to his boss. "Nobody said nothing about no intruders. You said everything was okay."

Zia said nothing, but her expression was set, her eyes still hidden behind her goggles, despite the gloom. Ida glanced down and saw she had one hand resting on the handle of a pistol hanging from her belt. He hadn't noticed her wearing it before, but even with it mostly hidden in a holster, Ida could see enough of its curved back and handle to recognize it: a Yuri-G, a small but incredibly powerful pistol. They said it had enough kick to send a man into orbit, hence the nickname. Illegal for civilians. Restricted even for Fleet use. A stray shot would punch a hole straight through the *Coast City*'s herculanium shell. How a celebrity star-miner had one strapped to her hip was a mystery to Ida, one that was more than a little alarming. Zia Hollywood moved in unusual circles; the pistol plus the alcohol—perhaps people like her really could operate above the law.

The sentient tattoo on Zia's arm swirled, perhaps showing annoyance, impatience, neither of which were evident on Zia's forever-cool features. Ida tried not to think about the way the tattoo's curling motion matched the way the shadows in the corridor swam out of the corner of his eye. His mind went back to Astrid. Then the image dissolved, almost without conscious thought.

There is no such thing as ghosts. There is no such thing as ghosts.

"I can help," said Ida, watching his own reflection in Zia's goggles. He turned to Carter, who seemed ready to keep arguing, when the fourth scream came. It was male, close, and terrible.

Zia stepped around the group and jogged ahead, Fathead on her heels. Carter glanced at Ida.

"Come on," the marine said. As he turned and headed down the passage, he touched the commlink on his belt and started calling for more backup.

Ida let one of the armored marines go first, then followed, the second bringing up the rear.

Ida struggled to keep up, his bare feet aching on the decking, the marine following behind forced to check his step. Zia, still at the front, clearly knew which direction to head in.

The auxiliary air lock. Her own ship, the *Bloom County*.

Ida and the second marine finally caught the group as they stopped by the air lock door. It was open, and dark beyond, and Ida was surprised to see the group hesitate. Zia was staring into the void, into her own ship, one hand resting on the bulkhead frame, the other on the butt of the Yuri-G.

"Ivanhoe?" she called out into the air lock. "What's happened? Day?"

Ida brushed past Carter, who caught him by the arm. Ida shrugged his hand off. He reached forward and touched Zia's shoulder, but recoiled almost instantly as her tattoo responded to his touch, crawling back up her arm toward Ida's fingers. The idea of an intelligent swarm of dye particles having free rein of her epidermis made Ida's own skin crawl.

"What's wrong?" said Ida.

Zia turned around to face him, and he once more found himself staring at a stereo reflection of himself, bed hair and all. He couldn't see her eyes, but her mouth was open, finally betraying her uncertainty and fear.

Ida pointed to the air lock. "Whatever's going on in there, we need to check it out. People don't scream for no reason."

He moved forward to take the lead, but this time it was Zia's hand on his shoulder. He turned.

"It's… it's dark."

Ida frowned and turned back to the passage ahead. It was short and unlit, but at the far end, no more than a few meters away, the lights were on at a junction, a service ladder leading up out of sight and down to a recessed hatch. There seemed to be options to turn left and right as well.

"Which way is the bridge?"

Zia hesitated. Ida watched the pulse in her neck twitch.

"Zia, which way?"

She nodded ahead. "Up. It's up and forward."

"Fine," said Ida. Without waiting for the rest of them, he turned and jogged down the passage toward the junction. The dark around him seemed to crowd in, blurring the lights ahead of him, but he kept his gaze fixed ahead and three seconds later was at the ladder. The metal rungs were icy against his bare feet and hands, but he powered upward and through the open ceiling hatch. Behind him, he heard the others rattle down the passage in their mix of heavy boots. Zia had been right about the dark. It was like moving through smoke. It crossed Ida's mind that maybe someone with a gun should be the one going first, but they were being slow enough already.

Ida emerged into a junction similar to the one he'd entered. The ladder continued upward to another hatch, and behind him a second black passage leading to a room, dim yellow light spilling hardly any distance at all from the opening. The flight deck. The yellow light shifted like someone was crossing in front of it.

"Hello?"

Nothing. Underneath his feet he saw Zia's reddish hair approach. He stepped off the ladder, and the others appeared one by one. It was cold—no, *freezing*—up here, Ida's breath pluming in front of his face and drifting outward, melting into the thin black mist that hung in the air. It was like standing in a walk-in freezer in a ship's galley.

Ida slowly approached the bridge, his bare feet on fire on the cold floor.

"Ivanhoe? Dathan?" Zia called out.

The passage was well insulated with a soundproof wrapper to keep vibrations from the mining machinery beneath their feet from rattling the crew's brains to gray paste when they were at work. In the dark, the complete non-echo of her voice was disconcerting. The bridge doorway was just a few meters away, but Ida had the feeling that Zia's voice had not even traveled that far.

Ida looked back as Zia took a step forward, but Carter held his hand up and shook his head. He raised the sight of his gun to his eye and took aim at the empty doorway. Following his lead, the two marines behind him did the same.

"This is the Fleet Marine Corps. If there are any unauthorized personnel on board this vessel, you are required to approach and identify yourself. Now!"

Carter waited a beat, then raised his head and looked out around his gun with his naked eyes. The yellow light continued to flicker, like someone had set up a campfire in the middle of the flight deck.

Carter sighted the gun again.

"You are in a Fleet-restricted area. We are authorized to use deadly force. We are entering the flight deck in five seconds."

The two marines clicked the safeties off their guns, the light on their barrels flicking from blue to red. Fathead pointed his weapon at the ceiling and stood back against the wall, ready to let the marines charge in before him.

Ida stood firm next to Carter. He could feel Zia tense beside him; he supposed she wanted to get into the flight deck first in case Carter started shooting her crew. Ida didn't like what was going on. He was glad the *Bloom County* was so cold, his shivering disguising his fear.

There is no such thing as ghosts. There is no such thing as ghosts.

Zia unclipped the Yuri-G and slipped it from the holster. Ida watched as her thumb flicked the safety off. The barrel of the tiny pistol lit an angry red.

Carter began his countdown. Ida readied himself, knowing this time he really did need to let those armed go first.

"One!"

Carter sprang forward, the two marines at close quarters. Ida waited, but then Zia swore and sprinted forward, the Yuri-G swinging as she ran to overtake Carter. Carter saw the movement out of the corner of his eye and sidestepped to let her pass, swearing as he did so, never once breaking his perfect combat crouch.

"Ivanhoe!"

Ida was at the door as Zia ducked ahead, crouching at the side of her crewman on the floor. He was alive, lying on his back and convulsing.

Carter signaled the marines to fan out and begin a search of the flight deck room as Ida joined Zia on the floor. Fathead rapidly paced about, his huge gun pointed skyward, checking computer readouts and flicking switches.

"Come on, baby, come on…" whispered Zia. She'd dropped the Yuri-G and was holding her crewmate's bald head, trying to stop him banging it against the hard decking. Her fingers came away bloody, and his eyes rolled as a white foam trickled from the corners of his mouth and into the edges of his beard.

Ida looked at Zia, then over at the discarded gun. He picked it up carefully.

"Does he have a condition? Medication?"

She shook her head. "No," she said. "Not that I know of."

Ida was aware of military boots dancing around the small bridge. He looked up to see the two marines slowing their frantic patrol, Carter stationary in the center of the room. Carter swept his rifle around one more time; then he lowered the gun and relaxed his posture.

"Clear," he said. He glanced down at Ivanhoe and his two attendants. "What's wrong with him?"

Ivanhoe's seizure had stopped, and he now lay flat on the deck, head lolling to one side, breathing heavily and out cold.

Ida stood, hands on hips. "Don't know. Nothing here?"

Carter shook his head. "Small bridge, only one door out. No one in here except him."

Ida sighed, and crouched back down next to Zia. "He was fixing the nav pod, right?"

Zia stroked Ivanhoe's forehead. "Yes. Dathan was supposed to be helping him."

Ida nodded. Then he froze, his eyes wide. "So where's Dathan?"

Zia's head snapped up, and Ida blinked at his reflection. Zia looked back down to Ivanhoe and gently stroked his cheek with the back of her hand.

"Ivanhoe? Ivanhoe, where's Dathan? Where did Day go? Can you tell me, honey?"

Ivanhoe twitched, and his eyes flickered open. He licked his lips and looked around the flight deck, but his eyes were dull and unfocused. Zia pointed somewhere across the room and clicked her fingers. She looked insistently at the nearest marine when nobody moved.

"Water, over there!"

The marine went to investigate, and after fumbling with a wall-mounted dispenser, returned with a small plastic bag of water. Zia took it, uncapped the tiny spout at the top, and offered it to Ivanhoe's lips. He sucked greedily for a few moments, but then pulled away.

Zia leaned over him again. "Ivanhoe, where's Day? What happened?"

Ivanhoe coughed and rolled his head around. His lips moved, mumbling something, but Zia just shook her head and continued to stroke his cheek, repeating her question.

Suddenly he jerked and grabbed her wrist. Zia cried out in surprise as Ivanhoe pulled himself up on an elbow, pushing his face to within an inch away of his employer's. His eyes were wide, wide, wide.

"They took him, Zia, they took Dathan. They took him."

Then he flopped back down, agitated, flexing his free hand while the other continued to grip Zia's wrist.

Then his expression changed, and he looked... sad. Ida folded his arms and watched, uncomfortable, as the man's face twisted into a grimace and he began to cry and shake his head.

Zia pulled his fingers off her wrist. "Who took him, Ivanhoe? What happened?"

Ivanhoe sniffed and wailed, his sobs choking any attempt to speak. Finally he took a deep breath and said it.

"They came. Zia, they came. All of them. All dead. They came and took him. They took him. They took Dathan." He twitched and grabbed at Zia's arms, eyes wide. "Where's Momma? Tell me, please, where's Momma? When can I see Momma?"

Behind him, Ida heard two guns being released from their safeties. Turning around, he saw the indicator on the side of Fathead's absurd cannon light up as he began sweeping it back and forth into the dark corners of the bridge. Carter had raised his rifle again, but not to eye level. The marine stood, face bleached of all color. When he met Ida's gaze, his jaw was slack.

"The fuck is going on?" the marine asked.

Ida shook his head. That was a very good question.

30

They carried Ivanhoe to the infirmary and hooked him up to a monitor, one of the marines, Ashworth, volunteering to keep an eye on the otherwise automated systems as the others returned to their stations. Ida went back to his cabin to get dressed; while there, he tried to raise Izanami on the station's comms, thinking she should really go take a look at Zia's crewman. But there was no response, just more interference. When Ida returned to the infirmary he found Fathead and Zia by Ivanhoe's bedside, Ashworth still by the monitor. Fathead held his cannonlike weapon in both hands, the lights on the barrel an angry, dangerous red.

Zia watched her crewman sleep for a few minutes, then turned and left the infirmary at practically a run. Ida glanced at Fathead, but the man didn't seem to notice his boss's departure.

Ida quickly ducked out and found Zia farther along the corridor, marching with some determination. She looked back at him as he approached but said nothing. Ida didn't know what to say either, so he kept his mouth shut. She was going to see the marshal, that much was clear; standing in the elevator, Zia waited impatiently as Ida realized she needed him to punch the access code to the bridge.

Her meeting was brief. Provost Marshal King sat alone in the middle of the ready room, computer pad on his lap. Marines guarded the door on the outside, but not within. Ida thought maybe they should be.

The marshal looked at his computer pad but his eyes were unfocused. He looked ill to Ida. So did everybody else left on the *Coast City*.

Zia stood and shivered. The room was cold and her face was white and shiny. The famous pout was gone, her once ruby red lips dull and dry.

King glanced up at her, flexed his fingers, then looked back to the computer pad.

"I'm sorry for the loss of your crew member, Ms. Hollywood." His voice was low, quiet, not a whisper but close enough. "All attempts will be made to locate him. For the moment, I'm assigning you a Fleet security detail—"

Then she spoke. She said: "We're leaving," and then turned on her heel and walked out.

King didn't reply, his gaze fixed somewhere beyond the computer pad. He flexed his fingers again. It was an odd, mechanical motion, beginning with the little finger and ending with the thumb. Ida hadn't noticed King do it before.

Dumbfounded, Ida turned and watched, through the still-open door of the ready room, Zia stride across the bridge, toward the elevator.

"What just—?"

"Thank you, Captain. Dismissed."

Ida stared at the marshal for a second. Then he went to follow Zia. But when he stepped out onto the bridge, she was already gone.

As the door to the ready room closed, the marshal twitched in his chair, eyes flicking to his left, toward a shadowed corner of the ready room. But it was a movement driven purely by his autonomic nervous system. If Ida had been able to look him in the eye before he walked out, he would have seen the marshal's pupils contracted to pinpricks, his eyes glazed, unfocused.

Out of the shadows stepped Izanami. As she moved, the shadows seemed to kick up around her like dust.

She laid a hand on King's shoulder, and the marshal twitched again, flexed the fingers of his empty hand, and stared at his knees.

Izanami smiled. In the dark her eyes burned blue as she bent down, her lips almost touching his ear.

"You can't keep him from me forever, my dear Roberto. Not now that I took your book away, your precious book of secrets and codes. Did your commandant really think that would be enough, that if he wrote it all down in cipher like a child, that someone like you would be able to understand it? Would be able to carry on, as if the secrets in the book were enough? Perhaps he did." She laughed. "The Fleet is indeed full of the weak and the foolish."

King's eyelids flickered, but he did not respond. Izanami straightened and watched the main door. She stroked King's head with her hand, her smile widening.

31

Serra had been sleeping when Carter returned. It was real, uninterrupted sleep; a rare thing, sleep to be treasured, free of shadows and purple light and the voice of her grandmother and from the *other* thing, the noise, the roaring of the ocean that filled her head—the sound of the Spiderbaby sleeping in Zia Hollywood's hybrid ship. It was a sound Serra was familiar with from dozens of sorties where she had to infiltrate and disrupt Spider networks with her mind. But out here it was different. Spiders were never alone, and they never slept. And this one… this one was *dreaming*. And this close, the Spiderbaby within touching distance, Serra could see into those machine dreams and hear the sound of—

She rocked on the bed as Carter jogged her shoulder. She tried to ignore it until Carter did it again.

And then he said, "I saw her," and Serra was bolt upright in a second, as alert and ready for action as when the gunnery sergeant blew the trumpet to announce incoming Spiders.

Carter paced the small cabin. Serra watched as the sweat glistened on his forearms as he walked under the fluorescent strips. He moved his hands as he paced, like he was sculpting the description out of thin air. But Serra already had a fair idea of what he was talking about.

"On their ship?"

Carter nodded vigorously but didn't stop walking. "It was there, on the bridge. Back in the corner, against the wall. The shadows hid it—" He moved his hands as though kneading dough. "—like smoke, or dust."

Serra swung her feet to the decking and pulled the sheets over her lap. "Why the fuck didn't you challenge, or tell the others?"

Carter stopped and looked at her. He was pale and his eyes were wide, his brow creased as he struggled with what she'd just said. "What do you mean?"

"You found the intruders, why didn't you challenge them?"

Carter's mouth twisted into what might have been a smile. Serra didn't like it.

"No, no," he said quickly. "They weren't there. That's the whole fucking point. Nobody else could see them, only me, because they weren't there."

He stopped, and Serra saw that he was shaking. His bottom lip began to quiver; he looked like a lost child.

Serra stood and took his cheek in her hand. "What is it, baby? Tell me."

Carter took her hand in his, and she winced, just a little, as he squeezed too hard. He looked into her eyes, and she saw them wet with tears. "She said I could see them again."

Serra blinked. "She? The intruder spoke to you?"

Carter nodded. "It's a woman. She's from far away. She said I could see them again."

The final barrier came crashing down, and Carter sobbed into Serra's shoulder. She brushed his hair and pulled him backwards toward the bed. He was leaning on her, and he was very big and very heavy but he moved without resistance when she pushed him to one side to sit on the bed next to her. His sobbing died but the lost look on his face remained. Serra was frightened and her thoughts were being drowned out by the white noise of the

Spiderbaby dreaming. She focused, trying to cut the sound out before it gave her another migraine.

"Who is she, and what did she say?"

Carter sniffed loudly and wiped his nose with his hand. "She's from far away. But she can bring them back." Carter turned and looked at Serra. She winced again at his too-strong grip.

"For fuck's sake," she said. "Who?"

"My parents. I can see them again, speak to them. She'll bring them here."

Serra's heart rate went up by half in less than a second. She shook her head and ran her hands over Carter's regulation crew cut. "Nene, you've had a shock. Ever since the security breach. You shouldn't have gone back to duty so quickly."

Carter snarled and yanked his head away. Serra wasn't surprised at the reaction and let her hands fall into her lap.

"She can bring them back," he said. He stabbed a finger down toward the floor, like his parents could materialize right in their cabin, right now.

But they couldn't. They couldn't.

Serra shushed her lover but he flinched, so she got to the point. "They can't come back, baby. They're dead. You know that."

Carter nodded, the snarl replaced with a smile. He sniffed again. "Yes, yes, they're dead. They're all dead, all of them. But they can come back. She can bring them back."

Serra shook her head. Carter had snapped. Spooked by the shadows and the environment failures and the general what-the-fuckery that had gone on for the last two months.

Serra reached down to pick up her discarded clothing. As she moved, Carter hopped from the bed and grabbed her arm. He squeezed and pulled her to her feet, the bedding falling away. Serra snarled at him. "What the fuck are you talking about, Charlie? Your parents are dead. You know that. They're dead."

But Carter just nodded. "Yes, they're dead. They're all dead— DeJohn, the commandant, the marines. She can bring them all back here. The gift, you gotta use it, for me. You can help me."

Serra searched his face for any hint of sanity, but saw nothing but eyes wide and wet and a rictus grin. She didn't like the way he called her wild talent the "gift." It was the word her grandmother used for her precious Carminita, a description of the raw, hereditary ability the Fleet had enhanced to a finely tuned battle sense. Serra had never called it that, not to Carter. She didn't like the way the conversation was going.

She pulled her arm free and turned to reach for her clothing again, but Carter grabbed her a second time.

"Charlie, let go!"

He shook his head. "You can do it," he said. "You can help me. Please, you have to help me. You can use the gift." He tapped his own temple.

She moved to sit back on the bed, and he let her this time.

The gift? In the middle of all this, he wanted her to reach out and make contact? Even the thought of it made the static in her ears rush in, like a gate had been opened. She closed her eyes and pressed the heel of her hand against her forehead, and listened to the noise.

"Who is 'she'?" she asked eventually.

Carter sat next to her. "She's from far away. From the other side of space. She's dead too."

Serra gulped and felt faint. She opened her eyes and saw Carter looking at her.

"She's dead, and she can help us. She can help all of us. She can help *you*."

Their eyes remained locked.

Help... me? At this thought, the static swirled, like the machine was listening in on their conversation. Watching from the dark. Giving approval.

Then Serra nodded.

"Okay."

32

The corridor swam with static, which made Ida pause, half-in, half-out of the elevator. The space radio had been off when he left his cabin, he was certain of that, and the first thought that jumped out at him was that someone was messing in his private space—again. Ida clenched his fists and his jaw and headed down the passageway.

It took Ida a few moments to realize how cold the air was and that the pain in his knee that had started back at the elevator was ramping up. He stopped mid-stride, his breath catching in a white cloud before him.

Not again.

"Ida? Ida, where are you?"

Ludmila calling, her voice punching holes in the white noise that surged and rolled to fill the gap when she was silent.

"Ludmila?"

"Ida, I can't stop them, I tried—"

Ida broke into a run, his artificial joint screaming. Ludmila's voice was different: it sounded even farther away, and the hard edge of fear had returned.

Ida's cabin was empty and dark, lit only by the half light from the passageway as he stood across the open doorway. The blue light of the space radio was piercing.

"Ludmila? What's wrong?" Ida moved to his desk, pulled the chair in tight, and hunched over the radio set. He tried adjusting the signal, but the static just popped and crackled and settled back into its usual pattern.

"I tried to stop them, I tried to stop them, Ida, but I couldn't, I couldn't—"

Another noise now, a chirping or clicking. Ida frowned and closed his eyes. Then he realized what it was, distorted by the bad signal. Ludmila was crying.

"Stop who? Ludmila, tell me what happened."

Ludmila sniffed, the sound of dry paper being torn.

"They're coming. It's sooner than I thought. I've tried to hold them back, but it's not working. They're getting stronger."

"Who is?"

"Ida, you must stop them."

Ida sighed and rubbed his face. "Who?"

"Your friend, Carter. And the others. They're going to try to bring them in. It's too soon, too soon."

Ida sat up. Carter? Friend was not the first term that came to mind. But, more important, how did Ludmila know what the marine was doing? How did she know anything about what went on in the *Coast City* outside of Ida's cabin?

"What's Carter doing?"

The rush of white noise snapped like a gunshot, making Ida jerk back instinctively from the radio set. When Ludmila spoke again her voice was loud and crushed.

"Stop him! Stop them all!"

Ida hopped to his feet and looked around, searching. Then he saw it. The Yuri-G was sitting on the bed. In the confusion aboard the *Bloom County*, Zia hadn't seen him pick it up. He grabbed it and checked the charge, almost telling Ludmila to wait there. He stopped, and had the oddest feeling that she really was in the room.

"Go," she said. "He's on Level Twelve, Mess Deck."

"How did you—?"

"Go!" Ludmila screamed. Her voice, meshed with the interference across the radio, was like a banshee's cry. Ida felt the hairs on the back of his neck stand up.

Without saying a word, he sprinted out.

In the empty cabin, the static died down to a baseline level, punctuated by the occasional pop as Ludmila cried. Then it snapped again, as it had before.

"Contact has been established… contact has been established," Ludmila whispered to the empty room.

33

Knock-knock-knock-knock-knock-knock-knock.

Hands clenched.

"It's not working—"

"Marine, shush."

"Sir."

Knock-knock-knock-knock.

"You really know what you're doing?"

"It's fine. It always starts like this." Serra fidgeted on her chair. Carter's hand was like sandpaper in hers.

Knock-knock-knock-knock.

"This is fucked up."

Someone else moved, knocking a knee against the table, rocking it.

"Carter, shut the fuck up. You were the one who asked me to do this." And now, sitting in the dark, in the circle, she wondered why she'd agreed so easily.

Then the machine sound was there, creeping in at the edge of her mind, and she knew she'd made the right decision.

"Fine," Carter whispered.

Knuckles white. More knocks.

"Carter," said Sen, thrown out of bed by Carter to complete the circle, "you are so fucking full of shit."

"That so, gunner?"

"It sure is. Just wanted you to know."

"Duly noted."

Someone snickered. Serra's eyes flicked open but the canteen was lost in pitch black. It was amazing, breathtaking, how dark they had managed to get it. Not even the night-lights in the passageway outside sent a single sliver sliding under the canteen door.

She closed her eyes again and concentrated. She wasn't that familiar with the rituals of Santeria, and she hadn't done this for… well, forever, really. And only one time before that, when she'd been six. Her mother had been furious, but even she bit her tongue. Her mother had been scared of Grandmother, always, of the things she could do. But it was working. The white noise in her head was clearing, slowly.

"This better work."

Serra's eyes snapped open again. It was ridiculous. Just an hour ago Carter had been a wreck in her cabin, crying for his mother. Now he was acting like she was *making* him do this.

"Are we going to keep trying, or do you children want to go play somewhere else?"

Someone yawned, and someone coughed. The blackness was like a blanket, enveloping, soft.

Nobody said anything for a few seconds, but nobody let go of her hands either. Finally Carter hissed; Serra could just imagine his face, teeth clenched, lips drawn, ready for anything the enemy could throw at them.

"Do it," he said.

Serra screwed her eyes tighter and tried to remember what her grandmother had taught her, twenty years ago. That it had been in the old house in Puerto Rico and she was now on an old station a thousand light-years away shouldn't matter. Carter had made direct contact. That was much more than her grandmother ever had, and she'd made a living out of the "gift."

She was old by the time Serra hit recruitment age, but cane in hand she'd stood by her beloved Carminita as she took the oath, as tall and as proud as her bones would allow. Next to her, her mother was also proud, but there were tears in her eyes and her hands shook. She was scared for her daughter. Service with the Fleet was honorable, but with Spider aggression increasing daily, the survival rate was enough to make any mother weep.

A sigh in the dark, from her left. Someone jumped in his or her seat and someone snickered again. This wasn't going to work. They needed a focus. They needed a light. They needed gifts.

Ida's booted feet pounded the crosshatch decking. It made a racket, which was fine by him. If the marines were in trouble, he had no problem letting them know someone was coming.

He came out of the elevator and headed left. The canteen was a quarter-way around the hub, between him and the next elevator lobby. For a change the passage lights were operational, the night glow flaring to regular operational white as Ida raced around the curved corridor. The environment control was holding as well.

Neither of these facts entered Ida's mind until the lights failed. He careered to a halt, animal instinct stopping his run as the darkness of the next passageway section reared up at him like a physical object.

Ida swore and, arms swinging, carried on.

It was all they had, but it would do. The lighter—illegal on the U-Star, but smuggled on board by someone—provided a tiny flame but one that burned with a yellow so dazzling in the complete dark of the canteen that even with Serra's eyes closed, the shapes moved brown and red behind their lids. Next to the lighter stood a plastic cup of canteen coffee, the steam rising in mesmerizing waves in the flickering light. The only thing missing from the offering was a cigar, but Serra was amazed enough that someone in the circle had produced the lighter. The gifts were better than she could have hoped for.

Serra exhaled, shook her sweaty hands, and then completed the circle again. All at once, everyone around the table jolted, like a circuit had been completed and an electrical charge conducted.

"What the fuck—?"

"Quiet," whispered Serra. Behind her closed eyes she watched the flame dance.

Knock-knock-knock-knock.

"This still ain't working. I gotta be on shift soon."

KNOCK-KNOCK-KNOCK-KNOCK.

Everyone jumped as the rapping sounded on the table in front of them.

"What the fucking fuck?"

The knocking continued, fainter. Serra leaned down toward the table, concentrating.

"Please, we have a code. One for no, two for yes. Do you understand?"

Knock-knock-knock-knock-knock.

Serra felt Carter's grip relax. He moved his fingers, threatening to break the perfect circle. They were so close.

KNOCK.

"What?"

"Wait."

KNOCK-KNOCK.

"Do you understand us?"

KNOCK-KNOCK.

Someone on the opposite side of the table drew a breath in sharply. One of the marines, another woman. Serra didn't really know her. She seemed quiet and timid, but she had more Spider kills notched on her rifle butt than the rest of the squad put together. Always the quiet ones.

"Is someone there?"

KNOCK-KNOCK.

Backs straight. Knees together. A gasp in the dark.

"You asked us to come, didn't you?"

KNOCK-KNOCK.

Serra opened her eyes, just a crack. Lit by the steady flame of the lighter, Carter's face was a grimace, sweat dripping down his forehead. Serra licked her teeth and watched Carter's eyeballs moving rapidly behind his eyelids.

"Is there someone there?" she asked. "Is someone coming?"

Nothing. Serra repeated the question, and then closed her eyes. As soon as she did, the red and black shapes reappeared, dancing with the flickering flame.

She took a breath and held it; then she opened her eyes again. The flame was still, steady, strong.

Then she looked up. Standing behind the group, in the gap between Carter and the protesting Flyeye, stood DeJohn.

Except... maybe it was the light, the way he was illuminated in yellow from the front and from down low, maybe it was the way the light flickered even though the flame was steady and true. Maybe it was the way that the blackness behind him moved. Whatever it was, the figure looked less like DeJohn and more like a photograph, or some weird mannequin. She realized DeJohn had his eyes closed.

"Hey—" Carter whispered, eyes closed. Immediately the darkness seemed to bulge, partially obscuring DeJohn's head. Serra pulled on Carter's hand.

"Quiet, dammit."

Carter did as he was told.

Serra closed her eyes. "Who is there? Do you know us?"

KNOCK.

KNOCK.

The raps came slow and deliberate. Somebody whimpered and Serra felt Sen's grip slip in the fingers of her left hand. She turned her head instinctively toward the sound, but kept her eyes closed.

She sat and watched the shapes moving in the flame light behind closed eyes, hypnotized by their dance.

The door was open, but the canteen beyond was just an empty black void. Ida stopped again, and listened. He could hear something, a knocking sound, far away. The temperature in the passageway was approaching freezing. Standing motionless, he could feel his eyeballs drying out.

The darkness had gotten thicker somehow as he approached, filled with a substance as thin and insubstantial as gas but impenetrable to light. It had no substance, no taste, no smell, and Ida knew full well that it wasn't gas or mist or smoke. It was shadow.

Ida was scared. Scared of what the shadows hid, of what might come out of the shadow, of going into the shadow and not returning.

"Ida... Ida..."

Her voice was caught on a nonexistent breeze, painted light and thin onto a background of static. The echo of subspace.

Ida spun around. The shadow had surrounded him, but back the way he had come the passage lights, now returned to their baseline nocturnal setting, were faintly visible. The passage looked old and granular through the fog.

She was there. Standing where he had come from. He wondered how long she'd been following him, but then he realized that she hadn't at all. Beyond, the elevator door remained open. It was possible she'd come around from the other side of the hub, but he knew she hadn't really.

Ludmila.

Her suit was silvered, her closed visor golden. Across her chest were four bold red letters.

CCCP.

And when she spoke, it was across the eternity of subspace. Ida wasn't sure whether it was sound acting on his eardrums or whether she'd tuned in to his very thoughts. But she spoke, and he listened. If he was afraid, she was terrified.

"I can't stop them, Ida, I can't stop them. Go, please."

And then her voice dropped to a whisper, reduced to a sibilant hissing against the interference.

"They are coming... They are coming..."

Ida needed no further encouragement. He spun on his heel, yelled blue murder, and dived into the black portal of the canteen.

* * *

"Carter?"

Someone sobbed. One hand, rough, grabbed Serra's hard enough, it felt, to snap bone. Another hand, soft and wet, twisted and slipped away. The circle broke.

KNOCK.

KNOCK.

Slow and sure.

She dared not open her eyes.

Dared not.

"Who is there? Who are you?"

A sigh—long, high, not from someone who sat around the table. She must not open her eyes.

Must not.

But...

KNOCK KNOCK.

But she must...

"I feel..." said someone not at the table. "I feel the darkness *breathe*."

The voice was female, accented. Far East. Asian. Japanese. The voice spoke the last word like it was a blessed relief. She must not open her eyes.

KNOCK. KNOCK. KNOCK. KNOCK.

A breeze. Ice. The flame flickered.

The voice was as cold as space as it asked, "Where is he?"

She opened her eyes, and it began. One scream, then another.

The light danced and the shadows swirled and the flame on the table was still, steady, small.

Between each sitter, a face. DeJohn. An older man in round glasses. Men in Fleet marine helmets reflecting the light that guttered and flared from nowhere.

Serra tried to close her mouth, tried to stop the scream, but she could not. Wide-eyed and wide-jawed, she turned her head, left to right, left to right, like a fairground attraction from old-time Earth.

And then she turned again, to the left. The chair was empty. Sen had gone.

And to the right. Carter crying.

And to the left. The chair was no longer empty. A woman sat demurely, hands in her lap. Dressed in white, with hair long and black. Skin as white as her tunic. Her eyes, oval, Japanese, closed.

They opened, and the woman smiled. Her smile was the death of a thousand children under a hot desert sun. Her eyes were blue voids in which stars exploded

Serra's jaw clicked as it opened beyond normal endurance. The scream she uttered came from the ancient part of her brain. It was old and green, the sound of the Earth being split in two.

And the flame burned, white, steady. But it could not fight the darkness, the shadows. The blackness spun around the table, around the sitters, around the uninvited guests.

The Japanese woman held up her hands. One was empty, the palm facing forward. The other clutched a handle, long with a woven cover. Pointing downward, something long and silver sparked in the night.

She whispered, and the whisper became a rush of sound, a wind from nowhere, the static white noise howl of subspace. The Japanese woman stood and raised her sword.

"Where is he?"

Serra stared into the light.

"Where is he?"

Serra stared into the light and screamed.

Ida looked around, sweeping the Yuri-G in front of him. It had a white light on the front of it that projected a bright cone in front of the barrel, mixing with the red safety-off warning indicator and illuminating the table and chairs and the canteen's serving bar at the back in a washed-out pink.

The room was empty.

Careful to keep his senses alert to anything that might be hiding in the corners, Ida played the light from the Yuri-G over the table. There was a plastic cup filled with something black that had frozen into a solid block, and something smaller, metallic, that glinted. He leaned forward and snatched it up—a cigarette lighter. He held it close and shook it. It was still nearly full of fuel, and the cap and striking wheel were hot to the touch but the metal of the body was icy. He closed the cap and squeezed the lighter in his fist. His knee banged one of the chairs; he winced at the sudden sound.

He didn't know why he wanted to be quiet, but he did. There was something about the canteen. Not just the darkness, now that he'd passed through the strange blackness that had hung like a mausoleum curtain over the entrance, but something else. He turned to look back at the door, but the shadows seemed normal again.

Mausoleum. He turned back to the canteen and pointed the gun around slowly, rolling the word in his mouth like a glucose tablet. The canteen was the canteen, and he knew it well. But somehow, whether it was the harsh light of the Yuri-G against the soft blue of the night-lights, whether it was the odd way the shadows flitted around his peripheral vision, he couldn't tell. But the empty tables and chairs were... spooky.

Especially the table in front of him. With the chairs arranged like a group had just been sitting there. With the frozen cup and the lighter, the closed cap still hot in his hand.

It was like walking into a tomb. He'd experienced the sensation before, on several planets. Action against the Spiders meant infiltration or outright conquest of people and places, on both sides. He'd walked through enough sacred places, forbidden temples or tombs of kings, where the very fabric of the place pushed at you, telling you to turn around, warning you to go no farther.

And he felt it here. The canteen had become an alien landscape, a sacred, secret place. Ida had the feeling he'd interrupted something, something important, something of which he wasn't supposed to be a part. Something that, he knew, was terrible and dark and old, the result of foolish meddling by people who had no clue at all.

Had no clue, or were led into a trap.

Ida kicked a chair and shouted and recoiled at the sound, so loud and sharp in the cathedral silence of the canteen.

It was empty. He'd been too late.

"You couldn't stop it."

Ida turned. When he saw Ludmila in the doorway, he lowered the gun. Its flashlight spotlighted his feet absurdly.

She was getting stronger. As he stood there, watching the slim figure in her silver spacesuit, Ida felt the hairs on his arms and neck prickle. Fear, yes, but cold as well. It seemed that to manifest like this, Ludmila was sucking the energy from the very air. Any kind, whatever was available. Light and heat. His robot knee ached like someone had hit it with a hammer.

"Where are they?" was all Ida could manage. His face was stiff with the cold, his words sending clouds of steam billowing into the air between him and her.

She moved a gloved hand by her side so that the palm faced him. Maybe moving was difficult. The room reverberated with the faint sound of the ocean.

"They've been taken."

"Taken where?"

"I thought they were coming," said Ludmila, "that this would hasten their arrival. But someone stopped them. Not you, someone else."

"I'm afraid."

"So am I."

Ida's throat was dry. "I'm afraid of you," he said.

The gloved hand dropped.

"So you should be," Ludmila said.

Ida stared at the apparition. She was real, solid, three-dimensional. And then he saw that her golden visor was not reflecting the room or him, standing right in front of her. It showed a starscape and the edge of a blue-green orb. The Earth.

Ida jumped as the scream punched through the fog in his mind. His intake of breath was sharp and the cold air stung. He knew that voice.

Zia.

He turned back to the woman in the spacesuit, but she was gone. The canteen was empty once more.

When Zia screamed a second time, Ida flicked the safety off the Yuri-G and left the room at a run.

34

He found her in the corridor outside, halfway between the canteen and elevator lobby. She was curled into a ball and pressed into a corner, arms wrapped around her knees. One arm was bare but the sentient tattoo on the other had stretched out, enveloping the limb in a black sleeve. It made Ida feel sick to look at it.

"Zia?"

She flinched at his voice, and as he knelt down she crawled backwards even farther, trying to telescope her body into the smallest bundle possible. Small, safe, out of reach.

He caught sight of his own face looming toward the reflection in her goggles. At least that meant she was real, and she was here. Then he blinked and looked away. The reflection showed only blackness behind him. He had the irrational, childish fear that something was going to swim out of the darkness and grab him from behind; a single white hand with claws, creeping out across the floor to grasp at an ankle and pull him away.

He shuddered and then took a breath. "Zia, what happened?"

He gently took one shoulder—above the arm without the tattoo—and squeezed. Her curled form seemed to relax, and the tension in her forehead eased. Her lips parted, and she tilted her face up to his. Then her lips began to move, mouthing words that, somehow, Ida didn't feel were hers.

"Where is he? Where... Where is he?"

Then she let out a cry and jerked forward, pushing Ida away. He rocked on his heels as she scrambled forward on her hands and knees before she seemed to relax again and sat on her haunches.

"What's wrong?" Ida realized he had a fair idea. "What did you see?"

Zia coughed and brought her knees up to her chest. Her goggles were pointing dead ahead, but Ida had no idea where she was looking. Then she spoke in a small voice.

"Nobody. I didn't see nobody."

She fumbled on the floor; Ida backed off to allow her to push herself to her feet.

"You all right? Because you sure screamed like you weren't. And where is who?"

Zia paused as though considering an answer while she brushed herself down. Her glasses were now pointed right at him.

"I don't know what you're talking about. I'm fine."

Ida frowned.

"We have to leave. Now," she said, and she headed toward the elevators.

"Wait," said Ida, but she ignored him. He jogged to join her and touched her shoulder as he pulled level, but she jerked away. As she moved her other arm to rub the shoulder where he had touched, Ida noticed the tattoo springing to life, curling and swirling like an agitated eel in a tank.

Zia Hollywood hit the control panel and stepped through the sliding doors, Ida close on her heels. Ignoring Ida, she touched the personal comm unit on her wrist.

"Fathead, we all set?"

The comm clicked and her crewman's voice came through, acknowledging. Zia nodded.

"I'll be at the *County* in five. Start the engine warming." She released the comm and dropped her arm.

"So that's it? You're off, just like that?"

Nothing.

"Zia—"

She tapped her foot three times and then spun on her heel. Her mouth was set.

"Yes, Cap'n, I'm leaving." The elevator dinged. She shifted the weight on her feet, and the corners of her mouth twitched. "And if you had any sense, you would too."

Ida took a step forward. "What does that mean?"

Zia shook her head. "I need to get the fuck off this ship. You do too. Everyone."

The elevator doors snicked open. Zia's level, one floor up from Ida's hidey-hole. She made a line for the doors, forcing Ida to sidestep. By the time he turned around, she was already halfway down the corridor. And then the light panel behind her faded off as the one ahead faded on, and Ida watched as she became a series of vignettes disappearing toward the guest quarters.

She was waiting for him in his cabin. She sat on the bed and was smiling, like there was nothing wrong at all aboard the U-Star *Coast City*.

"What's the matter?" Izanami asked. The smile didn't leave her face.

Ida paused at the threshold, one hand on the doorframe, one hand rubbing his forehead. He was getting a headache, a real thumper. It was cold and there was a sound in his head, the rushing noise of subspace like some kind of tinnitus, echoing in his ears.

"I saw her," he said. He gasped for air. His body felt like it was made of herculanium armor.

Izanami hopped off the bed and went to Ida, her hands behind her back. She peered at his eyes. Ida held the back of his hand over his mouth like he was going to retch, but nothing materialized.

Izanami's smile grew a little at the corners. "You look like you could use a rest, Captain."

Ida shook his head and tried to straighten up, but his vision was going black and red at the edges. The shadows, crowding in. He turned to Izanami and was surprised by the blue light in her eyes.

"She's here," he said, shaking his head again. "And Zia's gone... going... she saw... I..."

Ida screwed his eyes shut. It felt like hot metal was being pressed against his temples. He staggered to the table, where he sat heavily in the chair.

Izanami turned but stayed by the door. "Who's here?"

From Izanami's tone, Ida thought for a moment she was addressing a small child. He opened his eyes, but she was looking at him. The room flipped momentarily in front of his eyes, and nausea crawled up his chest from somewhere lower down. He grimaced and gripped the arms of his chair so hard, the edges bit into his hands.

He closed his eyes again. The last thing he saw before he did was Izanami's eyes. They were blue, as blue as the sky, as blue as the light on the space radio and just as bright.

Behind his closed eyelids he wished for the purple shapes of summer, the breeze on his face, and the grass in his nose, but all he got was black shapes on a black background. They shifted, squirmed, rolled.

The *sound* filled his head. He sucked a breath in that was colder than he thought it should be.

"Where have you been, anyway?" he asked. He kept his eyes closed. He didn't want to look at her. There was something about her eyes... "One of Zia's crewmen needed attention." He opened his eyes. The cabin was still dark, and Izanami was hidden in shadows. Ida stood, waiting a beat to make sure he wasn't going to keel over. Then he hobbled to the bed and lay down.

She shrugged. "I'm not the station's official medic. You should get some rest."

Ida turned over, the effort titanic. He opened his eyes and looked up and saw two Japanese medics sitting on his bed, the black shadow of a translucent third orbiting above them. He blinked and rubbed his eyes, and the image refocused. Izanami was still smiling.

"Sleep, Ida. Sleep."

Sleep. Yes. He was tired, very tired, and cold. He thought about Zia and about the empty canteen, but the roar of subspace was like a blanket, enclosing, enveloping, smothering his thoughts.

"Good night, Ida."

"Guuhnmm…" he said into the pillow, and she was gone.

On the table, the blue light of the space radio shone, but there was no static, no interference, no noise.

After a while, Ida jerked awake, but the room was empty. When he looked up, the radio's blue light shone straight into his eye, and he let his head drop back to the pillow.

"Good night, Ludmila," he said.

There was no answer, but Ida was asleep. In his dream he saw himself holding a gun and looking around an empty room. Red paint flakes fell like snow, and Astrid called his name.

As he was lying on the bed, his left hand unclenched, finally releasing the small, silver object onto the olive green blanket. Ida sighed in his sleep and turned over, knocking the lighter to the floor. It banged dully as it hit the rubberized decking, but not enough to wake him.

35

Ida woke and the nausea hit him like a punch in the stomach. He got to the communal bathroom down the passage just in time. After he threw up he felt better, at least physically. He knelt in the stall for a few minutes, collecting himself. He had to see King straight away, insist he put the station on full alert, get everyone available to work on clearing the lightspeed link. The *Coast City* and everyone in it— everyone *left* in it—were in danger.

As he shuffled back to his cabin, he found himself checking over his shoulder more than once, more than twice. The environment control had settled into a low twilight, which wasn't helping his state of mind.

Ida rushed into his cabin, immediately shutting the door behind him and leaning back against it as he took deep breaths, waiting for the panic to abate. He closed his eyes but that seemed to make it worse, and he quickly turned around to check through the frosted window. The corridor beyond was empty and silent. Ida exhaled loudly and rolled his neck. He had to see King, yes, but right now he didn't really feel like venturing out in the corridor again, not just yet.

The cabin was cold, so very cold. Ida scrambled to the bed and grabbed the blanket to wrap around himself; then he saw something glinting on the floor in the low light, a bright white-blue sparkle like a tiny star. He reached down and picked it up.

The cigarette lighter: old-fashioned, either a replica or maybe an antique, forbidden on a U-Star as part of standard protocol (no naked flames). Ida flipped the cap, shook it—nearly full—then flicked the wheel. The flame was short and shone brightly in the twilight.

"Ludmila?"

Ida's eyes flicked toward the space radio. It was on, the blue light shining. But the speaker was dead. Suddenly Ida missed the hiss and pop and crackle.

"Ludmila, are you there?"

Nothing. Ida dropped into the chair in front of the table. He adjusted the set, altering the volume, the gain, the everything.

Silence.

Ida swore and quickly pulled the radio set toward him so he could access the back panel. Nothing. It was all the same, all the jumpers were in the right place, the tune controls aligned. He pushed the box back and ran a finger over the manual controls on the front. All fine.

Ludmila was gone.

Ida pushed away from the table with a shout, allowing the momentum to spin his chair around and around, his face in his hands.

Had she ever been there? Maybe she'd been a product of his imagination, a voice conjured from the dark shadows of his mind. Maybe she'd never answered back. Nobody else had heard her, after all. Ida wasn't even sure now that he'd told Izanami it.

Maybe he was cracking up. Maybe he already had. Maybe the same thing had happened to DeJohn before he vanished. Being alone in the dark could break a man.

But… no, he'd *seen* her. She'd been there, an apparition, a warning. And Carter had seen her too, earlier. He'd described the red CCCP insignia on her spacesuit.

Ida flicked the lighter closed and swore.

The blue light of the subspace radio. Ludmila. She *was* real, and she was connected to whatever was going on aboard the station. Ida knew that now—she'd died when her capsule burned up a thousand years ago; what was left was an echo in subspace, some part of her personality imprinted on the fabric of that bizarre dimension. Intelligent, self-aware survival after death. A ghost in the machine. And right now, the only person—alive or dead—who knew what was going on.

He waved his hand in the air above the space radio. The blue light flickered as the set recognized his commands and the three-dimensional holographic control panel materialized in the air. Ida began scrolling through frequencies; every few seconds the radio auto-locked onto something, but it was all garbage, the signal destroyed by the interference from Shadow.

He searched, lower and lower. Ludmila's signal had been at the very bottom of the set's range, where it shouldn't even have been able to pick anything up: subspace, where the frequencies were thin and the signals weak, meshing with the background noise of the dimension itself.

Finally he was there, and the voices died down to be replaced by the roaring ocean of white noise that was so familiar, the roil of metallic static tinged with danger. He sighed and sat back, letting the sound roll over him and bounce around the room.

He was close. Close to her, he knew it.

He opened his eyes and scrolled farther, the noise, the poisonous, hypnotic, *addictive* pulse of subspace ebbing and flowing like a tidal current.

There. He jerked his head up. The patterns in the static had changed. Another signal, buried deep in the roaring. His eyes narrowed in concentration as he tried to focus on the sounds.

More pops and crackles and… a voice. His back went straight.

Ludmila.

He pulled himself closer to the table and yanked the radio closer to him so it practically hugged his chest. He carefully scanned the region he was tuned to.

"Ludmila? Ludmila, can you hear me? Come in, please."

Something there, scrambled. A woman's voice.

Ida's heart raced. The answer was within reach.

"Ludmila? It's Ida. You're very faint. Can you hear me? Over?"

"*Ma... Y... this... ty...*"

More fine-tuning. The voice started to pull itself together like a jigsaw. A woman, yes, but the accent... Ida frowned.

"Ludmila?"

"*Mayday... mayday... mayday...*"

Ida gasped, hands busy on the ethereal control panel. "This is the U-Star *Coast City*," he said, his training kicking in. "Please state the nature of your emergency."

The static surged like a wave, and the voice was lost. Ida tuned some more, rotating an invisible dial between finger and thumb.

"Come in, please. Ludmila, is that you?"

He knew it wasn't. When the voice returned, it was loud and crystal clear. His heart raced and there was a cold, hard ball in his stomach.

"Mayday, mayday, this is the P-Prof *Bloom County* requesting urgent assistance. We are drifting and need rescue. Mayday, mayday."

Zia Hollywood, surely not more than a few million klicks away. Ida wasn't sure what the *Bloom County*'s speed was, or how long he'd been out, but the ship couldn't have left any more than a few hours ago, at the very most.

"*Bloom County*, this is Captain Cleveland aboard the U-Star *Coast City*. Zia, it's me, Ida. What's happened? Where are you?"

Static lapped at Ida's ears like waves rolling on a beach. There was something else buried under the aural junk, and Ida realized it was Zia crying.

"Ida? Ida, help us. Help us, please."

"We're coming, Zia. Hold tight."

Ida stood, the blanket falling away as he sprinted out of his cabin. Zia said something else, but it was lost in the interference. It popped and crackled and fizzed in the empty room.

Izanami stepped from the shadows, her eyes blue spinning diamonds of night. With each slow step she took toward the table, the white noise pulsed.

"Who's there? Ida? Ida?" Zia's voice came thinly over the air. Izanami stepped up to the table.

"They're all dead, Ida. All of them. They were taken. They're dead." Izanami waved a skeletally thin arm over the radio set. The static roared as her hand approached the receiver, and the last sound that came over the speakers before the set overloaded and turned itself off was Zia Hollywood, alone in her spaceship, screaming.

36

Darkness. Darkness and sound; enveloping, surrounding, penetrating. Pink noise and square waves and saw waves. Nothing random, nothing natural. A pattern: information, data. A *code*.

The language of machines.

Frequency modulation. The machine was awake.

Ahí estás, Carminita.

The roar of the ocean. The roar of language, ancient, artificial. Alien.

The sound was all around her and it was inside her. Nobody could hear it except her. This was what she was born for, born to do. A gift, a wild talent honed by training, polished and sharpened until it became a tool, until the tool became a weapon.

And she was the best of the best.

Contact has been established. Contact has been established.

In the darkness, Carmina Serra smiled and turned over on the hard floor.

In the darkness, the machine clicked and whirred and lights flashed, once, twice, and then went out.

AOKIGAHARA AND THE GIRL WITH BLUE EYES

She was there the next day too, standing by the tall pines that marked the edge of Aokigahara, the Sea of Trees. Tsutomu stood by the well and watched her for a while. Behind the forest, Fuji's perfect cone pierced a sky that was blue and clear. It was still cold that day, unseasonably so; the water from the well was so cold, it should be frozen, Tsutomu thought as he filled the two buckets and lifted their yoke onto his shoulders. Some in the village said it was the falling star that had brought the cold, but at this, most laughed.

And then she was there, watching him. For five days she had watched in silence. He didn't hear or see her arrive, or see her leave, for that matter. She never spoke and never seemed to move. She was wearing white, and her eyes were blue and bright, but Tsutomu knew that was just the strange cold playing tricks. People didn't have blue eyes.

He bent down to adjust his load, and when he looked up, she was gone and the forest was once more empty and silent. A cold wind blew across the black rocky ground and Tsutomu turned to start the long trek back to the village. Maybe today he would tell the elders at the village and they could go and ask the daimyo. The daimyo would know what it meant.

The girl had appeared the morning after the star fell from the heavens. The star roared as it fell, as loud as the scream of a shisa, and everyone came out to look toward Fuji. Perhaps the mountain was angry, angry as it had been before, when the gods rained fire on the Earth and turned the sky thick and black with rage.

But the mountain was still and in the morning the air was cold, like the winter so recently passed had returned anew. Tsutomu was sent by his mother to the well, and there he had seen her for the first time. Except she hadn't been a girl then, not on the first day. She was a... thing, something white, a light and a shape that slid along the ground and then stopped by the edge of the trees.

He had been surprised and wondered if perhaps he should have been afraid. Aokigahara wasn't cursed, not really, but it was said there were caves lost within the trees, caves in which *things* lived, things that slept but which sometimes woke, and when they did, they fed on those foolish enough to venture beyond the pines, into the forest proper. He wondered if the shape was one of the cave-things, but it didn't move from the edge of the forest and then it was gone, so perhaps he hadn't seen anything at all.

On the second day he returned and so did the shape. This time it stood, and it had arms and legs but no face. It stood by the tree and even though it had no eyes, Tsutomu knew it was watching him. He watched it too, and then between the blink of an eye it was gone and he was alone with his task.

On the third day he returned and she was there, dressed in white, by the tree. Now it had become a girl, no older than he, with long black hair like his. But her eyes were different. They were blue, and in the shadow cast by the tree they shone like coals.

Tsutomu returned home with his water and felt afraid. His mother hit him when he didn't do his chores properly, but he was distracted by his thoughts of the girl in the forest. And then his mother was distracted by the news that quickly spread through the village.

Hideo and Aki had gone. The two brothers had not returned from the woods. Not Aokigahara, never Aokigahara, of course. The other woods, the ones on the other side of the hill where the soil was rich and brown and where birds still sang. Hideo and Aki went to cut wood and never returned. That night a search party set out: seven men, with torches and axes and swords.

They were the next to go. When morning broke, the village was less nine souls.

But his mother still needed water and Tsutomu still made the journey, even though it took him near to the Sea of Trees and its strange black ground. Near to where they said the star had fallen over Fuji.

That night, Tsutomu told his mother about the girl, and she hit him over the head and told him not to talk of such things. But there was something in her voice and in her face that Tsutomu hadn't seen before. Later, when the village was quiet, he lay awake, unable to get the image of the girl's burning blue eyes from his mind, and he heard his mother talking to someone. It was Kanbe, one of the elders. He sat in silence as his mother spoke, and he left without a word. In the dark his mother wept and Tsutomu went to bed.

The next day the girl was there. Tsutomu set his empty pails down beside the well, and across the rocky ground the two watched each other.

Then she smiled, and there was suddenly someone with her. A young man, standing behind her in the shadow of the fir tree.

Aki.

Tsutomu recognized him at once, and he called out, but Aki moved back into the trees, into the shadows. The girl with blue eyes was smiling, and Tsutomu knew something was wrong. That day he ran back to the village without his pails of water.

And he returned, and soon, leading the men of the village to the edge of Aokigahara. Kanbe said Tsutomu was a good boy and had done well, and patted him on the shoulder as he drew his own sword and ordered his men to follow him into the Sea of Trees.

Tsutomu waited, and eventually the day drew in and the sun set behind Fuji, making it look in the cold clear sky as though the mountain were alight. And as the stars came out, there was a sound in the air, a roaring, like a waterfall, like the sound of the ocean far away, like the scream of a shisa. More stars fell that night. Tsutomu counted four, and then he screamed and turned as the girl stepped out of the forest, her blue eyes burning in the dark and behind her a group of men, more than two, more than seven, more than twenty. Aki and Hideo and the men of the search party and Kanbe's warriors. But now they were clad in dark shadows spun from the night itself, and when they stepped from the trees they moved quickly, flashing in time with the blink of Tsutomu's eyes.

Tsutomu ran back to the village, the demons of Aokigahara and those that had fallen from the heavens close on his heels.

PART FOUR

AND YOU WILL KNOW US BY THE TRAIL OF DEAD

37

She was quiet after that.

Gone were the black coveralls, the tight singlet. Instead she sat in the canteen, clad in a spare pair of blue and green marine overalls. They were the right size and she carried them off like the supermodel she might have been had her father been in a different business. Ida was perhaps surprised the most by the fact that she had covered up her bare arms—the right, which was elegant and beautiful and tanned, and the left, which was covered by the ever-changing tattoo.

That was just as well. He didn't like the tattoo, the way it damn well knew what was going on around it, and the way it moved to suit the mood of its wearer and, perhaps, those around her.

But gone too were the big square mining goggles, and without them, Zia Hollywood's face looked small. Here was her real face, naked, unhidden. And she looked unhappy. People tended to avoid her, though that wasn't difficult, considering Ida had counted less than a hundred remaining crew members. On a U-Star the size of the *Coast City*, that figure gave a very low population density per square kilometer.

The station's shuttle, the U-Star *Magenta*, had picked her up. Ida had wanted to travel on board the small patrol boat himself, but when he finally got the comms Flyeye on the bridge to tune in on the *Bloom County*'s distress call, echoing weakly over the lightspeed link, interference crawling over the signal only just strong enough to be picked up by the station, the *Magenta* was already out on its regular, routine patrol. Ida was happy at the response speed, but he knew that if he hadn't been scanning the illegal subspace frequencies, Zia's signal would never have been picked up.

King didn't seem to care anymore. He dragged himself from the ready room, but he seemed tired, worn out, just the shell of the blustering bureaucrat he had been. It was understandable; everyone left on the *Coast City* was on edge, going through their routines, carrying out their duties on autopilot as the undercurrent of tension and fear steadily grew. They were stuck, isolated. There was nothing left to do but just survive until the final transport arrived.

As for Zia's signal, King blamed it on Shadow, and perhaps he was right. The *Bloom County* sure as hell wasn't equipped to transmit over subspace, so what Ida had picked up was a freak occurrence, a random reflection of Zia's call. The light of Shadow, said King. Does strange things. Bounces a signal around to God knows where.

That Ida wasn't going to argue with. He thought back to Ludmila and wondered if she had had any reality outside of his own head.

And now Zia Hollywood sat in the canteen. She sat still and in silence, although she ate standard protein rations. They were a far cry from the real food stowed on the *Bloom County*, but after the marines dragged her screaming from her ship—which had been towed back to the station and now sat in the spare shuttle bay—she had refused to return to it.

Ida had stayed by her side since she returned to the station. She was unhurt, according to the automated scan in the infirmary. She and King had a debriefing that lasted no time at all, Ida waiting in the bridge, watching the closed door of the ready room. He wondered what they had talked about, or if Zia had said anything at all. As she exited the ready room, King stood in the doorway and glanced at Ida. Ida frowned, and the marshal, pale, looking ill, turned around and closed the door behind him.

Ida watched Zia in the canteen. There were four others eating: a pair at a nearby table and two others spread out across the large communal space.

He needed to talk to her. She *knew*; he was sure of it. There was something out there, hiding in the purple space between the station and the star. She'd seen it. As Ida had. As Carter had. And maybe like Serra and Sen and the others, before they'd vanished.

Ida grimaced. Now Zia was also alone. Her message had been no exaggeration. Her remaining crew members were gone, just like the others. Just like *that*.

When the *Magenta* docked, according to Private Chan—Ida had eventually cornered the Ops on the bridge as he waited—the *Bloom County*'s distress call had stopped. Zia, the only person aboard, was busy at the control deck erasing things—erasing everything, as it turned out: navigation files, computer drives, and the ship's log, all of it. All illegal acts: treason, conspiracy with the enemy, an automatic death penalty. But so intent had Zia been on her task that she had actually asked the marines to wait a moment before they realized what she, celebrity or not, was doing.

She hadn't finished erasing the log, so when the marines picked her up by her arms and carried her off the bridge, the screaming had begun.

Aboard the *Coast City*, the screaming stopped and the silence began. As she sat in the canteen, her eyes moved, left to right, up and down, like she was sitting in the dark, waiting for the bogeyman to appear. She'd moved her chosen table closer to the far wall, with just enough of a gap to allow her to squeeze in, her back hard against the wall. Even so, she'd occasionally look over her shoulder at the featureless gray green expanse behind her, like there might have been someone—some*thing*—there.

Ida frowned. He had no idea what to do.

"Are you going to talk to her?"

He jumped and his plastic chair banged against the floor of the canteen. Izanami was right behind him, had practically whispered in his ear. Across the canteen Zia started at the sound, but then she returned to her curled posture and closed her eyes.

Ida lowered his voice to a whisper. "I'm not sure she wants to talk. Not to me, or to anyone. She's traumatized."

Izanami straightened up, and didn't make any attempt to lower her voice. "With no medic on board, I doubt she's getting the proper care. She needs counseling."

Ida turned and looked up at Izanami. Clad in her medical whites, she had her arms folded and was regarding Zia like a specimen to be observed.

"Jesus Christ," Ida hissed through his teeth. "You're a medic. Can't you do something?"

Izanami smiled, still looking at Zia. "I'm not part of the crew, Ida."

Ida tapped the table impatiently. Keeping his voice down became an effort. "I'm pretty sure the marshal won't care if you volunteer your services."

Izanami turned to Ida. Ida didn't like her look or her smile. Something at the back of his head began to hurt. Her eyes, they were blue ovals, burning bright, drawing Ida in. As he looked, his vision unfocused and her eyes seemed to spin with stars.

"Who are you talking to?"

Ida blinked and jerked his head around. At the opposite table, Zia still sat, knees drawn to her chest, heels balanced on the lip of her chair. Her arms were wrapped around her shins in a way that didn't look comfortable.

"Zia Hollywood, welcome back," said Ida with a nervous smile that didn't convey the relief he felt inside. "I was just thinking that Izanami here could help out. She's not part of the crew, but she's the only medic we have until the last transport arrives." He laughed lightly but it sounded fake, so he stopped.

Zia smiled, a shadow of her former, knowing grin. "And you think *I* need help?"

Ida's smile flickered. "I'm sorry?"

Zia lowered her legs to the floor and leaned forward on the table. "Who's Izanami?"

Ida gestured to the Japanese woman standing at his shoulder. "You weren't introduced before? Zia Hollywood, Izanami, the best neuro-psycho-physio-therapist this side of Fleetspace."

Izanami bowed slightly.

Zia's smile turned to a frown, and she rubbed her forehead with the heel of one hand. "You hum it, I'll play it."

"Ah. Pardon?" Ida felt confused.

Zia shrugged an apology. Then just said, "Okay."

"Okay?"

Zia nodded. "Okay."

Ida frowned. He had an odd feeling that he was listening in to only half of a conversation he'd thought he was taking part in. He glanced up at Izanami beside him. "Ah… is there anything you can do for Ms. Hollywood at the moment?"

"Ida—"

"Yes, Ms. Hollywood?"

"Who are you talking to?"

"Ah… what?"

Ida watched as Zia's eyes moved to the space over his right shoulder, and then back to his face. "There's no one there."

Ida coughed. His headache was starting to return. He turned and looked up at Izanami. The Japanese woman began to laugh, and this time her eyes really did spin into pools of pale blue light, scattered with diamonds and stardust. As Ida watched, she melted away, becoming nothing more than a black-silhouetted afterimage on the insides of his eyelids.

"You feeling okay, Cap'n?"

Ida stared at where Izanami had stood. When he blinked, he could see her outline, but then even that faded. He closed his eyes and screwed them tight and wished the shadows away.

"Oh, just fine, thanks," he said. Then he took a breath as the world wobbled around him. "Zia, what happened?"

The miner sighed. Ida's eyes were still closed, and he never wanted to open them again.

"We were attacked. They—"

"No, no. Before. Here. What made you leave early?"

"Oh, that," said Zia lightly. "I saw my father. He's dead, you know. Ain't that just a fine thing."

Ida exhaled, long and slow.

"He was with someone." Zia's voice got higher, and the words got faster. Ida shook his head, refusing to look. "There was a woman, behind him."

Something clicked in the back of Ida's mind. "A woman in an old-fashioned spacesuit?"

"No. She was laughing. Dressed in white."

Ida's stomach did a flip-flop. He opened his eyes to stop a sudden wave of dizziness and felt hot bile in the back of his throat.

He turned to look at Zia. She was sitting calmly, but her eyes were wide and she was as white as a ghost.

"Describe her."

Zia's eyes unfocused; although they remained on Ida, he didn't think she was looking at him. "A white dress, short. She had black hair, long and straight. And blue eyes, pale baby blue, very bright, as bright as the stars. She was Asian... Japanese or Korean. I don't know."

Ida swore, and prayed to whatever gods were listening to stop the walls of the world crashing in on him.

"She knew my name," said Zia. "She called to me. My father asked me to come with them. And then... then they changed. Became... I don't know... She's looking for someone too. She asked me if I knew where he is..."

She was shaking now. Ida watched her lips move, although no more words came. Then she squinted and pressed the heel on one hand to her forehead. Ida knew exactly how she felt.

Ida's mind raced. "When I found you," he said quickly, "before you left, that's what you said. You said, 'Where is he, where is he.' Who?"

Zia shook her head. "I don't remember that," she said. She closed her eyes tight, and her shivering increased.

He stood, pushing his own chair away noisily. She jumped at the sound but didn't open her eyes. He walked over, ignoring the way the shadows moved like smoke in the corners of the canteen. The others in the canteen had gone; Ida just hoped they had walked out rather than been... *taken*.

Ida grabbed Zia's shoulders firmly, not sure what he could do other than to let her know that he was here, that *they* were here, together.

Zia screwed her eyes even tighter, and her hands shot up and grabbed Ida's forearms. She squeezed them hard, hard enough to hurt. Ida grimaced, but then she opened her eyes.

"They're watching," she said, her voice a whisper.

38

They locked themselves in Ida's cabin.

It had been hours, although it was hard to tell, as Ida's override meant the automatic night cycle never came. For all he knew, the station was back in twilight outside. There was no way in hell he was opening the door to check. The frosted window was just a vaguely orange opaque square.

The shadows were dangerous, and they weren't *just* shadows. This they both agreed on.

And Izanami. He'd seen her fade with his own eyes—the only pair of eyes, he now realized, that had *ever* seen her aboard the *Coast City*. Individual ideas and suspicions finally coalesced in his mind, forming a picture he didn't want to see. The malfunctioning life scan that never showed Izanami in his cabin. Interrupted conversations. Izanami's insistence that she wasn't a member of the crew. It turned out she was telling the truth.

"Not sure we can count on the marshal, either."

Zia looked up. "Do you think he's a part of it all?"

"Maybe," said Ida. "He knows something, I'm sure of that. He's been frosty since I arrived, but the last few cycles it's like he's not really here."

Zia shrugged. "Sure he isn't just buckling under the pressure?"

"No, seems more than that. Like he's... I don't know, fighting something."

"What about the others on the station?"

"Well, there aren't many left. At first it was just a bug in the manifest, but now we know that crew members are disappearing. Carter and Serra were taken in the last group I know of. Six in total."

"Like Dathan and my crew."

Ida grimaced. "Like them."

"What happened to your commandant?"

"When I arrived, he'd already gone. But he'd managed to get off the station *between* transports."

"And we know what that means..." Zia sucked in a breath.

"Maybe he was the first," said Ida. "I heard his voice later—calling over the comms, during the first security breach. The ready room was attacked at the same time."

Zia shifted forward on the bed. "But if you heard him, doesn't that mean that he's... well, that he's out there, somewhere? And the others too?"

"Maybe," said Ida. He rubbed his face and spoke into his hands. "They were taken to somewhere. Maybe they're still alive." He dropped his hands and watched the dark space under the bed, thinking back again to Zia's account of what happened on board the *Bloom County*.

Zia's crew were not only highly trained but highly paid as well, and when their employer told them to jump, they asked for the height, distance, and details of the bonus remuneration offered for the task. At Zia's call, Fathead had dragged Ivanhoe from the infirmary and readied the *Bloom County* without pause or hesitation. When Zia joined them, they didn't speak unless spoken to, and the trio blasted off to their destination ahead of the official schedule. Neither Ivanhoe nor Fathead asked about Dathan, and Zia didn't mention him. The only thing her two remaining crew members knew was that they had to get away from the *Coast City* quickly. As well as miners and pilots, they were bodyguards and minders. Zia Hollywood was one of the most valuable private assets in all of Fleetspace, and protecting her was a deep-drilled instinct. They were a three-person self-preservation society. Saving their asses was the prime directive.

The slowrock field lay on the other side of Shadow, forming a cone-shaped spearhead of rubble powering cometlike toward the star. Perhaps it *had* been a comet, one that had broken up into its constituent rocky parts. Over time, if it wasn't engulfed by Shadow or vaporized by its strange light, the field might separate until its density became almost undetectable in deep space. This was the bounty Zia had come to hunt. The readings were off the chart, making it a prize worth crossing half of Fleetspace for. Each bite-sized chunk, according to the data leaked to them by the Fleet, was composed nearly entirely of lucanol, a metalloid that, when combined with herculanium, made an alloy strong enough to construct the core filaments of quickspace drivers. Half a standard mining hopper of rough lucanol ore could buy you a small asteroid of your own to call home. A *Bloom County* skipful of the pure metalloid meant Zia could buy the Fleet itself. Maybe that was her plan.

Or had been. The new plan was to get the hell out of the system, and fast. The question of the slowrocks hadn't even entered Zia's mind until they came up close, quite by accident as the ship curled away from the *Coast City* and into a trajectory that would take them away from Shadow. The ship's mining computer got a lock immediately and started pumping out data without anyone even asking.

The readings were impossible. Lucanol was soft, reactive; that's what made it so rare. So either the readings were subject to the same kind of weird interference from Shadow's radiation... or they were being altered somehow. Deliberately.

Two hours later and they'd swung by the leading asteroid's perihelion, the debris looming large on portside as they raced along. It was black, solid, a single triangular wedge, something too perfect, too regular.

Then the Spiderbaby under their feet had begun to twitch. It was unusual, but within bounds, and probably due to the light of Shadow as they skimmed its corona. They were close to the star, far closer than they'd intended.

The first sign of trouble had been when the movement of the mining legs had stopped. A minute later and the *Bloom County*'s engines cut out. As Fathead scrambled over the controls, they went dark. The control cabin cooled a little as the environment systems shut off, giving Zia's crew just a few hours of life support before they'd freeze in space.

Ivanhoe worked on the engines while Zia and Fathead got the backup systems online. Minimal life support and emergency communications, and that was it. The flight deck was dark, lit by the weak orange of the emergency communications screen and the dull purple glow of open space coming in from the large window. Zia thanked the stars for their light, and the fact that their ship had real windows and wasn't reliant on viewscreens.

She'd seen it first. The starlight itself began to dim. The debris field was suddenly looming over them, much closer than it should have been as they'd drifted unpowered toward it. It was impossible. Unless the great black nothing had steered toward them itself.

As Zia watched, the window went dark, leaving them with nothing but a sick orange from the comms channel as it sprang to life, filling the cabin with a hard-edged roar of white noise. Then the light from even that dimmed, as the darkness came through the window and filled the cabin like a heavy, black gas being poured into a tank.

Fumbling in total blackness, Zia called for Ivanhoe and Fathead. At first her crew replied and Zia walked and stumbled, arms outstretched, the small flight deck impossibly large in the dark. Then the voices stopped. Zia realized then that there had been three responses: Ivanhoe and Fathead... and Dathan.

As her eyes adjusted, Zia could make out the comms deck ahead of her. The shadows seemed to move at her peripheral vision, black-on-black shapes darting out of sight as she turned her head.

And then a new voice.

Ida scratched his chin and looked at Zia. "The voice," he said, waiting a moment as Zia tilted her head quizzically. "You sure it was him?"

"On the ship?" she asked. "I know my own father's voice."

Ida nodded.

"Y'know," she continued, "the very worst thing is that part of me wanted to go."

Ida glanced at her. She sat cross-legged on the bed, her hands twisting at the sheets beneath her. Ida thought back to his own temptation on board the *Coast City*, in the lifetime ago before Zia had even arrived.

Zia sighed. "D'ya think it was really him?"

Ida didn't answer for a long time. "It's either him, or something pretending to be him. Whatever it—they—are, they can get into our heads, into our minds."

"You've seen 'em too?"

Ida nodded. "I saw someone who was once very close to me."

"Dead?"

"Yes, she's dead."

They sat in silence for a while. The shadows under the bed didn't move.

"I couldn't go," said Zia eventually.

"No," said Ida. "Me neither."

"He said he'd forgive me if I came."

Ida looked up. "Forgive you for what?"

But Zia wouldn't meet his eye.

39

Quicker than Ida expected, Zia changed the subject. "What makes us so damned special?"

"What do you mean?"

Zia shifted on the bed. She let go of the bunched-up sheets and began gesturing with her hands as she spoke. It was good, Ida thought. She was focusing on solutions, not problems. First step: gather data.

"They... she... *it*—whatever 'it' is—is taking people. The marines, the commandant, everyone on this fucked-up space station. Fathead, Ivanhoe, Dathan. And who knows who else. How far does this go? How many people have vanished in Fleetspace?"

Ida frowned. "And this station—or rather, this system—is at the center of it. Must be. Shadow is an unusual star, unique. Can't be a coincidence. But more important, what are people being taken for? There must be a reason."

They fell into silence. For once, Ida didn't miss the static roar from the space radio.

Zia unfolded her legs and lay down. She looked at the ceiling, and then crossed her arms behind her head.

"So did all those fancy heroics really happen?" Zia asked.

Ida coughed, his train of thought broken. "Tau Retore? Yes," he said, looking at her. "It really happened."

"So if you saved an entire planet from the Spiders, how does something like that get erased from Fleet records? What I heard, the war isn't exactly going as planned. Win like that would be shouted to the heavens."

Ida felt the panic rise in his chest. Just a twitch, just enough to remind him that, weirdness aboard the good ship *Coast City* aside, there was plenty else wrong with the universe.

Unless, of course, they were connected. Another unlikely coincidence.

Zia sat up and leaned forward. "No, I'm serious. Damn thing never happened. I ain't never heard of it, and none of my crew have either. It's just smoke in the wind."

"What do you mean? How do you know?"

Zia raised an eyebrow. "I checked. We were given a crew list of the station when our stop was approved. It was a long flight. I looked you up."

"What did you find, exactly?"

Zia shook her head. "Nothing, is what. There ain't nothing recorded. No name, no rank. No record. Nothing at all. You, my fine Cap'n, don't even exist."

Ida laughed, but the laugh died and he stared at the floor. Zia shook her head again. "But…"

"But?"

"Well, here you are." said Zia.

"Here I am," said Ida, throwing his hands open. "Stuck out in the back end of nowhere, surrounded by shadows and ghosts. Tau Retore happened, and then I was sent here."

Zia blew out a lungful of air between pursed lips. "And so was I…"

Ida straightened in his chair. "You were sent here? I thought you came of your own free will?"

"Well, yeah, but only because we were fed the readings on the slowrock field. If those readings didn't show a whole damn gold mine floating out in this fucked-up system, I wouldn't be here."

"So you and me—"

Zia nodded. "Yep."

"We were both sent here."

"Yep."

"For a reason."

"Yep."

Ida stretched his arms in front of him, turning his palms inside out and cracking his interlocked fingers. Then a thought occurred. A connection made, perhaps.

"I'm not the only one who seems to have dropped out of the history books," he said.

"What do you mean?"

Ida spun the chair around slowly until he was facing the table. There sat the space radio, narrow and silver, the blue light now a dead black dot on the front of its shiny casing.

"I made contact with someone with this thing, just before you arrived. Caught a signal and then found a voice."

"And?"

"And she didn't exist. The transmission was from a thousand years ago and had been bouncing around subspace ever since. The sender was a cosmonaut, mid-twentieth century. Except not one that ever existed."

"Subspace?" There was something in Zia's voice that made Ida want to sit very still, very still indeed.

"Ah… yes. Some malfunction, the set could pick up—"

"God*damn* it, Ida, you've been listening to a voice from fucking *subspace*?"

Ida turned the chair, surprised at Zia's outburst. But there was something else too, that cold fear again, somewhere in his middle. He could feel his heart kick up a gear and he watched Zia. She was sitting up on the bed again, her eyes wide.

Zia swore. "Jesus, Ida, don't you *know* about subspace? Didn't the Fleet send you a fucking memo?"

"I know subspace frequencies are illegal, but—"

"Holy crap. You know why they're illegal?"

"Um." Ida's breathing was fast and shallow. The quiet, creeping fear grew and grew and grew. His mind tripped over memories, trying desperately to claw back what he'd learned at the academy, searching for answers, facts that he felt he should know but that he now realized hadn't been taught by the Fleet, not to him, not to anyone.

The stories. The half-remembered whispers about subspace, about how it was dangerous. About what lurked below. Hellspace.

"Um," he said again. His throat was dry.

Zia sighed and slouched back on the bed, shaking her head. "Things," she said, like that explained everything.

Ida let out a breath and blinked. "Things?"

"Damn *it*." Zia rubbed her forehead. "There are things in subspace. Bad things. You could say they lived there, but they're not alive, not really. They live in subspace and deeper too. Hellspace. *Fuck*."

Ida swallowed. His throat felt tight, the sound so terribly loud in his ears.

Hellspace.

He rolled the word around in his head, trying to convince himself that this conversation wasn't happening.

"You've been hanging out in too many colonial bars, Ms. Hollywood," he said quietly, but he knew he was out of his depth.

She turned her head to look at him. "Don't you get it?"

"Get what?"

"Subspace is illegal because the *things* that live in it got out once. Followed a signal. Back in the early days of the Fleet, before the Spiders. Took everything we had to push them back, and then subspace was closed off. No one went near."

Ida stared at her, his mind racing. Then he shook his head and laughed—a nervous reaction, the laugh of a man afraid, one that quickly died in his throat. He closed his eyes and held up a hand.

"And how do you know this, exactly? I'm an officer of the Fleet and even I don't know—"

"Look," said Zia, and Ida opened his eyes. She was leaning forward, toward him. "Someone like me, I get to see a lot of things. *Hear* a lot of things. There's a whole lot of people, all of them want a piece—of me, of my money, everything. They want my ship, they want to be friends, business partners, lovers. When you're rich and you're famous, then doors get opened, you get to go places most people don't, not even officers of the Fleet. And you're told things, shown things."

Ida shook his head. "Told things?"

"You'd be amazed at how willing people are to talk when they think they can impress someone like me, thinking it can get them *in*, get them close. Trust me when I say that those stories about subspace and what lives there are all true."

Ida sighed. He believed her. And if what Zia said was true, then the stories, the rumors, about subspace and hellspace, they didn't even cover the half of it. There was something out there. Something the Fleet didn't want anybody to know about. Something that, Ida thought, was now stirring.

"What if they're coming back?" he asked. "What if someone made contact again and what if they're following the signal back out?"

"Then we're all dead," said Zia.

40

With only a fraction of operational personnel on board, the *Coast City*'s hangar was a rare hive of activity, the crew busying themselves with familiar routines and protocols, trying to keep order, control. It was the Fleet's way. In the middle of a difficult and protracted war, this is what you did. You carried on, and maybe you told yourself that the final transport was already on the way, having headed out early, as soon as the lightspeed link had gone down.

Maybe. But until it arrived, the crew went about their duties, running the hangar bay and readying the station's shuttle for its routine patrol of the system.

The *Magenta* was illuminated from underneath by landing lights, and from their position behind a row of empty loading pallets, Ida and Zia could see two crew members sitting at the flight controls.

Ida and Zia had a plan.

In his cabin, they'd patched into the comm channel between the bridge and the hangar and listened to the chatter between the two for nearly half a cycle before heading down to the hangar. Most of the talk had been the usual system updates and routine checks, although they learned that two crew members who were due on duty were not responding to calls and couldn't be found on the hub. More taken.

They waited, listening, until the *Coast City* cycled into night. The dark was dangerous, the domain of Izanami—the thing from subspace, Ida now knew. But they needed to risk it, because they had to get to the *Magenta*. Their objective was clear.

The debris field.

They'd pored over data from Zia's wrist computer. The field density readings originally supplied by the Fleet said the slowrocks were pure lucanol—a gold mine, as Zia had said, but one that was impossible. As Zia had seen firsthand, whatever was floating out on the other side of Shadow wasn't a cluster of asteroids at all, but something regular, artificial: a single solid object, one that had moved toward the *Bloom County* like it was being piloted.

Piloted… like a ship. Another coincidence too far. The answers lay aboard it. Ida knew it and Zia knew it and they also knew they had to get back there. They were clean out of options on the station.

They couldn't take the *Bloom County*, not without people noticing. And Zia had refused to get back on board it. But the *Magenta* was due to make its regular, routine flight. If they could get on board and bide their time as it went about its patrol, they could take the ship over and be at the target before anyone knew about it. Before Izanami knew what they were doing.

Space Piracy 101: Secrete yourselves on board, wait for the ship to blast off, count to a thousand, and, bingo, hijack. It was so simple, it might just work.

Zia was restless, and Ida didn't blame her. They'd been crouched behind the loading trays for more than an hour now. Ida flexed his fingers around the Yuri-G's molded grip; he looked back at the shuttle.

"Here we go," he whispered.

Two hangar crewmen walked down the *Magenta*'s rear ramp and headed toward the stairs leading to the control room, a large cuboid box that hung on one side of the bay. They looked tense, anxious, and as they walked in silence they both glanced around, into the shadows that draped the far corners of the hangar. The *Coast City*'s crew was holding on, but only just. The Fleet's training was good.

"Preflight routine complete," said Ida into Zia's ear. "The shuttle will be empty for less than an hour."

Zia nodded. Ida watched the hangar crew move up the stairs and into the control room. After disappearing around a door, they appeared briefly at the main window as they completed their check, then turned and walked out of view. Just to be sure, Ida counted to twenty, but nobody reappeared on the stairs.

"Go!"

Zia led the way, crawling around the side of the loader and then ducking under the superficial railing that separated the cargo pads from the shuttle landing pad. She dropped the three-foot step silently, and ran at a crouch to hide behind the *Magenta*'s front landing gear. She waited a count of three, just like Ida had told her, and then scrambled to the rear of the craft and up the exit ramp.

Ida counted to three himself, and then followed her pattern— railing, check; landing gear, check; exit ramp, and on.

Time to fly.

She fell asleep in the power conduit. Pressed against her, Ida watched as her gentle breathing bounced a strand of her hair against her lips. He hoped she wasn't dreaming.

They'd been in the conduit hatch for only another twenty minutes before Ida heard the *Magenta*'s crew climb the ramp and fire up the craft. Ida had tried to count the footfalls on the floor above their heads, but he hadn't been expecting so many and had lost count. It sounded like a whole squad of marines. Ida knew that this was standard, in case the *Magenta* was required to board any other craft in the vicinity, but with the *Coast City* at such reduced manpower and the Shadow system devoid of other activity, Ida was surprised they kept to the book. With King still locked away in the ready room, and without orders to the contrary, Ida imagined the marine commander on duty was just trying to do his job as usual.

The *Magenta*'s orbit would be short. It was pure routine. A single perfunctory sweep of the station's immediate vicinity, maybe out to a quarter of a million klicks. It crossed Ida's mind that the shuttle might not even be fully fueled, without enough energy to get them to the debris field on the other side of Shadow. But if everything was being run to routine, then there was no reason to suspect the shuttle didn't have a full complement of power cells loaded. More than enough to get them halfway to Earth, let alone a few million klicks around to the far side of the sun.

Ida pressed an ear against the metal panel beside him. The shuttle was small with disproportionately large engines, and every part of the ship was a perfect sounding board. He listened, and with a lifetime's expertise judged the engine throttle. It was slowing, imperceptibly at first, the drone of the drive system lowering in pitch as the shuttle approached the far side of its orbit. There the *Magenta* would pause, like a ball at the top of a throw, and then curve a graceful arc back around to the other side of the *Coast City*. The edge of the orbit was their target. It was nearly time.

He nudged Zia, and she jerked awake. He shushed her and raised the Yuri-G as much as he could in the cramped compartment.

"Did you dream?" he asked, hooking fingers into the webbed underside of the floor panel that was their temporary ceiling.

"No," she said, but she said it too quickly and Ida guessed it was a lie.

The short corridor that connected the shuttle's hold to the bridge was empty. The flight was running as normal: marines strapped into their flight harnesses in the troop compartment next to the hold, the four crew members (pilot and copilot, navigator and commander) in the cockpit flying the shuttle around the preset course, mostly on automatic, mostly in silence.

Ida crept down the corridor. The cockpit door was open, and he could see the back of the pilot and copilot's Flyeye helmets. The commander's chair was just out of sight, as was the navigator's.

Zia moved silently back along the corridor, toward the troop compartment. Ida glanced over his shoulder and nodded, and then watched as she gingerly pressed the hatch lock. The troop compartment would now open only from the outside, but they probably had only a minute before one of the marines on the other side noticed the lock status light change color. Zia returned to her position behind Ida and tapped his shoulder.

Eyes front, Ida held up a hand, three fingers extended. At an even pace, he dropped them one by one; when his fist was closed, he darted forward, Zia on his tail.

He burst into the cockpit so quickly that at first only the commander and navigator registered his entrance. Both reacted in the same way, moving quickly to leave their posts and confront the intruder, but Ida held the Yuri-G in front of him and they both gently sank back into their seats, hands raised in surrender. Zia saw the pilot twist his head around and jumped forward, pulling the commander's pistol from his belt as she passed him and moving around to stand directly in front of the freestanding control console, in the gap between it and the forward viewscreen.

"Everybody stand for the man with the gun in his hand!" she said, waving her own weapon at the pilot and copilot.

With Zia covering the cabin, Ida lowered the Yuri-G to a more comfortable position to cover the commander and navigator, now standing as Zia had instructed.

"This is treason," the commander said, looking Ida up and down. Ida recognized him from the groups that used to congregate back in the canteen. A noncommissioned officer—he couldn't remember the name—but one who had taken pleasure in sending sour looks over to Ida when they were in the same room. Ida squeezed the grip of the Yuri-G just that little bit harder.

"Technically, you're right. But you might just thank me later." Ida moved around the chairs at a sidestep so he was standing in front of the navigator. He wiggled the end of his gun, gesturing to the pair to return to their seats. He heard the Flyeyes move behind him, Zia having followed his lead.

"Navigator, you've got some new coordinates."

* * *

The copilot saw it first. They'd reached the approximate location recorded on Zia's wrist computer; dead ahead the violet disk of Shadow burned in the center of the viewscreen. As Ida watched tendrils of blackness curl from the pale star's horizon, he was grateful the *Magenta* had no actual windows.

And there it was: in the middle of the sun's disk, impossibly close, a black mark that could have been a sunspot if Shadow had had any blemishes at all on its perfect purple skin. Ida followed the copilot's pointed finger and watched with growing dread as the black shape steadily grew in size. Like it was coming out of the star itself.

The pilot had his eyes glued to the forward sensor reading, Zia standing at his shoulder. There, at least, the object was as large as life. Dead ahead.

"Is that another ship?" asked the *Magenta*'s commander. Ida glanced at the man and scratched his own temple with the barrel of the Yuri-G, safety on, before turning back to the screen.

The safety had been on the gun for a while now. Ida was pleased that the crew had offered only a token resistance. You didn't argue with a man holding a Yuri-G. The marines locked in their troop compartment had been somewhat more vocal, at least until Zia had told the commander in no uncertain terms to kill the comm link with them. The manifest scanner on the control desk showed the life signs of ten marines sitting in their harnesses along each wall, one standing by the door, and one pacing up and down.

"Now what?" The shuttle commander drummed his fingers on the arm of his chair behind Ida.

"We get close, we find out what that thing is," said Zia.

The commander snorted. "That's some plan, lady."

Ida turned back to the screen. "The best defense is a good offense. Didn't they teach you anything at the Fleet academy?"

The pilot slowed the *Magenta*. The black wedge ahead of them got larger, nothing but a deep silhouette against the star behind. Then he leaned forward over the control desk and flicked a couple of switches. "Manifest failure, sir."

The commander creaked forward in his chair, but Ida waved at him to sit back. Ida stood over the pilot's shoulder and glanced over the screens.

"Report, pilot."

"Sir… ah, I mean…"

The commander began drumming his fingers on his chair again. "Go ahead, pilot," he said.

"Tracing the fault now, sir. Manifest scanner is misreporting crew complement."

Zia stepped forward to look at the pilot's display, upside down, from the other side of the console. She and Ida exchanged a look.

Ida looked at the small square display panel set into the desk that provided the standard shuttle system report. Energy reserve, engine throttle, and core temperature, a dozen other mysterious technical parameters that Ida once understood but had long since lost interest in. As on the *Coast City*, the ship's crew were counted among its equipment and assets.

The troop compartment was showing as empty. Where twelve life signs had showed as bright orange dots just a few moments before, the diagrammatic representation of the harnesses showed them all to be empty. Gone also were the two others who had been moving around.

An alarm chimed, and the pilot flicked another switch. The status screen refreshed, but the manifest report stayed the same.

"Can't trace any computer fault, sir. Trying again."

Ida felt his skin grow cold. "Don't bother," he said. "That's not a fault. That's the manifest report."

Zia swore. The commander leapt out of his chair and pulled on Ida's shoulder, ignoring his own gun held in Zia's rising arm.

"Do you know what's going on, Captain Cleveland?"

Ida licked his dry lips and glanced at the viewscreen. Shadow was nearly all gone, obscured by the black nothing.

Another alarm pierced the silence, loud enough for everyone on the bridge to jump. The commander grabbed Ida's arm instinctively, but Ida threw him off and pushed him back into his chair. The commander made to stand again, but found the hot end of the

Yuri-G in his face, the red light in the barrel indicating that the safety was now off.

The high, bell-like alert sounded again. Ida looked at the ceiling.

"U-Star *Magenta*, stand down and prepare for boarding. Do not deviate from your present heading or we will open fire."

The voice that came over the ship-to-ship was female, the accent American. Ida spun around and leaned on the control desk to stare at the viewscreen. There was nothing but an empty black void, lit violet white at the edges of the screen.

The alarm sounded a third time.

"Proximity alert, Commander," said the pilot, and the commander, navigator, Ida, and Zia all crowded the pilot's position. The sensory display showed the object ahead, close enough now to get a better reading: an oblong outline, with a set of three narrow trapezoids at one of the short ends. The shape was distinctive, recognizable to any Fleet personnel.

"What is it?" Zia looked at Ida.

Ida stood and pointed at the forward viewscreen. As the object blotted out the light of Shadow behind it, it came into sharp relief. It was metallic, silver, and very close, filling the entire forward view. "It's a U-Star. A Destroyer."

The ship-to-ship sprang into life again.

"U-Star *Magenta*, boarding in two minutes. Present yourselves at the loading bay air lock immediately, seated with hands on heads. Failure to comply will result in the use of lethal force."

The *Magenta*'s commander swung back into his chair and snapped on the personal comm panel in the arm.

"This is Commander Van Buren of the U-Star *Magenta*. You will identify yourselves."

There was a pause, but the comm channel stayed open. Very faintly, at the edge of hearing, there was a rustle, something like dry paper being crushed or someone walking on small pebbles. Or static, white noise, the sound of nothing. The sound of subspace.

"U-Star *Magenta*, this is Commodore Manutius of the U-Star *Carcosa*. You will stand down and prepare for boarding in one minute."

"Jesus Christ have mercy on our souls," Ida whispered.

Zia's eyes were wide. "Ida, what is it?"

Ida looked at Zia, and then the others on the bridge.

"That's not Manutius, and that's not the *Carcosa*. It can't be."

The commander and navigator exchanged an uncertain look. Zia stepped up and stared into Ida's eyes.

"How do you know?" she asked.

"Because," Ida said, "the *Carcosa* was lost with all hands."

"What? When?"

"At Tau Retore. The *Carcosa* was my ship."

41

They were kept in darkness for a long time. There was no need for hoods or blindfolds. As soon as the *Carcosa* had docked and its marines stormed the *Magenta*, the lights were killed. Standard Fleet procedure—the marines could all see in their helmets, but the prisoners were blind. In a way it was worse than being hooded, because with eyes wide in the total dark, the blackness became almost a physical object. It loomed right into your face, giving you the feeling you were about to walk into something very hard and very painful.

That was the idea. At the end of a march through darkness, prisoners would be in a state of near-panic. Considering most of the Fleet's human prisoners were civilians, it worked too. Captured Fleet troops were unusual, and for Ida and the crew of the *Magenta*, it was unpleasant but quite bearable if you knew what to do. Except as far as Ida and Zia were concerned, the darkness itself was dangerous, and both of them kept their eyes screwed tight.

Ida had got only a glimpse of the boarding marines. They were what he expected, helmeted and armored, although he wasn't sure if it was his imagination or whether there was something else there, something dark, misty, smokelike; shadows that moved with the men.

When the lights came on, Ida needed a few moments to adjust to the glare. Sitting cross-legged on a hard ceramic floor, Ida guessed before he opened his eyes that the flare of lights meant that they were now in the holding cages. He lowered his hands from behind his head and looked around.

Zia was sitting immediately on his left, the commander, navigator, and two pilots behind them. They were sitting in the middle of a cube made of a fine wire mesh, big enough to stand in and walk around comfortably with a dozen people in it. But if you strayed too close to the mesh, you could hear an unsettling buzzing coming from the wire. The walls of a standard Fleet holding cube were not something you would want to touch.

Their cube sat in a large, hangarlike room, and was just one of fifty identical cages set in a regular grid, filling the space. The holding cells of a large U-Star. Ida knew the design well. It looked like half the cages were occupied, a sea of blue and olive figures, some standing, most sitting, blinking as they adjusted to the lights. All Fleet personnel.

"So they got you in the end, huh?"

Ida turned at the voice. The next cube along the grid was three meters away, and was occupied by a full dozen. Hands on hips, Carter stood as close to the wire wall as he could. He shook his head, like a teacher disappointed with a problem student yet again.

Ida unfolded himself and stood quickly. "Carter, you're alive?" He ran his eyes over the other occupants of the cage. "Serra! Your whole squad?"

Carter nodded, and behind him, Serra's face broke into a grin. Carter looked back over his squad, and when he turned back to Ida, his smile curled up at the corners. He really seemed pleased to see Ida. Or, Ida thought, pleased to see his nemesis stuck in the same position he was.

"All but DeJohn," said the marine. He nodded, indicating the other cages. "They're keeping about half of us here."

Zia paced their cage, looking out at the other cubes. Ida knew what she was looking for.

"No sign?"

Zia's pace increased. She swore impatiently. "Nothing."

"They were here," said Carter.

Zia stepped up close to the wire next to Ida. "Were? You've seen them?"

"Your crew? You betcha. They were taken out a while ago. Look." He pointed.

Between the holding cubes and the far wall of the room was a gap of twenty meters, an assembly ground where prisoners were brought in and sorted—in the dark—into their cube groups. The far wall had a large double door, the very one Ida's group had been marched through. This had now opened again, and a group of people walked in. Ida's jaw loosened as he watched.

They didn't really walk. They *glided*, their movements somehow in time with the blinking of Ida's eyelids. One moment they were ten meters away, the next five, and yet they didn't seem to be moving at all. Their edges were blurry and seemed to streak away to the left, like a faint smoke trail being pulled in a nonexistent wind, like the shadow figures he'd seen on the station—like the marines who had boarded the *Magenta*. Except these were no shadows; they were people.

In single file, ten figures—eight men and two women—traveled across the assembly space.

Carter folded his arms as he watched. "Looks like they're coming to get some more."

As the people approached, their forms shimmered like the guttering flame of the lighter in Ida's pocket. Ida found himself stepping back from the wall of the cage. Were they still people at all?

They were all Fleet marines. None of Zia's missing crew were among them.

Ida looked at Carter, but the marine just shook his head. Serra caught Ida's eye, and she nodded, just slightly before quickly looking away. Ida frowned, unsure what she was trying to tell him.

The figures separated, each heading toward a different cube, including Ida's. As the shadow-man approached, Ida could read the name tag stitched onto the marine's fatigues.

"Garfield? Garfield, it's me, Cleveland? Remember?"

The marine that had been Garfield made no indication he knew Ida was there. Close up, he looked as real as anyone, except for an odd halo of darkness that seemed to outline him, a shadow clinging to his figure.

Zia joined Ida at the wire, peering closely at the marine.

"What the hell's happened to them?"

Ida stood. "Carter?"

Carter was sitting on the floor again, next to Serra. A shadow-man had gone to their cage too, and was now standing, waiting for something.

"Every now and then they take people out," he said. "Sometimes they come back, and when they do, they're like this. Sometimes we don't see them again."

"What about the crew of this U-Star?"

"What crew? We haven't seen nobody."

"The commodore spoke to us, on board the shuttle."

"You came here by shuttle?"

Behind Ida, Commander Van Buren laughed. "Not by choice."

Ida sighed, but Van Buren told Carter about the hijacking.

Carter laughed. "The resourceful Captain Cleveland. Maybe you really are a hero."

Ida ignored him. "What did you see on the station, marine?" he asked.

Carter stopped laughing, and the smile dropped from his face. "What?"

"Back on the station," said Ida, "I saw someone... someone I knew. Someone I know is dead. She spoke to me, even."

Carter's eyes widened.

Zia stepped forward. "So did I."

Ida smiled at Carter. "So, who did you see? What sent you to the infirmary for a whole cycle?"

"I don't think that's your business, *sir*."

"Come on!" Ida slapped his arms against the sides of his legs in frustration. "You may not have noticed, but we're kinda in trouble here."

Carter sat back down. Ida looked around and realized the shadow-men had vanished. He turned, looking around his cage. The two pilots from the *Magenta* had gone, leaving him and Zia with Van Buren and the navigator. In Carter's cage, half of the dozen prisoners had vanished. Ida was pleased to see Serra was still there. She sat cross-legged on the floor, her eyes closed, a smile playing over her lips. She was a psi-marine. Maybe she'd gone too, inside her head.

Ida whistled. "Hey, listen to me. You know where we are? We're on a ghost ship, marine. The U-Star *Carcosa*. That's a ship I happen to know very well. It was my ship, the one that didn't make it through quickspace when we hit Tau Retore."

Carter shuffled on the hard floor. "Didn't you say the *Boston Brand* was your ship?"

Ida shook his head. "I was on the *Boston Brand*, but I was assigned to the *Carcosa*. Commodore Manutius and I swapped commands for our attack. The *Boston Brand* had a few tricks the *Carcosa* didn't, and I wanted the *Boston Brand* out in front."

Zia's eyes widened. "So if you'd stayed on your own ship—"

"Yes," said Ida. He cast his eye over the interior of the hangar they were now in. "If I had stayed on the *Carcosa*, I'd be dead. Or not, as the case may be."

He raised his hand to the cage wall and felt the tingle of the charge play across his palm.

"Only delaying the inevitable," said Carter quietly. Ida pulled his hand away from the wall of the cage and turned to the marine. Sitting on the floor behind him, Serra laughed and opened her eyes.

"You okay, marine?" asked Ida.

Serra nodded. Carter uncurled himself to turn around, and peered into her face. Serra smiled again.

"It's okay," she said. "She won't get it."

Carter jerked back in surprise. "What?"

"The shadow demon. She thinks she has her prize within her grasp, but she doesn't."

Carter leaned forward and snapped his fingers in front of Serra's face. "Hey! Snap out of it. You've been funny since we got here."

Serra blinked, and her smile dropped away. She scooted back on her hands, shaking her head.

"She's here," she said, and then she screamed, and then the lights went out.

42

The dark was absolute, abyssal. Around him, Ida heard the other prisoners murmur and move in their cages.

"What's going on?" Zia at his shoulder.

"No clue." Carter in the other cage. From the same direction, Serra's breathing, quick, fearful.

Ida held his breath as he heard something else. Footfalls. He stood as still as he could, trying to locate the sound in the dark. Someone was walking between their cage and the one holding Carter and Serra's group.

"Hello?" His voice sounded uncomfortably loud. The footsteps continued, coming around to the front of his cage.

"Who is it?" Zia had her hand on the small of his back. Ida shook his head, then realized nobody could see him.

"Serra? You with us?"

"Yes." Her voice came softly from the other cage.

"Who's here? Izanami?" Perhaps Serra knew about her. Perhaps Izanami had made contact with her, a psi-marine. Perhaps Izanami had followed the signal Serra's mind had sent out into the dark.

Ida's thoughts turned to another kind of signal. Was... was he responsible?

"Who's Izanami?" asked Carter, breaking Ida's train of thought. Ida heard the squeak of Carter's boots and the rustle of his uniform as he stood up.

The footsteps were soft, rubbery, accompanied by a sliding sound, like someone wearing something bulky.

Ida turned over his shoulder. "Van Buren?"

"I'm here. Koch?"

The *Magenta*'s navigator confirmed he was still with them.

The footsteps stopped, right in front of them. Ida balled his hands into fists, not sure where to plant them and not sure there would be anything physical to hit. He closed his eyes to blot out the disorienting depth of the dark around them and concentrated on the sounds instead.

The buzzing of the cage's energized mesh walls increased gradually, like someone turning the gain of an antenna up. As the pitch increased, it began to break up into rough noise. White noise, like static, the rolling of an ocean. Ida felt his heart leap at the familiar sound.

The sound of—

There was a click, and then, "Ida."

A voice, far away but right in front of him. Tinny, thin, coming through an old-fashioned speaker. A female voice, accented. A voice brushed with interference.

Ida let out his held breath and choked in the process. He swallowed the ball of spit quickly.

"Ludmila?"

A ghost ship filled with... ghosts.

"Come," said Ludmila.

Ida opened his eyes. There was a light, yellowish orange, in front of him. He blinked and watched as the light moved, lighting up the cage. The light blinked, and then a brighter, white beam snapped on. A lantern, fixed to the left breast of the spacesuit.

Ludmila stood outside the cage, her golden visor catching enough light from her flashlight that Ida could see himself and Zia reflected in the mirrored surface, superimposed over other shapes that moved and swirled. It looked like the reflection of stars and a planet spinning beneath. The curve of the Earth.

Ida sighed. She was real, solid, a person in a spacesuit. The suit was some kind of metallic silver cloth, quilted in fat bands, with the red letters CCCP boldly printed across the chest. In one hand she held Ida's space radio, the light on the silver box a bright baby blue. With her other hand she reached forward to touch the cage. Ida watched, spellbound, as the silver fabric of her suit creased at the elbow as her arm moved, as her hand raised to show Ida the black fabric that covered the palm and underside of each finger—

Zia called out just as Ludmila's gauntlet touched the cage. There was a pop, and the entire framework of the cage flashed blue for a second. Zia flinched, but Ida stood rock still, watching himself in Ludmila's helmet.

Was there anyone there, behind the curve of the visor? Did Ludmila exist?

She withdrew her hand and turned, heading back to the holding bay entrance. "Come," she said, her voice crackling through the space radio.

Her pool of light was small but the floor was reflective enough for it to light a wide stretch of the hangar. Ida glanced over at Carter and saw the marine was watching Ludmila too. He could see her. They all could.

Ida pushed at the front of the cage. The mesh was warm and rough. He pushed again, and the door flicked open silently.

"Hey!"

Ida turned. Carter gesticulated at the cage around his group. Serra stood at his shoulder.

Zia pulled on Ida's sleeve. "We're going to need all the help we can get."

She was right.

"Ludmila!" he called. The flashlight's beam turned slowly until it was directed at them. Ida pointed at the other cage as the prisoners shielded their eyes.

"Can you release them?"

The light bobbed forward slowly. It was like she was walking against a high wind, or in low gravity. Maybe that was exactly what it was like, moving through a world you were not supposed to be in.

When she got to the cage, Ida watched as she touched the mesh. There was a flash, and Ludmila stepped back. Carter wasted no time in shoving the door open and releasing his squad.

"Come," said Ludmila. "There is not much time. The harvest has begun."

"What about the rest?" Carter gestured to the other cages that filled the holding zone. The shallow light of Ludmila's lantern caught the glittering eyes of those prisoners closest.

"We have no time," said the voice from the crackling speaker.

Carter began to protest but Ida raised his hands. "We'll come back for them. Let's just do as she says and see if we can't figure this mess out first."

He turned back to Ludmila, who was walking away at her infuriatingly slow pace. Ida, Zia, and the others followed, forming a single file as they quietly left the cells. Behind them, shouts erupted, the other prisoners protesting at being abandoned. Ida ignored them. He had no choice. None of them did.

They walked in the dark, Ludmila's lantern lighting the way, illuminating metal corridors in an eerie white yellow glow that bobbed up and down and left and right as she walked in her bulky suit. It felt like walking into a tomb, ancient and cold, except for the occasional wall panel with bright LED lights. Their footfalls were soft but they echoed oddly. It was as though the whole of the *Carcosa* had powered down to system minimum, the ghost hulk drifting toward its destination.

But it was real, all of it. It might have been dark, but it was solid. The metal floor, the walls. The same as any other Fleet U-Star. Ida touched the walls, trailing his fingers along the metal and plastic panels. Cool to the touch, as they would be on any ship. The metal was hard and shiny, with the finest of grains running horizontal to the floor. The rivets were perfect, almost seamless at the panel edges.

It was real. The *Carcosa* was part of the First Fleet Arrowhead. They'd all entered quickspace near Atoomi, and they'd all exited near Tau Retore—all, that is, except for the *Carcosa*. There was no engine failure. The ship had been taken, wholesale, as it sailed close to Izanami's domain. Ida's escape on the *Boston Brand* had been coincidental and, as he now realized, only temporary.

And Ludmila? She was right in front of him. He could reach out and touch her. He raised his arm to try but then changed his mind. She was real, as real as the passageway along which they now crept. A real person, taken a thousand years ago.

Zia's question resonated in Ida's mind: How many had been taken, and for how long? And the ultimate question—for what?

Ludmila's lantern beam diffused suddenly, and she stopped. They'd come to a larger space, a wide, low room. Ahead were a set of heavy doors. An air lock. Ludmila turned around, and Ida stared at himself and Zia and the rest of them in her golden visor. Her chest radio popped.

"This ship is now attached to the auxiliary docks of the space station. This will lead you back to it."

Zia stepped forward. "What? We can't just leave. We gotta spring the others, and find the ones they've taken away."

Ludmila said nothing. Zia's reflected face loomed as she leaned toward the cosmonaut, and then turned to Ida. Ida studied the reflection, lost in thought.

"It's not that easy, is it?" he said at last, eyes still on Ludmila's visor.

"The harvest has begun," said Ludmila. "She has enough power now to make her last moves before she returns. Time is short. We must act soon."

Carter gestured over his shoulder with a thumb. "We've got enough personnel locked away down there, and enough weapons on the station, to take this ship over from any hostile alien force, easily."

Ida watched it all in the helmet reflection.

"Ludmila?" he asked quietly. "They're not aliens, are they?"

"They are not anything," she said, the radio spitting the words out in a trebly squawk. "The Funayurei are neither alive nor dead. They are the souls of those lost at sea. They are her army. They wait, trapped like her, eager for release. And soon she will be free. She will, in turn, release her army, and her army will march."

Carter frowned. "This is no time for riddles, ma'am."

Zia exhaled softly. "Hellspace. She's talking about hellspace. That's where her army—these *Funayurei*—are."

A hundred thoughts entered Ida's head, all of them bad, all of them leading to the same conclusion.

"So that's where she takes them." He stared into the visor. "She's built an army, pulling people down from our world into hellspace. The souls of those lost at sea."

Zia caught his eye in the reflection. She looked very pale.

"I told you they were real."

Carter looked between Ida, Ludmila, and Zia. "What the hell are you talking about? Who is building an army? And what for?"

"*She* is," said Ludmila. Carter blinked and the crackling voice over the radio continued. "Izanami-no-Mikoto. She is almost here."

Ida shook his head. "But Izanami was my medic. She was on the station, looking after me."

"Shadow is *Ame-no-ukihashi*, the bridge between subspace and this universe. Here she could wait—still imprisoned, but able to move among you as her power grew."

Ida's heart raced. "How?" he asked. "How does her power grow?"

The radio clicked. "Before, she was nothing. A thing from subspace. Centuries ago she fell to the Earth and became Izanamino-Mikoto. Others of her kind followed. Then she died, leaving only an echo in subspace where her husband, Izanagi, found her. She begged him to take her back into the world. She grew angry and tried to follow Izanagi out, but he sealed the gateway, trapping her forever."

"This is some fairy tale," said Carter. He huffed and folded his arms.

"Izanami vowed revenge. To rebuild herself and escape, she needs to eat a thousand souls a day. They nourish her, provide her with the energy to cross the bridge, to return."

Silence. The space radio crackled and Ida realized the truth. He turned to the others.

"The Fleet. They're in on it—they sent me here. You were tricked into coming," he said, looking at Zia before gesturing to Carter, Serra, Van Buren, Koch. "They were sent here too, as part of their tour." He turned back to Ludmila and looked at his own reflection. "We were *all* sent by the Fleet. The Fleet, who placed this station around a very particular and unusual star." Ida rubbed his chin. "And the war isn't going so well…"

The space radio hissed and Ludmila spoke. "Izanami wields the power of subspace, if only she could be released."

"Are you out of your minds?" Carter stepped forward. "Are you saying that the Fleet sold us out to whatever it is trapped behind the star, in exchange for victory against the Spiders?"

Ida nodded. "The Psi-Marine Corps. Commandant Elbridge is from the Psi-Marine Corps. So are all the Fleet Admirals. The… whatever they are, the things that live in subspace, they escaped into the world once before, right?" He glanced at Zia. "And then the Fleet banned all subspace technology. But it was too late. They knew about what lived in subspace. They knew about Izanami."

Carter frowned. "So the Fleet cut a deal? This is insane."

"The souls she consumes become her army," said Ida. He looked up at the ceiling. "They even gave her a ship."

Zia swore, but Ida was already nodding. "And," he said, "the only Spider tech in human hands. The *Bloom County*."

Carter glanced at Ludmila. "And where does she fit in?"

Ida frowned. "The original incursion from subspace?"

Ludmila bowed her helmeted head.

"But there was no Fleet when she was taken," said Zia. "The Fleet wouldn't have been around for another, what, hundred years?"

"January the first, 2050," said Ida. "But there would have been records of the incursion—classified, but records all the same. And then the Fleet runs into trouble with the Spiders and the old project is opened up. The Psi-Marine Corps."

Ida turned to Serra. The psi-marine stood at the back of the group, her eyes downcast. She hadn't said a word since they left the cells. He remembered the odd look she gave him earlier, like she knew something.

She was smiling.

"They evacuated all of the psi-marines off the station," said Ida, taking a step toward her. "All except one."

The crackle of the space radio. "The commandant knew the plan," said Ludmila. "But he also knew that Izanami would not stop with the Spiders. She would destroy everything. All life is energy to be consumed."

Ida nodded. "So he was taken, but he made sure someone was left behind to fight. Someone with the right skills."

Serra looked up, her eyes bright in Ludmila's lantern light, but she didn't speak. Ludmila's voice crackled from behind Ida. "He ordered a psi-marine be left on board," she said. "The best psi-marine." Her helmet clicked as she turned toward Serra. "Is it ready?"

Serra nodded. "Almost."

"Good," said Ludmila.

Serra walked to the front of the group. "Come on," she said. "We need to get to the *Bloom County* before it's too late."

"The *Bloom County*?" asked Ida. Then he smiled. The only Spider tech in human hands, of course. "Right, let's go," he said, but when he turned around, there was no sign of Van Buren or Koch.

Carter cracked his knuckles. "Come on," he said, "before we disappear too."

43

"Sections Five and Six to embarkation point. Embarkation at oh-seven-oh-seven."

It was the third time the announcement had been broadcast to the crew of the *Coast City* since Ida's group had returned to the station, and it was just one of many instructions echoing over the internal comms. Ida was shocked to find the station's passageways glaringly bright, the hub alive with people—marines, Flyeyes, technicians, support staff. Everyone walking briskly in one direction. Ida knew the leftover crew of the *Coast City*—those who hadn't already been snatched by the Funayurei—must number only between fifty and one hundred, yet there appeared to be many more on the move. Such was the pace of the traffic that Ida feared they would be called out purely because they were walking slowly and uncertainly.

Ida, Zia, and Serra crouched at the corner of a side passageway as it curved away from the main thoroughfare. There was just enough cover provided by the curving wall that they could observe the main corridor without being seen. Ludmila had vanished as soon as they returned to the *Coast City*—Serra, in contact with her thanks to her remarkable abilities, telling the others that Ludmila hadn't wanted to slow them down. If the plan worked, she would meet them later. Ida asked what the plan was, exactly, but Serra just smiled. But he trusted her. He didn't have a choice.

"Here he is," said Zia. A moment later Carter was striding briskly toward them. He kept his eyes ahead and didn't slow as he approached, only turning and dropping into a crouch to scoot down the side passage when he had passed the group. They gathered around him.

"Everyone is being assembled for evacuation. They think the *Carcosa* is the last transport."

"But who are all these crew?" asked Zia. "There weren't this many when I arrived."

"They're from the *Carcosa*," said Ida. "I recognize them."

"Well, that means you're a liability," said Carter. "They'll recognize you too."

Serra shook her head. "They're not really people anymore."

"The Funayurei," said Ida, and Serra nodded.

Zia frowned. "But what are they doing? There's hundreds of them."

"Remember what Ludmila said." Ida rested his artificial knee on the floor and leaned around the curve of the passage; the knee now ached constantly, a low, dull pain. In the main corridor there was no letup in the foot traffic. Fleet personnel passed by in a near-continuous stream.

"The harvest," said Zia. "They're swarming."

Serra shuddered. "Like locusts, coming in to eat."

"Something tells me the Fleet's plan isn't going so well," said Carter.

"We have to make sure ours does, then," said Zia. She turned to Serra. "You can talk to my ship?"

Serra nodded; Carter's eyebrow went up.

"I really wish you'd tell us what was going on," he said.

"Can't risk it," she said. "I'm talking to the ship, but others may be listening."

"Well, that's just dandy. So what do you want us to do?"

Serra scanned the corridor ahead of them. "Nothing at all," she said. "Just follow my lead. Help is nearby."

"Help?" Carter asked. Serra met his eye and nodded.

"You were wrong, before," she said.

Ida pursed his lips. "Wrong?"

"There are two members of the Psi-Marine Corps left aboard."

"Two?"

Serra nodded. "Two: me and the commandant, Elbridge. And this is our battle now."

44

They resumed their journey down the corridors of the *Coast City*. They made **good** progress at first, the standard Fleet garb of the group blending in **easily** with the multitude of personnel rushing here and there. Together, the four of them looked like any other crew.

But as they got closer to their destination, it got more difficult. They started getting looks, a group of four not moving with the rest of the crew. They kept quiet, kept walking, trying to ignore the crew around them; the crew that stopped and stared, their faces hard, their outlines flaring with black light.

No, not crew. Not anymore. The Funayurei. The U-Star *Carcosa* had been plucked out of quickspace by Izanami-no-Mikoto, the crew within consumed, their souls absorbed to rebuild their demon queen, the remnants regurgitated to add to the ranks of her army of ghosts in hellspace. The things that watched them now were projections, incomplete, but growing in power along with their queen. None spoke or moved to stop Ida's group, but he couldn't help but wonder. Was Izanami watching them, through the eyes of her legion? Did she know what Serra's plan was? Could she hear what the psi-marine was saying to the *Bloom County*?

Ida scratched his cheek and noticed his hand was shaking. He risked a glance sideways at Serra, and although she kept up the pace, she was squinting again, like she was in pain. Ida imagined she was. She was a psi-marine on a ship full of the dead, talking to an alien machine intelligence while one of the devils from subspace was getting closer and closer to corporeal existence in their universe. Ida didn't want to dwell on what Serra might be hearing in her head.

They approached the service doors leading to the back of the hangar, which, they hoped, would let them slip in unobserved. Ida motioned for the others to wait around the corner of the passage as he jogged forward and reached for the control. He paused, his hand an inch away from the panel.

Carter hissed from the shadows opposite. "Problem?"

Ida's breath came out in spurts. Carter had broken his concentration. He sighed, and exhaled again, and noticed the breath gathering in front of his face in a great white cloud.

The temperature was dropping. Fast. Ida's knee protested, and he gasped in pain, then pressed his palm against the bulkhead control.

The door opened. The hangar beyond was dark, and a cold breeze came from within. It ruffled Ida's hair as he looked down. Something as light as anything tapped at his boots.

"Please tell me you can see this," he said, his eyes fixed on the floor. The breeze from the hangar carried with it big leaflike flakes of red paint, shiny white on one side, desiccated, like they'd peeled off an old barn in a hot summer long ago.

Ida closed his eyes, and Astrid's image loomed behind his closed lids, so he opened them again.

"See what?" asked Carter. He joined Ida and looked at the floor, but it was clear he could see nothing.

Ida closed his eyes and felt a hand on his.

"She's pulling images from your mind," said Serra. "She sees the dead in all of us. They're just more lost souls for her to use against us. Whatever you see, it comes from within."

Ida opened his eyes and looked at the floor. There was no paint from the barn. He looked up and Serra nodded. Behind her, Zia had her arms wrapped tightly across her front, shaking her head slowly. If he had seen a reflection of a lost summer, Ida wondered what it was that Zia had been shown just now.

Ida kicked at nothing on the floor and took a deep breath.

"Come on," he said, and he went through the door.

45

Ida stepped into the *Coast City*'s hangar, the others close behind. The space was lit in an eerie purple twilight, which Ida had thought was the station's fritzed environment controls, but which he now knew was the same color as the light of Shadow, the light that would fuck you up, penetrating the supposedly shielded U-Star along with the interference on the comms and the roar of subspace, flooding the corners of the station like a ship taking on water. As Ida blinked, the edges of the hangar flickered with black shapes; darkness that swam, darkness that *watched*. The souls lost at sea. The Funayurei.

Ahead, the two shuttle bays were occupied—the *Magenta*, nearest, and, beyond, the *Bloom County*, crouched on the cradle of Spider legs. And in the cavernous space between the two craft was *her*.

Izanami sat on a great pyramid of red, brown, and olive green. At first it was just a tangled collection of shapes and colors, but as he got closer in the dim light Ida could make out an arm, a leg, a head, all clad in the scraps of Fleet uniform and soaked in blood. It was a pile of corpses, Ida realized, torn apart. The empty, discarded husks of those taken by the demon queen.

Izanami was still clad in white, but the medic's tunic was now a long flowing robe. Her hair was tied back, and across her chest was the black strap of a sword, the long red handle visible over her right shoulder. She sat at the apex of the corpse pile, ten meters from the hangar floor. Her robe was immaculate, and her eyes were burning blue coals, energy coursing out of them like smoke in the cold, still air.

"Welcome, my captain," she said, smiling.

Ida tore his eyes from her and glanced around the hangar. "There's no one else here," he said to Serra. "If you were expecting help—"

Izanami's laugh interrupted him. At the edge of the hangar, the dancing shadows parted and DeJohn stepped forward, his hands resting on the shoulders of two men shuffling along beside him. The pair stared straight ahead, their arms by their sides, their faces slack, though their eyes were moving. They were caught, trapped by Izanami's will.

It was Provost Marshal King, and another man: older, his hair gray but full, small circular glasses still clinging to his face. The commandant of the *Coast City*, Price Elbridge.

DeJohn directed them to the front of the stack of bodies, then pushed them to their knees. He stood, swaying, his bulging bloodshot eyes staring somewhere into the space between him and his queen, a thick tentacle of drool escaping his slack jaw to pool on the floor.

King looked up at Ida and then at Serra, who stepped toward him. DeJohn jerked around, lurching toward her like a zombie. Serra stopped where she was, her eyes locked with the provost marshal's.

"No farther, psi-marine," said Izanami from her corpse throne.

Serra tilted her head at DeJohn. The marine rocked on his heels, seemingly unaware of his surroundings.

"What happened to him?"

"I was promised the best," said Izanami, "but this man was weak. He broke easily." She looked down at the humans below her. "But he still has limited use."

"Promised the best?" asked Ida. In the gloom on the other side of the hangar, he could see small yellow lights flickering inside the *Bloom County*'s flight deck. Serra was quiet and so was the ship, but he knew they were talking. He knew he had to play for time. "I can't speak for the others, but I think you got the bad end of the deal. I'm a washed-up captain with a robot knee. I should be a damn colonel, at my age."

Izanami laughed. "Oh, Ida, my dear, handsome Ida, war hero and space captain. My poor, poor, Ida."

The demon's smile vanished, and this time the flamelike radiance from her eyes seemed to spread out around her, enveloping her in a glowing, curling halo of blue fire, her hair and the trailing ends of her white robes billowing out around her.

"But you *are* the best. Your Fleet Admiral has done well." She pointed to the group one by one. "The best marine in the Fleet—Charlie Carter, who won the Fleet Medal for services rendered, who obeyed his orders and betrayed those he loved. Carmina Serra, the best psi-marine in the corps, her battle sense beyond the knowledge of even the Fleet Admiral himself, though her own power scares her, stunts her potential.

"The Fleet's best officer, Abraham Idaho Cleveland, and his ship, the *Carcosa*. A man who saved a planet even when it meant the death of those he loved, an officer never promoted, because the Fleet were desperate to keep him on the front lines, where the war was being fought and lost."

Izanami's smile returned. "And the final prize, Zia Hollywood, lost in space, running from her past in her remarkable craft. The Spider I shall study and study until I have found its secret." She laughed again. "Oh, such prizes as these. Nothing will stop us."

Carter found his voice. "What for? Why are you here?" He glanced at Ida out of the corner of his eye. Carter was in on the game, stalling for time.

"The Fleet has bargained for its survival," said Izanami. "The Spider war goes poorly and soon all of Fleetspace will be consumed by the machine gestalt. But now the Fleet has given me my freedom. You shall lead the Funayurei, and together we will all burn in the darkness."

Carter swore. Ida shook his head. "You really think the Fleet knew what they were dealing with? They thought they could get the genie back in the bottle." He looked at the two prisoners on the floor in front of DeJohn. "But someone knew that was impossible. The commandant. He knew."

"He thought he could stop me," said Izanami. She was amused, patient. Confident. Ida felt ill. "He was sent here to oversee the bargain—the very reason this station was built. But he realized what his Fleet Admiral had not, and he fought. I took him first, but he had anticipated this. He prepared instructions for the one he knew would replace him, one who was not a psi-marine but who could perhaps learn from the messages written in a book. The marshal learned well, learned how to resist, to fight. So I destroyed the book and then I took him."

"So," said Zia, "you're gonna eat your way through the whole universe, top to bottom. And then what?"

"I am looking for my husband," said Izanami. "He will suffer for his betrayal." Izanami looked past the group, as though her husband had just walked into the hangar. "He trapped me behind the star, behind the gateway. I shall have revenge on life itself for this!"

In the *Bloom County*'s cabin, yellow lights flashed again, and Serra spoke.

"No," she said. She stepped forward and DeJohn jerked, but he seemed unable to move. He shuddered on the spot, his eyes unfocused, a quiet moan escaping his throat.

Izanami's smile vanished, and she appeared on the hangar floor. In one swift movement she drew the sword from her back and swung it forward. The tip of the blade spit electric blue in the dim light and stopped a hair from Serra's throat.

The lights inside the *Bloom County* flickered, brighter this time.

"*No farther!*" Izanami had both hands wrapped tight around the sword's handle. Serra didn't move, but she smiled. The blue flame in Izanami's eyes flared brightly.

"You are not free yet," said Serra. "The gateway can still be closed."

The commandant pulled himself awkwardly to his feet, King close behind. Izanami swept the sword in an arc toward the two men.

Serra stepped forward. Carter went to follow, but Ida grabbed his arm and pulled him back. In the dark, the *Bloom County*'s windows were filled with flickering yellow light as the machine awoke.

"You've miscalculated," Serra said. "You've put two psi-marines and a *Spider* in the same room."

Serra turned to the commandant, then to the marshal. They all took a step forward.

Izanami swept the sword back and forth, stepping backwards as the trio moved toward her. Her face was a twisted visage of hate, but there was something else. Hesitation.

Fear.

A sound filled the hangar: a roaring, mechanical and deep; pink noise and square waves and saw waves, in a pattern, repeating. The machine code of the Spiders.

The two psi-marines and the marshal stepped forward and Izanami stepped backwards, toward the *Bloom County*. Her sword was still raised but she seemed reluctant, unable, to act. Around the edges of the hangar the shadows seemed to thin, the purple light growing brighter.

Zia grabbed Ida's arm. "What are they doing?"

Serra answered, keeping her eyes fixed on the enemy. "She's not here, not fully. Izanami is still in subspace. The three of us can interfere with her projection into our universe, for a short time."

Ida glanced at the *Bloom County*. The mining legs were moving now, tapping against the hangar floor like an agitated insect, making the whole ship rock gently.

"And then what?"

"And then—"

Izanami screamed and lunged forward. Serra ducked to one side as the sword flashed past her, but Elbridge was not as fast. Izanami thrust her weapon through the commandant's chest. He staggered back and looked down at her hand pressing the hilt of the sword into his chest, as if surprised that the blade was somehow real enough to be used as a weapon. Then Izanami pulled the sword free and, even as Ida, Zia, and Carter darted forward to help, spun on her heel and sliced diagonally through King from shoulder to waist. The two men toppled over; Serra cried out and dropped to her knees, her hands pressed against the side of her head as the machine roar that filled the hangar increased in volume, the mining legs of the *Bloom County* adding to the metallic cacophony.

Something grabbed Ida and nearly lifted him off his feet as his forward momentum was checked. He swung around, one arm held fast by DeJohn. Carter lunged forward and grabbed Serra, the pair falling backwards as he pulled. Zia dodged DeJohn's other roving hand and reached for Carter, helping him drag Serra away from Izanami.

Ida dipped his head as DeJohn swung awkwardly with his other arm, like a puppet operated by a blind master. DeJohn's haymaker sailed cleanly over Ida's head as Ida threw a punch into the marine's stomach. The attack did nothing, but DeJohn overbalanced, his grip on Ida's arm loose. Ida pulled free and scrambled out of the way as the marine fell like a tree to the floor and didn't move again.

Ida spun around, fists clenched for a fight, and found himself face-to-face with Izanami.

She smiled and raised the sword above her head. Ida was lit in the burning blue of her eyes as the blade came down.

Someone screamed his name.

46

There was a flash of white light, and the roaring static snapped like a gunshot. Ida toppled backwards as something silver and cold appeared directly in front of him, pushing him back.

Ludmila.

She collapsed onto one knee, her arms raised, Izanami's blade gripped in her gauntlets, the space radio set she had been holding skittering across the hangar floor. Izanami screamed and Ludmila pushed forward against the blade, pushing to her feet.

"Now!" she said, her voice echoing from the space radio a dozen meters away. "It must be now!"

Serra moaned in pain in Carter's arms, and as Ida ran toward them, the Spider legs of the *Bloom County* thumped once, twice on the floor, the vibration nearly enough to send him tumbling again. Serra struggled to rise but then arched her back, her face distorted in pain.

"It's too much for her!" Carter yelled into Ida's ear. "Without the other two, she's on her own!"

Ida looked over his shoulder. Ludmila and Izanami were locked together. Around the hangar, the shadows spun faster and faster. Time was running out.

"Ida," said Serra. Her hands grabbed at his legs, and he quickly dropped to one knee.

"The… Spider," she said, hand flailing toward Zia's ship. "Spiders consume stellar cores. Fly it… fly it into Shadow, it'll collapse the gateway. Trap her."

She pulled again at Ida, but he ignored her. Instead, he looked up at Zia. She shook her head. "You ain't flying that thing into a star, peaches."

Serra jerked her head and hissed in pain. "No," she said. "The Spider will fly it. It just… you just need to release it… release it and it can be guided in."

Ida and Zia looked at each other. Zia was shaking her head.

Ida frowned. "Release it?"

Zia pointed at the ship. "There's a quantum dampener around the Spider's CPU, to stop its psi-fi field interfering with the ship's systems. Fleet standard unit. That must be what she means."

Serra moaned again.

Ida turned. The space radio. It lay on the floor just a few meters away. He started toward it when Zia grabbed him. He turned and pointed at the *Magenta* behind them. "Warm up the shuttle," Ida said. "Get them out of here."

"What are you going to do?"

Ida ducked forward and grabbed the radio set. The light on the front was bright blue, like the flames that haloed Ludmila and Izanami behind them. He turned and saw Izanami's blade inch closer to Ludmila's golden visor.

"Take this," he said, passing her the radio. "Serra can guide the Spider in from the shuttle."

Zia clutched the radio to her chest and was about to speak when Ida waved her off.

"Go! I'll release the dampener. *Go!*"

She nodded finally and ran back to Carter and Serra. Ida watched as Zia and Carter lifted Serra between them and carried her toward the shuttle.

Ida stood and took a breath. He was the best captain in the Fleet. He wasn't known for taking risks, but he was known for thinking outside the box. He'd saved Tau Retore, earned the Fleet Medal. And then the Fleet had erased him from history, handing him over to an entity from another dimension in exchange for victory over the Spiders.

It was time to set the record straight.

The hangar shook. Ida ran toward the *Bloom County*. As he did, Izanami pushed Ludmila to her knees, but Ludmila twisted her hands sideways and the demon's sword dropped to the floor. Ludmila fell sideways with it and Izanami turned, floating a meter from the hangar floor, her outline blazing, blue and awful.

Ida's foot hit the edge of the *Bloom County*'s ramp and he tripped, his robot knee hitting the decking, jarring his whole body. Ida yelled out, seeing his own shadow cast in front of him by the blue light, fierce and terrible behind him. He turned, and Izanami floated toward him quickly.

Behind her, Ludmila was already on her feet. She picked the sword up from where it lay. Ida blinked and she was closer, then closer again—one moment far away, the next close enough to touch, close enough to see one eye, see her face, through her smashed visor.

Close enough to push the sword through Izanami. Ludmila moved forward again, walking this time, until Ida imagined the hilt of the sword was hard against the demon's back.

Izanami reached for Ida and paused, the blade of the sword protruding cleanly through her torso, the tip stopping just short of Ida's face. There was no blood, just a faint blue light leaking from her. Izanami smiled and looked Ida in the eye, and for a moment he saw the medic he'd met an eon ago, the only friendly face in a hostile world. Then her expression darkened, and she snarled as cracks appeared across her face, and then across her body. She began to flake away, like ash from a fire. The cracks widened, a burning blue light shining through the channels, the same as the light in her eyes, the same as the light of the space radio.

Ludmila yelled and pulled the sword out, and Izanami shattered and was gone. Ludmila fell to her knees, the sword bouncing across her legs and to the floor before it too broke into a thousand shards, the pieces salting the floor before vanishing in an instant. The roar of subspace was louder than ever, meshed with the hard staccato of the Spider code. Around the edges of the hangar, the Funayurei swarmed in anger at the defeat of their queen, and under Ida's back, the *Bloom County*'s ramp bounced as the mining legs twitched and twitched again.

Ida dragged himself to where Ludmila knelt. He cradled her cracked helmet in his hands, ignoring the white pain of cold that seared his palms. He watched his reflection in the part of the golden visor that was intact, and met her eye through the part that was broken. He fumbled for the helmet's catch, his fingers on fire. Finally, the helmet twisted and the catch came free.

"Hello, Ida," she said.

Her helmet clattered to the floor, and Ludmila—the first woman in space, the cosmonaut lost one thousand years ago, the pioneer who had burned in the atmosphere over Siberia in her capsule, the hero erased from all history and memory—smiled at Ida.

Her smile was the most beautiful thing in the world. He wanted to touch her skin but he was afraid that she would break, that she would tear like tissue paper. Her hair was short and spiky. Her eyes were blue and her teeth were white, and Ida almost passed out.

He felt a touch on his face, slight pinpricks of contact that burned like fire. He opened his eyes and found she had managed to take her gloves off, her long, delicate fingers on his cheeks, their icy touch like a flaming brand. Her face drew close, and he could feel no breath, smell no scent. She smiled and kissed him lightly. It was like kissing the terminal of a battery, and afterwards his lips were dry and numb.

Ludmila. Dead and alive at the same time, a soul lost at sea, like the others.

"Are you really here?" he asked, and he felt foolish for doing so.

Ludmila nodded. The hangar shook as the *Bloom County* thumped the floor, and she stood, pulling Ida up with her, his arm aching where she held him. Over her shoulder, Ida could see the lights of the *Magenta* flick on, piercing the purple haze of the hangar with brilliant sharp white.

"The Spider," he said. "We need to deactivate the dampener, then get back to the shuttle. We—"

"I cannot come with you," Ludmila said. "I don't belong here."

"What? But you're real, aren't you?"

She shook her head. "Someone needs to direct the Spider toward the gateway while Serra blocks Izanami. Her projection may be lost, but that won't stop her trying to pull herself across the bridge."

"But the Spider can fly this ship, can't it? Serra said—"

Ludmila shook her head. "The Spider is not awake, not truly," she said. "I will try to show it the way."

"You sure *you* can pilot it?"

Ludmila hesitated.

"I'll fly it," said Ida. Ludmila gasped in surprise, but Ida just nodded. "We can't take the chance. Go on." He gestured up the ramp just as the hangar shook again. "Go!"

Ludmila ran up into the *Bloom County*. Ida turned. On the other side of the hangar, Zia appeared on the *Magenta*'s ramp, waving furiously at him.

No. There was too much at stake. Izanami had to be stopped.

Ida stepped up onto the rising ramp of the *Bloom County*. He turned in time to see Zia yell something and move away from the shuttle before a thick hand caught her arm and pulled her back inside. She fought, but the effort was token.

Ida saluted Carter. Carter hesitated, then perhaps realizing Ida's plan, saluted back, and then the ramp was closed.

Ida stood in the passageway inside the *Bloom County*, took a deep breath, and then jogged toward the flight deck.

47

The main viewscreen of the U-Star *Magenta* showed the aft view as the shuttle limped away from the *Coast City*. The disk of Shadow convulsed as a giant flare of solar material was ejected from its surface. Silhouetted against the star, the incomplete torus of the space station looked tiny.

"Come on, come on," Carter muttered, knuckles white as he pushed the main thruster controls. Next to him Serra sat motionless, her eyes closed, her skin pale and a layer of sweat across her brow. On her lap sat the space radio, the blue light illuminating her slick skin, making her almost glow. She moaned in pain.

Zia clutched the arms of the commander's chair as she watched Carter wrestle with the controls.

"Can't this piece of junk go any faster?"

"Engines are still cold," said Carter. "Shuttles aren't known for their quick getaways."

Zia glanced at the viewscreen. She assumed the shuttle's computer was filtering the light from the star, making it safe to look at, but after a moment she closed her eyes, just in case. She imagined her own ship, the famous P-Prof *Bloom County*, racing toward the star as they pulled away, the Spider at the heart of the craft waking, sensing the star nearby with a terrible hunger. She only hoped that it would all work. Otherwise, they weren't making it out of the system alive and would join the others taken by Izanami to fill the ranks of the Funayurei.

Serra cried out. Her scream was primal, animal, full of pain and despair. Zia's eyes flew open and she saw Serra jerk back in her chair, her back arched, before she slumped into it and didn't move. Her breathing was shallow and fast.

"Hey, Serra! Hang in there!" Carter risked letting go of the uncooperative yoke with one hand as he reached over and rocked her knee.

Something flared on the viewscreen, white and red and expanding, flooding the shuttle's control cabin with blinding light. Zia squinted into the screen, one arm raised instinctively against the light. The violet white disk of Shadow had gone, replaced by a rippling mass of colors as the star went nova.

"Bingo," Zia whispered. The gateway was closed; it had to be. She only hoped Izanami had still been behind it.

"Shit," said Carter. "Hold on to something."

A few seconds later, the *Magenta* was pitched forward at forty-five degrees as the shock wave from the stellar explosion reached them. An alarm sounded, and the control cabin's lights flicked to an angry emergency red.

The trio bounced in their seats as Carter pulled at the controls, helpless as the shuttle rode the leading edge of the explosion.

On the viewscreen, the *Coast City* and the *Carcosa* boiled away into nothing but hot atoms in space a hundred thousand klicks behind them. Another alarm sounded, and Carter swore as the yoke kicked in his hands. Then the *Magenta* righted itself and the emergency lighting switched back to white. On the viewscreen, the nova slid out of the bottom of the picture as Carter pulled the shuttle up and accelerated, just enough to escape the explosion, the still-cold engines screaming in protest.

Serra sighed and rolled her head against the back of her seat. Carter reached over to Serra and squeezed her hand.

It was over. Shadow was gone, along with the space station, along with, Zia realized, everyone still held captive aboard the *Carcosa*. They couldn't have saved them, that she knew, but she also wished there had been some other way.

Zia watched the empty viewscreen for a moment. Then she stood and left the control cabin without a word. In her hand she held the space radio, which she had picked up from where it fell as the ship had bucked.

In the *Bloom County*, there was—had been—a window directly above her cot. It was a custom installation, but it let the starlight fall on her as she slept.

The *Magenta* was Fleet-standard modular design, and had no such customization in its simple, functional crew quarters.

But there were inspection windows in the cargo hold, which is where Zia had dragged her bedding and mattress, making herself a nest under the angle of the ceiling on a high shelf on one side of the hold, directly underneath the porthole. It wasn't that comfortable, but it would do for the long haul back to the nearest way station— they had discovered the *Magenta*'s drive had been damaged in the shock wave from Shadow's explosion, and Carter had estimated the crawl to port would take ten cycles or more. If they were careful with the shuttle's standard emergency supplies, they would make it. Just.

But she had the starlight, and that made her happy. That, and something else.

Zia rolled over and reached forward to adjust the controls of the silver space radio set that sat on a shelf on the wall beside the makeshift bed. After a second or two there was a pop and a crackle and the room was filled with the rolling sound of the ocean. There was another sound too, of someone breathing, faint, thin, and far away.

Contact had been established.

"Good night, Ida."

Hiss-pop-crackle-pop.

Zia lay back, closed her eyes, and listened to the echo of stars as the *Magenta* powered out of the Upsilon system, the system that had once been bathed in the strange light of Shadow, the light that would fuck you up. But now the star field was a dazzling spectrum of color as the remnants of the star glowed in space.

A voice spoke, thin and reedy and an infinite distance away, but Zia was sleeping under the stars and dreaming of her mother, of her father.

"Good night, Zia Hollywood," said Ida.

Somewhere in the roar behind him, a woman laughed.

MAY 19, 1961

Five... four... three... two... one...
One... two... three... four... five...
Come in... come in... come in...
LISTEN... LISTEN!... COME IN!
Come in... come in... Talk to me! Talk to me!...
I am hot!... I am hot!
What?... Forty-five?... What?... Forty-five?... Fifty?...
Yes... Yes... Yes... Breathing... breathing... oxygen... oxygen...
I am hot... This... Isn't this dangerous?... It's all... Isn't this
dangerous?... It's all...
Yes... yes... yes... How is this?
What?... Talk to me!... How should I transmit? Yes... yes... yes...
What? Our transmission begins now...
Forty-one... this way... Our transmission begins now...
Forty-one... this way... Our transmission begins now...
Forty-one... yes... I...
I feel hot... I feel hot... It's all... It's hot...
I feel hot... I feel hot... I feel hot...
I can see a flame!... What?... I can see a flame!... I can see a flame!...

I feel hot... I feel hot... Thirty-two... Thirty-two... Forty-one...
Forty-one...
Am I going to crash?
Yes... Yes... I feel hot!... I feel hot!...
I will reenter!... I will reenter...
I am listening!...
I feel

ABOUT THE AUTHOR

ADAM CHRISTOPHER is a novelist and comic writer. In 2010, as an editor, Christopher won a Sir Julius Vogel award, New Zealand's highest science fiction honour. His debut novel, *Empire State*, was *SciFiNow*'s Book of the Year and a *Financial Times* Book of the Year for 2012. In 2013, he was nominated for the Sir Julius Vogel award for Best New Talent, with *Empire State* shortlisted for Best Novel. Born in New Zealand, he has lived in Great Britain since 2006.

For news and information about upcoming books and events, sign up to Adam Christopher's author newsletter at www. adamchristopher.ac.

THE DIRE EARTH CYCLE

JASON M. HOUGH

The Builders came to Earth and constructed an elevator from Darwin, Australia into space. No one knows why, or if they will return.

Years later, a virus ravaged the planet. The rare immunes survived, others became something less than human. The elevator protected from the virus. The rich colonised the cord as the city below collapsed.

But now the alien technology is failing. Will humanity survive?

THE DARWIN ELEVATOR
THE EXODUS TOWERS
THE PLAGUE FORGE

"Claustrophobic, intense, and satisfying. I couldn't put this book down. *The Darwin Elevator* depicts a terrifying world, suspends it from a delicate thread, and forces you to read with held breath as you anticipate the inevitable fall."
Hugh Howey, *New York Times* bestselling author of *Wool*

TITANBOOKS.COM

VICIOUS

V.E. SCHWAB

Victor and Eli started out as college roommates—brilliant, arrogant, lonely boys who recognized the same ambition in each other. A shared interest in adrenaline, near-death experiences, and seemingly supernatural events reveals an intriguing possibility: that under the right conditions, someone could develop extraordinary abilities. But when their thesis moves from the academic to the experimental, things go horribly wrong.

Ten years later, Victor breaks out of prison, determined to catch up to his old friend (now foe), aided by a young girl with a stunning ability. Meanwhile, Eli is on a mission to eradicate every other super-powered person that he can find—aside from his sidekick, an enigmatic woman with an unbreakable will. Armed with terrible power on both sides, driven by the memory of betrayal and loss, the arch-nemeses have set a course for revenge—but who will be left alive at the end?

"Supremely plotted and incredibly well-written."
The Independent on Sunday

TITANBOOKS.COM

KOKO TAKES A HOLIDAY

KIERAN SHEA

Five hundred years from now, ex-corporate mercenary Koko Martstellar is swaggering through an easy early retirement as a brothel owner on The Sixty Islands, a manufactured tropical resort archipelago known for its sex and simulated violence. Surrounded by slang-drooling boywhores and synthetic komodo dragons, Koko finds the most challenging part of her day might be deciding on her next drink.

That is, until her old comrade Portia Delacompte sends a squad of security personnel to murder her.

Now Koko is on the run in the sky-barges of the Second Free Zone—dodging ruthless eye-eating bounty agents dispatched by Delacompte and falling in with Flynn, a depressed local cop readying his nerves for a sanctioned mass suicide known as Embrace...

"Brutal, smart and wickedly funny."
Stephen Blackmore, author of *Dead Things*

TITANBOOKS.COM

For more fantastic fiction, author events, exclusive
excerpts, competitions, limited editions and more:

VISIT OUR WEBSITE
titanbooks.com

LIKE US ON FACEBOOK
facebook.com/titanbooks

FOLLOW US ON TWITTER
@TitanBooks

EMAIL US
readerfeedback@titanemail.com